Frost At Midnight

Elizabeth Falconer

BLACK SWAN

FROST AT MIDNIGHT
A BLACK SWAN BOOK : 0 552 99839 7

First publication in Great Britain

PRINTING HISTORY
Black Swan edition published 2000

1 3 5 7 9 10 8 6 4 2

Set in 11/12pt Melior by
County Typesetters, Margate, Kent.

Black Swan Books are published by Transworld Publishers,
61–63 Uxbridge Road, London W5 5SA,
a division of The Random House Group Ltd,
in Australia by Random House Australia (Pty) Ltd,
20 Alfred Street, Milsons Point, Sydney, NSW 2061, Australia,
in New Zealand by Random House New Zealand Ltd,
18 Poland Road, Glenfield, Auckland 10, New Zealand
and in South Africa by Random House (Pty) Ltd,
Endulini, 5a Jubilee Road, Parktown 2193, South Africa.

Reproduced, printed and bound in Great Britain by
Cox & Wyman Ltd, Reading, Berks.

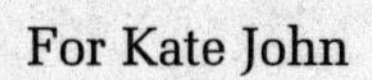

For Kate John

Elizabeth Falconer lives in Gloucestershire and spends part of the year in the south of France. *Frost at Midnight* is her sixth novel; her first five novels, *The Golden Year, The Love of Women, The Counter-Tenor's Daughter, Wings of the Morning* and *A Barefoot Wedding*, are also published by Black Swan.

Also by Elizabeth Falconer

THE GOLDEN YEAR
THE LOVE OF WOMEN
THE COUNTER-TENOR'S DAUGHTER
WINGS OF THE MORNING
A BAREFOOT WEDDING

and published by Black Swan

Chapter One

Misha ben Bella, at thirty-seven years old, would certainly have described her life as pretty nearly perfect, had she been interviewed on the subject. Named for her father Michel, an immigrant from the Maghreb who had settled in Marseille and married an Irish go-go dancer, Misha was small and slender, with short black hair and the large, intelligent green eyes of her mother. She also had a remarkably high forehead, and long-fingered, extremely beautiful hands.

Having completed medical school, and qualified as a doctor, she had spent the usual gruelling years working her way steadily through various hospital appointments, until she reached the level of senior house officer. It was at that stage that she had begun to have serious ambitions, and decided to apply to do surgical training.

Unmarried, and apparently destined to remain so, Misha had neither husband nor children to consider, which left her entirely free to focus on her career, as well as having time for the enormous amount of studying she would have do, in order to qualify as a surgeon.

The decision taken, she was currently employed as a trainee member of a celebrated neurosurgeon's *équipe* in one of Paris's most prestigious teaching hospitals. The work was fascinating, extremely exacting and precise, and suited Misha's temperament perfectly. For her, the long afternoons in the operating theatre, assisting, sometimes even carrying out part of a procedure under the watchful dark eyes of Professor de Vilmorin, were her idea of heaven.

Far from being the chaotic scene so often represented on the TV screen for the entertainment of the viewers, the theatre was a cool, peaceful oasis, the silence broken only by the hum of machines, the bleep of the heart monitor and the calm voice of de Vilmorin, explaining his every move as he removed an undesirable object from the brain of a patient. After the position of the tumour had been identified with the aid of the CT scans displayed on the light box, the hair had been shaved from one side of the patient's head, and the rest dowsed with disinfectant. A circle had been drawn on the shaved area to mark the tumour's exact position, and Misha watched with admiration as de Vilmorin drilled tiny holes around its circumference, and then sawed through the cranium until he was able to lift away a circular piece of bone, revealing the tumour below. He glanced towards the anaesthetist: 'Everything OK?'

'The patient's comfortable, sir.'

'Good.' Scalpel in hand, the surgeon addressed his students. 'What we are about to do has to be very slow and painstaking, and is of crucial importance,' he said quietly. 'If one were to remove the tumour quickly, and in one piece, the displaced brain tissue would spring back into its original position, almost certainly causing subsequent paralysis or epilepsy. It is, therefore, vital that we carry out the procedure as slowly as possible.' He lifted his scalpel. 'First, we remove the centre of the tumour to reduce its size: like this.' With gentle precision, his gloved hands steady in the beam of brilliant light that illuminated the field of battle, he cut into the core of the tumour, scooped it out, and deposited it into the waiting dish, ordering its immediate despatch to the laboratory for analysis. 'Now comes the tricky part,' he said. 'We work round the edges of the remaining tissue, removing exceedingly small pieces at a time, again as slowly as is humanly possible. By doing this, the brain will return to its normal position almost imperceptibly, and, with any luck, we should be able to avoid any kind of permanent damage to the patient.'

The procedure took almost seven hours from start to finish, and by the time the last tiny piece of tumour had been meticulously removed the entire team was beginning to feel the pressure. None the less, de Vilmorin offered his most senior pupil the chance to close the wound, once the missing piece of cranium had been eased skilfully back into place. 'Right, we can close. Jean-Luc, do you want to do it?'

'Thank you, sir.' The team watched critically as Jean-Luc, with only one mild correction from his mentor, carried out his task.

'Well done, team; a good afternoon's work. The poor chap will feel a lot more comfortable in a week or two, I've little doubt. Have a good weekend, all of you.'

Paul de Vilmorin left the theatre, followed by his pupils, except Misha, who accompanied the patient and the nursing staff to the ITU and double-checked that everything was functioning perfectly before removing her scrubs, mask and gloves, then collecting her jacket and bag from her locker, signing off and leaving the hospital.

She took the Métro to Bastille, changing at Châtelet, finally emerging from the crowded, noisy station into the comparative tranquillity of an early summer's evening. In rue de la Roquette she did her shopping, buying two tender young pigeons, salad leaves, cheese and a crisp fresh baguette. Carrying her purchases in a plastic bag, she turned into an alleyway, passage des Ebénistes, a dark, narrow street of industrial buildings, formerly the workshops and warehouses of furniture-makers, now converted into fashionable boutiques and bistros, with apartments on the upper floors.

When she reached number sixteen, Misha unlocked

the glossily painted black door. She stepped into the hallway, letting the door swing shut behind her, and took the high-tech lift to the top floor, and the loft apartment she shared with Giles, her partner of seven years.

Giles Murray-Williams was an associate in Cunningham's, a firm of international auctioneers, with offices in London, Geneva and New York as well as Paris, so that he was in fact rarely in his favourite city for very long at a time, a circumstance that did not seem to dull or diminish the flames of desire between the lovers. On the contrary, each opportunity to be together was like a honeymoon. Giles was a very private man, almost obsessively so. Misha knew that he had a house in London – in Chelsea – but she did not know exactly where it was, and in any case the telephone and fax numbers seemed to her to be perfectly adequate points of contact. She had never questioned him about his life in London or New York, and felt no particular curiosity about it.

They had met when Giles had been laid low by a burst appendix while in Paris, and Misha had been a junior doctor in the hospital to which he had been taken. Even in the unglamorous circumstances of a sickbed, Misha had found the thirty-five-year-old Englishman incredibly attractive. He was of medium height, with the wavy auburn hair that goes with a very pale, freckled skin. A man of self-indulgent habits, and a cocaine user, Giles rarely walked if he could take a taxi, and his poorly maintained musculature bore witness to his slothful existence. In spite of these physical defects, however, he had one exceptionally redeeming feature: his eyes. They were almond-shaped, lion-coloured, and fringed with chestnut lashes under delicately marked eyebrows. Aware of the penetrating gaze of those eyes as she supervised the dressing of his wound, Misha had felt herself responding in the predictable classic manner, and longed to have sex with him. She felt sure that he would be seriously good in bed, and a week later, when he suggested that they dine together as soon as he was discharged from hospital, she did not decline the invitation.

On that first date it had not been possible, so soon after the appendicectomy, to consummate their mutual attraction in the fullest sense, but what did occur had been quite enough to convince Misha that she had found the man of her dreams.

Letting herself into her apartment, she was pleased to see that the cleaning lady had performed excellently. The salon sparkled with polish, and the air was filled with the subtle scent of new-mown hay. Although, technically, the place belonged to Misha, the large, rather stark L-shaped salon had been largely refurbished by Giles, and had become the setting for his formidable collection of twentieth-century furniture and artefacts. Of all his extremely valuable possessions, the most cherished by him was his superb collection of drawings and paintings by Braque.

Giles had also taken charge of the decoration of the salon, and had arranged for the original oak floorboards to be sanded and repolished, and the walls and ceilings painted a soft neutral shade called Mouse's Ear. This English National Trust colour was much admired by Giles and his colleagues, and the iron pillars that supported the building were finished in a gloss paint of the same colour. Giles was an ardent fan of the art deco period and the loft was furnished with the designs of Eileen Gray, Chareau and Mallet-Stevens. A long black-leather sofa, soft and comfortable, was fronted by a stunningly beautiful low table of immensely thick glass supported on a chrome frame. The floor was absolutely bare, without carpets or rugs of any kind, and along one wall Giles had installed a storage unit, the visible surfaces finished with white glazed tiles. This clinical-looking fitting had asymmetrically spaced gaps for the accommodation of books, compact discs and videotapes. It was topped with a wide shelf on which several beautiful objects were displayed, notably Giles's valuable collection of Japanese netsuke: small, exquisitely carved pieces in ivory or aromatic wood. In addition there were three small sculptures by Giacometti, five large nautilus shells and a set of contemporary silver candlesticks. Each piece had its own precise position, and after the twice-weekly visits of the cleaning lady, Misha took care to correct any small carelessness in respect of the arrangement that might have occurred. For herself, it was not a matter of vital importance. For the sensitive perfectionist Giles, she knew that it was.

The room was lit by narrow slits in the walls, through which could be glimpsed the rooftops of Bastille. In the centre of the ceiling, strong white light poured from a glass lantern, altering completely the ambiance of the loft, according to the weather. In sunlight, the place took on a brilliant black-and-white exuberance; in dull weather, the mood seemed introspective, even depressed.

Misha passed through the room and turned into the concealed part of the L. It was furnished with a small black-lacquer table and a pair of black 'sphinx' armchairs, and it was here that Misha and Giles dined, when they felt like eating at home.

She opened the door to the kitchen, her favourite room in the apartment, her heart lifting at the sight of the blue sky visible through the glass roof and walls, and the small gravelled roof-garden, bright with flowering shrubs in pots. It's been pretty hot today, she thought; I must give the poor things a drink. She dumped her bag on the grey-marble café table, and her shopping on the white worktop that ran along the length of the room, beneath its sloping glass canopy. Then, from force of habit, she switched on the small TV that sat at the end of the counter. Briefly, she watched the news, in case there should be anything worrying about Algeria. All seemed well, so she turned off the set and went out into the garden.

Small, and simply furnished with blue-painted metal chairs and a table, it had been made private with panels of woven willow, over which climbed jasmine and roses. In spite of this, one or two neighbouring chimney stacks could still be seen through the exuberant plantings, but they did not detract from the charm and quietness of the place, and Misha spent many happy hours there, particularly when, as so often, she was alone.

She looked at her watch: five to seven. Giles would be here by eight-thirty. Punctilious about such things, he always told her his intended time of arrival at passage des Ebénistes, and he was almost always exactly on time. I'd better get the pigeons on first, she thought, then I'll water the pots.

She returned to the kitchen, unpacked the shopping, and sautéed the pigeons with lardons of bacon, new spring garlic and herbs. She put them into a small casserole with a glass of Médoc, and left them to cook in a gentle oven. She washed some new potatoes and left them in cold water in a shining stainless steel saucepan. That done, she went out to the roof-garden and spent a soothing ten minutes watering her plants.

Misha's second-favourite room in the apartment was the bathroom. An extension of the only bedroom, its walls, shelving, window-sills and bath-surround were immaculately tiled in the same white porcelain that Giles had specified for use in the salon. Long and narrow, the bathroom had windows along one wall, overlooking the little garden, and facing a large reflecting mirror on the other side, behind the bath. This light-filled, pristine space, far from being cold and harsh in feeling, was given a magically tender and romantic atmosphere by the translucent blinds that hung at the window. Made of antique organdie, with deep bands of heavy guipure lace, Misha had found them in a flea-market one Sunday morning, and had had them restored and hung before Giles's next visit, replacing the simple cream linen store blinds of his original choice. To her surprise and pleasure, he had raised no objection to the change, even grudgingly commenting that they looked 'quite pretty'.

Misha showered, washing her hair at the same time to remove the smell of hospital, then wrapped her large, dark-blue bath towel round her wet body, and applied a little make-up to her face, using the round, chrome-framed magnifying mirror fixed to the wall. Dry and naked, she ruffled her damp hair and went into the adjoining bedroom, equally plain and white, with a dark-blue carpet, and a wall of mirrored cupboards which housed both her and Giles's clothes. She chose to wear a string-coloured knitted linen sweater, with matching linen trousers, and, on her feet, soft red Moroccan slippers. She tidied the bathroom, and turned down the bed.

In the kitchen, she made a dressing for a salad of mixed leaves and rocket, decanted the wine, set the table in the dining area with the Sèvres plates that Giles adored, and put fresh candles in the silver candlesticks. By eight o'clock everything was ready, the pigeons simmering perfectly. She put the potatoes on a low flame to boil, made herself a kir, and went out into her garden to enjoy the mildness of the evening.

Eight-thirty came and went. Misha went back to the kitchen, turned down the potatoes, and took the pigeons from the oven. She had no wish for her careful cooking to disintegrate into mush; she would reheat the food when Giles arrived.

At nine-thirty she began to be slightly worried. At ten-thirty, she sat down on the leather sofa, looking thoughtfully at the cordless telephone waiting on the coffee table, beside a glass chemist's beaker containing a single lemon-yellow rose. She touched the rose gently with a long slender finger, then frowned, glancing at her watch yet again, trying to decide whether or not there was any point in calling Giles in London.

She waited another half-hour, then dialled his Chelsea number, but all she got was the message service, inviting her to leave her number, so that her call could be returned as soon as possible. Sick with anxiety, and with her appetite completely gone, she cleared the table and put the uneaten food into the fridge. She drank a glass of wine, pacing up and down the salon, willing the telephone to ring. Finally, she went to bed, unable to believe that Giles would simply not turn up. Never in all their long relationship had he failed to let her know if there had to be a change of plan. Increasingly convinced that something serious must have happened, she tossed and turned miserably in the bed that should at this moment have been the setting of their joyful reunion.

Early next morning, Saturday, Misha telephoned the London number again, and every two or three hours thereafter, but with no success. This pattern was repeated on Sunday, and on Monday morning, in desperation, she phoned the London offices of Cunningham's and asked to speak to Mr Murray-Williams.

'I'm so sorry,' said a cut-glass English female voice, 'but Mr Murray-Williams is not available at the present time.'

Misha drew a deep breath. 'I see. Can you tell me when he *will* be available, please? It's important.'

'I'm afraid that's not possible.' The woman paused briefly, then continued, 'Mr Murray-Williams has had an accident. Unfortunately.'

'What kind of an accident?'

'I understand he was para-gliding.'

'I see. What injuries did he sustain?'

'I believe he broke both his wrists, and some ribs. He hit his head against a stone on landing, and was badly concussed, I understand. It seems that he's not very well at all.'

Misha took a deep breath, and forced herself to speak calmly. 'When did the accident happen?'

'On Thursday, I believe.'

'Could you tell me which hospital he's in, please?'

'Yes, of course. Hold on, I'll make enquiries.'

Misha entered the address and phone number of the hospital in her organizer, thanked the woman for her help, and hung up. For a couple of minutes she remained where she was, cold, shivering slightly, filled with panic. Then she picked up the phone again, called her own hospital and asked to speak to Professor de Vilmorin's secretary. 'Lisa? It's Misha ben Bella.'

'Hi, Misha.'

'I have a problem, Lisa. I need to go to London urgently. We're not operating today, but I was wondering if you could arrange for someone to cover for me tomorrow?'

'Would you like to speak to Professor de Vilmorin yourself? He's right here; he's on his way to his clinic.'

'Oh. Right. OK.'

'I'll put him on.'

'Thanks.'

After a moment, Paul de Vilmorin came on the line. 'Misha? What's the problem?'

'I'm sorry to be a nuisance, but my partner has had a bad accident. He's in hospital in London, and I wondered if I could have a couple of days' leave, to go to him? I was asking Lisa if someone could cover for me tomorrow.'

'How serious is the trauma, Misha?'

'Multiple fractures.' Misha's voice shook. 'And depression of consciousness, so I understand.'

'I see. Right, don't hang about, my dear. Go. Stay as long as you need. Don't worry, we'll sort something out here, I'm sure.'

'Thank you so much. If you're quite sure?'

'I'm quite sure. Goodbye, Misha. Good luck.'

'Goodbye, and thanks again.'

Misha arrived in London in the late afternoon, and took a taxi straight to the hospital. At the reception desk she was told that she could not see Giles: 'Mr

Murray-Williams is not well enough to receive visitors.'

'I'm not just a visitor, as a matter of fact. I am his doctor in Paris. It's possible that I may be able to help.'

'I see.' The efficient young woman on the desk looked at Misha, as if doubting the veracity of this claim. Nevertheless, she picked up the internal phone and spoke to the sister in charge of the private wing. 'There's a doctor from Paris to see Mr Murray-Williams, sister. Shall I send her up?' She nodded, glancing at Misha. 'Yes, she's a woman. Yes, OK.' She replaced the phone, and turned to Misha. 'You can go up, doctor. The private wing is on the top floor. Sister Becket will be expecting you.'

Sister Becket, when Misha located her, turned out to be a well-groomed, middle-aged woman who looked as though she ran a very tight ship. She made brief but thorough enquiries in respect of Misha's identity, status and relationship to the patient. On being informed that Misha's acquaintance with Giles was of long duration and stemmed from his emergency appendicectomy in Paris, she seemed reassured and began to divulge the nature and extent of his recent injuries. 'Mr Murray-Williams has sustained multiple rib fractures, and we are treating these with intercostal blocks, analgesia and physiotherapy. He has fractures of both wrists and was severely concussed. There was some depression of consciousness, together with amnesia.' Sister Becket frowned, and pursed her lips to signify disapproval. 'It is difficult to assess whether the patient's symptoms are the result of injury to the brain, doctor, in view of the fact that he appears to be a regular user of an illegal substance. However, an X-ray has not revealed any fracture to the skull, but we are keeping him under observation, as a precautionary measure.'

'I see.'

Sister Becket stood up. 'I'll take you to see him.' She led the way to a small private room, where Giles lay, apparently asleep. Left alone with him, Misha sat on the chair provided and gazed at the face of the man she loved. The thick chestnut lashes of his closed eyelids seemed like shutters of his soul, maintaining his privacy, excluding intruders, even herself. Tiny red hairs sprouted on his lip and chin. He'll hate that, she thought, he's so fastidious about that kind of thing. What where you doing, *para-gliding*, you silly man? she scolded silently. You should know better at your age, and with your pathetic musculature. Who were you trying to impress, for heaven's sake? Giles's arms lay on either side of his inert body, the forearms in plaster, the fingers protruding from the snow-white casts. Gently she reached out and stroked his bristly cheek. 'Hello, darling,' she said softly. 'What on earth have you been up to, crazy man?'

The chestnut lashes fluttered, the tawny eyes opened, and he turned his head slowly towards her, frowning, as if he had difficulty in getting her face into focus. 'Who are you?' he croaked.

'It's me, darling, Misha.'

'Oh? Do I know you?'

'Of course you do, Giles. We have an apartment in Paris, remember?'

'Don't be ridiculous. I've never seen you before in my life. Go away.' He turned his face away and closed his eyes.

Dismayed at his failure to recognize her, but mindful of the sister's remarks about his confusion and amnesia, Misha immediately withdrew her hand from Giles's face. She sat silently in her chair, trying to decide what to do next, in his best interests. Presently, a nurse came into the room and whispered to her that Mrs Murray-Williams had come to see the patient. Misha looked up at her, startled. 'Mrs Murray-Williams? You mean his mother?'

'No, his wife. His mother came yesterday.'

Misha swallowed, her lips stiff with shock, momentarily unable to speak. Then she stood up uncertainly and followed the nurse to the reception area. Seated on a bench, she saw a tall elegant woman. She had very fair hair, smoothed with gel, and combed flat against her skull. Her dark-blue eyes dominated a pale pointed face that seemed vaguely familiar. She would have been extremely beautiful in a very English way, had her body language not been full of tension and anxiety.

'You can come in now, Mrs Murray-Williams,' said the nurse. 'I'm afraid he's still quite poorly, so you shouldn't stay long.'

Torn with indecision, full of fear, confusion and a mounting sense of disbelief, Misha paced up and down the reception hall, staring out of the solitary window from time to time, unable to sit down, and equally incapable of thinking clearly. Should she leave at once, go straight back to Paris, or should she wait and try to speak to Giles's wife, try to piece together some sort of logical explanation for the situation in which she found herself to be drowning? Struggling to keep calm and maintain some control, she told herself that it would be foolish and immature to run away. She should, *must*, first satisfy herself that there was not some perfectly plausible reason for Giles's apparent marital status. Perhaps he had been married once and was now divorced? This simple answer made her heart leap. That could easily be the case, couldn't it? So why did the beautiful fair-haired woman look so anxious? Well, of course she would, wouldn't she? Even divorced people still have feelings for each other, in a civilized society, don't they? Of course, she'd want to see him, and be deeply concerned about him.

After twenty minutes, Mrs Murray-Williams re-appeared. Her face was pale and her eyes serious, but her bearing was impressively calm and dignified. She came at once to Misha, and held out her hand. 'Dr ben Bella? I understand that you've come from Paris to try to be of assistance to poor Giles. It's very good of you to go to so much trouble.'

'Not at all.' Misha took her hand. 'It's a terrible thing to have happened. I've known Giles for some time, since he was in hospital in Paris.' She smiled diffidently. 'I came in case I could help, but obviously he's in good hands; they don't need me here.'

'How long are you staying in London?'

'Until tomorrow, I thought. I must get back to my own hospital.'

'Have you got somewhere to stay?'

'I expect there's a hotel nearby. I'll ask at the desk.'

'Well, if you haven't booked in anywhere, I suppose you could stay with us, if you like. It's not far, and I'd be quite glad of your company. It's rather reassuring, for me, that you're a doctor. It would make me feel a bit less hysterical about Giles, if you were with me.'

'Are you sure? Wouldn't it be a nuisance, at such short notice?'

'No, not at all, if you don't mind dossing down on the sofa-bed. Dorothy will have supper ready; one more won't make any difference. It'll be fine with her, I'm sure.'

'Dorothy?'

'She's Alice's nanny. She's utterly brilliant, and takes care of everything for me, when I'm working. I couldn't cope without her.'

'Alice?' asked Misha, her heart sinking, guessing the probable response.

'She's my little girl. Mine and Giles's, that is.'

Punch-drunk, stunned by the unfolding revelations of Giles's secret life, sick with inner anxiety about his physical and mental health, Misha felt powerless to resist the arrangements being thrust upon her by her lover's wife. Numbly, she allowed herself to be taken down to the car park, installed in the passenger seat of Mrs Murray-Williams's car, and driven to St Peter's Square. They crawled under the Hammersmith flyover, frequently brought to a halt by the rush-hour traffic. Misha stared through the window at the unfamiliar London streets, beginning to regret that she had accepted the invitation, and wondering whether she could politely say that she had changed her mind and would rather take a taxi to a hotel. Suddenly, she received another shock.

'It was really weird, being called Mrs Murray-Williams at the hospital! I always think of Giles's *mother* as that! As a matter of fact, Giles and I aren't actually married; we're just a long-term item. Always will be, I expect.' She laughed. 'I don't think Giles is the marrying kind. Come to that, neither am I.'

Misha blinked hard, and rearranged her thoughts. 'I see. So what's your real name?'

'Mowbray. Juliet Mowbray. What's yours, apart from ben Bella?'

'Misha.'

'Mm; cool name.'

'Thanks.' After a pause Misha asked, 'What about Alice? Isn't it a problem not being married to her father?'

'No, not at all. He's a good father; he's not stingy with support, and he's put her down for Wycombe Abbey, so she'll be OK.'

'I see. Well, that's good, if *you* don't mind, Juliet.'

'The only person who minds is Dorothy, and you'll see why when you meet her. She's a real old-fashioned Bible-basher, and can't be doing with modern morals, or lack of them. She thinks I'm a terrific whore. I can't think why she stays with me.' Juliet negotiated her way across the lanes of traffic into King Street, and the car picked up speed.

I can think of lots of reasons, thought Misha, and smiled, almost light-headed with relief that this beautiful and charming woman, the mother of Giles's child, was not in fact married to him after all, and appeared to be in no particular hurry to tie the knot herself. She's in exactly the same boat as I am, Misha reassured herself. Giles doesn't feel entirely committed to either of us, apparently. The only difference is that she doesn't seem to care too much, whereas I do; I care like hell.

Juliet drove into St Peter's Square and parked outside a large town house. They got out of the car and went down a steep flight of concrete steps to the basement flat. The ugliness of the steps was ameliorated by a set of matching terracotta pots, planted with dwarf conifers and variegated ivy, and through the brightly lit, uncurtained window Misha could see a large room, furnished in the style of a country kitchen, complete with a china-filled pine dresser. Seated at a long, scrubbed pine table, a small girl, with copper-coloured curly hair, was vigorously applying red paint to a picture of Postman Pat's van. One end of the table was laid for a meal. At the stove stood a massively built woman with strong black arms, and black hair plaited into many tiny braids. She was frying onions, to judge by the smell when Juliet opened the door and they went in.

'Hi, Mum,' said the child. 'How's Dad? Is he awake yet?' She got down from her chair and ran to her mother's side, holding out her arms. Juliet picked her up, and Misha saw that the little girl had enormous, chestnut-fringed, lion-coloured eyes, the eyes of Giles, her father. It was too much for Misha. The whole nightmare situation burst upon her; her stomach turned to water, her legs to cotton-wool. I can't handle this, she thought, clutching the back of a chair; I must go. If I stay here, and they're nice to me, I'll only blurt everything out, tell them what a two-timing bastard Giles is, and their lives will be in ruins as well as mine.

She drew a deep, steadying breath. 'I'm sorry, Juliet,' she said, 'but I'm afraid I've changed my mind. I can't stay. I really ought to get back to Paris tonight.'

'Oh, *why*?' exclaimed Juliet, putting the child down. '*Please* don't go. It was so good of you to come and see Giles, the least I can do is put you up. We'd love you to stay, wouldn't we, Alice?'

Annoyed at being set aside by her mother, the child looked mutinous. 'No, we wouldn't!' she said rudely, and stuck her tongue out at Misha. 'Go away!'

'No, really,' said Misha, her spirits slightly stiffened

by the child's brutal honesty. 'It's better if I leave. You need to be alone with Alice just now.'

'That's the God's truth, and no mistake.' Dorothy's dark-brown voice matched her impressive physique, as, spatula in hand, she turned from the cooker. 'Alice needs all her mother's attention to herself, ma'am. You're not wrong about that.'

'You're bullying me, Dorothy.' Juliet made a brief attempt at imposing her authority, but knew that she was on a loser. 'If you're sure, Misha?' she said.

'I'm sure. It was nice of you to ask me.' She took Juliet's hand. 'Can I get a taxi in the street?'

'Yes, there are usually loads of them in King Street at this time of the evening.'

'Good, that's fine.' Misha hesitated. 'I wonder. Could I give you my phone number, so that you could let me know when there's an improvement, or any change in Giles's condition?'

'Yes, of course. Here, let me write it down in my Filofax.'

'Mummy's an actor,' said Alice, staring at Misha with her yellow eyes. 'She's quite famous. Did you know?'

'Um, no, I didn't know,' said Misha. 'How lovely for you, Alice.'

'It's not lovely at all. She goes away all the time and dumps me with Dorothy. It's not fair.'

'Really, Alice,' said Juliet lightly, 'how you do exaggerate.' She repeated the number Misha had given her. 'That's right?'

'Yes, that's right.'

Juliet insisted on walking Misha back to King Street, and waiting with her until a taxi had stopped in response to her signal. 'Goodbye,' she said. 'It was nice meeting you, Misha. I'll call you as soon as there's any news.'

'Thank you, I'd be glad to know.' Misha told the driver to take her to Waterloo and got into the cab. She waved through the window as the vehicle moved away, then sank back into her seat, exhausted.

Thoughtfully, Juliet walked back to her house, asking herself all sorts of questions as she did so. Wasn't it rather curious that this strange woman had suddenly arrived out of the blue to see Giles in hospital? Apart from everything else, how the hell did she know that he had had an accident in the first place? I don't really buy that story about her being his doctor in Paris, that doesn't explain anything. His doctor, and what else, I'd like to know? I wasn't born yesterday, Giles, you philandering brute. You've been up to your tricks again, haven't you?

Misha slept in the train, but the rest did nothing to alleviate her distress.

Images of Giles filled her dreams: Giles snorting coke, laughing at her for warning him that he should kick the habit; Giles in bed, naked, soft-skinned, silkily gentle but incredibly exciting, able to delay the climax of the act of love almost to the point of agony; Giles hung over, petulant, demanding drugs that she flatly refused to supply; and finally, Giles strapped into his para-glider, floating high in the sky, above the world; out of reach; probably stoned; in heaven, feeling no pain.

She woke with a headache and a vile taste in her mouth, as the train pulled into Gare du Nord. Unwilling to face the night-time Métro alone, she took a taxi to Bastille, and it was after midnight when she reached the sanctuary of her apartment. She made some tea, poured herself a small cognac and took the tray out to the roof-garden, feeling the need to fill her lungs with as much fresh air as possible before going to bed.

It was a beautiful night, the air still and balmy, leaf-scented. The sky, purple above the lights of the city, was sprinkled with faint, pale stars. In the country, she thought, the sky would be black, the stars like enormous diamonds. She saw herself as a child, in the walled garden of her parents' *auberge*, the gravel paths bordered with low box hedges, clipped and pungently aromatic in the hot summer sunshine. She could smell the flowerbeds filled with herbs, scented-leaf geraniums and the tall spikes of martagon lilies, their maroon Turks' caps curled voluptuously back, revealing their curved pollen-heavy stamens. The two cats, Minou and Minette, both fat, grey and brindled, followed her as she toured the small garden, turning over stones to discover nests of scuttling earwigs, lifting flowerpots to uncover the great fat Roman snails that it had once been her job to collect every morning, afterwards incarcerating them in wire cages on trays of salt. This was to ensure that their systems were purified before their final trip to the garlic-infused pan, for the *menu gastronomique* of her father's restaurant.

Dragging her mind back to the present, Misha felt actual physical pain rise within her, a wave of acute misery. She swallowed the cognac, and the raw spirit hit her stomach like a bomb, but at least had the merit of giving her temporary courage. She drank the tea slowly, and asked herself bitterly how it was that a man, a civilized, educated and confident man such as Giles, should feel the need to cheat on two women for as long as seven years, becoming a father in the process, without either of his victims having the least idea of the existence of a rival. How could you do it, my dear love? she thought sadly. How could you?

It seemed to Misha utterly unbelievable that he had ripped the heart out of their perfect partnership for ever, for that was how she was already seeing her situation. Even if Giles recovered his memory, and acknowledged her significance in his life, it was increasingly obvious to her that the only honourable course was to walk away from the relationship, if only for the sake of the child, Alice.

And what of Juliet, innocent and beautiful, hardworking apparently, as well as undemanding in her relationship with Giles? In spite of herself, the image rose in Misha's mind's eye of Giles and Juliet making love together, not merely going through the motions for the sensual pleasure of it, but passionately, urgently, without any form of birth control, with the express intention of making a new human being in their own image. Tears of humiliation, jealousy and ultimately rage spurted from Misha's eyes, as she forced herself to admit the truth, that she had been little more than a bit on the side as far as Giles was concerned. There had never been so much as a *discussion* about children between the two of them. They had never even spoken to each other about their own childhoods, and she knew nothing at all about his background, or his parents. Their relationship had been one that concerned the immediate present; now. The past or the future had had no part in their way of living.

Misha blew her nose with unnecessary force, making herself gasp, gathered up her glass and cup, and went back to the kitchen. It was almost two o'clock. She must go to bed; try to sleep. In the salon, she gazed around her at the precious artefacts, at the beautiful sombre paintings of Braque, and the Japanese netsuke. So, she thought, if I was so unimportant to him, why did he go to so much trouble to make this place so special? Probably thought of it as a good cheap place to store his investments, came the depressing answer. She sighed, took her organizer from her bag and dialled the number of the private wing of the London hospital.

'Staff nurse speaking.'

'This is Dr ben Bella. I'd like to know whether there's any change in Mr Murray-Williams's condition.'

'I'm afraid not. There's little change.'

'Thank you. I'll call tomorrow.'

Misha switched off the phone, and took it with her to the bedroom, where she put it carefully on the night-table. Then she undressed, got into bed, and, pulling the sheet over her head, wept as though her heart would break.

Chapter Two

For the next few days, Misha went through the motions of her daily routines, operating on autopilot. She got up, drank some coffee, went to work. Her head felt fragile, as though made of eggshell, and her nervous system was in shreds. Every day, she telephoned the hospital in London, and received the same non-committal report, that the patient was stable, and making slow progress. She heard nothing from Juliet, though she eagerly checked her answering-machine each time she came home.

One afternoon, she was part of the team assisting Paul de Vilmorin as he inserted a shunt to drain fluid from the brain of a hydrocephalic baby boy. Normally fascinated, and closely observing each new procedure in which she was involved, Misha was experiencing some difficulty in focusing her complete attention on the job in hand. She felt cold, and at the same time clammy with sweat. Like an automaton, she did what was expected of her without incident, and was thankful that the operation went unusually smoothly, and that it was not in her remit to accompany the small patient to recovery. Slowly, her legs like lead, she followed the team from the theatre. Washing at the sink, she found herself standing next to Professor de Vilmorin.

'How is your friend, Misha?'

'I don't really know,' she stammered, surprised at his

remembering. 'He's still in hospital, and they won't say very much, except that the X-rays were OK, but it seems to me obvious that he must have a primary brain injury.' She looked at de Vilmorin, and bit her lip. 'You see, Giles couldn't remember me, not at all. He didn't know who I was.'

'How very distressing for you.' He smiled at her kindly, as he dried his hands under the hot-air machine. 'No doubt that explains your appearance?'

'My appearance? Is there anything wrong with it?'

'No, of course not. You don't look at all well, though. Are you feeling ill, Misha? Do you need a few days' sick leave?'

'No, I don't think that would be a good idea. The last thing I need just now is a lot of time on my hands.' She turned towards him anxiously. 'Unless, of course, you think I'm not fit to be in theatre?'

'Do *you* think you're unfit, yourself?'

Misha looked up at him uncertainly, meeting his steady dark eyes, concerned and sympathetic. 'I think I'm probably useless, as a matter of fact,' she said, and burst into tears.

'Oh, come, it's not as bad as that, don't cry.' He tore off a large piece of paper towel and gave it to her. 'Did you have any lunch?' he asked.

'No, I don't think so. I can't remember.'

'What do you mean, you can't remember?'

She blew her nose, and wiped her eyes without replying, and threw the sodden paper in the pedal-bin. 'I'm sorry about that. I'm OK now.'

'When did you last eat?'

'I've had quite a lot of tea, and cups of coffee.'

'Anything else? Medication? Booze?'

Suddenly feeling herself to be on trial, Misha frowned uneasily. 'I might have had the odd drink, and a few sleeping pills. Is that a crime?'

'No,' he said gently, 'it's not a crime, Misha. But it's extremely foolish on an empty stomach, don't you agree?'

'I suppose,' she muttered, rather resentfully.

'Come on, it's not the end of the world. What you need is food, and I'm pretty hungry myself. We'll go and get something to eat.'

Feeling as feeble in the matter of asserting herself as she had when Juliet had insisted on taking her home, Misha took her jacket and bag from her locker and followed de Vilmorin out to his car. 'Won't your wife be expecting you?' she asked, as he drove the sleek dark-grey Mercedes coupé swiftly through the evening traffic to the Right Bank, and the Marais.

'No, not this evening. She's at a première, with friends. Not really my scene, I'm afraid.'

'Oh.' She looked at his profile, at the watchful dark eyes beneath strongly marked black brows, and the short, smooth silver hair, and thought that he must have been extremely attractive as a young man. 'What is your scene, then, Professor de Vilmorin?'

He smiled. 'Work, I suppose. And goats; I like them a lot. My son keeps a herd of goats, and makes cheese. I rather envy him his lifestyle.'

'Wouldn't you find it dull, compared to surgery?'

He glanced at her briefly. 'No,' he said. 'I don't believe I would, as a matter of fact.'

He parked the car in a side street near place des Vosges, and they walked to the beautiful seventeenth-century square, its four sides filled with identical houses built of pink brick and stone, and embellished at street level with low arcades, housing boutiques, antique shops and restaurants, the central gardens cooled by fountains, the arcades shaded by trees. It was nearly eight o'clock, and the fountains were illuminated, the water jets sparkling irresistibly in the warm evening air. In spite of herself, Misha felt her spirits lift.

'Let's see if we can get a table at Ma Bourgogne. I quite often come here; it reminds me of my home.'

'What a coincidence,' said Misha. 'I'm from Burgundy myself.'

'Really? Were you born there?'

'I was. My parents had a restaurant. They lived in a very small village near Villefranche. The place was a derelict mill when they found it, and they converted it into a little *auberge*; a restaurant with rooms.'

'Sounds delightful.'

'It was.'

'Are they still there, Misha?'

'No. My mother died a couple of years ago, and my father sold up and went back to his family in Algiers.'

A table for two at Ma Bourgogne was quickly forthcoming, under the arcade, and the waiter, well known to Paul, a regular client, brought bread, the menus, a bottle of water and two *flocs* with impressive speed. Paul pushed the basket of freshly cut bread towards Misha. 'Eat,' he said.

Obediently, she tore apart and ate a large chunk of bread, then looked at her glass of *floc*. 'Is it OK if I have a drink?' she asked.

'Yes, but take it easy. I don't want you passing out on me.'

They consulted the menu, and Misha chose steak-*frites*, and a salad. 'Very boring of me, but it's what I feel like,' she said.

'I'll have the same.' Paul gave the order and asked for a small carafe of the house claret to drink with it. Then he turned to Misha. 'Now,' he said, 'tell me all about it, please.'

Misha frowned. 'Tell you all about what?'

'Misha, your life is in crisis, right?'

She nodded, miserably.

'You have no particular friend to talk to, right?'

'Right.'

'OK. I'm old enough to be your father. I feel a certain responsibility towards you, as my pupil. You need to talk. I am happy to listen, if it helps. Is there a good reason why you can't confide in me?'

'No.'

'Well, then. Fire away.'

'Where shall I begin?'

'At the beginning, of course.'

Slowly, hesitatingly, twisting the stem of her glass between her long fingers, Misha told him the story of her only real love affair. Too busy, and too ambitious, first as a student and then as an overworked hospital doctor, she had had little time and less inclination to indulge in any deeply committed relationships. Marriage, or even a long-term liaison, had simply not been on her agenda before Giles had entered her life, sick and vulnerable with his burst appendix. 'You'd probably think him rather eccentric,' she said softly. 'For a start, he's English. He's not very tall, but he wears beautiful suits, from Savile Row I believe, and hand-painted bow ties, very elegant. He has curly red hair, rather long. I suppose you'd call him the arty intellectual type.'

Paul de Vilmorin did his best to look serious. 'And what was it about this man that so appealed to an intelligent woman like yourself, Misha?'

'I think it must have been his eyes,' she replied, ruefully. 'They're a wonderful amber colour, with long fox-coloured lashes.'

'I see. In such matters, eyes are important, are they?' He smiled, with a hint of irony.

She returned the smile. 'In my case, crucial, it seems.'

'So, what happened next?'

'Um, we became lovers.'

'Was that wise?'

'It was bliss.' Curiously, telling the story seemed somehow to restore her confidence; in herself, in Giles, and in the validity of their love. 'I was never so happy in my life as I was then,' she said. 'That is, until last Monday.'

'That was when you found out that he had been involved in an accident, and was in hospital in London?'

'Yes.'

The food arrived, and for a few minutes they ate in silence. Surprising herself, Misha found that she was ravenously hungry, the rare steak and crisp golden potatoes exactly what she needed at that moment. Paul de Vilmorin watched her covertly, relieved to see her eating, touched by her fragile appearance; the dark smudges under her bloodshot eyes, the lids puffy and swollen. 'A little wine?' he offered, picking up the carafe.

'Thank you.' She watched as he poured the wine into her glass, then into his own.

'So, what did you find in London?'

'I found Giles in quite poor shape. He has multiple rib fractures and a lot of superficial laceration to the face and chest. Both wrists are fractured and he was badly concussed, with some depression of consciousness and amnesia.' Misha looked steadily at de Vilmorin. 'There is no evidence of damage to the skull that could explain this, but they are unwilling to commit themselves to an accurate diagnosis, because Giles uses cocaine, and was in fact high at the time of the accident.'

'How very unfortunate.' Paul took a sip of his wine. 'Were you aware that he took drugs, Misha?'

'Yes, I was.'

'You never tried to stop him?'

'Yes, of course I did, frequently, but it was a pointless waste of time.'

'It's often the case, isn't it?' He looked at her thoughtfully. 'Obviously all this stress and uncertainty is proving difficult for you to sustain. You must have a very deep attachment to this man, my dear. So why didn't you get in touch with us, and ask for leave to stay with him?'

Misha swallowed nervously, stared into her glass, then looked at Paul, her tired eyes huge in her small pale face. 'This is the hardest part,' she said, her voice little more than a whisper. 'When I was at the hospital I met Giles's wife. Well, not his *wife* exactly; they're not married.' She lowered her eyes and smiled timidly. 'I could have handled that; I'm not a complete doormat, you know.' She paused, and drank a little wine. 'What I can't handle, and can't compete against, is the fact that they have a six-year-old child, a little girl called Alice.' Again, she raised her eyes to Paul's, and he gazed back at her, his expression grave and concerned, unsmiling. 'The child is a carbon copy of Giles. She has exactly the same unmistakable eyes, and red curly hair.' Unwisely, Misha attempted to make a small joke: 'At least, now, I know what he looked like as a little boy.' Then her head drooped, tears filled her eyes and fell unchecked onto her plate.

Quickly, Paul reached across the table and covered her hand with his. 'Don't cry, Misha. It's obvious to me that he's not worth your tears, or your love.'

Misha wiped her eyes on her napkin, and did her best to smile. 'I know that. Don't you think I've told myself exactly that, a million times?'

'But love's not like that, is it?'

'No, it isn't.'

They finished the meal, deliberately avoiding the subject of Giles. To fill the vacuum thus created, Paul told Misha about his son, Pascal, and his daughter-in-law Emma. 'They live in a tiny village called Mas les Arnauds, near Manosque, in Haute Provence. He makes goat's cheese, and she makes frescoes.'

'Frescoes?'

'Paintings in egg tempera, directly onto damp plaster walls.'

'How fascinating. How does she manage to do that, if they live in such a remote place?'

'There are quite a lot of eighteenth- and nineteenth-century small chateaux and *maisons de maîtres* in the area, and a good many of them were originally decorated by itinerant Italian fresco-painters. What Emma does is to restore them.'

'What a terrific way to spend one's life.'

'That's true, of course. But it's hard, too, sometimes.

The winters can be terribly cold and windy; the region's not called the Alpes de Haute Provence for nothing. Their house is beautiful, but has no heating other than the stove in the kitchen. They've only just installed electricity, and a proper bathroom upstairs.'

'Still, if that's what they like?'

'They do, though I have to admit that I sometimes do the unforgivable thing in a parent, and worry about them. Especially now that Emma is pregnant.'

Misha smiled. 'Is it so unforgivable, worrying about your grown-up children?'

'Absolutely. Your grown-up children should be like your patients, Misha. You're supposed not to be too closely involved with them. It's the cardinal rule, isn't it?'

The waiter brought coffee, and Misha put a lump of sugar in hers, stirring it carefully. 'Haven't you broken the cardinal rule, by trying to help me sort out my private problems?'

'Would you have preferred that I hadn't interfered?'

She looked up, and smiled. 'No, I wouldn't. I'm very glad you did.' She drank some coffee, and put the little cup carefully back in its saucer. 'As a matter of fact, I was pretty much at crack-up point, when you spoke to me. I feel better now. Not good, but not so confused, either. It's comforting to feel I can talk to someone, when things are going badly wrong.'

'Good. If you need me again, you know where I am, OK?'

'OK. Thanks.'

Paul paid the bill, and they walked back to the car. He drove her to Bastille, and dropped her at her door. She thanked him for her supper, said good night and got out of the car. He watched while she unlocked her door, and waited until the lights appeared in the top floor of the building. Then he drove slowly out of the narrow street and back to the hospital. He took the lift to intensive care, and checked that all was well with his small patient. The baby was sleeping peacefully, his cheeks rosy, a slight sweat on his upper lip. 'Well done,' he said to the young nurse who sat beside the child's cot. Then he returned to the car, and drove slowly home.

The de Vilmorins lived in an extremely grand house in the Marais, one of a seventeenth-century development of *hôtels particuliers* in a small square off rue de Thorigny, and a short walk from the Musée Picasso. Paul, himself the son of a country doctor and his English wife, brought up in a large rambling fortified farmhouse in the Yonne district of Burgundy with his brother and sister and their many cats and dogs, had never had any great inclination to live in such magnificent urban surroundings, and the fact that he did so was entirely the choice of Blanche, his wife.

Paul's mother, Jane de Vilmorin, had been an amateur botanical painter of some distinction, and their house had reflected the same faded charm, restraint and absence of ostentation as her pictures. In her world, only three elements were of any real significance – her husband, her children and her painting. Of her three children, two sons and a daughter, Paul, the youngest, had probably been the most aware of his mother's special talents and had enjoyed the forays into the fields and woods with her, carrying her killing-bottle, nets and jam-jars, in search of specimens for her camera and paintbrush. For him, too, the beautiful untidy house, always full of sunlight in his memory, had seemed the perfect place for the raising of children, and when he married and had children of his own he had assumed, wrongly as it turned out, that such a house would be where his own family would grow, in clean air and with woods and fields in which to ride and roam.

When Blanche had informed him, not entirely thrilled about it, that she was pregnant, Paul was already making rapid progress towards his goal, neurosurgery, and they were living in a small rented apartment in St Germain. Delighted at the news, Paul immediately suggested that they look for a house in the country, but this idea was quickly dismissed by Blanche. 'Absolutely not,' she said firmly. 'I would die of boredom, Paul. We'll find a bigger apartment, near here, where all my friends are. A city can be a good place to bring up children, more stimulating. Much more fun.'

Within a month, she had found a fairly large apartment, near to the university, and one which they could afford to buy, with quite a lot of help from Blanche's father. Blanche turned out to be extremely good at buying, doing up and selling very desirable apartments. By the time her second child, Pascal, was five years old the family was installed in the small but beautiful *hôtel particulier* in the Marais, and Blanche had established herself in a thriving business as an interior decorator. As a concession to Paul's love of the country, and because it was in any case a fashionable thing to do, she also bought a farmhouse in the Vaucluse and turned it into a comfortable *maison secondaire*, where they spent the long summer vacation each year.

In fact, Blanche had been perfectly right in her assertion that children can be successfully reared in the city, and both Nina and Pascal had done very well at school, passing their 'bacs' with flying colours. To her great satisfaction and pride, both had followed in their father's footsteps by reading medicine at university, and Nina had lived up to all her mother's ambitions for her. She had qualified, practised as a GP, and become engaged to a surgeon. She was now successfully combining marriage and career, and her life was full and happy.

Pascal, on the other hand, had proved a serious disappointment to his mother. He had dropped out of medical school and moved south to Provence, choosing to live in a village about an hour's drive from the de Vilmorin summer home. Blanche had never forgiven her son for his rejection of her plans for him, but his father had secretly encouraged Pascal in his bid for freedom, and had lent him money to buy his shabby old house and few hectares of land. As Paul had told Misha earlier in the evening, he envied Pascal his way of living, and often thought longingly of his two favourite people, deeply in love, at ease with their world in that wonderful landscape, but too far from Paris for him to see them as frequently as he would have wished.

Paul parked his car, and walked the short distance to the imposing iron gates that guarded the small square in which his house, and the seven others exactly like it, were situated. As he closed the gate, he glanced upwards and saw that the lights of the salon were not lit. Presumably Blanche had gone on to supper with her friends, after the show. White Versailles boxes stood on either side of the impressive front door. They were planted with clipped bay trees, illuminated by two large glass lanterns fixed to the stone walls of the house. Exuberant white petunias tumbled through the wrought-iron balconies of the first floor, slightly scenting the surrounding air. Paul inserted his key into the lock and went in, the door closing behind him with a heavy, voluptuous, rather satisfying clunk, as ancient wood and meticulously oiled specimens of the locksmith's art were reunited, functioning as flawlessly as they had when first installed, three centuries ago.

The hall in which he stood was the only part of the old house that Paul still felt comfortable with, and really liked. It had a pale-grey stone floor, laid in large diamond-shaped tiles, plain white walls, and very little furniture. It smelt cool and damp, like an ancient church. High on the walls hung two enormous rectangular landscape paintings, 'school of Poussin', with heavy black frames. Under one of the paintings stood a long cedarwood coffer, with a heavily engraved steel lock, and arranged on its lid was a collection of antique terrestrial globes, together with what appeared to be a small armillary sundial, but was in fact a perpetual calendar, painted with the signs of the zodiac. To one side of the coffer stood a tall Chinese jar of the Kangsi period, containing a collection of antique walking-sticks, umbrellas and parasols. On the opposite side of the hall, facing the front door, a curved flight of stone steps, supporting a graceful iron baluster, rose elegantly to the first floor and the principal rooms of the house.

It was at this point that Paul's feelings for his home became somewhat negative. When Blanche had first discovered the place, although it had been in an advanced state of neglect and near disintegration, the little house still had the romantic atmosphere and magical associations of its seventeenth-century origins. The *boiseries* that lined the walls, the parquet of the floors, and the plasterwork of the ceilings, although in a poor state, had survived, just, and Blanche had set about the task of restoration with an almost religious fervour. For several years the little *hôtel particulier* had been a perfect family home, beautiful, relaxed and full of Blanche's ever-increasing collection of furniture, books and pictures.

Then Nina and Pascal had left home, and everything changed. Blanche decided to open a shop, in order to run her expanding business more efficiently. She also redecorated the bedroom vacated by Nina, and moved in there herself. This action on her part did not come as any great surprise to Paul, and was in some respects a relief. It was as if she had silently acknowledged the demise of their marriage, without indulging in the crude weapons of angry words or accusations. While the children were still at home, and needing her motivating force to push them up the academic ladder, she had been content to overlook her husband's lack of any real interest in herself or her friends, and the busy social life they so much enjoyed. Now, she felt entirely free to do precisely as she chose, in all respects.

It was difficult for either of them to remember when

the break-up of their marriage really began, or for either of them to point the finger of blame at the other, but Paul was aware that Blanche felt that he had failed her badly in the matter of their social life. In spite of all her efforts to make him take such things seriously, as a means of furthering both their careers, Paul had stubbornly resisted, denouncing the social scene as a ludicrous waste of an intelligent person's time. After the birth of their children, his workload had increased along with his growing celebrity in his chosen field, so that even if he had wished it, his schedule left very little space for activities which he regarded as both frivolous and boring. It was for this reason that Blanche had become bosom friends with a pleasant, childless couple, Olivier and Catherine St-Denis, and it was in their company that she attended private views, the *défilés* of all the grand couturiers, theatrical first nights and similar social functions, and was from time to time photographed at some glittering soirée or other, a circumstance that afforded her intense gratification.

Equally, from time to time, Olivier, a gentle soul in his late fifties, urbane and paunchy, smelling deliciously of Givenchy's Monsieur, visited Blanche at her home, alone. These assignations usually lasted for about two hours, and were supposed to be a closely guarded secret, for neither of them wished to cause pain to their respective spouses. However, Olivier's vanity in the matter of his scent gave him away, and Paul had little difficulty in putting two and two together at such times. The sad thing was that he did not actually care, and was in fact rather pleased that Blanche was able to satisfy her sexual needs, or rather, he guessed, the desire to prove that she could still attract a man if she so wished. For himself, any such feelings towards his wife had long since withered and died.

He went upstairs, opened the door to the salon and went in. Blanche was at that time in her fashionable grey period, and the walls of this beautifully proportioned room were hung with silk damask, the colour of a town pigeon, with a pattern of urns and acanthus leaves in a paler shade of grey. The curtains that hung from ebony rings at the tall windows were made from the same fabric, and so were the covers of the two immense sofas flanking the grey-marble chimney-piece. Fixed to the chimney-breast was an impressive eighteenth-century gilded mirror, and on either side of it hung sanguine drawings by Holbein, mounted in grey and framed in distressed gold leaf. On the ledge of the chimney-piece were two Sèvres plates and a pair of Rockingham vases converted into electric lamps, their shades made from the ubiquitous grey silk damask. On the floor, beside the fireplace, was a set of brass fire-irons and a basket of logs. Quite what was the point of either, Paul had no idea, for the fire was never lit. All in all, he thought it the most depressing room in which he had ever had the misfortune to spend any time.

He drew the curtains, and went into the small ante-room that served as his study. He listened to his messages, checked his diary for the following day, poured himself a whisky and went upstairs to the bedroom he had once shared with his wife. Since the redecoration of the salon, this room, too, had received the grey treatment. Walls, curtains and counterpane, as well as the floor-length cloths that covered the small round tables on either side of the double bed, were of the same boring material used in the salon. Blanche must have bought several hundred metres of the bloody stuff, he said to himself, as he ripped the cover off the bed and bundled it into the cupboard where extra pillows and duvets were stored. At least, thank God, the bedlinen was plain and white, and the blanket blue.

He took off his jacket and hung it over the small Gothic oak chair that stood beside the door to the bathroom. Then he kicked off his shoes, took his glass of whisky from the night-table, and made himself comfortable on the bed, leaning back against a heap of pillows. He picked up the remote control and aimed it at the small TV set that stood on a padded bench at the foot of the bed, along with piles of books and papers. This was the single area in which he had energized himself sufficiently to challenge Blanche's strict rules on the subject of litter, in the shape of personal possessions, papers and books, all of which, in her view, should be tidied away on a daily basis. After several acrimonious arguments on the subject, Marie-Claire, the live-in help, had been instructed not to touch anything in his study or bedroom without his express permission.

Slowly, Paul drank his whisky, and flicked through the TV channels, finally settling on a late newscast. He watched the screen with little interest, and in his head played back the events of his own day. He saw himself and Misha ben Bella in the washroom at the hospital; driving through the traffic to place des Vosges; sitting on the terrace at Ma Bourgogne. He saw Misha's sad green eyes in her pale, tense face and her long-fingered hands twisted tightly together on the table, as she told her story. Poor girl, he said to himself, what a terrible humiliation to have to endure. The man must be an absolute bastard, or barely sane. I would've thought she'd be well shot of him, though I imagine it's going to take quite a time for her to work that out for herself.

He sighed, finished his drink and turned off the TV. He went to his bathroom, showered and cleaned his teeth. He returned to his bedroom and put his watch on the night-table, along with his bleeper. He got into bed, enjoying the coolness of the sheets on his naked body, then switched off the lamp, closed his eyes, and slept.

His sleep was not particularly restful, for he dreamt that he was driving his father's old Peugeot through the narrow lanes of the Yonne, with fields of oil-seed rape, grown tall and heavily scented, on either side of the road. On the back seat of the car was a baby, wrapped in blood-stained newspaper, like a parcel of raw meat, though whether the child was dead or alive he had no way of knowing. What he did know was that he had an urgent need to get somewhere in a great hurry. Then the country lanes grew dark, and turned themselves into the narrow streets of Bastille, and he found himself parked outside the building that housed Misha ben Bella's apartment. He got out of the car and looked up at the top floor, silhouetted blackly against the night sky. He saw a slight, dark figure standing on the roof, then leaning into the air, arms outstretched, falling, falling. 'STOP!' he yelled. 'DON'T DO IT!'

He woke, sweating, his heart hammering. He turned on the light, and peered at his watch: three-twenty. Fool, he thought, that's what happens when you bring your work home and allow yourself to fret about the patients, and your colleagues, isn't it?

He drank some water, switched off the light, and turned onto his side, settling the pillow under his cheek. He stared into the darkness. Poor girl, he thought, I hope to God she's all right.

Giles Murray-Williams lay on his hospital bed, feeling ill and tired, and refusing to get out of bed, in spite of the strenuous efforts of the nursing staff to encourage him to do so. He was dismayed at his physical weakness, his helpless dependence on others, and his inability to focus his mind on the urgent necessity of dreaming up a foolproof method of maintaining the distance between the two women in his life.

'What a nice person Misha is, Giles,' Juliet had said, during a recent visit. 'You never told me about having a doctor in Paris – especially such an attractive one, darling.'

'I've absolutely no recollection of the bloody woman,' he had retorted sharply. 'I told you that.'

'How strange.' Juliet had smiled, shaking her head. 'She seemed to know *you* awfully well.'

'In her dreams,' he had replied sulkily, and she had laughed.

Giles could not know that, driving home on that same night, Juliet had congratulated herself on making the decision to forget about keeping Dr ben Bella informed about Giles's progress. Let sleeping dogs, and all that, she had said to herself, sensibly. She knew Giles very well indeed.

Miserably, Giles contemplated his enforced convalescence in St Peter's Square, bossed by Dorothy, irritated by his small daughter, with Juliet out at work all day. He thought longingly of his own little garden flat in Chelsea, the place he adored and in which he felt completely free, unencumbered by either women or children. In his mind's eye he saw the discreet street door, with its pretty Georgian fanlight, illuminating the narrow passage that served as a hall. Deliberately undecorated, the wallpaper faded and peeling, the glue eaten away by insects, this dark, claustrophobic space led to a small, very masculine bedroom and bathroom, and thence to a minimal kitchen, from which a bare wooden staircase descended to a panelled room of medium size and extraordinary beauty. It was fitted on every suitable wall space with purpose-made bookshelves, filled with leather-bound volumes in several languages. On the floor was a large, threadbare, once brightly coloured Turkey carpet, on which stood a dark-green leather chesterfield. There was no other form of seating, except for a set of antique library steps.

French windows led into a small garden, introduced into the original stone walls of a much earlier building. Connected by a steep stone stairway, the garden was on two levels, and was Giles's greatest interest, even passion. Hart's tongue ferns grew in the cracks of the stones, and blue campanula cascaded down the steps in spring and summer. An ancient fig clambered around the grey enclosing walls, doing its best to reach the light. It produced very little in the way of fruit, but provided welcome shade in summer, wonderfully soothing to Giles's spirit as he chilled out in his secret haven, overjoyed to be alone, free to get hammered with drink or drugs if he felt so inclined, without the intrusive fussing of his womenfolk.

Lead urns, containing woodruff, nicotiana and other sweet-smelling plants, were grouped around the lower level of the garden, and scented the air around the solitary grey-painted wrought-iron garden chair in which he loved to sit alone on summer evenings. 'Oh God! I wish!' he groaned loudly to his empty hospital room, visualizing himself in his cool, damp paradise, with a plate of oysters and a bottle of chilled Chablis at his side, a copy of the Eclogues of Virgil in his hand. *Latet anguis in herba,* Giles recited silently, with a cynical smile. Dear little snake in the grass, he said to himself; just like me.

Sadly, he reflected on the distressing changes to his way of life that would necessarily occur as a result of his accident, with an emotion as near to anguish as he could persuade himself to feel. He realized that once the physical pain of his injuries ceased to occupy his mind, he would begin to miss Misha very much; horribly, in fact. She had been, for him, the perfect lover. Cool, well groomed, clever and beautiful, her attitude to sex had always been refreshingly unclinging, as well as athletic and inventive. Like himself, she greatly enjoyed the act of sex in itself, and never demanded from him more of himself than he was prepared to give. He had always felt liberated by the games of secrecy between them, and made a virtue of their frequent and lengthy separations, knowing how sexually explosive their reunions would be. In addition to her prowess in bed, Misha was an excellent cook, so that he had not found it necessary to take her to expensive restaurants all the time. He was going to miss that element of their association very badly indeed, he knew. The food at Juliet's wasn't bad, but the problem was having to eat with the cook all the time. All in all,

Giles felt extremely badly done by, and cursed the day he had taken up para-gliding.

Wrapped in his self-pitying isolation, he entirely failed to recognize that for Misha the areas of personal privacy had been a question of trust and generosity of spirit, never an excuse for cheating.

Juliet raised the subject of Giles's release from hospital after she had settled Alice for the night, and she and Dorothy were ready to sit down to their supper. 'I know it'll make extra work, darling, but he'll have to be here full time for a bit. He couldn't possibly manage on his own in Chelsea.' Dorothy, carving a guinea fowl breast into generous slices, looked singularly unimpressed. Juliet smiled at her, appeasingly. 'All those stairs, you know?' she suggested, hopefully.

'Yes, well, that's as maybe.' Dorothy spooned a pile of celeriac mousseline onto each plate, handed one to Juliet, and passed a sauceboat of hot cranberry sauce. She sat down, and looked severely at her employer. 'You're too soft,' she said, pouring wine for them both. 'Will he be going to work, or will he be expecting round-the-clock unpaid nursing? And where's he going to sleep, may I ask?'

'Where does he usually sleep when he's staying here, Dorothy? With me, of course, where else? And I'm sure he'll be going back to work pretty soon; he's bored stiff already.'

'Just so long as I know,' said Dorothy huffily. 'You let that man walk all over you, you really do.' She took a large mouthful of guinea fowl. 'It would be another thing if he married you.'

'So you keep saying,' said Juliet.

'Only considering the child.'

'Mm. I know you are, darling.'

A month passed, and gradually Misha began to accept that she was not going to receive a progress report from Juliet, and believed she understood the reason for this.

After two weeks she had stopped phoning the hospital, estimating that Giles would by now be well enough to go home, wherever 'home' was, for him. She did her best to put him out of her mind, to concentrate on her work, volunteering for overtime whenever the opportunity arose. Nevertheless, each night, on her return to the apartment, she eagerly checked her messages, her heart in her mouth, desperate for news.

One evening, in late June, as she got out of the lift, she heard the telephone ringing inside the apartment, and rushed to answer it. 'Hello?'

'Misha, it's me.'

'Giles! Where are you?'

'I'm in bloody St Peter's Square, where else? I'm going out of my mind with irritation and boredom, but I don't have a choice, short of checking into a private nursing home.'

'Oh dear, I'm sorry. What is it, darling? Your wrists?'

'Yes, and my fucking ribs. They're agony, most of the time. I'm still on painkillers.'

'Poor you.' There was a pause, and she asked, 'Is it OK, phoning from Juliet's place?'

'No, it isn't, absolutely not, and I won't be able to do it again.'

'Are you alone, just now?'

'Yes, I am. Juliet's working late, and dread Dorothy has taken Alice to a movie, something about bloody dalmatians, I believe.'

'I see.'

Giles cleared his throat. 'Actually, Misha, I'm afraid this is a "dear John" call. It's not an easy thing for me to have to do, my dear, but there's no alternative, I'm afraid. In any case, I'm unable to write just now, as I'm sure you'll appreciate.'

'Giles! What the hell are you talking about?'

'I'm talking about *us*, darling. It's over, Misha, kaput, fini. You get the picture?'

Slowly, Misha sat down on the sofa. 'Why?' she asked, very quietly.

'Because Juliet is my common-law wife, and Alice is my daughter. She bears my name, and I love her, so I don't want to rock the boat. You are only my mistress, Misha, so if something has to be sacrificed, I'm afraid it's you. It's a pity because you're a bloody good screw and it's nice having a place in Paris. Juliet can be quite vindictive, as a matter of fact. She'd go spare if she knew about us; she'd probably throw me out, and she'd certainly deny me access to Alice.'

'Giles,' said Misha, 'what makes you think that Juliet hasn't already guessed?'

'Shit! I hope not! No, I don't think she has, she'd have said something by now. I know her.'

'What about your things, Giles?'

'My things?'

'All your pictures, books, and stuff.'

'Oh. Yes, of course. Well, hang on to them for the moment, and I'll send for them later, OK?'

'Very well.'

'I'd better go now. I can hear Alice in the kitchen. They're back. Well, goodbye, Misha, it's been—'

'GILES!' screamed Misha into the telephone, causing him to suffer acute aural trauma at the receiving end. 'Don't you *dare* say it's been nice knowing you, you poisonous little creep!' And before he could gather his wits, she slammed down the phone.

Feeling cold, her fingers clumsy, she poured herself a large whisky, and took a long hot bath. She tried to relax, to think about the situation calmly and without overreaction. She forced herself to be realistic about Giles's behaviour, doing her best to despise him, to get really angry with him. Since he was no longer in any kind of danger, she found this comparatively easy to do. 'Bloody short-arsed little shit!' she said aloud. 'Bloody fucking two-timing bastard, I hate you!'

I don't hate you, darling, she thought, and tears filled her eyes. I love you; you bloody know I do. How can I stop loving you, just like that, Giles, you brute? Into her head came the clear image of Giles in the bosom of his family in Hammersmith, his lion-eyed little girl at his side, while Dorothy, in the kitchen, prepared something tempting for his supper. I have to let him go, she thought sadly. It's where he belongs, really, if he has to make a choice. She sighed. For the sake of the child, I can't fight him, or her. It's a question of ethics: mine, if not his, she thought bitterly. And even if I did succeed in getting him back, how could I ever trust him again? At least, if Juliet really doesn't know about me, I suppose she could still have a chance of happiness with him, who knows?

Had she been a fly on Juliet's wall, however, she would have laughed, for she was only human, and the idyllic scene she had imagined was far from the actual truth. Giles was, in fact, ensconced on the sofa in Juliet's sitting-room, complaining of the cold and demanding loudly that Dorothy light the fire, while Alice, unmoved by her father's raised voice, continued to tell him the story of the hundred and one dalmatians.

'DOROTHY!' shouted Giles, for the third time.

Dorothy stuck her head round the door. 'What?' she asked belligerently.

'Please light the bloody fire. It's freezing in here.'

'We never light the fire in summer!'

'I don't care. I'm bloody cold!'

'Come in the kitchen, then.'

'Certainly not!'

'Please yourself.'

'LIGHT THE BLOODY FIRE!'

'I WILL NOT!' Dorothy withdrew, slamming the door behind her, and returned to the kitchen to the pork and dumplings she was preparing for supper. She floured her hands, dividing the dough and rolling it into balls between her palms. Either he goes, or I do, she said to herself, her ears blazing with indignation. I'll not be spoken to like that; not by him, not by anyone. What does he think I am, a slave?

Through the window, she saw the little car draw to

a halt, then watched as Juliet ran down the steps to the kitchen door and came in, looking rather tired. Dorothy's face broke into a pleased smile. 'Hello, darlin',' she said. 'Had a good day, then?'

'So-so,' said Juliet. 'How was everything here?'

'Like you, so-so. You better ask him.'

'Shit,' said Juliet, and poured herself a drink.

'He wants the fire lit in the sitting-room.'

'Why can't he come in here?'

Dorothy shook her head, and said nothing. She dropped the little balls of dough into her simmering pork casserole.

Juliet sighed. 'OK,' she said wearily, 'I'll go and do it.'

Chapter Three

On the morning of the *vernissage* of her Paris exhibition, in late June, Olivia Rodzianko woke very early, disturbed by the song of a blackbird in the tree outside her open window. She was staying with her mother-in-law, Hester, in her apartment on the Ile St-Louis, and sleeping in the childhood bedroom of her husband, Basil. She looked around the small room, dim in the blue early light, her eyes wandering over the familiar objects: the small Russian ebony writing-table, inlaid with mother-of-pearl, which stood beneath the uncurtained window, along with a rush-seated, blue-painted country chair. On the desk was a brass student's lamp, with an adjustable green-glass shade, the twin of the lamp that stood on the chest of drawers beside the bed.

Olivia stretched out an arm and switched on the lamp. She gazed with admiration at the set of silver-framed miniature portraits, hanging on the wall behind the lamp. Formidable-looking bewhiskered men in Cossack uniforms, and frail-looking women with corkscrew curls, wearing high-bosomed gauzy ball-gowns, these were the Rodzianko forebears, practically the only remaining evidence of Basil's Russian ancestry. Close to the miniatures hung an ancient silver icon, elaborately moulded, chased and incised, with holes cut in the silver to reveal the faces and hands of the Virgin and Child painted on the wooden panel within.

Before the icon hung a silver votive lamp, suspended by three fine silver chains from a hook in the ceiling. A purple glass shielded its tiny perpetual flame, and Olivia got out of bed, crossed herself before the icon and said a prayer for Basil's preservation and safe return from his current overseas assignment.

She had been only nineteen at the time of their marriage, while still a student at the Beaux-Arts, and he thirty-three, a television foreign correspondent. At the time, some anxiety had been expressed by her family about the wisdom of marrying someone so much older than herself, but she had never felt a moment's regret, in spite of the inevitable loneliness and worry his postings to the hot-spots of the world often brought with them. In the event, the circumstances of Basil's career had taught her very rapidly to become independent, to do her own work, and lead her own life.

In the beginning, they had lived in a rented studio in Pigalle, so that Olivia had been near to her own parents, as well as close to Basil's mother, on the Ile St-Louis. Hester Rodzianko, now seventy-five, still earned her own living by painting bogus icons and selling them to the dealers in such things, and Olivia, though she would never have considered doing such a thing herself, had the greatest love and respect for the older woman, and almost always stayed with her when she had to come to Paris.

After two years in Pigalle, Basil and Olivia had found a disused barn of monumental proportions in a quiet corner of the Sologne, and it was here that she now spent the greater part of her time, alone, isolated, but happy, content to devote herself totally to her work as a printmaker. She made etchings and lithographs, and a good deal of the living space was occupied by her large and cumbersome printing presses, together with the necessary acid baths, plan-chests and work-tables required for her work. At thirty years old, Olivia was already well established in her career, and exhibited regularly in Paris, London, New York and

Tokyo. As a consequence of this world-wide success, she had of necessity to travel overseas quite frequently, so that it was becoming increasingly difficult for Basil to be in the same place as herself at any one time, or for them to be able to spend much time together.

It would have been a bonus to Olivia if he had been able to come to Paris right now, and be with her for the opening of her show, but, as usual, this had proved impossible, since he was currently in Moscow, with no date set for his return. Olivia felt the usual pang of disappointment that he could not be with her, for she was immensely proud of him, and loved seeing him on the TV news, with his wild dark hair and beard, now sprinkled with a little grey, but still thick and curly, in spite of his forty-four years. Tall, powerfully built and handsome, with sad grey eyes, he had always seemed to Olivia the perfect foil to her own deceptively frail appearance, with her slightly androgynous body, her long pale-blond hair, and her eyes of an arresting kingfisher blue.

Olivia was not a vain woman, but she knew her own worth and understood the publicity value to both herself and Basil of being a very striking couple. In his absence, she had decided to boost her solo morale by making one of her occasional forays into the exquisite shop of Issey Miyake and buying for herself a stunningly simple black pleated-silk construction; frock being an inadequate description of the architectural genius behind this amazing piece of clothing. On a less elevated intellectual level, it was also a pleasant change from her usual garb: old faded jeans and a T-shirt, augmented in cold weather by socks and sweaters belonging to her husband.

She went to the window, leaning over the sill and inhaling the scent of the flowers of the lime trees that grew in iron grids, in the paved courtyard of the seventeenth-century mansion. The soft, bright-green leaves of the trees were still transparent, and a delicate contrast to the pale-grey stones of the building. Olivia reflected on its quiet, subtle harmony, and the good fortune of the Rodziankos in having occupied the apartment in the *entresol* for more than forty years. Nowadays, Hester continued to live and work there, quite alone, but evidently not lonely. She's just like me, thought Olivia, smiling. Well, nearly, anyway; we're two of a kind.

She found Hester already up, making breakfast in the diminutive kitchen. They sat together at the table, and drank their coffee out of thick white bowls. 'You'll come with me to the *vernissage*, Hester?' she asked, dunking bread in her coffee.

'Not unless you really need me, Olly. I don't much care for these affairs, as you know.'

'I don't *need* you, darling. But I'd *appreciate* it, if you would.'

Hester raised her grey eyes, Basil's eyes, to those of her daughter-in-law. 'I've nothing to wear, Olly,' she said. 'I'm no substitute for Baz, you know, darling. I'd let you down.'

'Bollocks,' said Olivia, and laughed. 'What an old fraud you are. You always look wonderful. You just want to hear me say it, don't you?'

Hester put a hand to her thinning grey hair, pulled back into a small tight knot, and looked down her nose disapprovingly. 'Well, all right, if you say so, dear. I'll wear the Arabian job Basil brought me.'

'And the emerald cross, too,' insisted Olivia. 'The full Monty.'

'I might get mugged.'

'No chance,' said Olivia. 'Anyone can see the stones are fakes.'

'Oh. Do you really think so?' Hester laughed. 'Well, that's all right then, isn't it?'

Paul de Vilmorin, breakfasting alone in the dining-room, flicked through his mail as he drank his coffee before leaving for the hospital. He found little of interest, except a letter from his son, addressed, with unusual tact for Pascal, to both himself and Blanche. Paul finished his coffee, and took the note upstairs to his wife's room, where she was in the throes of a session with her personal trainer. Paul knocked and entered the room, to find Blanche, eyes closed and semi-naked, face down on her massage table, in the process of being pummelled by the vast muscular hands of the handsome black man to whom she entrusted the maintenance and improvement of her ageing body.

Paul coughed discreetly, by way of alerting his wife to his presence, and advanced to the bed of torture. 'Good morning, my dear,' he said. 'There's a letter from Pascal.'

Blanche opened her eyes. 'Really?' she said, without much interest. 'What does he want?'

'I don't know. I haven't opened it.'

'Well, open it, then.'

Paul broke the seal of the envelope and extracted the letter.

'Dear both,' he read aloud, '*Just to let you know that Emma has had a scan, and they think it will be twin boys. Love, P.'*

He looked at his wife, but she had closed her eyes again and he could not tell what her reaction to these tidings would be. 'Pretty exciting news, don't you think?' he ventured mildly.

'Do you really think so? In my opinion, they're mad. Hardly any money, and living in that ghastly old house. Poor Emma, I wouldn't like to be in her shoes. *One* baby is bad enough, but *two* is quite obscene.' Blanche's eyes snapped open. 'Especially *boys,*' she added abruptly. 'They're by far the most difficult.'

'I don't remember Pascal being particularly difficult.'

'That's because you didn't have to get up to him in the night, Paul. Horrible little brute, he never slept a wink. He was absolutely vile.'

'Oh, well. I'm sure they'll manage.' Paul put the

letter in his pocket, and made his way to the door.

'Paul?'

'Yes?'

'Will you be coming to the Rodzianko opening tonight? It would be so nice if you could, for a change. People are beginning to think you're dead, or something.'

'Um, well, I wasn't actually planning to go, Blanche. I've got a full list today. I shall be pretty tired tonight.'

'You could put in an appearance, just for a few minutes, I'm sure. Why don't you bring someone? What about one of your team? Why not bring that nice young Daniel Poirier? I liked him. Very sympa.'

'He's qualified, and moved on now. We miss him.'

'Oh, well, someone else? It's always a good idea to include the young intelligentsia in things, don't you agree?'

Paul paused at the door, his hand on the knob, reflecting briefly. 'There *is* a young doctor in the team, who's been a bit down in the mouth lately. Perhaps an evening out might be appropriate.'

'Fine. Bring him along, and we'll cheer him up, Paul.' Blanche opened her eyes and smiled at her husband, then gave a yelp of agony as Ben dug his powerful knuckles into the small of her back.

'It's a she, as a matter of fact.' Paul returned the smile. 'A woman doctor, Blanche. Music to your ears?'

'Oh, really? Well, *good*. I look forward to meeting her, Paul.'

'I'll see what I can do, my dear. *A ce soir.*'

'*A ce soir.*'

The door closed behind him. Blanche shut her eyes again, and concentrated on persuading her muscles to relax, as Ben worked his way down her spine, applying deep pressure to the knots that caused the tension headaches to which she had become a martyr.

'You are so *tight*, Blanche,' Ben said in his soft, velvety voice. 'You need me more than three times a week, I think.' Gently, he stroked her bare, oiled back with the flat of his hand, and she clenched her teeth to prevent herself gasping with pleasure at the delightful sensation this action induced in the pit of her stomach.

'That's enough for today, Ben!' Blanche sat up hastily, wrapping herself in her towel, and got down from the massage table. 'You'll have to go now, or I'll be late for the hairdresser.'

Misha, alone in her apartment at Bastille, got up as soon as the sun rose and watered the pots in her roof-garden. The air was fresh and cool, and since she was not on duty until ten o'clock, she decided that it would do her good to walk or, rather, run to the hospital; certainly a better idea than moping around at home, fretting about Giles, working herself into alternating moods of anger and despair. She pulled on her old tracksuit and trainers, put her breakfast things into the dishwasher, and left the apartment with a feeling of escape. Once on the street, she felt better, and decided to walk to Pont Sully, then run along the quays of the Ile St-Louis, crossing the little bridge to Notre Dame, then along the quays of the Ile de la Cité to Pont Neuf, where she would take the Métro to the hospital. When she reached Pont Neuf, hot and out of breath, she stopped opposite the statue of Henri IV. Then, dodging the relentless stream of traffic, she ran across the bridge, and down the steps into the little garden on the western tip of the island. There, she sat down for a moment to have a rest, and watch the early morning activities of the Bateaux-Vedettes du Pont-Neuf, as the crews prepared for the arrival of the sightseeing tourists.

As she watched, Misha thought fairly dispassionately about her situation. I'm not a fool, she told herself severely, and neither am I a child. It seems pretty clear that my life with Giles is over, finished, and probably that's as it should be, in the circumstances. I've just got to get used to the idea, that's all. She sighed, got to her feet, climbed back up the steps and began to walk slowly towards the Métro. Standing in the crowded train, she suddenly recollected how pale and diminished Giles had looked in his hospital bed, and in spite of her serious attempts at self-control, she felt her heart contract and her eyes ache with unshed tears as she remembered both his horrifying appearance and his failure to recognize her.

The train arrived at her station, and she crowded into the lift to the street, bodies packed tightly together, the air thick with tobacco smoke. She crossed the road, trudged up the steps to the rear entrance to the hospital, and made her way to Neurology. How odd, she thought suddenly; he remembered Juliet straight away, didn't he? And Alice, too. Why was it that he didn't know me? Why?

She went to the locker room, took a quick shower, got into her hospital trousers and white coat, and hooked her stethoscope round her neck, ready for the consultant's rounds. As she hung up her tracksuit in her locker, the blindingly obvious answer to her question stared Misha in the face. He knew perfectly well who I was all the time, horrid little swine, she told herself angrily. It wasn't at all *convenient* for him to remember me at that particular moment, was it?

The afternoon's list took very much longer than anticipated, with the added stress of the cardiac arrest and subsequent death of one of the patients. Although of necessity inured to the inevitability of such occasional disasters, Paul, and to a lesser extent his team, felt a keen sense of failure and disappointment at such times, and he found it appallingly difficult to have to confront the deceased's anxiously waiting family with the news that would break their hearts, and probably destroy their lives.

As he left the hospital, depressed and exhausted, he remembered his half-promise to Blanche to attend the Rodzianko private view. Shit, he said to himself, and paused on the steps. I said I'd ask Misha to come, too.

God, how stupid I am; am I losing my grip? He turned, went back into the hospital, and found Misha, looking tired and dishevelled in a crumpled tracksuit, preparing to leave. One look at her convinced him that there was no way she would accept an invitation to one of Blanche's chic affairs, looking as she did, and obviously exhausted into the bargain. 'Misha,' he said, lamely. 'You look shattered. Are you OK?'

'I hate it when they die.'

Paul sighed. 'You have to bear in mind that none of us are gods, my dear. We can only do our best, and sometimes that's not good enough. Some things are out of our control.'

'I know. It's stupid of me to mind so much.'

'No, it's not. I feel rotten about it myself, as a matter of fact. It's a question of having to live with it, or else pack in the job.'

'Yes, of course. I see that.'

Paul looked at her, hesitating. He felt disinclined to say goodnight and walk away, leaving her to find her way to Bastille alone, looking as ill and tired as she did. 'Can I give you a lift, or were you thinking of running home?'

She smiled. 'I ran here this morning, but I don't feel much like running again. I was thinking of the Métro, but I'd appreciate a lift. Thank you.'

'Fine. Let's go.'

She was silent, preoccupied, as they drove through the late evening traffic. He drove into passage des Ebénistes, and stopped the car at her door. 'Here we are,' he said, putting on the handbrake.

She turned, and smiled, undoing her belt. 'Thank you,' she said. 'You're very kind.'

'How's your friend, Misha?'

Taken by surprise, the blood rushed to her cheeks. She stared stonily through the windscreen. 'He's OK,' she said coldly. 'He's left hospital and gone home.'

'That's good news, then?'

'Is it?' She turned her head and looked straight at

him, the pain in her eyes palpable. 'I had a call from Giles last week. He's dumping me, Paul. He says he doesn't want to put his domestic life in jeopardy. He's in denial, as far as I'm concerned, and I don't know what to do about it.'

She called me Paul, said de Vilmorin to himself, and a very curious sensation moved him, as though some long-closed door in his inner being had been opened a crack. He drew a slow, imperceptible breath. 'In what respect, Misha?' he asked quietly, not entirely sure what he meant by the question.

'Well, for one thing, I don't know what to do about his things.'

'His things?'

'Yes, his *things*; his possessions. If he's ditched me, I sure as hell don't want to be reminded of him all the time, do I?'

'Is there so much of his stuff?'

'You wouldn't believe how much.' Misha looked at the car clock: eight thirty-five. 'Are you too tired, or do you feel like coming up for a drink?' She looked at him doubtfully, her eyes luminous in the gloom of the car's interior. 'I expect you'll want to get home, though? You must be knackered?'

Paul remembered his promise to Blanche, then, realizing that it was too late to attend the show anyway, and that she and her friends would have gone on to dine, he smiled. 'Yes, I am knackered, and I'd love a drink, but on one condition.'

Misha looked faintly alarmed. 'What's that?'

'That I can have something to eat; some cheese, anything. I'm starving.'

She laughed. 'Of course. There's something in the fridge; sausage, and some cold rice, I think.'

'Sounds terrific. Can't wait.'

At half past nine the gallery was emptying, the last of the guests departing in search of dinner, and Olivia observed that there was a gratifying number of red stickers on the exhibits. Glen, the American dealer who promoted and sold her work, was in animated conversation with the art critic of one of the glossy magazines, though which one Olivia could not call to mind. Earlier in the evening, going round the exhibition with her, that same critic had made a polished little speech on the subject of her cleverness, youth and beauty, remarking that it was such a shame that Basil was so rarely in town, and adding that he would be more than delighted to stand in for him, if required. The offer had been made with what could only be described as a predatory leer, but Olivia, having no wish to jeopardize what she was sure would be a good notice in his publication, had thanked him very sweetly, and promised to bear it in mind. Now, as he shook hands with Glen at the door, he blew her a kiss. Olivia, smiling, raised her hand in farewell.

'Right.' Glen came to her side. 'An excellent evening's work, Olivia, if I'm not mistaken. I think we've said all the right things to all the right people. We deserve a good dinner, darling. I booked a table at Grand Véfour.'

'Golly, how posh!' exclaimed Olivia. 'Hester won't like that; far too grand.'

'Nonsense, of course she will. Where is she, anyway?'

'In the stock-room, having a sit-down. She doesn't do standing up for long, these days.'

'Very understandable.' Glen took his mobile from his pocket and called a cab. 'She's a very remarkable lady. I wish she'd let me sell her stuff for her. It'd go down a storm in the States. I could probably do a deal with one of the big Fifth Avenue stores, to flog them in the furniture department.'

Olivia laughed. 'No chance, I'm afraid. She's been working for the criminal Benoit for decades. He brings her the bits of wormy old wood-panel she uses for her icons. He even finds floorboards, rescued from derelict early buildings; it's amazing what he gets out of skips.

If she sold the end product to anyone else, he'd cease to supply her, no question. She likes the old devil, anyway – the elderly tend to hang together, I've noticed.'

'Oh, well, one can always hope, I suppose.' Glen smiled. 'I'll just have to go on making a profit out of you, darling.'

'Here's the taxi,' said Olivia. 'I'll get Hester.'

Once settled with due ceremony at a corner table in the softly lit restaurant at the far end of the gardens of the Palais Royal, Olivia and Hester studied the menu, while Glen, without consulting his guests, asked the waiter to bring three *coupes*.

'Really, Glen,' said Hester crossly, 'champagne gives me wind. I've had far too much already.'

'Never mind. We'll drink it for you, if you don't want it, darling.' Olivia looked round the elegantly restored restaurant, with its beautiful Directoire décor, intricately painted ceiling, mirrored wall-panels, ornate gilded light-fittings and richly embroidered golden-tasselled hangings. In spite of the opulent atmosphere of the place, the small, intimate tables were plainly dressed with white cloths, and comfortable gilded chairs.

'Have you chosen, Olivia?'

'Yes, I have. Smoked salmon, and sweetbreads *en croûte*, please.'

'Hester?'

'Smoked salmon, and the *chartreuse aux pointes d'asperges*, please.'

'That's two starters, Hester.'

Hester looked at Glen with cool grey eyes. 'I'm aware of that, young man,' she said. 'It's what I'd like, if you don't mind.'

The waiter arrived with the champagne, and Glen ordered the meal, and a bottle of Montrachet.

'Perfect,' said Olivia. 'Baz always tries to make me drink claret.'

‘And do you, my darling?’ Hester asked, looking slyly at her daughter-in-law.

‘No, I don’t,’ said Olivia, and the two women shrieked with laughter, like a pair of hyenas.

Glen shook his head, unable to understand the thought processes behind this burst of hilarity. He took a long cold swallow of his champagne. European women, he said to himself. They’re completely off the wall. I’ll never understand them.

At a table in the window sat another party of three, Blanche de Vilmorin and her friends Olivier and Catherine St-Denis, and they were already halfway through their dinner. At the gallery, Blanche had bought a number of etchings, and had had a brief but pleasant chat with the artist, but Olivia had not looked in her direction when she entered the busy restaurant, and was now completely engrossed in conversation with a very odd-looking old woman wearing some kind of ethnic robe and a really bizarre large silver cross, studded with obviously fake emeralds. The woman’s sparse grey hair was tied back in a chignon, but long wisps had escaped and trailed about her shoulders. The contrast with the stunning youthful perfection of Olivia Rodzianko in her glorious Issey Miyake creation was more than Blanche could bear. She shuddered, and took a deep swig of her excellent Margaux. ‘I don’t remember seeing that frightful old bag at the show, do you?’ she remarked to her companions. ‘I only hope they legalize euthanasia before I get to that stage.’

‘You’ll never be like that, Blanche.’ Olivier, his face flushed with devotion and good food, rose to the bait. ‘You take such good care of yourself, darling. You have wonderful bones, too, and that’s what counts, at the end of the day.’

‘Yes, I suppose it does make a difference.’ Blanche checked her reflection in the mirrored wall, admiring her own impeccably blond hair, and smoothing the black taffeta skirt of her Galliano frock. Reassured, she smiled gaily at Olivier, giving him the full benefit of her dazzling white teeth, framed within her scarlet lips.

Catherine, failing to be amused by this display of mutual admiration, twitched her snowy linen napkin with ill-concealed irritation. 'I've not the smallest doubt, my dear Blanche,' she said clearly, and with deliberate cruelty, 'that when the time comes, you won't have the slightest difficulty in persuading Paul to oblige you with the necessary lethal injection. No problem at all in that direction, wouldn't you agree?'

Olivier shot a reproving look at his wife, who smiled at him blandly. 'So, where is Paul, anyway?' he asked hastily. 'I thought he was coming tonight?'

'He was,' said Blanche, looking martyred, and deciding to ignore Catherine's unkind remark. 'It'll be the usual stupid excuse, I expect.' She laughed uncertainly, suddenly feeling hot, and slightly drunk. 'He'll have been giving some poor sod a head transplant, I dare say, and the procedure took longer than expected. That's what he always says, you know: I'm sorry, Blanche, the procedure took longer than expected. There's no answer to that, is there?'

'What about a pudding, Blanche?' said Olivier, gently.

'Fuck the pudding, darling. Let's have a cognac.'

Paul and Misha took the lift to the top floor, and they entered her apartment. Once inside the door Paul stood still, rooted to the spot, astonished at the elegance and intellectual rigour of the space in which he found himself. Quietly, Misha closed the door, and stood behind him, her arms crossed, waiting for him to speak.

Paul's eyes travelled rapidly round the room, absorbing the stark neutrality, the lack of colour, the grey brick walls hung with the sombre Braque paintings, the glazed-tile units full of CDs, videotapes and books, the intricate dark Japanese carvings, the Giacometti sculptures, the silver candlesticks, the nautilus shells. 'My God, Misha,' he said at last. 'It's like being in a gallery, or a museum, isn't it? It's quite beautiful, but don't you find it a little intimidating?'

She laughed. 'It's not all quite as challenging as this,' she said, and led the way to the kitchen. Through the glass walls Paul could see the garden, pretty and tranquil in the dusk, the first pale evening stars visible between the delicate young leaves of the vine trained over the glazed roof. 'Lovely idea,' he said. 'Reminds me of Provence.'

Misha opened the door of the fridge. 'I've got beer, or wine, or whisky,' she offered. 'Which would you like?'

'Whisky, I think.'

'Ice?'

'Yes, please.'

On a shelf she found half a *saucisson sec*, and the remains of a risotto in a covered bowl. She took them out and put them on the worktop. 'Perhaps this is too revolting?' she suggested, taking the lid off the cold risotto.

Without replying, Paul took a wooden fork from a jug full of kitchen implements, and helped himself to a large mouthful. 'It's delicious,' he said, and took some more.

She got plates from the shelf, and handed him a sharp little paring knife. 'Since you're the celebrated surgeon, Paul, you can cut up the sausage.'

She's done it again, he thought. Smiling, he took the knife from her and sliced the meat into paper-thin rounds, eating several of them as he did so.

Misha put everything onto a tray, and Paul carried it out to the garden. He put the tray on the table, and they sat down. She poured two whiskies, they filled their plates and ate hungrily.

'Wonderful. Exactly what one needs,' said Paul,

putting his plate back on the tray and picking up his glass. 'I never feel much like eating an elaborate dinner after a long spell in the theatre, do you?'

'No, I don't.' Misha swallowed the last mouthful of risotto. 'There ought to be a little surgeons' kitchen at the hospital, with a fridge full of ham and cheese and stuff. Bread, too.'

'Excellent idea. Perhaps I'll float the suggestion at the next meeting of the executive.'

'It wouldn't work, though. There'd be too much in-fighting about who pays and how great a share each person is entitled to.'

'Mm. You're probably right. It would soon turn into a cumbersome, self-defeating exercise, like most institutional ideas.' Paul stretched out his legs, and settled himself more comfortably in the metal chair. He took a sip of his whisky. 'What a soothing place this is, Misha,' he said, and smiled at her. 'I have to say, though, that taken as a whole, your apartment seems to me to suffer slightly from schizophrenia.'

Misha laughed. 'The reason's pretty obvious, isn't it? The salon is entirely Giles; the rest is me, though he did his best to minimalize that, too.' She stared into her glass. 'Giles is a control-freak, you know. He likes things to be in his own image; even me, in a quite insulting way.' She looked up, with a wry little smile. 'The fact is, I was overly impressed with Giles, from the moment I set eyes on him.'

'In what way?'

'I thought him amazingly cool, amusing and very, very clever. He has an encyclopaedic knowledge of the arts; architecture, painting, literature and music. You name it, Giles knows about it. But it's more than just appreciation of works of art with him, he understands not only their intrinsic value in monetary terms, but their deeper, much more important meaning, too. He adores those Braque paintings; absolutely worships them, one can tell, and when he handles his little Japanese netsuke things, it's almost as if he was making love to them. It's rather disturbing to watch him, as a matter of fact.'

'Disturbing'?'

'Sexually disturbing, if you like.'

'I see.' Paul took another sip of his drink, and cleared his throat. 'You seem to me to be under the spell of a strange and very unusual man, Misha. You've already told me about his other attachment, and his child, in London. You've also told me about his abuse of drugs, and his skilful manipulation of yourself, for a number of years.' He looked at her, his face serious. 'You'll probably tell me to go to hell, but he sounds to me to be quite a monster and seriously bad news, my dear girl. I would have thought that any future you might share with him would be a minefield of betrayal and misery: for you, at any rate.'

'I know that.'

'But you don't care?'

'I don't really *know* how I feel, that's the problem. Most of the time I feel furious, hurt and betrayed and want out.' She took a swallow of her drink. 'But then at other times, I long for him. I long to hear his voice, and feel him close to me again, especially at night.' In the darkening garden, she felt entirely relaxed in Paul's company, almost as if she were talking to herself. 'I ache to be in bed with him,' she said softly. 'It's as simple, and as humiliating, as that.'

For Paul, too, the shadowy garden seemed to unlock the self-imposed reserve, the shell of protective privacy he carried around with him most of the time, at work, as well as in his private life. Without asking her permission, he refilled their glasses, and returned to his chair. A bat zig-zagged erratically over their heads, its barely audible squeaks pinpricks of sound in the cool night air. After a long comfortable silence, he spoke, choosing his words carefully. 'What are your feelings about Giles's room, Misha, now that he is no longer here?'

She thought for a few moments. 'I used to love it,'

she said. 'It seemed to me quite strange, but beautiful. Perverse in a way, not at all friendly to live with, but exciting.'

'Just like Giles?'

'Exactly.'

'And now?'

'Now I dread coming back to it alone. When I come through the door, it feels like a nightmare, a mockery of everything I thought he and I shared.' She looked at Paul, and smiled in the dark. 'Quite often, I feel like trashing the place, as a matter of fact, but I know I could never do that. Even though that room has never felt like a real home to me, it would feel like an act of vandalism to wreck it.'

'It's a strange concept, "home", isn't it?' said Paul. 'I live in an extremely beautiful house, much admired, very fashionably decorated in excellent taste, and I detest it. When we first lived there, twenty-seven years ago, it was decrepit and run-down, but full of its own authentic atmosphere and I loved it. It was rather like the shabby old country house of my family, haunted by its former inhabitants, but full of love and optimism, in the shape of the children growing up there.'

'And now the children are gone, and everything has changed?'

'That's what happens, doesn't it?' said Paul, his voice sounding cold and bleak.

Covertly, Misha watched him as he slumped in his chair, his silver hair shining in the light from the kitchen, his long legs stretched out in front of him. He is lonely, like me, she thought sadly. He feels tired and old, and has no friends, like me. Why else would he be here with me, now? 'I expect your wife misses the children, too?' she ventured. 'Perhaps even more than you do?'

'No, I don't think she does, Misha. Blanche is a very energetic and busy woman, with an enormously full social life. I think she misses the children like a hole in the head, to tell you the truth.' He laughed. 'Of course, she is absolutely right in her attitude towards them. She has never allowed herself to become emotionally dependent on them – in that respect, she is, quite rightly, her own woman.'

'But you have?'

'I have what?'

'You have allowed yourself to become emotionally dependent on your children?'

'Yes,' he said quietly, after a moment. 'I have. Especially my son, Pascal, and his wife, Emma.'

'They're the ones you told me about, who keep goats? Aren't they expecting a baby?'

'Yes, they are.' Paul smiled, and got up from his chair, preparing to leave. 'I had a letter from Pascal today. Emma has had a scan, and they think it may be twin boys. Isn't that rather sensational, Misha?'

She laughed and got up from her seat. 'Yes, it is, if it makes you happy. Does it?'

'It makes me happy. It also makes me sad, and anxious.'

'More emotional dependency?'

'I expect that's it, yes.' He put a hand gently on her shoulder. 'Tomorrow is Saturday, Misha. Are you on duty?'

'No.'

'Short of an emergency, would you like to drive into the country, and have lunch somewhere?'

'Do you really think we should?'

'Is there a good reason why not? I need to get some fresh air, and I enjoy talking to you. Is that a crime?'

'No, of course not. I just thought . . . '

'Well, don't think. It's only *lunch*, Misha; nothing more sinister, believe me.'

'Yes, of course. Thank you, I'd love to come.'

Retracing their steps to the salon, Paul paused briefly before the Braque paintings. 'My God,' he said, 'these must be worth a fortune. Blanche would love them.'

'Only for that reason?'

'*Touché!* No, probably not; she is not a philistine.'

At the door, he thanked her for the supper, and she reached up impulsively and kissed his cheek. Briefly, his arms closed round her, and as quickly he released her. He said good night. 'I'll pick you up at ten, OK?'

'I'll look forward to it. Good night.'

The door closed behind him, and Misha went back to her garden, and stood at the railing, looking down into the narrow street below. She watched as Paul left the building, then unlocked the door of his elegant car. He looked up and raised a hand, and she waved back, then watched as he drove slowly away.

Chapter Four

At five to ten the following morning, Misha was waiting in the alley, and at ten o'clock precisely the car turned into passage des Ebénistes, then came to a halt at her side. She got in, and Paul, after a brief greeting, drove smoothly away from the kerb and began to thread his way though the Saturday morning traffic in the direction of the *périphérique* and the Porte d'Italie. From there, he took the road to Fontainebleau and the A6.

It was a beautiful day, cloudless and warm. Overhead, swallows wheeled high in the pale blue sky, and the countryside on either side of the *autoroute* unfolded itself before them in softly rounded undulating hills, studded with clumps of trees and the occasional huddle of a brown-roofed village. Misha sat back in her seat, enjoying the feeling of the breeze in her hair, and the warmth of the sun as it poured through the open roof.

'Not too windy for you, Misha?'

'No, it's lovely.'

'Don't you want to know where we're going?'

'Not particularly. I rather enjoy surprises, as a matter of fact.' She looked at him sideways. 'I guess it's in Burgundy?'

He laughed. 'Not much of a mystery, is it? You're right, of course. But you don't know exactly where, do you?'

'That's true.'

He drove fast; quite a lot faster than the speed limit allowed, Misha observed with amused detachment. They passed the signs to Nemours and Auxerre, then left the *autoroute* at the *sortie* Nitry, and were soon driving along a minor road through hilly, wooded country, empty except for an occasional old man on a bike, or a lonely tractor cutting grass for silage, on a distant hillside.

In another twenty minutes they had arrived in Vézelay. They parked the car and walked up the steep, cobbled pilgrims' way to visit the abbey. As they climbed the hill they could see above them the pale limestone walls of the magnificent building, thrusting into the blue summer sky, a clarion call to the faithful. Inside, a tour was in progress, and the guide's voice, though subdued and respectful, was clearly audible in the huge echoing spaces of the monumental church. Avoiding the tour, Paul and Misha walked past the soaring columns, touched by the calm and simplicity of the place, and its timeless atmosphere of confident, unswerving belief.

Outside, in the warmth of the sunshine once again, Paul looked at his watch. 'What do you think, Misha? Shall we lunch in a restaurant, here, or would you rather have a picnic?'

'A picnic, wouldn't you? It's such a beautiful day.'

'Good. That's what we'll do.'

They shopped in a small *alimentation*, buying ham, cheese, tomatoes and a bottle of water. At the *boulangerie*, they bought a baguette and an apple tart. Then they went into a tourist shop and bought a willow vine-basket, in which to carry the shopping.

They returned to the car and drove out of Vézelay, following a winding road through a wooded valley. After a few kilometres they crossed a canal, and continued through dense woodland along a rutted, single-track road. The unpruned branches of the surrounding trees met overhead, so that they drove through a leafy green tunnel. At the end of the tunnel, the trees gradually thinned and gave way to pasture, inadequately fenced with posts and rails. Within these flimsy enclosures grazed the solid-looking white Charolais cattle of the region, and some of them raised their heads in mild enquiry as the car passed.

Beyond the grazing, and half hidden by an enormous stand of black cedars, Misha could see the stone walls and russet-tiled turrets of a Burgundian fortified manor and its attendant farm buildings. Paul turned into a rough drive that led between the fields to the farm, drove through an ungated archway and came to a halt in an empty courtyard. The place was firmly shut up, the windows and doors heavily shuttered and barred.

'This is it,' he said, and switched off the engine. 'Froissy.'

'Froissy?'

'It's the name of the place, Misha.'

'Oh, I see. Well, how amazing, and how lovely. Is it really OK to have a picnic here, though? Won't someone come and tell us to shove off?'

'No, I don't think so, unless I were to behave in such a hostile manner.' He looked at her mystified face, and smiled. 'This is my family home, Misha. It's where I was born and brought up.'

They got out of the car, and Misha stood looking slowly around, at the battered and shabby but still beautiful house, at the cows knee-deep in the lush green grass, at the shimmering green-gold of the surrounding hills. 'With a place like this,' she asked quietly, 'why on earth do you live in Paris?'

'It's a question I often ask myself,' he replied. 'Every time I come down here, in fact. It's the usual complicated business of joint-ownership. The house belongs to three of us, my older brother and sister, as well as me. Robert is a career cleric and lives in Rome, and Marie-Christine is married to a banker in Switzerland, so neither of them has the time or inclination to worry about the place very much. None of us is able to live here, but equally none of us can bear the idea of selling it, either. The land is all let, and most of the barns and byres are, too. All that's left is the poor old house, rotting away, and my mother's walled garden and her *potager*, quietly going back to nature. If only one of us had the will to save the place, it would be an answer to prayer; my prayers, anyway.'

'Don't,' said Misha. 'I'll burst into tears if you go on like that.'

'Come inside,' he said, 'and I'll show you how bad things really are.'

He took a key from behind a loose stone in the wall, close to a modest-looking door, unlocked it, and they entered a cold, dark kitchen. 'I'm sorry to bring you in this way,' he said, 'but the grand entrance on the other side of the house is barred and bolted from the inside, in case of intruders.'

He led the way between a long farm table and a sinister-looking rusty wood-burning stove, then along a dark, flagstoned corridor which led to a high, square, stone-walled hall. 'I can't think why we go to such lengths to protect the place,' he said. 'It's so tucked away in this neck of the woods; very few people know that it exists.'

'In any case, I don't suppose it would take an experienced burglar very long to find the key, do you?'

'God, I hope not!' Paul crossed the echoing floor to a pair of tall glazed doors and opened them, disclosing the wooden double doors behind. He undid the heavy bolts, and knocked up the thick wooden beam from the metal clasps sunk in the walls on either side. Then he pushed open the doors, one heavy leaf at a time. Immediately, and dramatically, the hall was flooded with light, and a warm gust of wind from outside filled the air with the sweet smell of trampled meadow grass.

Misha gazed up at the bare stone walls, festooned with cobwebs, moist with condensation. A rusted iron chandelier was suspended on a chain from a boss in the intricately patterned plaster ceiling, far above her head. Hanging from the chandelier she noticed an enormous bunch of dead green twigs, with shrivelled and twisted leaves. 'What's that?' she asked, pointing.

'Mistletoe,' said Paul. 'It's a good-luck thing. We always gathered a new bunch every year, at Christmas. That one's been there for several years, by the look of it.'

'Oh.' She came and stood beside him, on the steps, in the warm sunshine. Below them, invaded by tall grass and scarlet poppies, a gravel drive formed a sweep, originally intended for the setting-down of visitors to the house.

'We never used it,' said Paul. 'We always came in and out through the kitchen. It used to drive the *bonne* mad, poor woman.'

Beyond the sweep was a wire fence, and beyond that the ruins of a sizeable vineyard, so old and neglected that scarcely a single leaf had appeared on the blackened, rotting vines. 'How sad,' Misha said.

'Indeed. I'll have to get them grubbed up, sometime.'

They walked along the drive, re-entering the courtyard, and got the picnic basket from the car. Once again, Misha followed Paul through the bleak kitchen, then along the corridor to the hall, where he opened the door to yet another darkened room. Swiftly, he undid the windows and shutters and opened a glazed door, giving onto a walled garden full of roses. 'This is the sitting-room,' he said. 'It's probably my favourite place in the house.'

'I'm not surprised.' Misha looked around her at the spectacular collections of butterflies, stuffed animals, fish, and even snakes that were displayed on the walls, in beautifully constructed glass cases. Interspersed among them were the most exquisite water-colour paintings that she had ever seen; birds, insects and flowers. 'Did your mother do all these, Paul?'

'She didn't stuff the wildlife, no.' He smiled. 'They were already heirlooms when she came here as a bride. She loved them, and thought them beautiful, though not everyone would agree with her, of course. They're mostly nineteenth-century, and were trapped or shot by my great-grandfather, I'm slightly ashamed to have to admit. Very politically incorrect nowadays, of course.' He laughed, not sounding particularly contrite about the misguided behaviour of his forebears. 'The paintings are all hers, though. It was her life's work, in between running the farm, doing most of the gardening, looking after us and coping with the patients, as well.'

'The patients?'

'My father was a country doctor.'

'Really? How could he afford to live in this lovely house, if it's not a rude question?'

'Of course it's not a rude question. He inherited it. His older brothers were both killed in the First World War; he was the only *héritier*, after my grandparents died.' He looked at Misha's serious face, and smiled gently. 'So you see, it was important to him, and to my mother, to carry on here if they possibly could. And of course, in those early days, labour was cheap and plentiful.'

'Not like now.'

'No, not like now; and quite right too, in my view.'

'Of course; I agree.'

'None the less, it makes it almost impossible to keep these old family places in good shape, much less heat them and pay the taxes.'

'I suppose.'

'Come on, let's go outside and have lunch. No point in dwelling on what might have been, is there?' He picked up a couple of cushions from the faded, chintz-covered sofa, and they went out into the garden. It was full of the sound of bees, and the long, thorny, overgrown stems of hundreds of climbing and rambling rose bushes festooned themselves up and over the walls, and stretched across the paths of the garden, so that walking along them was difficult, if not impossible.

They sat on the steps below the door, and Misha laid out the food on the patch of creeping thyme that formed a compact aromatic mat in the grass. Dwarf lavender hedges, grown old and straggly, grew along the paths of the garden, and their clean sharp scent filled the still, warm air. The roses, in their turn, released their floating clouds of perfume, magically defeating the atmosphere of futility and waste that should have pervaded that neglected and abandoned place.

They split the bread between them, and divided the ham and the cheese. Paul went back into the house and returned with glasses and a bottle of Chablis, cold from the cellar. Leaning comfortably against the door-frame, they drank the chilled, flowery wine and ate the fresh, clean-tasting food, and felt the sting of the first really hot sun of the year on their faces. Misha took off her linen jacket, and rolled up the sleeves of her shirt, and in five minutes she could smell the ozone scent of sun on her winter-pale bare arms.

'I've told you quite a lot about my family, Misha. Now it's your turn to tell me about yours.'

Misha took a sip of wine, and shook her head. 'There's not a lot to tell, really. My grandfather ben Bella was born in Algiers, and married a girl from a poor French mixed-race family. *Pieds noirs*, such people are sometimes called. I expect you know that? He started a business exporting olive oil to France. They did pretty well, and raised a family; three daughters and one son, and the son was Michel, my *papa*. At first when he grew up he worked with his father, then he moved to Marseille and got a job in a fish restaurant in the Vieux-Port. It was in Marseille that he met a young Irish girl, who was working as a night-club dancer, and running round two or three different *boîtes* every night, to make enough money to live on.' Misha looked at Paul, and smiled shyly. 'Do you really want to hear any more, or do you get the sordid picture?'

'It's not at all sordid, Misha. It's fascinating. Please go on.'

'Well, they fell in love, and she carried on working until they had both saved enough, and he had learnt the restaurant business well enough, to start on their own. First, they rented a little café in Nîmes. Then they bought it, and sold it on, then bought the derelict mill near Villefranche, and converted it into a restaurant. I was born there, and went to school there.' Misha's eyes grew soft, and she smiled, a little sadly. 'They were incredibly ambitious for me. They didn't want me to have to work every hour the Lord sends, like them. They encouraged me to try to get into a proper profession, like medicine, and that's what I did.' She gave an ironic little laugh. 'In the event, you probably work longer and tougher hours in medicine than practically anything else, don't you?'

'No question.'

'Anyway, they were absolutely thrilled when I qualified. I went down to the country to tell them. They were so proud of me that they cried, and after the last dinner guests had gone, we had langoustines for supper, and *Papa* opened a bottle of champagne.'

'Your father is comfortable with alcohol, then, Misha?'

'Oh, yes, of course. He doesn't drink very much himself, but he had become a non-practising Muslim in every respect. I think he so much wanted me to be *French*, not to feel like a *pied noir*, like himself, split between two cultures, not really belonging to either.'

'And did he succeed?'

'Not entirely. I certainly don't feel at all Irish, though I'm quite like my mother in some ways. I don't feel particularly Algerian, either. I suppose I do feel fairly French. It's what I am, officially, in any case.'

'We're in the same boat, you and I,' said Paul. 'My mother was English, and I feel a strong affinity to her genes, her culture. I think Pascal feels the same; he spent a lot of time with his grandmother as a child, and then chose to marry an Englishwoman himself. But if it came down to having to make a choice between my two countries, I'd probably choose France.' Paul gazed around him, at the ruined garden, filled with the ghosts of his childhood. 'I expect it's this place that would keep me here,' he said. 'Come hell or high water, as a matter of fact.' He poured the rest of the wine into their glasses. 'So, what happened next, Misha?'

'Just over two years ago, my mother developed a pain in her abdomen. She thought it was indigestion, but of course it wasn't. It was appendicitis, and it was the usual story; she refused to go to the doctor, it turned into peritonitis, and she died. It was tragic; a ghastly waste of a terrific woman. She was only fifty-six when it happened, and just when everything was going so well for them.'

'How terrible for you, Misha. And your poor father, what happened to him?'

'He stuck it out for three months, and carried on with the *auberge*, but the heart had gone out of him. He had a good offer for the restaurant, so he sold up, and went back to Marseille. Then, six months later, he surprised everyone by returning to Algiers. I think he felt he'd given life in France his best shot, and been defeated by the gods in the end. There was nothing more he could do for me, that could have given him the incentive to go on. He was unbelievably lonely without my mother, and all he could think of was going back to the sounds and smells of his childhood. He needed to disappear into the *medina* whenever he felt like it, to drink mint tea and listen to the Rai music that he loved. At the end of the day, he went to the place he really thought of as home.'

'And is he there, still?'

'Yes, he is, and I think about him all the time, and pray that nothing happens to him, in the riots and the terrible massacres.' She glanced at him briefly, the anxiety manifest in her eyes. 'I imagine him stepping on a landmine, and being blown to bits, or having his throat cut, things like that.'

'Yes, of course you do. How could you not?'

'Do you know,' said Misha thoughtfully, after a pause, 'you're the only person I've ever told about my parents, Paul.'

'Not even Giles?'

'*Especially* not him. He hated anything like that, anything sad or serious, anything that interfered with how he expected things to be.'

'But if you'd known him for seven years, Misha, and your mother died only two years ago, how could he possibly have failed to notice that you were mourning her loss?'

Misha stared at the flowering thyme beneath her feet, and felt her face grow hot with shame. 'I never told Giles anything at all about my parents. I think I was probably afraid that he would have the usual racist views on the subject, and that they would devalue me in his eyes, somehow.'

'He never asked you about your name, ben Bella?'

'No, he never did. He used to spell it with a capital B, all one word, Benbella, and I chose not to correct him. He probably thought it was Italian, or something.' She laughed. 'In any case, he never showed the slightest interest in my family, or my background; the subject simply never came up. As far as he was concerned, I was merely a classy bit of skirt, with a degree in medicine, I realize that now. Giles is the only Englishman I've ever known, so I'm not really qualified to judge, but I've noticed that men like him appreciate things that are rare, or beautiful or valuable, but they have to be things they feel confident about, that are approved of by their peers, and ultimately the establishment. It's not at all their style to discover things for themselves, and certainly not things from cultures other than their own.' She shook her head, and frowned uneasily. 'I'm probably being grossly unfair,' she said quietly. 'I expect my own insecurities are crawling out of the woodwork, don't you?'

Paul smiled, and changed the subject. 'Tell me about your mother, Misha. Do you look like her?'

'Yes, I do, quite. I've got her eyes and the same shaped face, but not her freckles and red hair.' She smiled. 'I'm quite glad I haven't got the freckles, but I would've loved to have inherited the red hair.'

'What was her name?'

'Josefina. My father called her Josie.'

'Was she small, like you?'

'No, she was tall and leggy, and bone-thin.' Misha laughed affectionately, remembering her mother's long legs, made even longer by high stiletto heels. 'I'm like my father, physically. I only came up to her shoulder, and so did *Papa*.' She stretched out her own legs, to catch the sun, and rubbed a scented sprig of thyme on her skin, bruising the leaves, releasing the smell. 'What a pity your son and his wife don't live here, and farm the land,' she said gently. 'Then you could see them quite often, and the house might be saved, mightn't it?'

'Lovely idea,' said Paul, 'but an absolute non-starter for Pascal, I'm afraid.'

'Oh? Why?'

'Too close to Paris, and his parents.'

'You mean too close to *Maman*?'

'Yes, I'm afraid I do. Blanche can never resist the temptation to try to boss and bully him, and subtly denigrate his wife; not so very subtly, either. At least in Provence he's far enough away to be left pretty much alone, and in any case, it's a stunning place. They live out of doors for eight or nine months of the year, and they love it.' Paul drank the rest of his wine. 'We do get quite a lot of rain here, you know, and grey skies in the winter. It's a lot like England, in many ways, so they're probably very wise to have chosen Provence.'

'But *you* love it here, don't you?'

'Yes, I do.'

'Aren't you going to show me the rest of it?'

'Yes, of course, if you'd like to see it. Let's go in.'

They went inside, and Paul led the way round the house, throwing open windows and creaking shutters, allowing the place to breathe and come alive. He showed her his father's consulting room, with its roll-top desk and swivel chair, its brown-leather examination couch, and the shelves packed with medical books. A small annexe, a combined laboratory and pharmacy, had fitted shelves and locked, glass-fronted cabinets containing every drug and herbal remedy available during the old doctor's time. On a bench stood a large marble pestle and mortar, together with rows of test-tubes in graceful wooden racks, and on the shelves, glass bottles and cardboard pill-boxes. A stone sink was fitted with a brass swan's-neck tap, and had a coarsely woven brown roller-towel fixed to the wall beside it. A perforated metal dish contained a piece of blue-streaked carbolic soap.

'Pretty primitive, don't you find it, Misha?'

'But probably perfectly adequate for most common ailments, I'd say.'

'I agree. Of course, after the war was over, this all changed. My father saw his patients in Vézelay, and he no longer made up prescriptions. I keep it like this for sentimental reasons, a sort of memorial to his war effort, if you like.' Paul looked at the drugs cabinet, and frowned. 'I really ought to destroy a lot of this stuff,' he said. 'Look at this bottle of chloral hydrate. Imagine if someone broke in and helped themselves to it, though I dare say it's lost most of its efficacy by now.' Carefully, he closed the shutters and windows, and checked the locks on the cabinets.

They looked into the drawing-room, comfortably furnished in the English style, the wood-ash from the big open fireplace spilling onto the floor as it always had done, the room smelling faintly of lavender and wet dogs. 'There were more animals than people here when I was a boy,' said Paul. 'Dogs, cats, squirrels, mice; you name it, we had them.' He grinned at Misha, suddenly looking about ten years old. 'You can still smell them, can't you? The whole place needs cleaning and airing.'

The dining-room was quite ordinary. It overlooked the courtyard, was papered in a William Morris design of willow-leaves, and had a heavy silver epergne in the centre of the long mahogany dining-table. 'We hardly ever used this room, especially during the war. We ate in the kitchen, with whatever help we were lucky enough to have at the time.'

'Did your mother cook, Paul?'

'Yes, she did. She made huge pots of *garbure*, with the vegetables she grew in the garden, and she roasted rabbits and pheasants, and anything else that my father and brother could trap, or catch in nets. She made bread, and cakes, too. It's my earliest memory of her; standing at the kitchen table stirring a Christmas pudding. It smelt delicious, warm and spicy, and alcoholic. She was wearing a blue dress with the sleeves rolled up, and a white apron, very long, and it was a sunny day in October; the leaves were falling, I remember it clearly. I must have been four or five, so it would have been about the middle of the war, and things must have been pretty difficult and scarce. I imagine it took her months to collect enough dried fruit for that one special pudding.'

They returned to the hall, and climbed the echoing wooden staircase to the gallery that encircled the hall below, and led to the first-floor bedrooms. 'After the collapse of France, and the German occupation, we were actually rather fortunate,' Paul went on, as they walked along the bare bleached boards of the gallery. 'My father wasn't taken into forced labour, as so many men were, but was allowed to continue his work as the local doctor. The Nazis stole most of my father's cellar, and cut down and took away quite a lot of timber, but otherwise we were left alone, and largely due to my mother's efforts we got by pretty well.'

He stopped beside a door. 'This is my room.' They

went in, and Paul switched on a light at the door to reveal a bare little room, with a grey-painted *lit bateau* beneath the window, a dustcover spread over the voluminous mounds of the fat duvet and pillows beneath. A folding chair, its seat made from a piece of cream-and-crimson striped linen, stood beside the bed, and a torn and faded ikat rug lay on the bare boards of the floor. On the lime-washed wall opposite the shuttered window hung an unframed nineteenth-century portrait of a middle-aged woman, painted in the manner of the pre-Raphaelites. She had the same black arched eyebrows as Paul, Misha observed, but she did not remark on the resemblance.

Leaning against a cupboard door was a pair of old-fashioned wooden skis, strapped together, and beside them lay a large model sailing-ship, resting on its side. The little room seemed to Misha to reflect exactly the spirit and soul of boys – grubby little boys; ink-stained schoolboys; gangling and sensitive adolescents – and she felt a small pang of sorrow and regret for the brother she would have liked to have had, but had been denied. She turned away from Paul, so that he would not see how the nostalgic room had affected her. 'What's in the cupboard?' she asked.

'Oh, the usual horrors, as far as I remember; football boots, honky old tennis shoes and stuff, and my gun, I hope.' He went to the cupboard and opened the door. 'Yes, look, here it is.' He took out a long, heavy, brown-canvas bag, and unbuckled the straps, revealing a sleekly oiled double-barrelled shotgun. 'Isn't it beautiful?' he said, stroking the butt lovingly. 'It's one of a pair that belonged to my mother's father. It was a miracle that they weren't confiscated by the Germans. My father hid them under the floorboards in the attic, and they never found them.'

Misha looked at the beautiful gun, admiring its craftsmanship, but repelled by it nevertheless. 'Trouble is, they can kill so easily, can't they?'

'So can cars, Misha, and practically any machine

you care to mention, unless they're handled with appropriate caution.'

'Like the way you drive your car on the *autoroute*, Paul?' said Misha, smiling, breaking the spell the room had cast on her. 'At a hundred and sixty kilometres an hour, for example?'

'Nonsense! Of course I don't!'

'Yes, you do!'

He laughed, put the gun back in its case, and replaced it in the cupboard. 'Come on,' he said, 'we'll take a quick look at my parents' room, then we should be heading back.' He looked at his watch. 'It's nearly five o'clock.'

'Are you going out this evening?'

'No. Are you?'

'No, I'm not.'

'Well, good,' said Paul. 'There's no hurry, then.'

He led the way to the last door in the gallery, opened it and unfastened the three tall shuttered windows of a large room overlooking the ruined vineyard and the fields of grazing cattle beyond. In spite of its shabbiness, the flaking distemper of its walls and the peeling ivory-coloured paintwork of the window frames and deep skirting-boards, it was one of the most beautiful bedrooms Misha had ever seen. The windows were extravagantly hung from ceiling to floor with curtains of pink-and-white *toile de Jouy*, which hung on steel rings and draped themselves in graceful heaps on the floor. Two Napoleonic armchairs were upholstered in the same fabric, and the gilding of the arms and legs had worn almost completely away, exposing the original wood, riddled with worm-holes.

Several of Jane de Vilmorin's paintings hung on the flaking walls, some of them quite badly foxed by the damp, but the real glory of the room was a spectacular double bed, made in Naples in the eighteenth century and bought at auction after the war. Jane had chosen not to have the voluptuously carved arabesques of the pine head- and footboards restored to their original gilded splendour. Instead, she had painstakingly rubbed away the remaining gilt and gesso with fine sandpaper, until she had achieved the look she had in mind: that of mellow age and distressed beauty. It seemed to Misha that the lovely bed looked like a marvellous piece of driftwood, bone-coloured and pale, its florid decoration subdued, its opulence tamed.

On the striped ticking mattress lay a pile of white square pillows and linen sheets, their corners embroidered in white thread with the initials J de V, and draped over the foot of the bed was a folded Black Watch tartan rug. A rosary, made of ebony beads with a silver crucifix, hung from the scrolled crest of the headboard. Entranced, Misha ran a hand over the carving, feeling the silken smoothness of the wood beneath her fingers. 'What a very beautiful room,' she said softly. 'Your parents must have been really happy here.'

'I'm sure they were. They must have slept in this bed for more than forty years.' He smiled. 'They were quite a boring couple, you know. Never a cross word, and all that. They adored each other, one could tell.'

'I don't think that's boring.'

'No, neither do I.'

They closed the windows, and went downstairs and out into the garden again. Misha looked at the extraordinary proliferation of the neglected roses, and inhaled their fragrance. 'I wish I could stick my nose right into the flowers,' she said, 'but it's impossible to get near them, it's such a thorny tangle.'

'Hang on,' said Paul, and disappeared into the house. In a couple of minutes he returned, carrying a pruning hook and a pair of stout leather gloves. 'You cut, and I'll pull the long bits out and stack them on the path, OK?'

Slowly and silently, they worked their way along the central path to the garden's axis, a lead statue of Leda with her swan. Then they stood together and looked back at the transformation they had wrought in the space of two hours. The gravel path, bordered by the extravagant roses, led the eye straight back to the house. The sun was beginning its descent of the western sky, bathing the stone walls in honey-coloured light and drawing dazzling scarlet reflections from the small unshuttered windows in the turrets. 'My God! It's so *beautiful*, Paul!' exclaimed Misha. 'What a magical place this is. I'm not at all surprised that your mother devoted her life to looking after it.'

'It killed her, in the end. Especially after my father died.'

'Oh, dear. Did it really? How?'

'Exhaustion, for want of a better diagnosis. She never stopped working, from early in the morning until she fell into bed, late at night. In the final analysis, she was incapable of sitting quietly, or reading, or even painting any more. She was on a hiding to nothing, poor old thing.'

The way Paul said 'poor old thing' seemed to Misha inexpressibly sad, and she could not think of anything comforting to say to him. Instead, she put on her gloves again. 'What about all the rubbish?' she asked. 'Shall we make a bonfire?'

'Good idea. But first, we need a barrow.'

'Even more, I need a drink of water.'

They walked back to the steps, and Misha took a long drink from the litre bottle. 'That's better,' she said, wiping her mouth with the back of her hand. She watched as Paul, in his turn, drank thirstily. 'How interesting,' she remarked. 'Did you know that you don't appear to swallow when you drink? The water goes down in one glug, like a drainpipe.' He laughed, but said nothing and screwed the cap back on the bottle. 'I suppose the house isn't connected to the mains water supply here?' Misha asked. 'How do you manage?'

'There's a spring, and it's piped to a very large storage tank at the top of that turret.' He pointed to one of the pepperpot roofs at the rear of the house. 'The water gets there by means of gravity, through a series of stone tanks in the fields, and since the spring is at the top of a hill and more than twenty metres higher than the top of the tower, the house tank is slowly filling itself all the time, as the water tries to find its own level.'

'What if the tank overflows?'

'There's a ball-cock, which I very much hope is still in good working order.'

'But presumably the water keeps on coming down the hill; it doesn't know that the tank's full?'

'Misha, you're teasing me?'

'I'm *not*, I promise!'

'OK. There's a hole at the top of the lowest stone tank, and when the stop-cock says the tank in the tower is full, the water flows through the hole, and into a hollow in the hillside, full of brambles.'

'Clever.' Misha looked at Paul, and grinned.

'You *did* know!'

'I didn't, honestly!'

'Liar!' He took a step towards her, took her face in his hands and kissed her gently. She did not pull away, but put her arms round his waist, her mouth soft beneath his. For them both, it was an impulsive exchange of tenderness, but equally a moment of tentative discovery.

They broke apart, smiled at each other, then went at once in search of the barrow, neither of them feeling the slightest inclination to comment on what had happened, or to express regret about it.

They found an old-fashioned wooden barrow, with deep extended sides, and a couple of pitchforks, and for the next half-hour they cleared away all the rubbish and burned it on a bonfire in the far corner of the garden, sending billowing clouds of white smoke into the still air. The silence of the early evening was broken only by the crackle of flames, the rumble of the wheelbarrow's iron wheel, and the occasional clonk of a cowbell in the nearby fields. They had finished the job, and were standing together, watching the sparks fly up into the fading lavender-coloured sky, when there was a heavy footfall on the path behind them. They turned, as a man approached.

'It's you, Mr Paul. Thank the good Lord; I thought the place had gone up in smoke!'

'Hello, Marcel. How's everything with you? And the family?'

Marcel assured him that the family was in excellent shape, shook hands with Misha, remarked that they'd done a good job, that it was a pity they didn't come down more often, and departed the way he had come.

Paul called after him. 'Marcel?'

'Eh?'

'When was the water last tested?'

'The water? Let's see. Couple of months ago, I think. Yes, the man came at the end of April, after I'd rodded out the system.'

'Everything was OK, then? The water's OK for drinking?'

'Yes, yes, it was fine, like always.'

'Good. Thanks very much, and thanks for keeping an eye on the place; it's kind of you.'

'Where does he live?' asked Misha, when Marcel was out of earshot.

'He's got one of the farmhouses, the one that used to be the manager's house, in my grandfather's time. It's over there, on the other side of the woodland.'

'So it would be quite a step for him to come over?'

'Yes, but it's his milking-time, so I expect he killed two birds with one stone.'

Slowly, the fire died down, and Paul meticulously forked into it every small unburnt branch and twig, until all that remained was a sweet-smelling heap of warm black ashes. Carefully, he raked through them, to be sure that the fire was completely out, stamping round the outer rim, and covering his trousers with black smuts in the process. 'God, look at us both,' he said. 'We're filthy. We'd better wash in the kitchen; there's probably soap there.'

They washed as thoroughly as they could, put the scraps from their picnic into the vine-basket to take back to Paris, then locked up the remaining windows and doors, leaving by the kitchen and putting the key back behind the loose stone.

'Does Marcel know it's there, Paul?'

'Yes, of course.'

A summer dew was falling, and the air felt fresh and cool. Misha put on her jacket, and they got into the car and drove away, back through the green tunnel, now so dark that Paul put on his headlights. Vézelay, high on its hill, across the misty meadows, looked like a Christmas tree, shimmering in the twilight. Tired, they drove in silence, and arrived at Misha's door just before nine o'clock. Paul switched off the engine, and turned towards her. 'Misha?'

'Paul?'

'Was it OK, that I kissed you? You weren't offended, or annoyed, or thought that I took advantage of you?'

'No, not at all. It was friendly, and kind.'

'Nothing more than that?'

'I don't think so, no.'

'And would you mind if it happened again?'

Misha smiled, and touched his cheek. 'No, of course not. Why should I?'

'And if one thing led to another, Misha? How would you feel about that?'

'I don't know. But one thing doesn't *necessarily* lead to another, does it, Paul? A kiss can be simply that, can't it? Just a kiss, between friends?'

'You're telling me that a friendly kiss is OK, but you're not ready for anything else, right?'

'Do you mind?'

'No, of course I don't.' He smiled and put a finger on the tip of her nose. 'Don't look so solemn, darling. Just a kiss is fine, though I'm a bit rusty in that department.'

'Hm,' said Misha, and laughed. 'You seemed pretty *au fait* with it, to me.'

'Come out to dinner.'

'Just dinner?'

'Yes, *of course*, just dinner! Aren't you hungry?'

'Yes, I am, ravenous.'

'Well, then?'

'OK.'

They walked round the corner to the next street, just as they were, and dined in a modest bistro, with checked tablecloths and candles stuck in wine bottles, a deliberate tourist cliché, but small and friendly. They chose the seventy-five franc menu, which was a warm salad of duck livers, followed by grilled chicken, with chilli, lemon and mint. 'I bet the cook's been to Algiers,' Misha remarked, helping herself to the fragrant couscous that accompanied the dish. 'This is just the sort of thing my father did in the restaurant.' She smiled at Paul, her eyes bright with nostalgia. 'It's the smell of burnt chicken and lemon, it's unforgettable.'

They talked about their day at Froissy, and Misha asked Paul to tell her more about his childhood; about his brother and sister, and especially his parents. Gradually, she was able to build up a very clear picture of that impoverished but happy family in her mind, and it seemed to her that Paul would have traded everything he had worked for, all his professional eminence and the rewards that flowed from it, to return to his childhood home, restore the buildings and make the gardens come alive again.

The waiter, unasked, brought a second pot of coffee, and Paul, in his turn, gradually extracted from Misha a lot more about her own childhood with her parents, and the visits to her grandparents in Algiers. As she talked, Misha began to enjoy an experience entirely new to her, that of being the focus of someone's undivided attention. For the first time in her adult life she felt herself to be really interesting, respected, taken seriously as a woman, and as a human being. It might have been just the good food and wine that induced the new feeling of confidence, even happiness that flowed through her, but she did not think so. 'I'd love to go again to Froissy, sometime, and do some more gardening,' she said impulsively. 'It was wonderful there, Paul. I loved it.'

He reached across the table and took her hand in his. 'We will go again,' he said. 'Whenever you say.'

They walked back to her door. She thanked him for a lovely day, and they said goodnight. Paul waited until he saw the lights go on in the loft, then drove back to the Marais. As always on a Saturday night, the house was dark and empty, for Blanche had not yet returned from her party. Since he did not feel particularly like being interrogated as to why a nearly-new pair of trousers appeared to be more or less ruined, as a result of his activities in the garden, he thanked his lucky stars and went swiftly up to his room. There, he showered and went straight to bed, feeling happier and more alive than he had for years.

Misha, too, took a shower and went sleepily to bed. She quite forgot that she had not listened to her messages.

Chapter Five

Basil Rodzianko and his camera crew arrived at Charles de Gaulle airport at three o'clock in the morning, were met by a studio vehicle and driven into Paris. Basil spent a busy morning debriefing from his assignment, had a late lunch with two other correspondents at Le Petit Zinc in rue de Buci, and called on his mother in the Ile St-Louis, where he drank a cup of Earl Grey tea. From there, he telephoned Olivia in the Sologne, to warn her of his homecoming, and took a train to Orléans, arriving at seven forty-five.

Having slept very little during the flight from Moscow, and consumed a good deal of wine with his lunch, the alcohol-induced exhilaration had passed and he was beginning to feel pretty tired. Outside the station, he looked eagerly around, trying to locate Olivia's estate car, but she was nowhere to be seen. Bloody hell, he said to himself, why does she *always* let me down? God knows, I don't ask much of her.

He took an expensive cab out to the barn, and the driver, an old man with a nicotine-stained white moustache, firmly declared himself to be incapable of unloading his passenger's heavy metal case from the boot of the car, so that Basil was forced to do it himself. He lugged it into the house, then went back for his cumbersome backpack. The old man sat in his cab, the meter still ticking over, staring morosely through the windscreen at Olivia's geese, which were huddled together in aggressive postures, making extremely unfriendly noises. Basil dumped his pack at the door, and walked back to the waiting cab. Silently, he peeled off the required number of notes from his billfold, added ten per cent and handed the money through the open window to the surly old man. Basil longed to give him a bollocking, and several childish expressions of disapproval sprang readily to his mind – useless old fart, for one – but knowing that it was quite on the cards that he would require the useless old fart's services at some future date, he sensibly refrained.

The cab drove away, and Basil, after shooing away the hostile geese, went into the house. He found Olivia hard at work, printing an edition of etchings. She was wearing jeans and a bra, and was barefoot. 'Hi,' she said, 'shan't be a tick. I'll just take this one off.'

He waited patiently, as, with the aid of paper fingers, she peeled a damp print from the bed of the etching press, and hung it to dry on a wire, with sixteen others exactly like it. Then she closed the press, put a plastic sheet over the stack of damp paper, and wiped her inky hands on a towel. She pulled on an old grey cardigan and came towards him, smiling. It's amazing, said Basil to himself, she hasn't changed at all. In eleven years of marriage, she still looks like a student. It was true. Olivia's face was absolutely flawless, her pale smooth skin the perfect foil for her astonishing blue eyes and the long tangle of pale-blond hair that sometimes fell in an extravagant cascade down her back, but was more often tied back with a bootlace, or the scrap of scarlet silk that had become a *fétiche* thing with her. Occasionally, as now, it was plaited into a thick braid that would have looked very severe on most women, but on Olivia merely looked beautiful.

She wound her slender arms round Basil's neck, and lifted her face to receive his kiss. At once he forgot his feelings of resentment and tiredness and held her tightly against his body in a rib-cracking embrace.

'God, I've missed you, Olly,' he said. 'Shall we go straight to bed?'

Olivia laughed, and disentangled herself from his arms. 'Are you mad?' she said. 'Can't you smell the terrific dinner I've cooked for you, Baz, you ungrateful brute? First things first, my darling.'

'Oh, well, OK; if you insist.' Basil took off his jacket and flung it over the back of the sofa, then looked longingly at the sofa itself, suddenly filled with an overwhelming desire to lie down and go to sleep.

'Baz!' Olivia spoke sharply, guessing what was in his mind.

'What?' He turned back to her, sheepishly.

'None of that crashing-out, Baz. Set the table, please, darling. I'll bring the food right away.' She went to the kitchen end of the long room in which most of the functions of their life took place, opened the door of the cooker, and took out a black-iron casserole. She put it down on the tiled worktop, and lifted the lid. At once, a powerful and delicious odour filled the room, for she had made one of Basil's favourite dishes, chicken cooked with forty cloves of garlic. 'Hurry up with the table, Baz, while I toast the bread. And open the wine, please, darling.'

Delighted that she had taken the trouble to cook especially for him, Basil's tiredness evaporated, he did as he was asked, and in ten minutes they were sitting facing each other across their pear-wood table, steaming plates of garlic chicken before them, glasses of good wine in their hands, happy to be together again. Olivia, her beautiful face flushed from the heat of the oven, her eyes soft and bright, looked at her husband with pleasure. She studied his dark curly head and bushy beard and reckoned that he had a few more grey hairs than he'd had three months before, on his last leave. He lifted his glass to his lips, and raised his grey eyes, black-lashed and sensuous, to hers. 'What are you looking at, my darling?' he asked, smiling.

'Nothing,' she replied, and took a mouthful of

chicken. 'Just thinking that for a bloke of your advanced years, you're still quite a sexy-looking old thing.'

'Well, *good*!' said Baz. 'I'm relieved to hear it.'

Olivia woke at dawn, looked at the motionless body of her sleeping husband, and got quietly out of bed. She slipped on her jeans and a T-shirt, and went downstairs. She opened the door to the yard, and stood on the step looking over the flower-sprinkled grassy meadow that was their garden, towards the marsh beyond, watery and reed-fringed, bordered by oaks and chestnuts, through which she could see the red ball of the rising sun. She could hear her bad-tempered geese complaining in the ugly little wooden shed in which they spent the night, and ran barefoot through the dew-drenched grass to let them out. Then she walked slowly back to the barn, made herself some tea, and finished printing her edition.

When she had finished the run, and cleaned the inking table, she looked at her watch: eight-twenty. She went to the kitchen, squeezed oranges for juice, made a pot of coffee and took the tray upstairs. She put it down on the table beside the bed, took off her clothes and got back into bed. She lifted Basil's arm, relaxed and heavy, and slid underneath it, moulding her body to his.

'God, you're freezing,' he said sleepily.

'I thought you might like to warm me up?'

He opened an eye. 'What, *again*?'

'Any reason why not?'

'None at all. Come here.'

Some time later, they drank the orange juice and the cold coffee. Basil, feeling wonderfully relaxed and extremely slothful, lay back against the pillows, and gazed at Olivia's beautiful naked body, at her still immature breasts and narrow hips, as she sat on the foot of the bed, brushing her long hair. Suddenly, impulsively, he spoke. 'What about a baby, Olly?'

'What did you say, Baz?'

'I said, what about a baby, darling. I've always thought of us as having a family. Isn't it about time?'

'No way.' Olivia shook her head. 'It's absolutely out of the question, Baz. I'm booked for two years ahead, you know that. I couldn't possibly spare the time. In any case, frankly, I can do without the hassle. I'm only thirty; there's loads of time.'

'But there isn't so much time for me, sweetheart. I'm forty-four. I don't want my children to think of me as an old man.'

'How absurd you are, darling. You'll never be *old*; you're not the type. Anyway, why the ugly rush to festoon ourselves with kids? Can't you see what a loss of freedom that would be for me?'

'Is that really how you see it, Olly?'

'Yes, it is.' Olivia looked at her husband, her blue eyes suddenly cold. 'Forget it, Baz,' she said.

Olivia's uncle, Giò Hamilton, was hard at work during the early part of July, regularly spraying his vines with Bordeaux mixture, and supervising the third cultivation of the soil against weeds. Assistance with this essential maintenance came in the shape of a couple of retired village men who helped Giò out on an ad hoc basis, since the death of his father Robert the previous year. The vineyard was situated on the edge of the village of Souliac, marooned like an island on its little hill, surrounded by the *garrigue*, a few kilometres from Uzès. Today, Giò was engaged in the task of cutting back the longest vine shoots, to encourage the formation of fruit.

Now in his middle fifties, and entirely responsible for the management of the vineyard, Giò went only rarely to Paris, and no longer bought and sold antiques for a living. Since the death of his father he had become a single-minded and committed *vigneron*, and was a comparatively happy man. Although he had never had the good fortune to find someone with whom to share his life and his bed, on a permanent basis, he took comfort in the fact that he dearly loved everything that he did have, including his family, his home, his cat, and his awkward old mother, Domenica.

The former presbytery in which they lived was situated in place de l'Eglise, a small tree-shaded square, dominated by a large, mossy, perpetually dripping fountain, and surrounded by tall village houses with graceful eighteenth-century doorways. The presbytery, half hidden behind a high green-painted metal gate, faced the church. The village was blessed with a *boulangerie*, an *alimentation*, a café and a *bureau de poste*, so that the inhabitants, snug within the encircling vineyards, had no need to travel to Uzès or to Nîmes for their daily needs, and the weekly outing to the market was as much an excuse for socializing as for the purchase of the necessities of life.

When the noon Angelus rang from the bell-tower, Giò raked his trimmings into a heap, ready for burning later in the week, put his secateurs into his pocket and walked back through his vines to the outer lane that ran right round the back walls of the village. Now that Domenica was too old, fat and arthritic to cope any longer with stairs, she and her son had exchanged houses and she lived in the small remise cottage that gave onto the lane, and was separated from the main house by a sunny courtyard, full of flowering shrubs in pots, and a huge, gnarled old fig. Rather than irritate his mother by taking a short cut through the remise, Giò, accompanied by his elderly cat, walked round the lane to the archway that led into place de l'Eglise, and went into the presbytery through the green iron gate. The gate clanged shut behind him and he crossed the small front courtyard to the double wooden doors that kept the kitchen cool in summer, and warm in winter.

Domenica may have been fat, old and arthritic but these misfortunes failed to spoil her pleasure in food and drink, and a good deal of her time was spent in the preparation and consumption of meals. Giò found her in the cool, dark kitchen, stirring a fragrant pot of *soupe au pistou*. 'Good timing,' she said. 'It's ready.'

He washed his hands at the sink, took a bottle of *pastis* from the fridge, and poured two slugs of the anis-flavoured aperitif, adding ice and water. Domenica, having taken the view that it was too hot to eat in the back courtyard, under the fig, had already laid the kitchen table with heavy white plates and bowls, a fresh baguette, cheese, olives and a tomato salad. She placed a steaming tureen of her brilliant green soup, smelling strongly of basil and garlic, on the table, and ladled it generously into the waiting bowls.

They had scarcely taken two mouthfuls, when their lunch was interrupted by the shrilling of the telephone. 'Bugger,' said Giò, getting up from the table. 'Who the hell is that?'

It turned out to be Basil, sounding bored and resentful. 'I wondered if I could come and stay for a few days, Giò,' he said. 'I've got a week's leave, but Olly's busy, she's working to a deadline, as usual. There's not much to do, here, except keep out of her way, and try not to get up her nose.'

'Poor old you!' said Giò, with heavy irony.

'Yes, well, you could say that, actually.'

'Sorry, Baz. Yes, of course, do come. You'll have to work, though. This is a busy time for me, too, you understand?'

'No problem. I'd love to help.'

'Excellent. When shall we expect you?'

'I could be at Avignon at half past six, and hire a car. I'd be with you about eight, Giò. Is that too soon? Would tomorrow be better?'

'No, no, today is fine. Ma will make a bigger salad, and bung in a couple more spuds. Come today, Baz, we'd love to see you.'

'Right, I will. Thanks, Giò. Love to your mum.'

'And love to Olly, of course. *A ce soir*.'

* * *

In the cool of the evening, Domenica, Giò and Basil enjoyed a long, leisurely dinner under the fig tree, and at ten-thirty, Domenica, sleepy after so much good food and wine, her arthritis soothed by the smoking of her evening joint, took herself off to bed, leaving the two men to their cigars and cognac in the scented, starlit garden.

Affectionately, and with gentle concern, for long ago he had been quite in love with Basil, Giò looked at his old friend, observing the sadness in his eyes, and the air of slight depression that hung about him. 'What's up, Baz?' he asked quietly.

Basil drew on his little black cigar till the end glowed red, then he let a thin cloud of blue smoke drift from his lips into the branches of the fig. 'Nothing, really,' he said. 'Just feeling knackered, and bloody old.'

'My dear old thing, compared with me, you're still in the cradle.'

'I'm forty-four.'

'So what? It's a number, Baz. Nothing else.'

Basil took a sip of his cognac. 'If you really want to know, Giò, I've fallen out with Olivia.'

'Shit! I don't believe you! What the hell brought that on, for Christ's sake?'

Basil smiled in the darkness. 'You'll probably think the reason pathetic in the extreme.'

'Try me.'

'It's children, Giò.'

'Children?'

'Yes, children. I would love to have them, and Olivia won't co-operate. It's as simple, and as stupid, as that. At present, her career is much more important to her, it seems.'

'Dear me, what a shame.' Giò shook his head, and refilled their glasses, thoughtfully. 'I suppose it's understandable, Baz. She's doing very well, and she's still quite young, isn't she?'

'But I am *not* so young, that's the whole point, Giò.

If Olly ever allows herself to be persuaded to have a child, I'll look like its bloody grandfather by the time the poor little thing goes to school.'

'Really, Baz, you're talking balls. Lots of couples put having a family on hold these days, even I know that. I've always thought you two were so impressive, not minding being apart so much of the time, each of you doing your own thing.'

'Well, now I don't think it's such a brilliant idea.'

'Isn't that a touch reactionary, Baz? What happened to your principles?'

'Up the spout, I expect. Whose side are you on, anyway, Giò?'

Giò laughed. 'Since you appear to have thrust the role of agony uncle on me, Baz, I shall remain strictly neutral, of course.'

'In that case,' said Basil with dignity, 'I won't burden you any longer with my domestic problems.' He rose unsteadily to his feet, then sat down again, clutching the table. 'You bastard, Giò, you've got me hammered! I can barely stand.'

'You don't think the damage is self-inflicted?' suggested Giò dryly. 'Come on, old dear, it's time you were in bed.' He hooked Basil's arm across his shoulders, and together they lurched unsteadily towards the house, leaving the bottles and empty glasses on the dew-drenched table.

It had become a habit for Paul, if he and Misha left the hospital at the same time, to give her a lift to her door, and frequently, on such occasions, they parked the car and walked to a nearby café to have a drink. On operating days, when they were both tired, they sat together comfortably, unwinding, saying little. Misha no longer felt the impulse to unburden herself on the subject of Giles and his treachery, and Paul was more than happy to let the matter drop. Quite often, they didn't even bother about having a drink, but just walked, for the sake of the fresh air and exercise.

For Misha, their friendship had become the essential key to the recovery of her confidence and belief in herself, as well as boosting her credibility as an increasingly capable member of the neurological team. On a more personal level, she took a great deal of pleasure in the knowledge that she had become somehow special to Paul, and he quickly became the dependable rock, as well as comforter, that her father had once been.

For Paul, their deepening relationship was far more ambiguous, and he realized that his growing feelings for her were not those usually felt by a father for his daughter. Quite aware of what was happening to him, he took care to conceal his emotions, not only from Misha herself, but even more from the colleagues around them at work. Constantly, he warned himself of the dangers inherent in the silent game in which he was engaged, having many times witnessed the destructive outcomes of similar liaisons. Nevertheless, he was incapable of suppressing the sensations of joy, light-heartedness and incredulous happiness that constantly bubbled up inside him, like a spring. He felt young again, and physically strong, and woke each morning happy in the knowledge that he would spend several hours of the day in Misha's company, with the possible added bonus, after work, of sharing a few minutes alone with her.

He longed to take her again to Froissy, and waited for her to suggest another visit, but she did not. On the night of the eleventh of July, he lay awake for some time debating the wisdom of raising the subject himself, finally deciding that, after all, she could only refuse, and that would be the end of the matter. They would remain friends and colleagues, nothing more.

He spent the day of the twelfth in a state of mild nervousness and excitement, though few would have guessed it from his manner, which remained quiet, cool and entirely normal. Everything went according to plan. The afternoon's list had been short and quite straightforward, and they left the hospital at half past six, Misha accepting an invitation to have a drink at the Vieux-Colombier, near St-Sulpice. The café was quiet, and uncrowded, and Paul ordered a carafe of chilled wine, and a plate of *charcuterie*. The food and wine arrived, and Paul watched indulgently as Misha piled sausage and gherkin onto a slice of country bread, and devoured it hungrily. 'Sorry,' she said, with her mouth full. 'I'm absolutely starving; no lunch.'

He poured two glasses of wine, and ate some sausage himself. Misha finished her snack, and took a swallow of her wine. 'That's better,' she said. 'I feel almost human again.'

'Misha,' said Paul, doing his best to sound as relaxed and unconcerned as possible, 'are you doing anything particular on Friday?'

'Friday? No, I don't think so. Why? Is there any reason why I should be?'

'Yes, there is. It's the Fête Nationale. Had you forgotten?'

'Good heavens, is it really?'

'If you're not on duty, or on call, I thought you might like to go to Froissy, and do some more gardening?'

'Just for the day?'

'Yes, if you like. Or the weekend, if you think that might be even better, Misha. It's entirely down to you.'

Misha took another sip of her wine, ate an olive, stared out of the window at the passers-by in the street, and was silent, so turbulent were the thoughts in her mind, and the pounding of the blood in her ears.

Paul, mortified to think that he had embarrassed her, put his hand on hers. 'It's OK; it doesn't matter. Of course you don't want to come with me, why should you? I'll go by myself.'

Misha turned her face towards him, and he saw that her cheeks were flushed and her green eyes shone in the subdued light of the café. 'But I do want to,' she said. 'I've only just realized it, but that's exactly what I want, Paul.'

'You mean, you'll come?'
'Yes, of course I will.'
'For the weekend, Misha?'
'Yes, for the weekend.'
He took her hand, turned it over and kissed the palm gently. 'I'm so glad,' he said.

They arrived at Froissy in the pouring rain, just after noon. In case the local shops would be shut for the Fête Nationale, they had gone to the supermarket in rue de la Roquette the evening before, and bought everything they thought they might need for the weekend. They carried the bags into the kitchen, then unpacked them in the walk-in larder. This useful room had several rows of slate shelves, as well as a cupboard for dry stuff, an ancient fridge, bought in the fifties, and a stone sink for washing vegetables. 'How sensible, and how well designed,' Misha remarked, putting eggs into a wire basket on the shelf, and butter onto a dish with a blue-and-white striped cover.
'We have a choice of cooking methods,' Paul told her. 'There's a rather clapped-out gas cooker, which one hopes still has some gas in the bottle. Failing that, we could light the Godin, which is probably the better option, because it not only cooks, but heats some not terribly hot bath water as well.'
'What does it run on?'
'Wood.'
'Really? And have we got wood?'
'Loads of it. I'll get some in, right away. Sooner the stove's lit, the better; give it a chance to get hot.'
He took a raincoat from a hook on the back of the kitchen door, and went out to the courtyard, leaving Misha to find her way round the kitchen cupboards, discovering beautiful old china and glass in the process, as well as heavy English silver cutlery, and drawers full of tea towels and table linen. In one cupboard she found cast-iron skillets and saucepans, lidded casseroles and a basket containing cake tins,

muffin pans and *madeleine* moulds. More kitchen tools, sieves, colanders and old-fashioned wire-mesh food covers hung from hooks in the beams supporting the ceiling.

Paul came back carrying a large basket full of logs, together with a bundle of kindling. 'Look in the larder, under the sink, Misha. There should be a small bag of coal. It makes it easier to get the fire going, especially if the chimney is cold.'

Misha found the coal, the firebox was quickly filled with paper, sticks, coal and logs, and a match applied to the paper. Gently, Paul closed the door and pulled out the damper. Immediately, there was a tremendous roar as the wood and coal caught fire, fanned by the draught in the flue.

'Won't the chimney catch fire?' Misha asked anxiously, slightly alarmed at the bangs and creaks emanating from the rapidly expanding metal flue.

'Certainly not,' said Paul robustly, then laughed. 'Or rather, I'm pretty sure not, unless there's an awful lot of soot up there.' Prudently, he closed the damper a bit, and the roar gradually subsided to a purring throb, with only the occasional muted bang inside the chimney.

He turned to Misha, and took her in his arms. 'Are you really here with me, my darling?' he asked, shaking his head. 'Tell me I'm not dreaming; that I'm not going to wake up and find myself in bed, alone, in Paris.'

'I hope you're going to wake up and find yourself in bed with me, here at Froissy.'

His arms tightened round her and he kissed her; on her forehead, on her closed eyes, and finally on her mouth, warm and yielding beneath his. 'That's more like it,' he whispered, and kissed her again.

'What do you mean?' She put a finger on his lips.

'I mean that we've moved on a stage from the good night kiss between friends, haven't we?'

'Yes, we have.'

'What changed your mind, to make that possible?'

'You won't laugh?'

'I don't know. I might.'

'OK,' said Misha. 'I won't tell you, then.'

'I promise I won't laugh. Tell me.'

'Well, it was last week, on Wednesday. We were scrubbing-up, and suddenly I found myself thinking how beautiful your hands and arms were, and then I began to fantasize about the rest of you, how you would look without your clothes on.'

'Misha! I thought it was only men who go around thinking naughty thoughts, not nicely brought up girls like you!'

'Ah, well, that goes to show how little you know about women. But there's a subtle difference, Paul. When men fancy someone, they make it pretty obvious with their body language. Women are less upfront. They keep these things in their minds, and their hands to themselves.'

Paul laughed, then looked worried. 'My God,' he said. 'I hope you're not going to be horribly disappointed when the depressing truth is revealed.' He looked at her, smiling, his eyes half-serious, questioning. 'How appalling to find the woman you love, and then she runs screaming from you, repelled by the wreck of the ageing flesh. Maybe I should have brought some pyjamas with me?'

Misha laughed and hugged him tightly. 'It won't be like that, I promise.' She looked up at him, her eyes soft. 'Is that true?'

'Is what true, darling?'

'Am I really the woman you love?'

'How can you doubt it? You know you are, Misha.'

She reached up and kissed him. 'You won't need pyjamas,' she said.

'Good.'

They drank a glass of wine, and ate a sandwich, then went outside to see whether the rain was showing any signs of stopping. It wasn't. In fact, if anything, the sky seemed darker and the rain heavier than before.

'What a bore,' said Paul. 'I was really looking forward to having another go at the walled garden.'

'Apart from the rain, what's stopping us?'

'What do you mean?'

'I mean, let's do it anyway. It's not *cold*, Paul, just wet.'

'Don't you mind getting wet?'

'No, not at all.'

They fetched the barrow and the tools, and set to work. For the whole afternoon they laboured together, Paul hacking, chopping, picking up great bundles of prunings with a pitchfork and dumping them on the bonfire, now revived and burning reluctantly in the relentless downpour. Misha, her hands protected by gloves and armed with a garden fork and a trowel, loosened the compacted earth round the newly cut-back roses, pulling out the encroaching brambles and nettles, and the huge clumps of comfrey that had established themselves where once had flourished hardy geraniums, alchemillas and violas. From time to time, she unearthed the dormant bulbs of muscari, bluebells and narcissi, and carefully marked the spot, covering them again with freshly turned earth. It must look lovely in the spring, she thought, seeing in her mind's eye the sheets of blue flowers appearing in the soft moist earth under the bare stems of the roses.

Paul had cleared the entire length of one wall, and he straightened his back and drew deep breaths of the moisture-laden air. He wiped the rain from his face, and looked at Misha as she knelt under the graceful white sprays of a Mme Alfred Carrière rose, ripping out brambles with her gloved hands, muttering words that sounded like 'thug', 'assassin', or 'brute' as she did so. He smiled, lifted the empty barrow, trundled it to her side and began to gather up the piles of weeds she had thrown onto the path.

'These are real sods to get out,' she said, between clenched teeth, and heaved out another bramble, her face red with exertion, her dark wet hair plastered to her skull.

'You look like a drowned rat, my darling. It's time we stopped, and got dry. We've done enough for one day.' They left everything where it was and went back to the house, going in at the French windows to the sitting-room, taking off their muddy shoes on the step.

'I am absolutely *soaked*!' Misha exclaimed, holding her filthy shoes at arm's length. 'I can feel the water on my skin, all over me. It's running down my back.'

'Me, too. We need a bath.'

Misha's eyes widened. 'What, a cold one?'

'No. Hot, of course. Let's see what the Godin has managed to produce in the way of heat, shall we?'

Dripping, they went to the kitchen to check the stove, which was extremely hot, radiating heat in fact, and the kettle on the top was murmuring in a friendly manner. 'Excellent,' said Paul. 'Tea.'

They removed their sodden raincoats and hung them on the rack suspended from the ceiling in the larder, then drank their tea as they stood, steaming, next to the stove. Then Paul picked up their bags, and led the way upstairs to his parents' room. He switched on the light at the door, for the place was still shuttered and dark, then crossed the floor to the tall windows, opening them all, and pushing back the shutters, revealing the misty, rain-soaked vineyard and the meadows beyond, the white cattle ghostly in the deepening blue twilight. Misha came and stood beside him, and he put his arm round her damp shoulders, drawing her to him. 'You don't mind sleeping in my parents' room, Misha?'

'Do you think *they* would mind, Paul?'

'No, I'm quite sure they wouldn't.'

'Well, that's OK, then, isn't it?' She smiled at him, a little shyly. 'You have the first bath; you're the one that needs it most.'

'Are you sure?'

'Yes, of course I am. And while you're having it, I'll unpack and make the bed.'

He went into the adjoining bathroom, and presently Misha heard the sound of rushing water, then several groans and gasps as Paul lowered himself into the hot tub, then silence.

She unpacked the bags, and hung the clean clothes in the armoire, then made the bed with the beautiful linen already waiting. In the armoire, she found a blue cotton bathrobe, and she stripped off all her clammy wet things and put it on, ready for her bath. She took a bottle of shampoo and a tube of bath gel from her bag, and sat down on the stool in front of the dressing-table.

'Misha?'

'Yes?'

'I've forgotten to get a towel!'

'Where are they?'

'In the airing cupboard, I think.'

'Where's that?'

'In here. Can you get me one, please?'

'Right.' She opened the bathroom door and went in. The towels lay in a neat pile on a stool beside the bath. Paul lay full length in the bath, up to his neck in the steamy water. 'There isn't any soap, either,' he said, and grinned.

Misha took the cap off the bath gel and squeezed some into the bath, then poured shampoo onto Paul's head and began vigorously washing his hair for him. Then she pushed him, spluttering, under the foaming water, let her robe fall to the ground and got into the bath beside him. He took her in his arms and held her naked body close to his in the warm, scented water and thought that he would explode with happiness. Gently he kissed her, and then not so gently as they explored each other's bodies for the first time. 'You smell of bonfire,' he said.

A little after nine o'clock, Misha was woken by the shriek of an owl in the trees, close to the open windows. She lay in Paul's arms, listening to his heartbeat beneath her cheek, and aware of the soft rise and fall of his stomach, beneath her hand. Carefully, she rolled away from him, and switched on the lamp on the night-table. She turned her head and looked at him, sleeping so peacefully, his face unlined, his body smooth and flat-stomached, graceful in repose. He opened his eyes and smiled at her lazily, still half asleep. 'What time is it?'

'It's late,' she told him, 'it's after nine. Aren't you hungry, darling?'

'Are *you*?' Eating was the last thing on his mind.

'Yes, I am. I could eat a horse.'

'Right. Supper. What've we got, that's quick?'

'Quails. They won't take long, will they?'

In the kitchen, Misha became a model of culinary efficiency. She stuffed the cavities of the plump little birds with garlic, thyme, juniper berries and lemon, and put them in the oven to roast. 'How come this old stove isn't all greasy and horrible?' she asked.

'It's how Godins are, I think. The fire never goes out; that's the theory, anyway. All the splashes and spills get burnt away to a powder. The original self-cleaning cooker, one might hazard a guess.'

'Brilliant! It's a rotten job, cleaning ovens.'

'I'm ashamed to admit, I've never actually done it.'

'OK, you can scrape the potatoes, as a penance.' She looked at him, quizzically. 'Don't tell me you've never done that, either?'

He smiled blandly, and forbore to tell her that Blanche had always made a tremendous fuss about his taking care of his valuable, heavily insured hands, and would have been angry if she had seen him hacking away at thorny rose stems, chopping wood and getting his hands filthy with kindling and coal as he lit the stove. 'I reckon I can manage that,' he said. 'Where are they?'

'In the larder. There are pans there, too, above the sink.' She searched in a shallow basket. 'Here's a knife,' she said. 'Choose small ones, so they cook quickly, and take care not to cut yourself.'

'Yes, ma'am! At once, ma'am!'

Misha laughed, and blew him a kiss. He took himself off to the larder, and found the potatoes. Standing at the sink, his hands in the freezing spring water, scraping potatoes as though it were an artform, so that not a mark of the knife-blade, or the smallest blemish remained, and each one lay in the pan of water, as bald and perfectly formed as a peeled hard-boiled egg, he was filled with a sensation of incredulous happiness, even ecstasy, as if he were drunk, though without the loss of control. It was a state of mind he had experienced quite frequently as a boy, but never before in his adult life. For the first time, he had chosen to listen to his heart, to behave entirely in his own interests, and in Misha's too, he hoped and believed.

It had been almost laughably easy to invent an excuse for not being in Paris for the holiday weekend – a university bash in Grenoble – and in any case, Blanche had shown no interest in his plans. Her own were keeping her fully occupied, and since they involved Olivier, she was not sorry to hear that Paul would be away himself. 'I might call in at Froissy on my way back from Grenoble,' he had remarked casually; 'just to check that everything's OK.'

'It must be ages since you went there?'

'Months,' he had lied. 'Far too long.'

'Oh, well, as long as you don't expect me to go with you, Paul. You know I can't bear the place.'

'Yes, Blanche, I do know.'

In the kitchen, he found Misha sitting at the table, shelling peas into a bowl. She was wearing the blue cotton robe, and her slim tanned arms were beautiful in the light from the lamp on the table. Her dark head was bent so that her face was hidden, and she looked up as he came into the room and gave him a slow, secret smile. He put the pan of potatoes on the hotplate, then knelt beside her. He pushed aside the loosely tied robe and kissed her breasts, first one, then the other. She held his head in her arms, and kissed the top of his head. 'Do I still smell of bonfire?' she asked.

'No, darling, you don't. You smell of love.' He looked up, she kissed him and thought that his mouth tasted of almonds, and cinnamon. The pan of potatoes boiled over, and reluctantly they paid attention to the preparation of supper. 'What about a drink?' Paul suggested, moving the potatoes to the edge of the hot-plate.

'A drink would be lovely.'

Paul went to the cellar, and returned with two bottles, a Vouvray, and a red Bourgueil to drink with the quails. He pulled the cork of the Vouvray and poured two glasses. They sat at the table, and drank the cold, slightly fizzy wine.

'Paul,' Misha said suddenly, surprising herself. 'I probably shouldn't ask, but I need to know.'

'Yes?'

'Have you ever slept in that bed before?'

'Yes.'

'When?'

'When I was about five, and used to get into bed with my mother and father, in the early mornings.'

Misha smiled. 'So, never with Blanche?'

He laughed. 'Darling Misha, Blanche only ever slept in a spare room in this house, and that only a very few times, and *never* with me. She loathed coming here, and found everything about the place a total bore, not her scene at all.' He looked at Misha, his face suddenly unsmiling, and serious. 'Blanche was the eldest daughter of a rich silk merchant, who supplied all the big couture houses. Her family had an impressive nineteenth-century mansion in a smart suburb of Paris, very opulent and well appointed; central heating; gold-plated taps; that sort of thing. Blanche thought Froissy incredibly old-fashioned and uncivilized by comparison, and didn't hesitate to broadcast her feelings on the subject, to anyone who would listen. It was her way of punishing my mother for being who she was. Blanche loathed her, and I'm afraid the feeling was entirely mutual.'

'How awful, for all of you.' Misha frowned, and took a sip of her wine. 'But if that's how it was, Paul, why did you marry Blanche at all?'

'You may well ask; it was stupid, foolish, wrong, a huge mistake. There were two reasons, Misha. The first was that Blanche was very pretty, and unusually sophisticated for a student. She was glamorous and extremely well dressed, a real Parisienne, and I was besotted by all that. I was in my twenties, and pretty emotionally naive. I might have grown out of it, except for one thing. Blanche goaded me constantly on the subject of being a mummy's boy, of being childishly close to my parents, of not having a mind of my own, and of being too tied to them and to Froissy. She never stopped reminding me that it was essential to be free of them, to leave my childhood behind for ever, and in the end I cracked, and asked her to marry me on her terms, just to prove that she was wrong about me.'

'And was she wrong, Paul?'

He shook his head, and laughed. 'No, of course not. She was right. This place is too deep in my bones and heart to shake it off, just like that. It's an integral part of me, and so is my family, it goes without saying.'

'And if Blanche had loved it here, too, and got on with your mother, what then?'

'Nothing would have made me happier, of course.'

'But it didn't happen?'

'No, it didn't.' He refilled their glasses. 'Let's not dwell on the past, please, Misha. Let's enjoy the present, shall we, darling?'

Misha twisted the stem of her glass. 'Just one more question, then we'll never speak of it again.'

'OK.'

'How long is it since you shared a bed with your wife?'

'Um, ten years, I suppose.'

'And have there been other women since then?'
'No.'
'None at all?' She found it incredible that a man of his looks and passion could make such a claim. 'Do you mean that I'm the very first one?'
'Absolutely. You're the first, and I very much hope, the last and only one.'
Misha laughed, leaned across the table and kissed him. 'I'd never have guessed that you were so out of practice, not in a million years.'
'Oh,' he said airily, 'I expect it's like riding a bike, don't you? Once you've cracked it, you don't fall off, do you?' He laughed. 'That is, if you can still manage to get your leg over the bike in the first place!'

Chapter Six

Blanche de Vilmorin was not a stupid woman, and she very soon noticed the change in Paul. They did not meet more frequently than usual, but when they did she could hardly fail to notice how cheerful he had recently become, how light was his step and how handsome and young he looked. With her quick intelligence, she drew the obvious conclusion: that he must be in love. As late July approached, and the annual trip south to Ménerbes drew near, she began to wonder whether he would invent some excuse not to accompany her to their summer home this year, and decided to broach the subject. 'I've told Mireille to expect us on the twenty-sixth, Paul. That's OK with you, I hope?'

'Yes, of course, Blanche, why not? Catherine and Olivier are coming with us, as usual, I take it?'

'Yes, they're coming, Paul.' Blanche smiled at her husband. 'Sometimes I quite wish they didn't always come, you know. It would be lovely to be by ourselves, for once, wouldn't it?'

If he was extremely surprised to hear this, Paul did not show it, but smiled non-committally at his wife, and went on reading his paper. He had already discussed the question of the summer vacation with Misha, and they had agreed that as neither of them wished to make an issue of Paul's family obligations, it would be best for him to go to Ménerbes, as usual, in order not to arouse suspicion. For the moment, they were anxious to keep their relationship a matter of secrecy, entirely between themselves, and would regard the summer break as an unavoidable hiatus, nothing more.

Blanche might have been reassured by Paul's confirmation of his intention to holiday with her, had not her suspicions been reinforced by other alarming pieces of evidence. Spurred on by some self-destructive impulse, she searched his clothes cupboard and chest of drawers while he was at work, and found several things that appeared to her to confirm her worst fears. Bundled up and shoved to the back of his clothes cupboard she found a pair of crumpled, dirty and rather damp trousers, as well as some extremely muddy brogues. These items she found deeply worrying; what possible reason could Paul have had to get his clothes into such a state on a professional visit to Grenoble? And always assuming that there was a plausible reason, why go to such lengths to hide the dirty things afterwards? Why not just put the trousers out for the dry cleaner, and send the shoes to the kitchen for cleaning? Carefully, Blanche stuffed the incriminating items back where she had found them, then searched the pockets of the jackets hanging in the cupboard. She found nothing except a copy of the sonnets of Ronsard, with a white rose pressed between two pages. Her eye fell on the verse beneath:

Quand vous serez bien vieille, au soir à la chandelle,
Assise auprès du feu, dévidant et filant,
Direz, chantant mes vers, en vous émerveillant,
Ronsard me célébrait du temps que j'étais belle.

Blanche frowned. What kind of sentimental rubbish is this, she asked herself uneasily. This is schoolboy stuff; what the hell is he up to? Severely tempted to mangle the rose and throw it in the waste basket, she nevertheless prudently returned both book and rose to the jacket pocket. Carefully checking that she had left no sign of her visit, Blanche left Paul's bedroom and went to her study.

It so happened that it was Olivier's day for his afternoon visit, and as soon as he arrived, in happy anticipation of a pleasant couple of hours' dalliance, Blanche quickly dashed his hopes by inviting him into her study. There, she revealed to Olivier her suspicions that Paul had a mistress, and offered him the evidence to support her conjecture. Rather taken aback, both by the news, and by Blanche's obvious agitation about it, Olivier hesitated for a moment. Then he said, 'I'm surprised that you mind so much, Blanche. Does it really matter?'

'Yes, it does. It matters a great deal to me.'

'I see.'

'No, you don't, Olivier. You don't see at all. You're just thinking of yourself, like most men.'

'I'm sorry, I just thought . . . '

'Well, don't think, stupid man! It has nothing to do with you and me, Olivier, nothing at all.'

'Oh.'

'The point is, I need to know how far this has gone, before I decide what, if anything, to do about it. It occurred to me that you would probably know of a reliable investigative agency, so that we could get Paul's activities checked out.'

'Blanche! Darling! You wouldn't do a thing like that, surely?'

Blanche's response was icily implacable. 'I most certainly would, and you are going to organize it for me, Olivier.'

'Oh, God, Blanche, must I? I'd hate it if Paul ever found out; I'd feel like a traitor. After all, he is my friend, isn't he?'

'Really? You seem to forget your friendship quite easily on most Thursday afternoons, my dear.'

'Yes, well.' Olivier's blush was deep and prolonged, and he fervently wished himself anywhere but in that room with Blanche. She stared at him coldly, determined to bend him to her will. It did not take him very long to agree to carry out the commission for her. 'I'll speak to someone I know, in the morning,' he said. He gazed at her, his eyes ashamed. 'Now, can we go to your room, darling?'

Blanche got to her feet, terminating the interview. 'Certainly not, Olivier. That sort of thing must go on hold until this crisis has been dealt with. Anything else would be in extremely bad taste; I'm astonished that you could even think of such a thing just now.'

She accompanied him to the door and they parted with a chaste kiss on the cheek. Disappointed, and not a little rattled by Blanche's disclosures, Olivier made his way back to his parked car. I sometimes wonder whether darling Blanche isn't very slightly mad, he said to himself sulkily, adjusting his seat belt. Why should a bit of a cuddle *now* be in bad taste, if it was OK before she found Paul out, I'd like to know?

A week later, and a few days before the date of their departure to Ménerbes, Blanche received a visit from Olivier. He brought with him a large buff envelope, which contained a typewritten report, and a sheaf of enlarged photographs. Silently, he handed the package to Blanche, and equally silently, she examined the contents.

First, she looked at the photographs, which showed Paul in the company of an attractive, quite young, dark-haired woman, walking along the banks of the Seine; sharing a meal in several different obscure-looking restaurants; driving together in Paul's car, with the hood down, laughing. Last of all and most importantly, there were many pictures of Paul with the same woman at Froissy, obviously taken with a telephoto lens. In some of them they were apparently working in the garden, for there were wheelbarrows, rakes and other gardening tools in evidence around them. Another picture showed them standing together beside a bonfire, and lastly a series of repeat shots showed them in a close embrace, clasped tightly in each other's arms, kissing.

'Have you looked at these, Olivier?'

'Yes, I have.'

'What did you think?'

Olivier had already decided to keep his thoughts on the subject to himself, since his own initial reaction to the photographs had been one of envy, rather than condemnation of Paul. 'Well, I expect much the same as you, Blanche. Shock and disbelief, really. I always thought Paul was too high-minded for involvements of that nature, actually.'

Blanche ignored this. 'Who is she, anyway?'

'It's all in the report, darling. Evidently, she's a doctor at the hospital. Her name is Misha ben Bella. It appears her family came originally from Algeria.'

'*Really?*' Blanche's expression was one of combined distaste and aversion. 'God, a *pied noir*, how could he?'

'Only too readily, Blanche, by the looks of things.'

Blanche felt a sharp stab of disquiet, even fear. 'You know, Olivier, now that you've raked up all this dirt, I'm not at all sure that it was such a brilliant idea.'

'I'm sorry,' said Olivier, feeling curiously guilty, 'I was only doing what you asked me to, darling.'

'Yes, yes, I'm not blaming you. Don't fuss.'

For several days, Blanche thought very carefully about what, if anything, to do about Paul and his lover. It was not her style to confront the enemy and force a showdown, in order to achieve her ends. She reminded herself how painless the transition had been, ten years ago, when she had decided to end the charade of her marriage to Paul, by the simple means of removing herself from their shared bedroom. It had not been necessary to indulge in tears or tantrums, or to make a drama out of an unsatisfactory situation. Rather surprisingly, and slightly insultingly, Paul had not objected to the new arrangement. In fact, he had made no comment, other than giving Blanche an ironic little smile, and raising his eyebrows in the way that had always infuriated her.

Blanche had not the slightest desire to divorce Paul, or to change their way of life in any way. She admired him, as a successful and rather celebrated man, and greatly valued the kudos of being married to him, as well as his financial contribution that made their lavish lifestyle possible. Deep inside herself, Blanche had been terribly wounded and humiliated by the slow painful realization that Paul had ceased to love her, and had probably never loved her at all. Nevertheless, she had never regretted marrying him, and thought of him as a valuable possession, in the same way that her children, her houses and her thriving business were the evidence of her successful management of her marriage and career. Now, it seemed obvious that something had to be done to save the marriage. The question was, what exactly should she do? For several reasons, she rejected immediately the idea of any kind of showdown with Paul. She saw at once that such an action was quite likely to force his relationship with his lover out into the open, almost certainly causing a scandal, and, ultimately, a divorce. The thought of Paul's departure from her life, and possible remarriage to a much younger woman, filled her with a slow-burning anger, and fear. She saw immediately that such an eventuality would cause her friends a good deal of secret amusement, and utterly destroy her current enviable status within their circle.

Blanche spent a sleepless night, sitting on her bed, endlessly re-reading the private eye's report, and looking at the incriminating photographs. It did not take her very long to recognize the unmistakable and powerful attachment between her husband and the dark-haired young woman. If this gets out, she told herself, it will do irreparable harm to his reputation at the hospital, that's for sure. Somehow, I've got to think of a way of ending the affair, but with no harm done. The ben Bella woman must be got rid of. Somehow, she must be made to leave of her own accord.

In the morning Blanche telephoned her daughter, Nina, and asked her to come to rue de Thorigny as soon as possible.

'What's up, Mother? You sound a bit agitated.'

'Never mind that, Nina. Just come.'

Nina Mansart arrived at rue de Thorigny in time to have lunch with her mother, having cancelled her appointments or rescheduled them with her partners in the practice. She had also arranged for her English au pair to remain on duty, collect the children from school, and give them their tea. Normally, Nina would have seen her mother at a time more convenient to herself, but, sensing the slight panic in Blanche's voice and deducing that the reason was probably a medical worry of some kind, she got herself to rue de Thorigny as soon as she reasonably could.

Marie-Claire had prepared a *salade niçoise* and mother and daughter ate their lunch in Blanche's study, overlooking the tiny formal garden at the rear of the house. Nina, in her brisk and professional mode, came straight to the point. 'What's the trouble, darling?'

'It's your father, Nina, I'm afraid.'

'*Papa*? There's nothing wrong with him, is there?'

'No, dear, there's nothing wrong with his *health*, as far as I know. I'm afraid it's not good news, Nina. He's having an affair.'

'He's *what*?'

'Having an affair, darling. You know: he's got a mistress.'

'I don't believe it,' said Nina flatly. 'Someone's been telling you malicious lies, Mother. He'd never do a thing like that, I'm sure. For a start, where would he find the time? He's exactly like Gérard. He never stops working, does he?'

Blanche looked at her daughter sadly. 'You medics are all the same; you have the idea that you're all saints, don't you? No time for anything but the patients, and all that crap.'

Nina pursed her lips, and took a sip of her mineral water. 'I'm sorry you think that,' she said stiffly. 'I always thought you were pretty keen on the medical profession?'

'I was. I am.' Blanche shook her head. 'Sorry, Nina, it was a foolish thing to say. It's just that I'm really sick with worry; I haven't slept for two nights.'

'OK. Let's start again. You'd better begin at the beginning; tell me what's worrying you.'

Blanche put down her fork, and told Nina everything that she had at first suspected, then discovered for herself, and finally had confirmed by Olivier's private eye. She went to her bureau and took the package of photographs from a locked drawer, and put them into the reluctant hands of her daughter. Slowly, Nina read the report, then looked through the photographs, examining each one closely, especially the one of her father kissing the dark-haired woman, Misha. Then she put everything back in the envelope, and looked at her mother with a small smile. 'He certainly looks very happy, Mother,' she said. 'So I guess you must be right; he is having an affair.'

'Are you being frivolous, Nina?'

'No, of course not. I'm just telling the truth, as I see it. He *does* look very happy, doesn't he?'

'What the hell has his happiness got to do with it?' asked Blanche furiously. 'It's a potentially damaging scandal, and a threat to my marriage. It's got to stop, that's all there is to it, Nina.'

'Yes, well, I quite see your point, Mother. What do you suggest?'

Blanche took a sip of white wine. 'I wondered whether Gérard might be in a position to get the ben Bella woman sacked?'

Nina frowned. 'In the first place, I'm quite certain he

wouldn't do such a thing, even if he could, Mother. He would consider such an action unethical. In the second place, it's not his hospital, as you very well know, so there's no way he'd be able to have any influence there.' She looked at Blanche, uneasily. 'Quite apart from all that, Gérard has enormous respect for *Papa*. Nothing would induce him to harm him in any way.' In her heart Nina knew perfectly well that if and when she told her husband about her father's extramarital activities, his reaction would be one of unqualified approval and support for his father-in-law. Gérard had never had a great deal of time for Blanche.

'Obviously, I have no wish to damage your father, Nina. All I want is to get things back to normal, and that's what I intend to do.'

'How?'

'By getting rid of this bloody woman, of course. What else?'

'Any ideas as to how to set about it?'

'Not really, but I thought you might have, darling?' After a pause, she added, 'I thought perhaps you might be able to have a word with her, after Paul and I have gone to Ménerbes?'

Bloody hell, said Nina to herself, what am I getting into? She got up from her seat and went to the window, and stood staring at the little cupid figure in the centre of the small stone fountain. In fact, she understood very well her mother's motives in trying to find a means of getting rid of the interloper in her marriage, and knew that in similar circumstances she would probably react in much the same way herself. Certainly, the concept of her father in bed with a woman almost as young as herself did make her feel a little contempt for him, and pity for her mother.

After a few moments, she returned to the table and sat down. 'Very well, I'll think about it, and see what I can do. What's her address? Do we have it?'

'Yes,' said Blanche eagerly, 'it's right here, darling. It's in Bastille. Sixteen, passage des Ebénistes.'

Nina listed the address in her organizer. 'I can't promise anything, Mother, but I'll do my best.'

'I know you will, darling. I'm so grateful, you've no idea.'

'As a matter of fact, Mother, I think I have a very good idea.' After a moment's thought, she added, 'I think perhaps I'd better take the photos with me. That way, she won't be able to deny it, or argue the toss, will she?'

The night before Paul's departure for Ménerbes, he slept with Misha at passage des Ebénistes. They dined in their local bistro, then walked back to the apartment, drank a cognac in the garden, and went to bed.

'I don't think I can bear to be away from you for a whole month, my darling,' said Paul quietly, as he held her in his arms, and kissed her gently. 'This is the first time I've actually felt desperately sad, after making love with you.'

'I feel exactly the same,' she replied, and he could taste the tears on her cheeks. 'I can't bear it, either, especially as you'll be so far away.' She smoothed his hair from his forehead and, holding his head in her hands, kissed him gently and languorously, as though she were trying to drink enough of the essence of him to last her for a month. Responding to her kiss, and without taking his mouth from hers, he folded himself over her warm body and they made love again, slowly, not hurrying, then with passionate urgency, as if it were for the very last time.

'I love you, Misha.'

'I love you, too.'

Paul sighed. 'It wouldn't be so bad if I could phone you at night, but it's out of range of the mobile, and the bloody phone box is miles away, in the village. Blanche would wonder what the hell I was up to if I kept making excuses to go there, and I wouldn't dare risk using the house phone.'

'Don't do it anyway, darling, please. If I thought you

might phone, I'd be hanging about, in agony, waiting for it to happen. It would be better not to call at all, till you get back. But you could write to me, Paul, couldn't you?'

'I will, every day.'

In the very early morning, Paul got up, took a shower, and, wrapping himself in Misha's blue bath towel, went to the kitchen to make coffee. He carried the cups through to the bedroom, and they drank the coffee together, saying little, for there was very little left to say. He got dressed, and prepared to leave.

Misha went with him to the door. 'Just in case you get back while I'm at work, and you want to come here,' she said, 'I'll give you my spare keys.' She took them from her key-ring. 'I'll write to Giles today and tell him to get his stuff out of here as soon as possible, so if you do come, don't be surprised if the place looks different, will you?'

Paul put the keys in his pocket. 'The sooner we're free of the presence of Giles, the happier I'll be, my darling.' He gave her a swift hard hug, and left.

Misha ran to the garden and leaned over the railing, as she usually did, to watch him drive away. As he always did, he looked up and waved, and she waved back, and tried to smile. She went back to bed, and held Paul's pillow against her face, inhaling the smell of him. Then, still cradling the pillow in her arms, she lay down on her stomach and wept.

Before paying the proposed visit to her father's mistress, Nina Mansart decided that in the interests of obtaining undeniable evidence of his adultery, she would go down to Froissy and have a good look round for herself, rather than relying on the rather inconclusive proof of wrong-doing to be deduced from the private eye's photographs.

She parked her car in the courtyard, then, vaguely remembering where the key to the house was hidden, she found it without difficulty, and entered the kitchen. There was a faint smell of cooking, and she saw that there were logs in a basket near the Godin stove, and a glass jar containing mint, a sprig of rosemary and two pink roses on the table. Nina observed that the roses were still fresh, so her father and his mistress must have been there very recently – followed from Paris by Blanche's photographer, no doubt. In the larder, washed plates and glasses were on the draining board, and several empty wine bottles stood on the stone floor beneath the sink. Well, she said to herself a little grimly, they certainly managed to make themselves at home.

As Nina went down the corridor to the hall, then climbed the staircase to the bedrooms, she reminded herself that Froissy was, after all, her father's home, and that he had a perfect right to be there. Ghastly place, so cold and damp, she thought. I'm not surprised Mother could never bring herself to live here. Wild horses wouldn't make me, either.

She looked into the bedroom she had stayed in from time to time, as a little girl, visiting her grandparents. Nothing was changed. The grey-and-white dappled rocking-horse still stood beneath the window, with his red-leather saddle and his long white mane and tail. Nina gave him a little push, and he moved silently on his rockers, his silky tail ruffled by his own breeze. He must be worth quite a bit, I suppose, she thought idly. She glanced at the little walnut *lit bateau*, with its English eiderdown, covered in pink-and-green paisley silk, and suddenly a vivid memory came to her. She saw herself, sitting up in that bed and reading *King Ottokar's Sceptre* to her little brother, Pascal, as he sat beside her, looking at the pictures, transfixed, his mouth open, his dark hair flopping over his huge dark eyes.

Nina looked in the mirror that stood on the small dressing-table, and sighed, remembering how much she had always envied Pascal for inheriting the looks of his father, and how much she had always resented the fact that she herself was blonde and blue-eyed, like her mother. She had chosen to marry a man who looked as much like a de Vilmorin as possible.

She left the room, closing the door gently on her memories, and went to her father's boyhood bedroom. There was nothing unusual to be seen in there; the place looked bare and unused. She continued on to the door of her grandparents' bedroom, hesitating for a few moments, feeling unaccountably nervous, before firmly turning the handle and going in. She closed the door, then crossed quickly to the windows, pulling back the *toile de Jouy* curtains, opening one tall window, and pushing back the shutters. She turned and surveyed the room, her heart beating uncomfortably fast, for she felt exactly like a thief breaking into a house.

Here, indeed, was all the hard evidence she sought, in order to condemn her father and his lover. Here were their clothes, hanging in the armoire, and visible through the half-open door. The beautiful big bed was made, but obviously being slept in, with a blue bathrobe draped casually over the foot. There were pots and bottles on the dressing-table, a pair of men's leather slippers on the floor beside the bed, and a pile of books on the night-table. The place felt lived-in, comfortable and full of love, exactly as Nina remembered it when her grandparents slept there. She felt angry, sad and curiously envious all at the same time. Quickly, she closed the shutters and windows, drew the curtains, and ran down the stairs and out of the house, locking the kitchen door and returning the key to its hiding-place.

Thoughtfully, she drove back to Paris, trying to make sense of her mixed emotions in the face of her father's treachery towards her mother, together with the rather moving evidence of his and Misha's clearly very serious attachment. It was as if they really were married, she said to herself.

* * *

In the end, common sense and loyalty to Blanche prevailed, and Nina came firmly down on the side of her mother. She waited until her parents had departed for Ménerbes, then chose the following Saturday to pay her visit to Misha, arriving in passage des Ebénistes at four o'clock in the afternoon. She rang the bell at number sixteen. There was no response, so she went round the corner into rue de la Roquette, and walked up and down for a while, looking into the windows of the local shops. After half an hour, she returned to passage des Ebénistes, telling herself that if the ben Bella woman was still not at home, she would not wait, but try again another day. Turning the corner, she saw Misha putting her key in the lock of her door, and hurried at once to her side. 'Dr ben Bella?' she asked, slightly breathlessly.

Misha turned. 'Yes?'

'My name is Mansart. Dr Nina Mansart.'

'Yes? How can I help you?'

'I think I should tell you that my father is Professor de Vilmorin.'

'Really?'

'Yes, really. May I come in? I think we need to talk, don't you?' Without replying, Misha opened her door, and Nina followed her into the lobby. Silently, they took the lift to the top floor, and Misha unlocked the door to her apartment. 'Please come in,' she said, politely.

Misha led the way through the salon to the kitchen, and after a startled glance at the Braques as she passed by, Nina followed her.

Misha put on the kettle. 'I am going to make a cup of tea,' she said quietly. 'Would you like some? Or perhaps you'd rather just say what you've come to say, and then leave?'

Rather taken aback, Nina blinked very rapidly at Misha, and said, 'Um, yes, I'd like some tea, Dr ben Bella, if it's not too much trouble?'

'Let's keep it informal, Nina. My name is Misha, as I'm sure you're quite aware?'

Nina swallowed nervously. 'Oh, right,' she said.

Misha made the tea, and carried the tray out to the garden. They sat down, and she handed a cup to Nina. 'OK,' she said. 'Fire away. Let's get it over with, shall we?'

'You know why I've come, don't you?'

'Yes, of course I do. Do you think I am a fool?'

'No, certainly not.' This was not at all the way Nina had planned the interview, and she felt herself to be very much on the back foot. She decided that the best method of defence had to be attack. She drew a deep breath. 'I've come here on behalf of my mother, Misha. She is completely devastated about the relationship between my father and yourself, and she has asked me to tell you that it has to stop, immediately.'

'Why should that be necessary, if she no longer loves him?'

'Why? Because of the scandal, that's why. Because it will destroy my father's reputation, and tear the de Vilmorin family apart, that's why. The medical establishment doesn't approve of sexual relationships between colleagues, one of whom is married and a grandfather, and the other a woman almost young enough to be his daughter. Put as crudely as that, it doesn't sound very attractive, does it?'

'That's not how it seems to me, or to Paul,' said Misha, but her voice shook, and Nina knew that the battle was over before it had properly begun. All she had to do was administer the fatal blow, and with a flash of inspiration she said, 'There is another reason why you must give up my father, Misha, and in many ways it's a much more compelling one. My mother has non-Hodgkin lymphoma; probably she has not much time left to her.'

'I'm extremely sorry to hear it.' Misha stared at Nina, horrified.

'And I am sorry to burden you with my family's

problems,' replied Nina smoothly. 'I felt sure you'd appreciate the situation, and do the right thing in order to relieve my mother's understandable anguish, and preserve my father's reputation.' She took from her leather satchel the photographs Blanche had given her, and silently put them on the table. 'I suppose it's only fair to let you have these,' she said coolly. 'We have another set.'

At the sight of the pictures of herself and Paul, tears filled Misha's eyes. 'You don't seem to understand, Nina. I love your father, and he loves me. Doesn't that count for anything?'

'No, it doesn't, from my mother's point of view, and I don't suppose it's strictly true, as far as my father is concerned, anyway. My parents have been married for more than thirty years, Misha, and your sordid little affair is exactly the sort of crisis that happens to many men of his age.' She rose to her feet, leaving the photos on the table. 'You have to understand that I mean you no harm, personally, but I'm sure you will soon begin to realize how much damage you are inflicting on my father's reputation, and my poor mother's peace of mind. Put yourself in her shoes, Misha. I'm sure you will decide to do the right thing.'

Misha did not go to bed at all that night. Instead, she sat in her garden, gazing at the photographs, knowing that her happiness with Paul was at an end, and that the only course of action left open to her was one of instant and civilized retreat. In the blackness of the night, she found it hard to understand why it was that disasters of this kind should be visited on her, and why it was that the man she had once loved, as well as the man she had come to love so dearly now, should be the sole property of other women. She did not weep, or scream or indulge in an hysterical reaction of any kind. She felt numb, and very cold, and had the strangest feeling that Paul had died, and that she had not yet been properly informed of the details of his death.

* * *

In the morning, she took a shower, dressed carefully in her most severe and professional-looking suit, and left early for the hospital. She went at once to the administration block, and asked to speak to the head of personnel.

Nicole Christophe was a charming, highly intelligent and very astute woman, and Misha found little difficulty in explaining the problem to her. She answered Mme Christophe's questions clearly and truthfully, and made no attempt to hide anything at all from her.

'So, Dr ben Bella, what do you think would be the best way of resolving this unfortunate situation? Are you telling me that you wish to resign?'

'No, I don't want to do that, unless the management think I should, and I would certainly hope to resume my surgical training, later on, when the timing is more appropriate.'

'Yes, I see. So, what do you have in mind?'

'I wondered whether it would be possible for me to take a sabbatical, for six months or even a year, and work overseas with a voluntary medical team of some kind?'

Nicole Christophe looked at Misha, and smiled. 'You've thought it all out, haven't you?'

'No, I haven't thought it all out, at all,' said Misha. 'At the moment, all I can think of is how to prevent myself damaging Professor de Vilmorin, any more than I already have, according to his wife and his daughter. Especially as it seems his wife is seriously ill.'

'And have you thought of discussing the matter with Professor de Vilmorin himself? Don't you think he has a right to an opinion, too?'

Misha hesitated, detecting the sympathetic note in the other woman's voice. 'The important thing,' she said, choosing not to answer the question, 'is surely one of damage limitation. If my involvement with Paul became common knowledge, it wouldn't be regarded in a particularly friendly light by the hospital, would it?'

'No, I don't suppose it would.'

'Well, then?'

'Very well, my dear. I think you are probably making the responsible decision, and a courageous one, if I may say so. As it happens, I know some of the people in Service Medical Outre-mer, and I'll find out whether they have a suitable placement for a doctor of your experience.' She stood up, and accompanied Misha to the door of her office. 'Goodbye,' she said, shaking hands. 'I'll be in touch, quite soon.'

And so it was that, at the beginning of August, Misha had an interview with SMO, and then learned that she had been appointed to a job, travelling first to Kenya, then on to Sudan. There, in the desert country of West Upper Nile, she was to supervise a feeding-station for refugees of the civil war, and do whatever she could to alleviate their suffering. Two days later, she boarded a plane that would take her to Nairobi.

The month of August passed very slowly in Ménerbes, and Blanche could hardly fail to notice how miserable Paul looked, and how extremely oddly he was behaving. He spent a good deal of his time swimming, or floating on his back, staring up into the olive tree that gave pleasant shade at one end of the pool. At other times, he lay on a sofa in the salon, reading. He seemed unwilling to talk to Olivier and Catherine, except at meals, and made no attempt to conceal the fact that he found them boring. Blanche found this behaviour embarrassing to herself and unkind to the St-Denis, as well as very uncharacteristic of Paul, for he had always managed to hide his lack of interest in her friends with normal good manners.

By the end of the first week, and in some desperation, she suggested that he drive over to Mas les Arnauds, to see Emma, who would very likely be at home, since she was now in the fifth month of her pregnancy. 'Stay the night, if you feel like it,' she said.

'The new people, the German couple from Bonnieux, are coming to dinner tonight. I don't imagine you particularly want to see them, do you?'

In view of the fact that it had never been Blanche's habit to consider his opinions in respect of the people they met socially, Paul was quite surprised to hear her say this. 'What makes you think that, my dear?' he asked, raising his eyebrows.

'Oh, no reason,' she said, and laughed nervously. 'I just thought you would enjoy a change of scene, that's all.'

'Very well, I'll go, if you want me to.'

'Stay if you want to, of course.'

'No, Blanche. I'll go, all right?'

He left immediately after lunch, with an overnight bag, and as soon as his car had disappeared down the drive, Blanche telephoned Nina, hoping for reassuring news. Nina was not in, but the au pair had been instructed to give Mme de Vilmorin a message, if she should happen to phone. 'Very well,' said Blanche. 'Tell me what it is, please.'

'Dr Mansart told me to tell you that everything is under control, and you have nothing to worry about.'

'Oh!' exclaimed Blanche. 'That's excellent news! Please thank my daughter, will you, and say I'm very grateful.'

At Mas les Arnauds, Paul found Emma alone in her kitchen, packing figs into jars, and filling them with *eau de vie*, adding a little sugar and a couple of cloves to each pot. She came straight towards him as soon as she saw him in the open doorway, and he embraced her rather carefully, for she already carried before her the evidence of her twin baby boys. 'Dearest Emma, how are you, darling?' he said.

She spread her hands over her stomach, and laughed. 'Apart from having a football team in here, that never sleeps, and getting heartburn every evening, I feel wonderful,' she said, and kissed him again. 'And you, Paul? How are you, darling?' She looked at him, and frowned. 'You look terrible; whatever is the matter? You've lost weight, too.'

'Overwork, and the heat, I expect.'

'Oh dear, poor you. I wish you'd learn to slow down a bit. You're quite a worry to me; and to Pascal, too, I might add.'

Paul laughed. 'Really? I don't believe you!'

'It's true. Sit down, let me give you some tea.'

'I'd rather have a drink, if that's OK with you, Emma.'

If Emma was surprised that Paul wanted a drink at three-thirty in the afternoon, she took care not to show it, and poured him a glass of wine. 'That OK?' she asked, sitting down, and continuing to pack her figs into their sterilized jars. After a few minutes she raised her beautiful grey eyes and looked at her father-in-law, noting his prominent cheekbones and sad dark eyes, with the blue smudges of insomnia beneath them. 'You look dreadfully unhappy, Paul,' she said. 'Is something the matter?'

Their eyes met for a long moment, and he smiled faintly. 'Yes, I am unhappy, Emma. I'm so desperately unhappy that I can't sleep at nights,' he said quietly. 'But it's only because something wonderful has happened to me recently, and I couldn't bring it with me to Ménerbes.'

'You're in love, aren't you?'

'Yes, I'm in love, and I never thought I could be so happy, or miss someone so cruelly, either.'

'And are you loved in return?'

'Yes, I am.'

'I'm so glad for you, darling.'

'Are you really, Emma? Don't you think it's completely inappropriate, at my age?'

'Of course not. Why should it be?'

'Two rather compelling reasons. One, I'm married, and two, Misha is thirty-seven, only three years older than Nina.'

'Are you having second thoughts already, Paul?'

He looked absolutely shattered. 'What a ghastly thing to say, Emma. No, of course I'm not having second thoughts. I love Misha, now and always, for ever, until I die. And I miss her dreadfully, every hour of the day and night; it's an actual physical pain in the gut.' He looked at Emma, and she saw that his eyes were bright and glistening. 'In Paris, it was wonderful, exciting and new,' he said slowly, and smiled. 'We were so happy, at work, in the evenings at her place, and sometimes we went to Froissy, too. I've rarely felt so alive, so confident that what I was doing was right for us, and I couldn't allow anything to get in the way of that.' He paused, and stared into his glass. 'The awful thing is that down here, alone with Blanche and her idiotic friends, and separated from Misha, I can't help seeing the downside of things, and worrying about the future.' He sighed. 'I don't have to tell you, I worry about the effect on Blanche, if she finds out about us. God only knows how she would take it.'

'She has no idea, then?'

'No, none at all.'

By the third week of August, Paul realized that he was in imminent danger of a serious breakdown, and decided that he must return to Paris without delay. He told Blanche that he had an urgent case to see to, and left her at Ménerbes, to finish her holiday with the St-Denis, and return with them, at her leisure.

He drove as fast as he dared up the *autoroute*, and arrived at passage des Ebénistes at five minutes past eight. Exhausted, but light-headed with relief and joy, he let himself into the building, went up in the lift and unlocked Misha's door.

'Misha?' he called. There was no reply. He went to the kitchen, and looked through the glass walls, in case she was in the garden, but it was deserted. He looked in the bedroom, which seemed bare and overly tidy, like a hotel room. He went back to the salon, and saw that there was a small black cassette-recorder on the glass table, with a white envelope beside it, marked 'Paul'. He ripped open the envelope, and took out a cassette. He put it into the machine, pressed the play button, and listened to the message.

'*I'm terribly sorry, Paul, but I had to go. I've gone to work with SMO for a while, six months probably, or maybe a year, which should give you time to sort things out with your family, and forget about me. I really didn't mean to use you in the way that I did. I do love you, darling, but if I stay it will just make things worse, won't it, and I can't bear the thought of being responsible for some kind of scandal, which would crucify you and humiliate your family and make you hate me in the end. Please use the apartment sometimes, if you need to be alone. Thank you for loving me when I needed it so badly. I will never forget your kindness.*'

The machine gave a click, and was silent. He rewound the tape, and listened to the message again. She spoke slowly, in a quiet, unemotional manner, and the sound of her hesitant, gentle voice filled him with despair. In the post-box, he found a pile of letters and cards, almost all of them from himself. With a shaking hand, he poured himself a whisky, and went out into the garden. He sat down and read his own letters and cards, one by one, until the writing became indistinct and blurred, and he could no longer read. He put his hand over his eyes, suddenly feeling extremely unwell. A terrible blackness filled his soul, and he knew that his heart was breaking.

Chapter Seven

For Giles Murray-Williams, too, the month of August passed with unbearable tedium. His convalescence had been prolonged and frustrating, and he was still heavily reliant on Juliet in the matter of his domestic comforts. He had returned to work at Cunningham's on a part-time-only basis, which was not at all what he would have chosen, had his health been up to speed.

Fearful of any possible threat to his future position in the firm's hierarchy, he had persuaded Juliet to let him use Alice's room as a study, an arrangement which made it necessary to move the little girl's bed into Dorothy's room. To make matters less tense for everyone during the school holidays, Juliet had rented a cottage on the Sussex coast for Dorothy and Alice, and there they had spent the whole of August.

Since Juliet was appearing in a play at the Edinburgh Festival, Giles had the flat to himself, and took the opportunity to have his new study redecorated, refurnished and equipped with every possible aid to his work, including the latest phone/fax/photocopying machine. He also bought a brand-new computer, and lost no time in getting himself on-line. Giles was delighted with this efficient arrangement, and kept in close touch with his colleagues at all times, in all parts of the world.

Secure in the knowledge that messages, e-mail and faxes would be delivered to St Peter's Square in his absence, Giles took a cab to Chelsea most evenings, sometimes picking up his quota of cocaine *en route*, as well as a Chinese take-away, and was thus able to enjoy a few hours of solitary self-indulgence in his private domain.

August came to an end, and Dorothy and Alice returned to St Peter's Square, in good time for the beginning of the school term. When Dorothy saw what Giles had done to Alice's room, she was beside herself with rage. She waited until Alice was asleep, then sought him out. She found him sitting at his computer, apparently surfing the net. Positioning herself firmly between Giles and the door, in case he might attempt a sharp exit, Dorothy wasted no time in telling him, in some detail, precisely what she thought of him. At the conclusion of this tirade, Giles, with an attempt at withering scorn, looked at her coldly. 'Have you quite finished?' he asked.

'No, I bloody haven't,' she replied, her black eyes blazing, her swarthy arms crossed belligerently. 'It's high time you stopped treating Juliet and Alice like second-class citizens,' she said. 'It's time they had a proper house to live in, not this rotten little chicken-coop. You must be loaded, you selfish bastard, so why don't you get off your butt and organize a proper way of life for your family?' She drew breath. 'Because that's what they are, young man, your *family*, whether you like it or not!'

'Thank you, Dorothy,' said Giles, trying to make it sound like a dismissal.

Dorothy gave a snort of derision, and left the room.

Fearful of unleashing yet another onslaught, Giles chose not to appear in the kitchen at suppertime, but slipped out of the flat, and took a cab to Chelsea, where he spent the night. After several hours of reflection, he decided that Dorothy might actually have a point, that a larger house might indeed be more convenient than the present arrangement. The question was, how to finance such an expensive change to his way of life?

He had received a curt note from Misha, some time ago, requesting him to remove his possessions from passage des Ebénistes, but, characteristically, had chosen to ignore her letter, and had torn it up angrily. Now, he realized that by complying with her wishes he could do himself a favour. He would go to Paris, see Misha, have his stuff removed from passage des Ebénistes, and arrange for most of it to be sold. Misha might even be persuaded to stump up for the fixtures and fittings that he couldn't take with him.

He picked up the phone, and dialled the Paris number. To his extreme annoyance and frustration, his call was answered by her message service. *Vous êtes en liaison avec un répondeur téléphonique*, an irritatingly precise French female voice informed him. *Laissez votre message après le bip*. If there was one thing about contemporary communications that really got up Giles's nose, it was the automatic message system. He waited an hour, then tried again, with the same result. He dialled the number, over and over again, obsessively, throughout the night.

He returned to St Peter's Square in the early morning, made himself a cup of tea, and wrote to Misha. At the end of a week, he had neither received an answer to his letter, nor got through to her on the phone. A cold anger had finally replaced frustration in Giles's mind, and he decided to go to Paris immediately. He had his set of keys, and could let himself into passage des Ebénistes whenever he wished. He could, in fact, arrange to hire a van, and get a couple of professional packers to crate up his precious belongings and remove them from the apartment, even if Misha was not there in person. Late that night, he telephoned Juliet at her lodging in Edinburgh, and told her that he was going to Paris for three days, on business, and would stay at the hotel Angleterre in rue Jacob.

Juliet was anxious. 'Are you really up to it, darling?'

'Yes, of course I am. Don't fuss. It's high time I got back to normal, anyway.'

'Well, OK. But look after yourself, won't you?'
'Don't worry; I will,' said Giles.
I bet you will, Juliet said to herself; that's what worries me.

In New York, Olivia was staying in Glen's Manhattan apartment, and spending her days in an air-conditioned warehouse, with her framer. Together, they were choosing the mounts and frames for the large collection of etchings she had brought to the States by air, ready for her autumn exhibition.

Normally, in September, she would have been in Souliac on holiday, and helping Giò prepare for the *vendange*, but she had chosen not to risk leaving the choice of mounts and frames to anyone other than herself, and had therefore reluctantly decided to give Souliac a miss this year. In any case, she loved New York, and always managed to enjoy herself there, especially in the stimulating company of Glen. Nevertheless, it *was* rather unfortunate that for once Basil was actually in France, having a few weeks' leave, and had been expecting her to go south with him, as usual. 'Come to New York with me, instead, darling,' she had said. 'It will be fun, you'll see.' Sulkily, he had refused, and had gone to Souliac alone, making no secret of his disappointment. Doesn't matter, said Olivia to herself; he'll be OK once he gets there. Giò will cheer him up. They'll have a great time together, I'm sure.

In West Upper Nile, at a feeding-station a hundred and fifty kilometres from the nearest settlement, a shanty-town called Talakal, Misha was busy from morning till night, weighing the horrifyingly malnourished babies and small children that arrived, glued to their mothers' empty breasts, in the endless queue of refugees that stretched into the dusty desert landscape as far as the eye could see. It was Misha's harrowing job to make the life or death decision concerning which children were sick enough to feed, and which were still well enough to be refused the nourishment their mothers so desperately sought for them.

Their lives torn apart by the civil war, effectively a question of the Muslim northern Sudanese against the predominantly Christian south, the perilous situation of the refugees was made even more fragile by the total failure of the rains, and the consequent loss of the crops that normally sustained entire villages. These pathetic women and children had frequently been robbed of their husbands, fathers and brothers, slaughtered by the marauding gangs of soldiers from the north. Their huts burned to the ground, their grain stores looted, and their goats slaughtered to feed the invaders, the terrified survivors had been forced to abandon their ruined villages and were now leading a nomadic existence, constantly on the move in search of water and food. Many small children were quite alone, evidently lost or orphaned, and frequently suffering from whooping cough or measles, as well as malnutrition.

To add to the general misery, the emergency food supplies dropped by the planes of the foreign aid agencies were often commandeered by gangs of soldiers, who seemed to have the gift of appearing out of nowhere whenever a plane appeared in the sky, ready to grab the rations to feed themselves. When she had time to think about it, which was seldom, Misha found the whole situation unbelievably horrible, not to say depressing. She found it impossible to understand why a once-prosperous and peaceful nation should find it necessary to tear itself apart in such a terrible and brutal manner.

For the past five weeks, she had lived with two other aid workers in a small hut, its walls simple screens of rush matting, with a corrugated-iron roof. Close to the hut, a similarly constructed and equally ramshackle building, with one wall open to the air, performed the function of surgery and field hospital. At a little distance, but still close enough to hear the wails of the sick children at night, was a long row of open sheds, roofed with corrugated-iron, which provided the only shelter for the refugees who arrived on a daily basis, many of them dying on their feet. Women, bone-thin, sat apathetically on the ground, nursing babies whose stomachs were grossly distended as a result of starvation, their limbs like sticks, their faces crawling with flies.

At night, Misha was guiltily conscious of the fact that she and her two colleagues were able to retire to the privacy of their hut and eat a proper meal. It was not a thing that she found easy to do, surrounded as they were by several thousand people desperate for food, or even a drink of water. As the weeks passed, however, she ceased to concern herself with the moral certitudes relating to her own right to eat, and by the end of each long, roasting day, she was so exhausted that she lay down on her camp bed after the meal was over, and fell into a deep, sweating sleep. Sometimes, towards the dawn, when the temperature dropped dramatically, Misha woke, and, staring through a gap in the plaited rushes at the brilliance of the starlit sky, she allowed herself to think about Paul. She visualized him going to look for her at passage des Ebénistes, imagined him playing back her tape, and knew that, listening to it, his heart would have broken.

Quite often, and equally painfully, Misha recalled her interview with Paul's daughter, rather admiring her for her courage in going to such drastic lengths to prevent the collapse of her parents' marriage. Extremely clearly, Misha called to mind every word Nina had said: 'They've been married for more than thirty years, Misha, and your sordid little affair is exactly the sort of crisis that happens to many men of his age. I'm sure you realize how much damage you're inflicting on my father's reputation, and my mother's peace of mind.'

She is quite right, Misha told herself as firmly as she could, and I'm sure I did the right thing by leaving without seeing him again. It was wrong of him not to tell me that Blanche has non-Hodgkin; I suppose he knew all the time that I wouldn't be able to ignore that, and just carry on as we were. Somewhere deep in her heart she asked herself coldly whether Paul had actually made any kind of effort to find out where she had gone. Surely, if he loved her as much as he had seemed to at Froissy, he would have moved heaven and earth to get in touch with her, or, at the very least, try to find a way of writing to her? After all, Charlotte was able to receive the occasional letter, with the airlifts of drugs and food, so there was no reason why she herself should not have mail, too. I suppose Paul decided that it was best that I'd left him, she told herself sadly. Maybe, in the end, he was quite relieved that I did. In the circumstances, Nina was probably right when she said it was just a predictable mid-life crisis, for him. Perhaps she decided to have a go at him, as well, after she'd got rid of me. I don't suppose she had much difficulty in persuading him that his love for me was just an old man's humiliating infatuation, and best forgotten by all concerned, for her mother's sake.

For one reason and another, mostly concerned with his job, Giles was unable to make the trip to Paris until mid-September. Juliet had returned from Edinburgh, and since she was at present unemployed was in a position to make life more bearable in St Peter's Square. When the time came for Giles's departure, she thought about offering to go with him, but decided against it. There's not an awful lot he can get up to in three days, she told herself philosophically. In any case, she was beginning to have the feeling that, on balance, she had invested far too much energy in sustaining Giles and his little ways, and that it was time she devoted much more to herself.

During the run of her play at Edinburgh, and somewhat to her surprise, Juliet had received a visit from an American movie mogul. He had taken her out to supper after the show, and offered her a supporting role in his next big production, which was currently in the development stage. Amazed and enchanted, she had responded eagerly, and had asked her new friend to contact her agent to discuss terms. At the back of her mind was the worrying thought that if a contract really were to materialize, it would mean moving to Los Angeles, and since she had no idea how Giles would react to the idea of her taking Alice with her to the States, she decided not to mention it to him unless, and until, there was a concrete reason to do so.

Now, looking round the dingy little flat in St Peter's Square, she could not help fantasizing about blue skies, even bluer swimming-pools, and spacious white houses in beautiful gardens. She also thought long and seriously about the financial independence such a contract would give her; the ability, in fact, to call the shots as far as her relationship with Giles was concerned. She did not realize it, but she was already falling out of love with him.

Giles took an evening plane to Paris, then decided to take a cab from the airport to the hotel Angleterre. Since he did not particularly want to barge into Misha's apartment in her absence, he thought it prudent to wait until she would have returned from the hospital before paying her a visit. He therefore had a leisurely bath, then dined in a nearby restaurant, before taking a taxi to passage des Ebénistes.

He let himself into the building, took the lift to the top floor, and unlocked the door of the apartment. Immediately, he saw that a lamp was lit, and that a strange, silver-haired man was lying on his, Giles's, beautiful black-leather sofa, with his feet on the cushions.

Paul, hearing the door open, sat up eagerly, his heart in his mouth, thinking that it must be Misha. Disappointed, he slumped back against the cushions, then, slowly taking in the red wavy hair and unusual ochre-coloured eyes of the intruder, correctly identified the man as Giles Murray-Williams. He got to his feet. 'Murray-Williams, isn't it? How do you do. My name is Paul de Vilmorin.'

'Oh, really? And what, may I ask, are you doing here?'

'Nothing. Waiting for Dr ben Bella.'

'Where the hell is she?' Giles's voice was unnecessarily loud, as well as aggressive. 'I've been trying to get in touch with her for weeks.'

'I believe she's in Africa.'

'*Africa?* What the hell's she doing there?'

'She's with SMO, so I've been told; in Sudan.'

On hearing this news, Giles, his blood pressure rising spectacularly, experienced a violent feeling of nervous agitation. His temples began to throb with pain, but, ignoring this warning, he glared at Paul in an accusing manner. 'If Misha is in Sudan, what's your excuse for being alone in her apartment?'

'No excuse. We are colleagues; close friends.'

'How close, may I ask?'

'You may ask, but I'm not going to respond to impertinent questions.' Paul looked coolly at Giles, staring him out. 'Suffice it to say that after your accident, and Misha's discovery that you already have a partner, as well as a child, in London, she badly needed a friend. She found one in me.'

'My private life is no concern of yours,' muttered Giles truculently.

'It most certainly is,' said Paul. 'As it happens, I love her.'

'Are you suggesting that I don't?'

'Of course you don't! It's obvious, isn't it? She was just a convenient sexual indulgence for you, wasn't she, you cruel bastard?'

'And you think that an old guy like you can give her what she wants, do you? Don't make me laugh, de Vilmorin. I'm surprised she let you into her bed at all. *If* she did. *Which* I doubt.'

Paul said nothing. He picked up the stack of letters and cards from the table, and put them carefully into his pocket. He stared at Giles for a long moment, then went over to the cassette-player, rewound the tape and pressed the play button. Misha's light, hesitant voice broke the silence.

'I'm terribly sorry, Paul, but I had to go. I've gone to work with SMO for a while, six months probably, or maybe a year, which should give you time to sort things out with your family, and forget about me. I really didn't mean to use you in the way that I did. I do love you, darling, but if I stay it will just make things worse, won't it, and I can't bear the thought of being responsible for some kind of scandal, which would crucify you and humiliate your family and make you hate me in the end. Please use the apartment sometimes, if you need to be alone. Thank you for loving me when I needed it so badly. I will never forget your kindness.'

There was a click, and the machine was silent.

'If you weren't at least twenty years older than me, I'd knock your fucking teeth in,' said Giles, his eyes blazing, his face red with fury.

'And if you hadn't sustained neurological damage comparatively recently, you conceited idiot,' replied Paul evenly, 'I'd do much the same to you.' Calmly, he removed the tape from the cassette-player, walked to the door, and let himself out.

Shaking, Giles went to the garden, and looked down into the alley. He saw Paul emerge from the door of the building, get into his beautiful car, and drive slowly away. Staring at the retreating rear lights of the car, far below, he suddenly felt his sense of balance dissolve. Trembling, he turned, blundered across the darkening garden, and made his erratic way back to the salon, knocking over one of his Giacometti sculptures as he did so. Quickly, he lay down on the sofa, feeling sick and frightened. He turned his head from side to side on the soft leather cushion, and became aware of Misha's scent, the smell of her hair. Anger, grief and jealousy filled his whole being, and he wept. Why isn't she here, the selfish cow? he asked himself. She's a doctor; she should be taking care of me.

In West Upper Nile, the black clouds that should have presaged the arrival of the rains had still not materialized. The sky remained a hard lavender-blue and the landscape for miles around was a tinder-box, the arid surface of the parched earth split into wide cracks by the drought, and every waterhole and stream long since bone-dry. The great yellow ball of the sun shone mercilessly down on the long queues of starving people, from seven o'clock in the morning until seven o'clock at night, when it set with surprising suddenness, after scarcely ten minutes of twilight.

From time to time, a plane appeared and made an emergency food drop, before continuing on its way to the next feeding-station. At such times, unless a gang of soldiers got there before them, the patient queue of slowly moving people was galvanized into a frantic determination to get at the rations, and they broke ranks, shambling across the cracked, stony ground towards the metal canisters that lay on the hard earth, waiting for collection. It was then the painful duty of Juma, the Kenyan orderly who was a vital authoritative figure in the SMO team, to produce his gun, and bring to an immediate end the unseemly scramble for nourishment that threatened to reduce the entire humanitarian operation to chaos.

Malaria and dysentery were now rife in the camp, and Misha's medical supplies, drugs and dressings were worryingly low, for they had not received a delivery for two weeks. The deaths of many of the smaller and weaker of the children were a daily occurrence, and Misha made the sad discovery that the Sudanese mother lives her whole life in the presence of death, even in normal times. She learned from Charlotte, her very experienced Belgian assistant, that the mortality rate for children under five years old was 40 per cent, and that it was the custom for the mother of the dead child to grieve for one day only. Charlotte appeared to feel that this put a less horrifying take on the death-rate in the camp, but Misha found herself unable to agree with her, though she did not say so. In all her years in medicine, the death of a child, of whatever race or creed, had always seemed to her to constitute an appalling waste, as well as a human tragedy. Sometimes such deaths could be blamed on lack of medical resources and skills; much less frequently, on simple ignorance on the part of the parents. Sorrowfully, Misha had to admit to herself that here, in this terrible place, no such judgements could possibly make any kind of sense.

As the days and weeks slowly passed, Misha became aware that she was losing her physical strength, so that even walking required a considerable effort. Working as she did out in the open, and beneath the ferocious sun all day, she was drenched in sweat for hours on end. She did not weigh herself, but reckoned that she was losing weight at the rate of two kilos a week. Her stomach had shrunk, she knew, for she never felt at all hungry, just incredibly thirsty all the time. Because water was at such a premium, she did not permit herself to drink more than her fair share of this precious element. Although the camp's water supply was warm as well as clouded and brackish, every small cupful that she did swallow seemed to her unbelievably delicious.

One morning, there was a commotion in the shelters, and Charlotte went to investigate. In five minutes she returned to the surgery, bringing with her a young woman of about sixteen years, wearing a filthy and evil-smelling black *basuti*, or sarong, with a flimsy piece of black cloth draped over her head. 'This is a very gross problem, doctor,' said Charlotte, standing as far from the young woman as she decently could. 'This girl has recently delivered a stillborn child, and has internal injuries as a result. Because of this, she is doubly incontinent, which is the reason for this terrible odour she is making.' Charlotte pursed her lips, and gave the girl a look of extreme distaste. 'The other women in the shelter won't let her stay there with them, which is not very surprising, I think.'

Horrified, Misha called Juma to come and interpret for her, which he did with commendable fortitude, in view of the revolting stench that emanated from the poor young woman. Quickly, she discovered that Ayuen's baby had been born, dead, two weeks ago, after three days of agonizing obstructed labour. Since then she had been losing a great deal of blood, as well as a constant and involuntary stream of urine and faeces. 'It's a classic case of vesico-vaginal fistula,' said Misha, and her heart sank. 'This is a condition which, untreated, leaves the patient permanently and doubly incontinent, as a result of the internal lacerations inflicted by the baby in its efforts to expel itself from the mother's body.' Misha smiled at Ayuen, and the young girl smiled back at her, her eyes full of trust and the expectation that help might be at hand for her. 'There are two things to be done,' Misha went on. 'First, we must build the girl up a little, and second, we must repair the wounds that are the cause of her problem.'

'How can we do that?' Charlotte demanded, still standing as far away as she could, close to the wall of the sleeping hut.

'It's a fairly simple procedure,' said Misha.

'You mean, an *operation*? Here?' Charlotte sounded horrified.

'Certainly, why not?'

'We're not equipped to do such things; we have nowhere sterile in any case, Dr ben Bella.'

'Well, we'll just have to do our best for her, won't we?' Misha turned to the orderly. 'We'll have to make a little shelter for her, Juma, otherwise we'll have problems with the other women. I'm sure you can make something suitable. We must give her powdered milk for two days, to build her up a bit, and then I'll operate.'

Juma, although deeply disapproving of the instruction to build a shelter, and even more disapproving of the intention to give the newcomer the precious milk intended for starving babies, carried out his orders to the letter, and by the evening Ayuen was installed in her little hut. Misha had removed her stinking rags, cleaned the poor girl up as best she could, and given her a clean sheet to wrap herself in, as well as a roll of lavatory paper. Last of all Misha brought her a pint of warm milk, and part of her own supper. Then she touched her hand, and wished her a good night's sleep. 'You will be better soon,' she said. 'I promise.'

In the hut that evening, the atmosphere was heavy with protest and resentment. 'I understand that you are in charge here, Dr ben Bella, but I really feel I have to register an objection in this affair.' Charlotte ladled rice and beans onto her plate, and glared at Misha, challenge palpable in every gesture of her body.

'Why is that?' asked Misha, mildly.

'Don't you feel it is not right to give special food and shelter to one woman, when many thousands are starving and dying out there, right beneath our eyes?'

'And if we don't treat her, what then?'

'What do you mean, what then?'

'She will continue to be shunned by her people; she will grow weaker and weaker, and then she will die. A simple operation will restore her to useful healthy life in a matter of days.'

Charlotte, her mouth full of rice and beans, looked deeply sceptical. 'I still don't see how you can allow so many of them to die, and make this one woman live,' she said obstinately. 'In any case, she will very probably develop septicaemia. We cannot be sterile here, can we?'

'This is all true, Charlotte,' said Misha quietly. 'But I still want to try, OK?'

* * *

Two days later, Juma and Charlotte, with ill-concealed displeasure, helped Misha prepare the operating theatre, which consisted of a scrubbed metal table, wiped over with disinfectant, under a tarpaulin shade. The procedure took a little over an hour, for the holes in Ayuen's bladder and bowel, once Misha had opened her abdomen, were seen to be pretty extensive, as well as putrid. Charlotte, overcoming her hostility and disgust, administered the primitive anaesthetic to the patient with admirable concentration, while Juma stood beside Misha, and held the enamel bowl for the used swabs, at the same time preventing the ubiquitous bluebottles from landing on either the surgeon or the patient, with the aid of a plastic fly-swatter.

Misha put the last stitch in Ayuen's abdomen, and covered the wound with antibiotic powder and a light dressing. 'With God's mercy, she should be OK,' she said. 'Thank you, both of you, you did a wonderful job.'

'No, doctor,' said Charlotte, stiffly. 'It is you who did the wonderful job, but I still think you were wrong to do it at all.'

'She is waking up now,' said Juma, his handsome black face breaking into a pleased smile. 'Maybe, in a while, she will like some milk?'

'Perhaps later on, Juma,' said Charlotte. 'Too soon you give it, and she will vomit.'

Giles, after an uncomfortable and sleepless night at passage des Ebénistes, returned to the hotel Angleterre, changed his clothes and went out for breakfast. As he sat in a café, reading *Le Monde* and drinking his coffee, he was humiliatingly aware of the sense of absolute mortification he had suffered throughout the long night, during which he had obsessively conjured up lurid images of Misha in bed with the elderly Paul de Vilmorin. Repeatedly, he told himself that Misha was just a woman like any other, and evidently a bit of a slag, too, if she could bed-hop quite as quickly as she appeared to have done. Unfortunately, the more furiously he silently abused her, the more he realized how incredibly jealous he felt about de Vilmorin's relationship with Misha, and how bitterly he now regretted dismissing her from his life.

Giles uttered a small groan, which he turned into a cough, then blew his nose, drank the remains of his coffee, folded his newspaper, and left the café in search of a taxi to take him to Cunningham's. There, he spent a busy morning renewing old acquaintances, and checking out the latest prices obtained at auction for art deco furniture and artworks. Filled with an aching self-pity, he also checked the current values of paintings by Braque, and sculptures by Giacometti, making a note of them in his organizer.

He lunched with a friend, went back to the office for a couple of hours, then returned to the hotel. There, he found a message from Juliet, asking him to ring her. He phoned her from his room, and she told him that she had received a terrific offer to play the second lead in a movie.

'Well, good, darling! That's *marvellous,*' he said. 'Congratulations.'

'The thing is, Giles,' said Juliet, 'it will mean my going to LA.'

'You must go, of course.'

'What about Alice?'

'Take her with you, darling, why not? Take Dorothy, too, to look after her.'

'You really wouldn't mind?'

'Of course not. It's a wonderful break for you, sweetheart. You deserve it.'

'Are you really sure, Giles? You won't be too lonely without us?'

'I expect I will, but that's not the point, is it?'

They talked for a little longer, Juliet barely able to conceal her excitement, then said goodbye and rang off.

Giles went to the window, and looked up at the sky,

and thought that maybe everything might work out rather well, if he played his cards carefully. There would now be no need to buy a bigger house for Juliet and Alice; everything could go on as before. He need not remove his treasures from passage des Ebénistes after all, or give up his place in Chelsea. Best of all, he felt entirely confident that he could patch things up with Misha, when she returned from this idiotic trip to Sudan. She adored me, he told himself, I know she did, and I bet that secretly she still does, silly girl. After all, we were together for seven years, weren't we? This has all been just a stupid blip.

He took himself out to an excellent dinner, all the while plotting in his mind the best method of removing the interloper de Vilmorin from the frame, once and for all. The last thing I need is for Misha to go back to him, before I have a chance to make it up with her. I'll sleep on it, he said to himself, as he returned to the hotel. I'm too bloody tired to think straight now, but in the morning something really clever will come to me, I feel sure.

In the morning, he made some enquiries, and had little difficulty in obtaining the address of the de Vilmorins, in the Marais. He sat down at the nice little antique *secrétaire* in his room, and wrote a letter to Blanche de Vilmorin, informing her that her husband had not only had sexual relations with his, Giles's, long-term partner, but was currently dossing down in her apartment in her absence abroad. He added that the property was full of his, Giles's, valuable art treasures, and went on to threaten that unless Paul ceased forthwith to break into the apartment, he, Giles, would not hesitate to inform the police of his activities. He gave his Chelsea address, in addition to 16, passage des Ebénistes, and signed himself very sincerely hers.

He posted the letter, and on the third day, as he had promised Juliet, he returned to London.

Chapter Eight

Ayuen's convalescence was remarkably swift, and her gratitude at being clean and odour-free again was as great as it was touching to Misha. After a few days, she was able to move around comparatively easily, and made it plain that she was anxious to help the team in any way she could. Quite soon, she had learned to detach the smallest and frailest of the babies from its mother's breast, slipping it skilfully into the sling suspended from the hook of the scales, so that Misha could measure and record its weight, and prescribe what medication, if any, the child should receive. Ayuen would then present the child, tiny bottom uppermost, to receive Charlotte's hypodermic syringe, if this was appropriate, afterwards returning it to the mother, with a docket stating how much daily rice the child should be given.

Quite often, the baby being examined was not ill enough or thin enough to warrant such a luxury, and Misha could tell that Ayuen found it very difficult to give the child back to its mother without a food docket. At such times, Ayuen would exchange a guilty glance with the woman she regarded as little short of a saint, and Misha would smile tiredly, and push the damp hair off her forehead, and wait silently for Ayuen to bring the next small candidate for survival.

Although Ayuen was clearly a great help in the daily work of the station, and Charlotte and Juma were very glad of the extra pair of willing hands, they had not forgiven Misha for her high-handed decision to carry out a procedure not in their remit, and it became increasingly obvious that they both thought her over-proud of her status, particularly in view of their far greater experience in the field, compared to hers. The weather got hotter and hotter, and tempers, already short, became explosive. The tense atmosphere in the cramped hut during the evening meal became progressively harder to tolerate, Charlotte in particular seizing every opportunity to make some sort of thinly veiled criticism, either of Juma, of Ayuen, or most frequently of Misha herself. 'I myself wouldn't have thought it advisable to give morphine to that old fellow with the broken hip,' she remarked to no-one in particular. 'Anyone could see he was dying, anyway.'

'Perhaps that was a good enough reason, Charlotte,' said Misha quietly, 'if it made his death a little easier.'

'And if the drugs run out, what then?' Charlotte looked at Misha's half-eaten supper, a greasy pile of rice and bits of bacon. 'You don't want any more of that, then?'

'No, I'm not hungry.'

'OK. I will have it, otherwise it is a waste.'

Misha, excusing herself, left the hut, and sat outside in the slightly cooler air, and drank her cup of tepid water. Idly, she watched the camp fires of the refugees, the small red pulses of flame illuminating the gaunt fatalistic faces of the families that sat round them, brewing tea to fill their empty stomachs, grateful for the water that made this possible. From time to time, a slender black silhouette would pass from one group to another, silently, a shadow in the greater darkness of the tropical night.

Gazing up into the sky, Misha studied the unfamiliar stars of equatorial Africa, and asked herself what she really thought she was doing here, and whether her presence had made the slightest difference to the fate of these tragic people, after six weeks of ceaseless toil on their behalf. I suppose I've made a difference to little Ayuen, she thought, with a wry smile, but what is one young girl among so many? Inside the hut, she could hear Charlotte's voice droning on, berating poor Juma for some imaginary sin, and wondered how much longer she could stick it out.

It's not the work that worries me, she thought, I can handle that. It's the heat, and Charlotte, and the awful feeling that I'm becoming brutalized myself by the whole thing. I didn't really care about that poor old man today; I only gave him the morphine as a reflex action. I probably killed him, if the truth were known. I'm sure Charlotte thinks I did, stupid woman.

I'd better get some sleep, she said to herself; it's pointless sitting out here, winding myself up. She tried to unfold her legs and stand up, but, to her consternation, her legs refused to obey her, and she remained where she was, sitting cross-legged upon the ground. Stay calm, Misha, she told herself. Firmly, she grasped first one leg, and then the other, straightening them out, then rolled carefully onto her knees, and very slowly, holding on to one of the poles of the hut, got to her feet. She stood for a while, clinging to the pole, waiting for the circulation in her legs to return to normal. She was not frightened, but realized that her loss of weight and wasted muscles were the reason for the weakness of her legs. I must be careful, she thought, and try to eat a bit more. I really can't afford to get sick out here, in this awful place.

In Souliac, the *vendange* was almost over, and Giò, with his village pickers and Basil to help him, was harvesting by hand that part of the vineyard dedicated to his superior vines, which produced the wine for his *appellation contrôlée*. The remaining crop, and by far the largest, had already been mechanically picked by the itinerant wine-maker, and the new wine was already in the fermenting vats. The weather was scorchingly hot, much hotter than it normally was in late September, and Basil, though quite used to the rigours of every kind of climate, was finding the going extremely tough.

In his current rather depressed mood, he could not bring himself to appreciate the beauty of the landscape, or to take much pleasure in the age-old activity in which he was engaged. He had received neither a letter nor a phone-call from Olivia, a circumstance that hurt his feelings more than he cared to admit, and although he longed to hear her voice, pride prevented him from trying to contact her by telephone.

Basil had not expected that his holiday with Giò and Domenica would be particularly stimulating, for excitement was never the point of a visit to the presbytery, but he had not anticipated that he would be really miserable, as well as bored out of his skull. At night, when he and Giò sat in the cool, peaceful courtyard after supper, he took care not to elaborate on the unsatisfactory state of his marriage, or to tell Giò how unhappy he felt, and how humiliating he had found Olivia's point-blank refusal to consider becoming the mother of his children. Giò, in his turn, although quite aware of Basil's wretchedness, thought it wiser not to encourage him to reveal things that he might later regret, and was careful to avoid the subject of Olivia.

One evening, as they sat together as usual, each of them smoking a cigar and drinking a cognac, Basil raised his sombre grey eyes to Giò's. 'I think I'll push off tomorrow, if you don't mind,' he said quietly. 'I've been a rotten guest here, Giò; a pain in the arse in fact. So I think I'll go to Paris for a couple of days; stay with the old girl, see a couple of exhibitions, if that's OK with you?'

'Whatever's best for you, my dear old thing.'

'The fact is, I desperately need to get back to work, Giò. Down here, in the peace and quiet, the days are so long, and there's so much time to think, that it's impossible not to let things get to you, if you know what I mean.'

'Yes, Baz,' said Giò, dryly, and emptied his glass. 'I do know what you mean. I've had a great deal of practice in that department, remember?'

On the last Sunday in September, Paul de Vilmorin drove down to Froissy, parked his car in the courtyard, and walked round the boundaries of his family's land. This was a task that he carried out twice each year, to satisfy himself that none of the estate fences needed repairing. It was the first time he had come to Froissy since Misha had vanished so suddenly and completely from his life, and he had anticipated that to go there without her would be painful, to say the least. In the event, he found being there curiously comforting, as if the ghosts of the battered old house touched him with sympathetic hands as he passed by.

After he had checked all the fencing, he walked up into the highest part of the woodland, and sat under a venerable walnut tree, leaning against its ridged grey trunk, and watching the first of the yellowing leaves detaching themselves and falling onto the mossy ground beneath its broad canopy.

Back at work at the hospital, and particularly in the theatre, Paul had found that he was able to function normally, as if nothing had happened, obliterating from his mind his agonizing grief and depression, as well as his constant anxiety concerning the state of mind and precise whereabouts of the woman he loved. During his off-duty hours, however, he found it quite impossible to control his thoughts and emotions so effectively, and spent most of his spare time lying miserably on the sofa in Misha's apartment, praying that a miracle would happen and she would call him from wherever she was. In the early hours of the morning he would leave the apartment, drive to rue de Thorigny, and let himself into the darkened house. There, he would take a shower, try to sleep for a few hours, and leave early for the hospital, before Blanche was up.

After his return from Ménerbes, and his first shattering visit to Misha's empty apartment, Paul had reasoned that the personnel department must have some idea of where she had gone, and after some hesitation had gone to see Nicole Christophe. From her manner, at the same time guarded and sympathetic, he guessed that she knew exactly what had happened between himself and Misha. 'Dr ben Bella is with SMO,' she had said, in reply to his enquiry. 'In Sudan, I understand.'

'I see.'

'I'm afraid that's all the information I have, professor,' Mme Christophe had said firmly, and smiled at him.

'That's OK. Thanks for your help, anyway.'

'Not at all. I'm sorry I can't be more specific.'

Now, sitting alone under the walnut tree at Froissy, in the fading blue light of a September afternoon, Paul asked himself whether it had been the formidable Nicole Christophe's decision that Misha should take leave of absence, in the interests of the hospital discipline, or whether the idea had come from Misha herself, in response to a threat of involvement in a damaging scandal, or pressure of some other, unknown kind. Either way, he had no way of knowing how best to resolve the situation, other than by backing off, and waiting for Misha herself to reveal her true feelings, in her own good time.

Under the trees, the air began to feel cooler, and he got to his feet, walked down through the darkening wood again, and crossed the pasture to the house. Quickly, he went through the rooms, to check that all was well, but could not bring himself to go into his parents' room, for fear that his memories of Misha would overwhelm him, and take from him the few remaining shreds of dignity and courage that he was still able to command. Instead, he went out to the walled garden. Most of the roses had faded, and in their place were brilliant red hips, like dabs of sealing-wax against the stone walls, but one tree still had a few perfectly formed, half-opened yellow buds with glossy dark-green leaves. Paul took out his pocket-knife and cut them from their branch, wrapping the stems in his handkerchief.

He drove slowly back to Paris, bought a sandwich in a café, and spent the entire night at passage des Ebénistes, alone in Misha's bed, with the yellow roses in a glass on the night-table.

Misha woke before dawn, chilled to the bone, her body wrapped in her cold, clammy sheet, which had been soaked by her own feverish sweating in the earlier part of the night. As silently as possible, she disentangled herself from her bedding, rubbed herself down with a coarse towel, then slipped into her khaki shorts, and a loose shirt. She went outside and saw Ayuen, enveloped in her sarong, lying close to the dispensary wall, fast asleep. The air was fresh and cool, and Misha took deep grateful breaths, doing her best to absorb as much oxygen as she could inhale, without hyperventilating.

In the shelter, the refugees slept beneath huddled heaps of brown rags, the only sound of life the occasional feeble cry of a baby. A faint pink light began to manifest itself on the distant eastern horizon; the stars grew dim, and went out, one by one. The red ball of the sun crept over the horizon and its shafts of light spilled over the arid plain, and ran towards the camp, like water running over a sandy beach at high tide. In ten minutes, the fiery ball had turned to a coppery gold, and was galloping up the sky. Misha could already feel its warmth on her skin, and sighed, thinking with longing of a nice, grey, rainy day in Paris. In the roof of the hut, the scorpions rustled and the cicadas began to sing, as if responding to an alarm call. Another day had begun.

Misha turned towards the surgery, and as she did so, she heard an unusual sound, which seemed to come from very far away. Gradually, the noise got closer and louder, then became a yellow speck in the distant sky. Misha's heart leapt as she realized that it was a light aircraft, and that it was heading in her direction. The little plane circled around over her head, then landed on the bumpy track that passed for the road to Talakal. It taxied to a halt close to the refugees' shelter, the engine cut out, and the pilot descended from the cockpit, followed by a tall, wild-looking, bearded man, carrying a large aluminium box. After him came two other men, carrying video cameras and canisters of recording equipment.

At the sight of four strong, fit men, Misha's spirits soared and she stumbled across the hot stony ground to greet them. She could hardly restrain herself from hugging them all, so relieved and delighted was she to see them. As it was, she shook their hands decorously, and asked them where they had come from.

'Nairobi to Talakal yesterday, then here,' said the tall, bearded man, laconically. He introduced the pilot, the camera crew, and himself. 'My name's Rodzianko, Dr ben Bella. We're here to make a film about the refugees, for TV. The people at Talakal asked me to bring you some stuff.'

'Really? What kind of stuff?'

'Drugs, I think. Your usual requirement, I believe.'

'Oh, thank you! What a relief! We're practically cleaned out here; I was beginning to despair of anyone turning up, ever again.'

Charlotte and Juma appeared from the hut, followed at a little distance by the shy Ayuen. Encouraged by the energetic Rodzianko, several other boxes were quickly unloaded from the plane and taken to the surgery.

'What about some breakfast?' suggested Misha, wondering what they could possibly offer the visitors.

'We've brought our own food, of course,' said Rodzianko. 'Coffee, even, if you'd like some?'

'I hope it is ground?' asked Charlotte. 'We do not

have facilities for the grinding, here, you know.'

'No,' he answered, seriously, 'I don't suppose you do.'

During breakfast, which they ate outside, since the hut was too small to accommodate seven people, Rodzianko explained that he and his camera team were to stay for two or three days, to record a piece about the plight of the refugees, and that the film would appear on TV in due course, in the hope of raising as much money as possible for the work of SMO in the region.

'Don't worry about us at all,' he said. 'We have our own tents, water, everything. We won't be a nuisance, I promise.'

Misha smiled. 'You won't be a nuisance,' she said quietly. 'It's wonderful that you're here.'

Blanche de Vilmorin, secure in the knowledge that Misha was no longer in Paris, had not been unduly worried by Paul's cutting short his holiday, and had little difficulty enjoying the rest of her own, in the company of Olivier and Catherine. It will give him plenty of time to make the necessary adjustment, before I get home, she told herself.

On her return to Paris she was therefore both perplexed and dismayed to find that Paul, far from coming swiftly to his senses, seemed to be even less prepared to communicate with her than he had been before his affair. When their paths did cross, which was seldom, he appeared cold and distant, and seemed anxious to avoid her. Occasionally, when she was able to study him covertly, she could not help noticing how old and depressed he looked, and, she had to admit, terribly unhappy.

After thirty-five years of a marriage, however unsatisfactory, only an insensitive and stupid woman could fail to understand these worrying symptoms, and Blanche was not stupid. She realized that her stratagem had failed, and began to feel that it might have been wiser to allow things to drift along, and let the affair take its course. After all, many men have younger mistresses, Blanche told herself, and the whole thing fizzles out when the girl moves on to pastures new, doesn't it? Perhaps I may have been a little inept over this.

She decided to try a different tactic. She cut down on her social life, told Olivier to stop coming to visit her for the time being, and got rid of Ben. She spent quite a few evenings at home, casually dressed, curled up on one of the sofas in the salon, with the logs burning in the fireplace in a homely fashion. She instructed Marie-Claire to prepare delicious food in covered dishes, and leave them in her study, kept warm in her hostess trolley, so that she and Paul could eat together, informally, when he got home from the hospital.

Unfortunately for Blanche, Paul appeared not to notice the changes that were taking place in rue de Thorigny. On the one evening that he actually did come home at a normal sort of hour, he refused her offer of dinner, saying that he had already eaten. They sat together in the salon, in an uneasy silence, Blanche finding herself unaccountably nervous, and Paul staring morosely into the fire, thinking his own thoughts. At half past ten, he rose to his feet and, saying that he felt very tired, went to bed.

Then Blanche received Giles Murray-Williams's letter, and all her good intentions in respect of the rehabilitation of her marriage flew out of the window. Immediately, she cancelled her appointments for the day, then telephoned Nina, but she had already left for her morning surgery, so Blanche left a message asking her to ring back. All day long, she wandered about the house, extremely agitated by the stranger's threat of involving Paul in a confrontation with the police. The man certainly sounded both malevolent and eager for retribution; she felt very sure that his ultimatum was not to be taken lightly. At four-thirty, Nina telephoned, and Blanche told her what had happened.

'Oh, God,' said Nina, a note of exasperation in her

voice, 'what a bloody nuisance, Mother. This ghastly little creep could easily wreck everything, by the sound of things.'

'That's exactly what I think, darling, but what on earth can I do, to stop him?'

'Well, for one thing, I'm afraid you're going to have to talk to *Papa*, aren't you? Otherwise, he'll just walk into the trap, and then we'll all have egg on our faces. You'll just have to tell him that he must never go to that woman's apartment again.'

'Oh, dear. I had hoped to avoid open warfare, Nina. It seemed so much more civilized just to pretend nothing had ever happened, and wait till everything returned to normal.'

'Sorry, Mother, but it seems we've got more than just Misha ben Bella and *Papa* to deal with here. This Murray-Whatsisname could really set the cat among the pigeons, you must see that?'

'Yes, darling. I suppose you're right.' Blanche sighed. 'I'll have to show him the letter, when he comes in. If he comes in.'

'It's like that, is it?'

'Yes,' said Blanche bitterly; 'it bloody is.'

'Well,' said Nina gently. 'Poor you.'

Blanche waited, sitting on her sofa in the salon, a glass of whisky in her hand, watching the television, normally concealed behind the doors of a walnut cabinet. The fire had burned low, but she could not be bothered to get up and put on more logs.

At a little after three o'clock in the morning, Paul came home. He looked surprised to see his wife still up at that hour. 'Hello,' he said. 'Is anything the matter, Blanche?'

She did not reply, but silently held out the offending letter, and he took it from her. He read it carefully, then tore it up and put it on the fire.

Blanche studied him coldly, her eyes hard. 'It's all true, then, Paul, isn't it?' He sat down at the other end of the sofa, and looked at her with a faint smile, his black eyebrows raised in the way she found so provoking. He did not look at all dismayed, or even disturbed by the letter. 'This man could ruin us all, Paul!' she reminded him angrily, her voice growing shrill. 'Why are you smiling? You must take it more seriously! You must promise me you'll never go to that woman's place again; you must stay away from there, like the man said.'

'I'm sorry, Blanche, but I can't do that.'

'Why not, for Christ's sake? Are you out of your mind?'

'No, I don't think I am. As a matter of fact, I feel more in my right mind than I have for years, and if Giles Murray-Williams were to cause this kind of trouble for me, it would be a relief, in many ways.'

'What the hell do you mean by that?'

'I mean that I could resign from the hospital without feeling guilty about it, and retire to Froissy.'

'With this bloody woman ben Bella, I suppose.' Blanche's confident, aggressive tone had subsided, and she sounded tired, defeated.

'Yes, with Misha, if she'd have me.' Paul looked at Blanche, feeling a momentary stab of pity at the sight of her hunched, skinny figure, and her pinched, bitter little face. 'I'm sorry, Blanche, but you don't seem to understand that something rather miraculous has happened to me, after all these years. For the first time in my life, I'm in love, and will be, until the day I die.'

'Really, Paul, you sound exactly like something out of a sentimental novel! In love for the first time in your life, indeed! What kind of a bloody silly cliché is that, coming from a man of your age? It's pathetic.'

'None the less, it's true. Expressions of real love always do sound like clichés, but I don't suppose you have very much personal experience of that.'

Blanche chose to ignore this insulting remark, and adopted an appeasing tone. 'It's just a question of mid-life crisis, Paul. You'll get over it, I'm sure.'

'No, I won't, Blanche. It's not an infectious disease, and in my case, it's terminal.'

'But she's left you, my dear, hasn't she?' she asked maliciously. Paul looked at her coldly, but did not answer her question. 'She's dumped you; the thing's over, finished. I can see it's making you unhappy at the moment, but that'll pass, you'll see.'

'I may feel unhappy, but at least I no longer feel dead.'

'What do you mean by that?'

'Work it out, Blanche. You're not without intelligence.' Paul stood up, went to the drinks tray, and poured himself a whisky. He picked up his briefcase and went to the door of his study. 'There's little point in discussing this,' he said. 'It's time we were both asleep, anyway. Good night, my dear.'

'Paul?' said Blanche suddenly, and he waited, his hand on the doorknob. 'Why was it that Misha left you? Did she say why?'

'Because, apparently, some poisonous bastard got at her, threatened her, warned her that she was damaging my bloody reputation and my marriage.' Paul looked at his wife, and his eyes were bitter. 'As if I give a toss about either of those things.'

'But I *do* care about those things, Paul! They mean everything to me, and it's because I care so much that I'm doing my best to preserve them, as a loyal wife should.'

Paul stared at Blanche, his dark eyes suddenly alight with comprehension, followed by disbelief. 'It was you, wasn't it, Blanche?'

'Yes, it was, indirectly,' said Blanche, defiantly. 'But it was Nina who went to see her, after you and I had gone to Ménerbes. She agreed with me that it was the only thing to do, Paul. Something had to be done, to end the affair, you must see that. Warning her off seemed an appropriate way to do it.' Blanche opened her bag, which lay on the floor beside the sofa, and took out a large brown envelope. From it, she took the sheaf of incriminating photographs, and threw them across the room in Paul's direction. They arranged themselves neatly at his feet, spread out like a hand of cards. He stared down at them for a moment, then went down on one knee and gathered them carefully together. Without another glance in Blanche's direction, he left the room, taking the photographs with him, and closing the door silently behind him.

Although Misha's spirits were lifted by the advent of Basil Rodzianko and his crew, it did not take him very long to realize how great a strain she was under, both mentally and physically. All day long, in the searing heat, he followed her as she carried out her work with the malnourished, the sick and the dying. With Juma acting as interpreter, he spoke sympathetically to the exhausted and emaciated mothers as they waited in line, drawing from them a few reluctant words. From time to time, holding in his arms a starving child with grossly inflated belly and stick-like limbs, he did a piece to camera, describing the appalling atrocities previously inflicted on these people, and their consequent desperate search for water, food and shelter.

He interviewed Misha and Charlotte as they worked, without disturbing their routine, and they described to him the difficulties of bringing help to the refugees with so little finance available for the drugs and food so badly needed by so many thousands of people. As the day progressed Basil observed with growing admiration the quiet sensitivity with which Misha coped with the moving tide of humanity that stood in line, desperate to receive her help. Calm and competent, making the life or death decisions required of her on a minute-by-minute basis, she seemed to him like a small beacon of humanity among the victims of a cruel situation. Charlotte, too, played her own important part in the collective effort to alleviate the general horror, but to Basil she seemed almost indifferent to the plight of the refugees. She's a true professional, carrying out her job, but she's not fully engaged, he decided. And yet, he said to himself, that's probably how it should be. She is able to stay detached, sensible woman, but the little doctor can't do that; she cares like hell. If one were brutal about it, she shouldn't really be doing this work at all; she's far too involved.

In the cool of the evening, the crew insisted on sharing their food with the SMO team, and while the supper was being prepared, Basil produced a bottle of whisky, and offered Misha a drink. 'You look as if you need one,' he said.

'What makes you say that?' she asked, slightly offended.

'You look knackered, that's why.'

'Oh.' She frowned, then smiled reluctantly. 'Well, you may have a point, Mr Rodzianko. I am knackered, as a matter of fact, but I wasn't aware that it was so obvious.'

Basil said nothing, and led the way to the far side of the surgery building, where they sat on the ground in the meagre shade of a scrubby little thorn tree. He poured two drinks, handing one to Misha. He raised his glass to hers. 'Let's dispense with the formality, shall we, since this place is hardly civilized enough to warrant it, don't you feel? *On se tutoie, n'est-ce pas?*'

Misha laughed. 'OK. My name's Misha. What's yours?'

'Basil, or more usually, Baz.'

'Right, Baz it is.'

Basil took from his pocket a half-consumed packet of cheese biscuits, and offered it to Misha. 'Here, take a few of these,' he said. 'You're so skinny that I don't want you passing out on me, as a result of one small whisky.'

Misha stared at him, then hung her head, her cheeks flaming, and did not take the biscuits.

'Shit!' exclaimed Basil. 'What the hell have I said? Did I say something, Misha? Tell me, please.' She looked up, shook her head and tried to laugh, but he saw that her eyes were bright with unshed tears. 'Please tell me what I said to upset you, Misha.'

'It's nothing, really. It's just that someone else said the very same thing to me, a while ago.' She brushed her fingers quickly across her eyes, took a couple of biscuits and ate them, then took a swallow of her drink. 'Not having whisky here is a serious mistake,' she informed him, quite cheerfully. 'I'm sure I'd feel a lot less knackered, as you put it, Baz, if I'd brought a few bottles with me.'

'Plenty more where this comes from,' said Basil, greatly relieved that his unintentional blunder was not, after all, so very serious. 'I never go anywhere without it, personally.'

'Very intelligent of you, if your assignments are usually as punishing as this one.'

There was a short silence, during which Basil studied Misha, taking note of her extreme slenderness, the filthy state of her short black hair, and the infected mosquito bites that disfigured her neck and her legs. 'How long have you been here, Misha?' he asked quietly.

She raised her eyes to his, and frowned impatiently, as if she thought the question rather stupid. 'A month? six weeks? two months? I don't remember,' she said. 'Does it matter?'

'I would have thought it mattered very much.' Basil hesitated, asking himself whether it would be cruel and unnecessary to tell her that he could see only too clearly how severely stressed she was, how ill she looked, and that he thought it would be extremely unwise for her to remain out in the field any longer if she were to avoid a total breakdown. Deciding that, on balance, any such interference would undoubtedly result in Misha's giving him a flea in his ear, he got to his feet, and held out his hand. 'Come on, I guess the nosh is ready. Let's go and eat, shall we?'

* * *

The next day passed uneventfully, assuming that one counted hunger and disease as non-events, and the little group of foreign aid workers and film people sat round the fire in the evening, saying little, listening to the strange echoes and distant ululations of the great African night, and marvelling at the size and brilliance of the stars.

On the following morning, when it was almost time for the noon break, an anxious mother forced her way to the head of the queue and thrust a grey-faced and gasping infant onto Misha's lap. Immediately, Charlotte snatched the baby away, and tried to return it to its mother, but Misha stopped her. 'The poor little thing is terribly dehydrated, Charlotte,' she said quietly. 'We must put in a line, and put the baby on a drip.'

'The child is dying,' said Charlotte severely. 'We should not waste the water. It is pointless, doctor.'

Misha sighed. 'We will put in a line, nevertheless,' she said. 'I'll do it, while you set up a drip, please, Charlotte.'

Basil and his cameraman moved quietly into position, and the camera whirred softly, to record the procedure, as Misha repeatedly stuck her needle into the back of the baby's hand, trying to locate a vein in which to insert a line. After the seventh or eighth attempt, her training and experience told her that she was extremely unlikely to succeed, but she kept on trying, becoming increasingly nervous and upset, until the baby gave a little gasp and a deep shudder and died. The mother snatched the baby from the table on which it lay and shook it as hard as she could, but the baby, as floppy as a rag-doll, could not be brought back to life. The mother broke into a loud, high-pitched wailing which quickly turned to hysterics. Juma stepped forward, gave the woman a hard slap across the face, and led her away, still clutching her dead child. Misha, completely shattered, burst into tears.

'Cut the camera,' said Basil, and, kneeling beside

Misha, held her in his arms until her sobs grew less violent. 'Don't cry,' he said. 'It's not your fault. You did your best.' He turned to Charlotte, who stood beside them, looking concerned, but unsurprised at Misha's behaviour. 'Charlotte,' he said. 'You carry on here. Dr ben Bella is ill; any fool can see that she needs a break.'

'Certainly,' said Charlotte. 'Juma and I can manage perfectly well, I'm sure.'

'I've no doubt that you can,' said Basil. He put his arm round Misha's shoulders and led her, still weeping, towards the hut, where he gave her a drink of water.

Misha drank the water, and gradually her tears subsided. She looked at Basil, red-eyed and apologetic. 'I'm sorry,' she said. 'I shouldn't have broken down like that, it was unforgivable. It's a cardinal rule, never to let a situation get to you, and certainly not in front of the patient, or the family. I feel so ashamed, Baz. I don't know how I could have been so utterly useless.'

'My dear girl,' said Basil, 'you're only human. Don't be so bloody hard on yourself. You're exhausted and ill, as well as half starved, it seems to me. Very soon, you really will be useless, as far as these poor devils are concerned.'

Misha turned her face to his, forlornly, and did not deny the truth of what he had said. 'I think you're right, Baz. I probably am pretty close to crack-up. But what the hell's the good of admitting that? I can't leave, can I?'

'Are you asking my opinion, Misha?'

'I suppose I am, yes.'

'I think you're very sick, close to collapse. You won't be much use to these poor sods, if you're lying in that tent, unconscious, will you?'

'I suppose not.'

'Would you object if I telephoned HQ, and asked whether they could send a replacement for you, Misha?'

Dumbly, Misha shook her head.

* * *

Basil went to the plane, and called HQ on the radio telephone. He explained the position, and told them he thought it desirable to pull out Dr ben Bella; would it be possible to send a replacement? To his considerable relief, they agreed, and that afternoon, the little plane took off for Nairobi, with Misha on board. As the pilot banked, and dipped his wings as they circled the camp, before heading south, she looked down at the endless black line of abused humanity, crawling like ants over the bleached yellow earth, and wept, cruelly aware of her failure to be of any real help to them. She did not see the tiny solitary figure of Ayuen, standing at a little distance from the huts, waving.

Chapter Nine

Olivia flew back from New York, and spent a couple of days with her mother-in-law in Paris, before returning to the Sologne. Always delighted to see her, and immensely proud of her achievements, Hester wanted to hear every detail of the trip to the States, and listened with close attention to Olivia's account of the opening of her show, her visits to museums and theatres, and the parties given for her by the great and the good of the New York art world.

They had supper in the kitchen, a wild-mushroom soufflé, a green salad and a *tarte aux poires*, bought at the local pastry-cook's. Olivia swallowed the last mouthful of the delicious tart, put down her fork, and took a sip of her wine. 'That was an absolutely perfect meal, darling Hester,' she said, 'thank you so much.'

'Have another slice, Olly.'

'I couldn't. I'm absolutely stuffed.' She smiled at Hester, her face rosy with good food and wine. 'What a tremendous treat real food is, when one gets home. I really ought to make myself cook more often. I only ever really do it when Baz is on leave. It's stupid of me – it's one of life's greatest pleasures, isn't it?'

'I've always found it so, even though I mostly cook just for myself, these days.' Hester drank some wine, and looked at Olivia. 'Baz came here for a couple of days, after he came back from Souliac. Then he left quite suddenly, and I haven't heard a word from him, not even a card.'

'Really? Did he say where he was going?'

'Rwanda? The Congo? Africa somewhere; I can't remember, Olly.'

'Poor old Baz,' said Olivia; 'how sad and ghastly for him.'

'It's what he does, dear.'

'Yes.'

Hester got up from the table to make the coffee. 'It's a great pity you're so often separated,' she said. 'Don't you mind, darling? Don't you get lonely?'

'Not really.' Olivia lifted her arms and pushed her long fair hair away from her face, then rested her chin in her hands, looking thoughtful. 'It's quite strange. I worry about his safety, all the time; whenever I turn on the telly to watch the news, I expect to see him being shot or taken prisoner or something equally horrible, but I don't really miss him. Too busy, I suppose.'

It was raining when the train arrived at Orléans, and dark by the time the taxi reached the barn. Olivia got quickly out of the cab, and feeling slightly vulnerable, alone with the driver in the rain-lashed darkness, handed over the fare, thanked the man curtly, and dragged her suitcase towards the kitchen door. She searched in her bag for the keys, and, reassuringly, the taxi-driver did a U-turn, then drove across the yard and out of the gate.

'Idiot,' said Olivia to herself, shoving the key roughly into the lock, and opening the door, 'I'm sure he's perfectly all right, really.' She switched on the lights, brought in her luggage, and locked the door, nevertheless.

The house felt cold and rather damp, after the few short weeks of her absence, and had the air of being abandoned, and unloved. There were no flowers to be seen, anywhere, and a thin film of dust veiled the surface of the long pear-wood table. On it was a large packet of hand-made paper, still in its brown-paper wrapping, with a delivery note on the top, initialled, Olivia noticed at once, by Baz. Just beside the package was a dark-green plate, one of a set they had bought in the market at St Tropez, some years ago. On the plate was a knife, and some crumbs. He must have made himself something to eat, she said to herself, and looked around for further evidence of his visit, but saw nothing.

She turned on the heating, looked in the freezer to see whether there was anything for her supper, then took out a frozen quiche and put it in the microwave to defrost. She took off her jacket, and carried her case upstairs to the bedroom. The room looked bare, and boringly tidy. There was no sign of anyone having slept there, least of all Baz. Throughout their married life, he had continued to leave a trail of wet towels and dirty socks behind him, and books and magazines on the bathroom floor, ignoring her angry complaints about his inconsiderate behaviour. At that precise moment, Olivia would have been quite glad to see such reassuring signs of his presence.

She went downstairs again, checked the messages, but there were none from Baz. She took the mail from the metal box behind the door, and found nothing from him among the bills and junk mail, not even a card. Pig, she thought, what's eating him? Is he still pissed off with me, or what? I suppose I didn't call him from Glen's place, she reminded herself. Oh shit, I suppose he's sulking, daft thing.

She reprogrammed the microwave, and in five minutes the quiche was ready to eat. Feeling uncharacteristically low, in fact bloody depressed, Olivia slid her not-very-interesting looking meal onto a cold plate, then opened a bottle of white Bordeaux and poured herself a glass. She found a fork in the basket on the tiled counter, and took her plate and glass and sat down on the sofa next to the fireplace. The fire was, of course, unlit, and a strong smell of wet soot emanated from the chimney. Bloody hell, she said to herself, hacking into the food, I wish he hadn't gone away like that, in a huff, without saying goodbye, and to her great surprise, tears filled her eyes and splashed onto the soggy quiche.

Olivia slept badly, and woke early in the morning, still feeling lonely and depressed. The rain continued to fall steadily, making a disturbing impact with the stone tiles of the roof immediately above her head. She could hear the rushing and gurgling of the rainwater as it forced its way along the gutters and into the downpipes. She sighed, and turned over with a groan of dismay, since a really heavy downpour usually meant a flood in the yard. If, as was more than probable, the soakaways were blocked, she would have to find a pickaxe and a mattock and unblock them herself, or face days of trailing liquid mud into the barn.

She turned onto her back and stared at the complicated pattern of the beams and rafters above her head. Normally she found the colour, texture and sculptural forms of these limbs of ancient trees both soothing and enriching to the spirit, but today she found no comfort in their strength and nobility. She stretched out her arm into Baz's half of the bed, trying to reconstruct in her mind the physical presence of the man she loved and knew she would always love, no matter what, but could not find him there. The bed felt empty, and cold. She lay for a long time, staring at Baz's pillow, remembering with regret their recent times together, and her harsh words on the subject of babies. I suppose it wouldn't really be so bad to have one, she thought. I don't suppose being pregnant would stop me working, and we could always have a nanny, couldn't we, right from the start? God knows, we earn enough between us; it shouldn't be that much of a problem.

She got out of bed, and pulled on her old jeans, and one of Baz's sweaters. She stared at herself in the mirror, trying to imagine herself fat, bloated, ungainly, and found it a totally alien image. It's weird, she thought; but I don't really feel old enough to be a mum. I still feel like a bit of a child myself. But I suppose if it'll make Baz happy, and make him spend more time at home, it might be worth a try.

She went downstairs and opened the yard door, and a stream of brown water flowed over the flagstones of the kitchen floor. 'Oh, shit!' she exclaimed, hopping from one bare foot to the other, trying to avoid the flood. She found her gumboots, and waded through the torrent to the shed to look for the pickaxe and mattock.

Locked into their shed on the previous evening by her helpful neighbour, her geese were furiously demanding to be released from their prison. 'Get lost, you boring old sods,' she muttered crossly, jamming the mattock into the largest of the blocked soakaways; 'you'll just have to stay there until I've got this sorted.'

After three days in hospital, during which she spent a great many hours asleep, only waking to eat several light meals each day, Misha felt considerably better, though still very weak. On the fourth day, she received a visit from the local SMO doctor, who told her that she could now return to the hotel, if she wished, but that she must take things very steadily. 'You are badly underweight, and suffering from nervous exhaustion,' he explained. Then, seeing her downcast expression, he smiled sympathetically. 'Don't take it to heart, Misha,' he said. 'It can happen to anyone; in fact, it happened to me. Not all of us have the ox-like constitution necessary for long spells of field duty in the tropics. I'm one of them, and so are you, it seems.'

'Trouble is,' said Misha, 'I don't suppose SMO needs another doctor working in Nairobi, with you already here?'

'Yes, I expect that's true. There are, of course, other appointments, but not suitable for someone with your skills.' He looked at her, his eyes full of admiration.

'We heard about you repairing the fistula. Very impressive, in the circumstances, I thought.'

Misha laughed. 'Not everyone would agree with you, I'm afraid. I got badly slagged off for doing it, by the rest of the team.'

'Really? Why?'

'Unfair distribution of available drugs, food and resources, in addition to rank-pulling on the part of the surgeon, something like that.'

The young doctor laughed. 'Forget it. You run up against that kind of prejudice all through your career, don't you? The also-rans don't care for breaking the rules, hadn't you noticed?'

Misha smiled. 'It's true. I shouldn't have let them get to me.'

'You didn't really, I'm sure. It's not the mind that lets us down, Misha, it's the frailty of the human body, I guess. In a place like Sudan, out in the bush, a week of dysentery will undermine the strongest constitution, as I know to my cost.'

He patted her hand, and got up to leave. 'You've done a great job, my dear, but in my opinion your contribution has been more than enough. Working out here can be an important experience in one's career, but it's certainly not a holiday. I shall advise the medical section that you should return to Paris, and that your next assignment, always assuming that you wish to continue with SMO, should not be in the tropics.'

Once back in her hotel room, Misha took a leisurely bath, washed her hair, and put on the cotton frock that the kindly chambermaid had ironed for her, then hung in the wardrobe. Feeling surprisingly exhausted by the small effort required to have a bath and change her clothes, Misha went out onto the narrow balcony of her room, sat down in a plastic chair to rest, and watched the traffic crawling by in the street, far below. In the distance, she noticed some vultures circling in the sky, presumably over a rubbish-dump, or an abattoir, she guessed. There's a lot about Africa that's cruel and unattractive, she thought, in spite of its Garden of Eden image.

The prospect of returning to Paris, after only two months, filled her with foreboding. With an intense uneasiness, and confused feelings of shame, she rehearsed the circumstances of her precipitate flight from the man she loved, and could not persuade herself that it was at all likely that Paul would wish to re-establish their close liaison, after what had happened. With as much strength of will as she could muster, Misha tried to convince herself that everything Nina had accused her of was true; that she *had* been very near to wrecking both Paul's marriage and his professional reputation. Fiercely, she told herself that she had done the right thing by withdrawing from a hopeless situation, and that in future she must take extremely good care not to embarrass Paul, or herself, in any way.

So, what will happen when I go back to work at the hospital? she asked herself. Nicole Christophe is a very sympathetic woman; perhaps she could organize a place for me in another *équipe*? That would be quite a neat way of avoiding any embarrassment, wouldn't it? Paul and I wouldn't be likely to run into each other, then. Misha stared at the lazily circling vultures, without seeing them. Or am I really just secretly praying that I *will* bump into him again, she asked herself sadly, and go with him to Froissy?

At six o'clock, feeling a bit less tired, she decided to go down to the bar, and see whether Basil Rodzianko was there. She found him, sitting at a table with one of the cameramen, drinking beer.

'Misha! You're out of hospital, that's terrific.' Basil got to his feet, and pulled out a spare chair for her. 'Sorry we didn't come to see you, but we did a quick trip to Rwanda. We've only just got back, this afternoon.'

Misha said hello to Thierry, the cameraman, and sat

down. 'A drink?' offered Basil. 'What would you like?'

'I'm a bit full of sleepers, so I'd better have orange juice, I think.'

Basil ordered her drink, and sat down again. 'It's great to see you,' he said. 'I thought you'd take much longer than this to get on your feet again.'

'It's surprising what sleep and food can achieve, with a few antibiotics to get rid of the bugs,' she replied. 'It's only a partial victory, though, Baz. I'm afraid they're going to send me home. The doctor seems to think I'm too much of a liability for the kind of work they have to do here.'

'Well, thank God someone's got a bit of sense. The chap's quite right. You've done a first-class job, but enough's enough, isn't it?'

'That's what they keep saying,' said Misha, taking a sip of her orange juice. 'But it doesn't actually make me feel any better about it, as a matter of fact.'

'Get real, Misha,' said Thierry. 'Stop feeling sorry for yourself. Sudan is no place to be sick, you should know that by now. Be thankful that you're still more or less in one piece, and do a runner.'

'Is that really how you see it, Thierry?'

'Yes, it is. Sorry to be rude, but it's a tough world out here.'

'Yes, I expect you're right.' Misha, feeling the humiliating tears of weakness pricking her eyelids, bit hard on the insides of her cheeks to prevent them falling.

Basil, seeing her looking so frail and downcast, found himself surprisingly concerned for the little doctor's well-being, and experienced a strong compulsion to take care of her, and make sure she got safely back to base. 'Tell you what,' he said. 'We're flying out tomorrow. Why don't you come back to Paris with us? I'm sure we can get you on the flight.'

Misha looked from one to the other, uncertainly, and suddenly the thought of getting out of the place that had almost broken her spirit seemed like a very good idea indeed. 'That would be wonderful,' she said, so quietly that they could hardly hear her.

'Is that a yes?'

Misha laughed. 'Yes, it is. Please.'

'Excellent,' said Basil. He looked at his watch. 'What about some dinner, you guys? I don't know about you, but I'm starving.'

The plane took off from Nairobi at noon. Basil insisted that Misha have the window seat, and as the flight path followed the Great Rift Valley, he pointed out the Ngong Hills, the beautiful profile of Mount Longonot, and the string of blue-green soda lakes, their algae-rich waters covered with thousands upon thousands of brilliantly pink flamingos. 'Quite a sight, isn't it?' he said.

'Yes, it is. It's amazing.'

As the plane approached the Kenya Highlands, it gained height and flew through the thickening cloud cover that now began to obscure the land spread out beneath them. Spots of water spattered across her window, reminding Misha of the plight of her unfortunate refugees, somewhere far below. 'I hope to God this means that it's raining in Sudan, at last,' she said.

'I wouldn't put money on it,' said Basil. 'It's absolutely heartbreaking. The clouds pile up over the horizon, and there's lots of lightning, but quite often only a few miserable drops of water fall, and it's back to square one.' He looked at Misha, and she saw that his grey eyes were sombre, and full of sorrow. She could tell that although it was his chosen profession to process their tormented lives into news items, the fate of such people was a matter of real concern for him.

'It's frightening,' she said. 'Until you've experienced it at close quarters, you've no idea how bad it can be, have you?'

He smiled. 'That's why I admire you for what you've been doing, Misha. I only have to deal with situations like that for three or four days at a time, but you stuck it out for nearly two months.'

'Charlotte has been at the feeding-station for *eight* months, Baz. That doesn't say much about me, does it?'

'That's a load of crap! Charlotte is not you, and you're not Charlotte, thank God. The woman may be tough, but she's a bloody tyrant as well as a pain in the arse, in my view.'

Misha laughed, secretly gratified by this analysis of Charlotte's character. 'Don't you like tyrannical women, Baz?'

'No, I don't,' he replied. 'I don't like tyrannical men, either, come to that.'

The plane flew steadily northwards for several hours. The sun slipped beneath the darkening cloud cover and the sky turned a lurid purple, with a vivid streak of orange above the western horizon. Suddenly, without warning, the plane began to throw itself about rather violently and they were told to fasten their seat belts, and extinguish cigarettes. Misha glanced at Baz, her eyes huge with alarm.

'Don't worry,' he said. 'It's only a bit of turbulence.'

As he spoke, there was a tremendous crack of thunder, and a simultaneous brilliant flash of lightning seemed to fizz through the plane, between the two rows of seats. 'Jesus!' said Basil. 'I think we've been struck!'

The terrifying storm continued to rage around them, and it grew dark. At last, the pilot's voice, calm and reassuring, came over the intercom. 'This is not a lot of fun,' he said, 'so we've got clearance to land at Tunis. Apologies for the delay this may cause, but better safe than sorry I always think. We're stacking just now, but we should be down fairly soon.'

He was rewarded for his coolness by a muted cheer, and a nervous outbreak of chatter. The hostess, looking reassuringly cheerful, came down the gangway, clinging to the seats as she passed, and distributing extra sick-bags where required. 'You OK, Misha?' Baz sounded anxious.

'I'm OK, Baz. Don't worry, I'm not going to throw up.'

In another twenty minutes, the ordeal was over; the plane had landed safely, and was taxiing up to the airport buildings. Thierry poked his head over the back of Misha's seat, grinning. 'Par for the course, eh, Baz? What was all that about getting Misha home in one piece?'

'I just hope we can find a decent hotel,' said Baz. 'And something fairly bland to eat.'

'And a drink, too, wouldn't you say?' said Misha, laughing, light-hearted with relief, now that the danger had passed.

'That, too. In fact, several.'

The taxi ride to the hotel was damp, but otherwise uneventful, and the hotel recommended by the driver turned out to be surprisingly luxurious, with a pleasant dining-room, which appeared to be empty and probably on the point of closing. The tired little group dumped their overnight bags in reception, though the cameramen decided to keep their equipment with them, and they all went straight in to eat. The maître d', a dapper little man with a large nose, black hair liberally coated with gel, and wearing an oversized white tuxedo, escorted them to a large round corner table, partially screened by real palm trees in enormous pots, and overlooking the busy street through a large plate-glass window. The menu offered either fish, fillets of mullet, or *moza*, which turned out to be roast lamb on rice.

'Sounds good,' said Misha, suddenly feeling very hungry. 'I think I'll have the *moza*.'

They gave the order, and Basil ordered the local wine. Looking at the doubtful faces of the crew, he laughed, and told them not to fuss, that it was excellent.

'Been here before, then?' said Thierry.

'Certainly have,' Baz replied, 'though I've only just realized it.' He looked speculatively at the plate-glass window beside their table. 'The last time I was here, some nutter let a bomb off, and that window blew in.'

'Now he tells us!' The second cameraman, Pierre, looked sternly at Basil. 'You're winding us up, Baz, aren't you?'

'No, I'm not.' Basil laughed. 'It's too bloody true, old dear.'

'But you weren't sitting at this table, were you, Baz?' asked Misha.

'No, thank God. I was right over the other side of the room, but I still got covered in glass.'

'What about the poor guys sitting here?'

'What do you think?'

The food arrived, smelling utterly delicious, and transporting Misha straight back to Algiers and her grandparents' home. She had eaten lamb many times in her life, and cooked in many different ways, but it had never tasted so good to her as the roasted lamb of the southern Mediterranean coast, its edges crisp and burnt, sharp with lemon and garlic, on its bed of soft rice, moist with the juices of the meat.

The young waiter, bending over, held the dish for Misha, and she gave herself a generous helping. '*Shukran*,' she said, and smiled at him shyly.

'*Afwan, lalla*,' the waiter responded politely, and moved on to her neighbour. Misha took a swallow of her wine, then picked up her fork, completely forgetting Basil's gruesome account of his previous visit, so comfortable did she feel in her own skin at that moment, so relaxed and profoundly at home in that Tunisian dining-room.

'How many languages do you speak, Misha?' asked Thierry, rather impressed by her apparent command of tongues.

'Only French and English, as a matter of fact,' she

replied, enigmatically, and turned her attention to the serious matter of enjoying her *moza*.

The next morning, after a rather disturbed night in her noisy bedroom, Misha came down to the dining-room to find Basil and the crew having breakfast, and in a very bad mood indeed. 'What's the matter?' she asked. 'You all look terribly glum. What happened?'

'I'll tell you what happened,' said Basil, crossly. 'The bloody airport's on strike, that's what happened.'

Chapter Ten

After a week of high tension, and frequent changes of mind about what it was absolutely vital to take with them to Hollywood, Juliet, Alice and Dorothy, together with a small mountain of luggage, were crammed into Juliet's little car, and driven to the airport by Giles. Though inwardly thankful to see the back of them all, he managed to put on a convincing display of sorrow at their departure, staying with them until their bags had been registered, and leaving them at the entrance to the departure lounge.

Just before she disappeared, Juliet raised her hand and waved cheerfully, and Giles waved back. Both of them knew that they had reached a crossroads in their relationship.

He turned away, walked briskly towards the short-stay car park, and drove straight to Chelsea. He bought himself a prawn sandwich and carried it home in a small carrier bag. Letting himself into the musty and dark hallway of his empty house was an indescribable relief, after the chaos and hysteria of the past few days. He sat on the stool in his tiny kitchen, poured himself a glass of decent claret and ate his lunch, revelling in the silence that flowed like a benison around him.

After he had eaten, he made some coffee and took the cup down to his subterranean sitting-room, where he made himself comfortable on the chesterfield, and began to formulate a plan for the reanimation of his love for Misha, and their former elegant lifestyle.

Giles had still not received an answer to his letter to Blanche de Vilmorin, and though he thought it quite possible that there would be a reply from her waiting at passage des Ebénistes, it had occurred to him that perhaps she might regard as something of a paper tiger his threat to inform the police that Paul was committing a felony. On reflection, he had therefore decided that a more subtle course of action might be more effective, and with this end in view, he had made arrangements to spend a week working in the Paris office of Cunningham's, and had already booked his seat on the Eurostar.

Confidently Giles told himself that if he found that Misha was still away, he would simply move into the apartment himself, and by this means prevent any further intrusion from de Vilmorin. If, on the other hand, Misha had already returned from her trip to Africa, a skilful pretence at grovelling on his part would soon repair the wounds he had inflicted on her. He had little doubt that she would quickly forgive him, and that their life together would then resume its former civilized pattern. He might even buy her an eternity ring, as a token of the renewal of their love.

He spent the afternoon rather happily, packing for the trip, then drove to St Peter's Square and spent a boring evening tidying away the stuff littered about the place by Juliet and Alice, knowing that on his return from Paris, he would find such squalor depressing. In the fridge he found a half-eaten dish of cauliflower cheese, and, with a shudder of distaste, put it in the oven to reheat.

In the morning, Giles caught the early Eurostar to Paris. He took a taxi to passage des Ebénistes, then manhandled his heavy luggage up to the top floor. The first thing he did was to check out the apartment, in case Misha had come home, but there was no sign of her at all, except, possibly, a glass on the night-table in the bedroom, containing a few fading yellow roses. He threw them in the bin. Then he looked in the post-box, and found it empty. He frowned, knowing that this probably meant that someone had been there since his last visit. Bloody de Vilmorin, no doubt, he said to himself. He listened to Misha's messages, and found nothing, except one from himself, demanding to know where she was, and what she thought she was playing at. Thoughtfully, Giles wiped the tape.

He spent a relaxed sort of day at the office, lunching with a friend, an expert in French eighteenth-century drawings. He left the office at five o'clock and took the Métro to Bastille, where he did a comprehensive food shop in rue de la Roquette, buying enough stuff to last him for a week. Back in the apartment, he put some Wagner on the CD player, and set about the serious business of making himself very much at home.

At eight-thirty, Paul de Vilmorin, after a fairly stressful afternoon in the theatre, and badly in need of the small amount of solace to be derived from spending a little time in Misha's empty apartment before taking himself out for a meal, drove into passage des Ebénistes, and parked outside number sixteen. He got out of the car, and from force of habit, looked up at the roof of the building. He saw at once that the lights were on in the apartment, and his heart lurched within his breast, the blood draining from his face.

He drew a deep breath, entered the building and took the lift to the top floor. As he drew near to Misha's door, he saw that a bulging blue plastic rubbish-bag had been dumped immediately beside it. This was something that Misha would never have done, and it made him hesitate for a moment. Silently, he approached the door, and laid his ear against the panel. From within came the portentous sounds of *Twilight of the Gods*.

Instantly, Paul withdrew from the door, and retreated to the lift. Misha's not there, he said to himself; she'd never be listening to that sort of heavy stuff, at least not if she were on her own. It's that bastard Murray-Williams again, he thought angrily, as the lift plummeted downwards. What the hell's he doing there, revolting little creep?

Back in his car, he asked himself whether it was at all possible that Misha could actually be up there with the revolting little creep, and then shook his head, recollecting the sordid bag of rubbish. No, she's not there, he thought. But he is, I'm sure of it. To satisfy himself, Paul took his mobile phone from his pocket, and dialled Misha's number. It rang three times. 'Yes?' It was the unmistakable English voice of Giles Murray-Williams. Paul, having no wish to communicate with him in any way at all, turned off his phone.

Marooned in Tunis, Basil spent a couple of hours on the telephone, angrily demanding that an executive jet be found to get him and his crew to France, with total lack of success. Frustrated, he called his company in Paris to rearrange the schedules, then ordered a cab to take them to Trapani-Tunis, in order to board the ferry to Naples. All things being equal, they would arrive there in time to catch an early plane to Paris the next morning.

After the boat sailed, the camera crew went below and settled down to pass the time with backgammon, while Misha and Basil strolled together round the decks, glad of the chance to get some fresh air. It was a lovely day, with a cloudless blue sky, and an even bluer ruffled sea. They stood at the rail of the poop-deck and watched the palm-fringed beaches of Tunisia growing smaller, shimmering in the heat-haze, and finally disappearing from view.

Misha sighed. 'It's beautiful, isn't it? But I can't say I'm sorry to be leaving. Africa's a tough place; one doesn't realize how tough before you get there.'

'What took you to Talakal in the first place, Misha?'

'My life was in a mess, I needed to escape from it. A

spell with SMO seemed like a good idea; it was as simple as that.'

'Tell me about it.'

Misha looked at Basil, her green eyes wary. 'Why should I, Baz? I hardly know you. It's none of your business, really, is it?'

'No, of course it isn't. Sorry. I didn't mean to intrude, Misha.' Gently, he took her by the elbow. 'Come on, let's walk for a bit, shall we?'

They walked in silence, side by side. After a few minutes Misha said quietly: 'That was rude of me, Baz. I know you weren't being nosy. I apologize.'

'Don't be silly. There's nothing to apologize for. You were perfectly right. Your private life is your own business.'

'As a matter of fact, I'd quite like to talk about it to someone, and as I'll probably never see you again after tomorrow, it might as well be you, if you see what I mean.'

'You make it sound as though you'd murdered someone, or robbed a bank, at the very least!'

Misha laughed. 'Nothing as dramatic as that, I'm afraid.' She glanced up at him, suddenly serious. 'But I *was* on the point of fatally destroying someone's life. I suppose that could be considered a kind of moral murder, couldn't it?'

They had walked right round the deck, and Basil pointed to two wooden folding chairs, sheltered from the strengthening breeze. 'Let's sit down, shall we? Or would you rather walk?'

'Sit.'

They sat down. Basil leaned back in his seat, closed his eyes against the glare of the sun and waited.

'Seven years ago,' began Misha in a low voice, 'when I was a hospital doctor, I fell in love with a patient, an Englishman. We became lovers, and he stayed in my apartment when he was in Paris. A few months ago, he had a serious accident and was in hospital for several weeks.'

'Poor guy.'

'Indeed. Naturally, I went to London to see him, and while I was there I discovered that he already had a partner. Not only that, he had a child of six, as well.'

'How rotten for you, Misha. What did you do?'

'At first, nothing. I was in shock, absolutely. Then I did a very stupid thing.'

Basil frowned. 'What was that?'

'I told someone all about it, just as I'm telling you.'

'Why was that stupid?'

'Because he was so sympathetic, so understanding, so kind, that I became completely dependent on him, emotionally.'

'And what was wrong with that, if you needed his support?'

'Three things were wrong, Baz. One, he is the Professor of Neurosurgery at my hospital, and I was a member of his team. Two, he is married, with a grown-up family. Three, his wife has cancer.' She raised her troubled eyes to his, and he saw that all the colours of the sea were reflected in them. 'So, you see, I had no choice but to get out before I completely wrecked his reputation, as well as destroying what was left of his wife's life.'

'Did he tell you that his wife was sick, Misha?'

'No, he didn't.'

'Who told you?'

'His daughter. She came to see me, when Paul and Blanche had gone on holiday.'

'I see.' He gazed out to sea, then turned towards Misha. 'Don't you think it was wrong of him not to tell you about his wife's illness, Misha? It seems clear to me that he was far more culpable than you, in the circumstances.'

'I knew he was married. He never tried to hide that.'

'But he didn't mention his wife having cancer?'

'No, he didn't.'

'Was that fair?'

'Probably not.' Misha looked down at her hands,

picking at her nails. She sighed. 'It makes no difference whether it was fair, or not, Baz. I was in love with him; I thought him the nicest and kindest man I'd ever met. I loved him; it was as simple as that.'

'And now?'

'It's over. It has to be, obviously.'

'Because of the wife, what's her name, Blanche?'

'Yes, of course.'

'And the man, Misha? What about him?'

'What about him?'

'Is he still in love with you?'

'I don't know.' She looked up, her small face drawn, as if in acute pain. 'I don't think so, as a matter of fact. He hasn't made any kind of attempt to get in touch with me, Baz. He easily could have found me, if he'd really wanted to.'

Basil took her hand, and squeezed it gently. At this sympathetic gesture, hot tears of anguish, regret and shame filled Misha's eyes and fell down her face. Basil did not realize it, but it was at that precise moment that he fell totally and irrevocably in love with her; it was a fatal condition that would possess him for the rest of his days. He knelt on the deck beside her chair and put his arms round her shuddering body, until her tears ran dry and all that remained was an attack of hiccups.

'Oh, God,' she mumbled. 'Have you got a hanky, Baz?'

He released her, and pulled a crumpled and rather grubby handkerchief from his pocket. 'Yes, if you aren't too fussy about its filthy state,' he said.

Misha blew her nose and looked at Basil, her eyes swollen, her face streaked with dirt and tears. 'I must look a wreck,' she said, with a shaky laugh.

'Since you mention it, yes, you do.' He smiled. 'What about something to drink, and a snack?'

'Good idea,' said Misha. 'But first I must wash my face.' She reached out and laid a hand gently on his wrist. 'Thank you, Baz. It was kind of you to let me bore you with my problems.'

'Isn't that what friends are for?'

'Are you my friend, Baz?'

'I'd like to be.'

Giles Murray-Williams spent a very agreeable week in Paris, both in the office, and plotting the discomfiture of his rival, Paul de Vilmorin, at passage des Ebénistes. With this end in mind, he set about the preparation of a nasty surprise for Paul, should he have the temerity to poke his nose inside the apartment after he, Giles, had returned to London.

Although the idea of deconstructing the impeccable atmosphere of Misha's apartment would normally have been anathema to his nature, he set about doing precisely that, with some enthusiasm. He began in the bathroom, scattering around his personal toiletries and medicaments. He looked into Misha's cupboards, found a nightdress, and draped it casually over the foot of the bed. He hung his own things in the wardrobe, and left his own crumpled pyjama bottoms on the floor beside the bed. Finally, and with what he regarded as a stroke of genius, he applied one of Misha's lipsticks to his mouth, then lightly pressed his lips to the collar of one of his shirts. He arranged it carefully in the laundry basket, taking care that the collar was clearly visible.

In the salon, he punched the leather cushions of the sofa until they looked as though someone had been lying on them, and sprayed a tiny squirt of Misha's scent on the one where her head would have been.

On his last evening, Giles sat down and wrote a long and rather maudlinly contrite letter to her, expressing his love for her, his regret at his behaviour towards her, his longing to be reconciled with her, and the hope that they would never again have to part. Carefully, he sealed the envelope, and put it on the glass table, where she would be sure to see it. This was a calculated risk on his part, for he realized that de Vilmorin might open the letter and read it, but, on balance, decided that this was unlikely to happen. Satisfied that he had cooked Paul's goose, he returned to London.

The hours passed slowly as the ferry surged ponderously towards Italy. Basil and Misha stood at the rail and watched the sun go down. They went to the bar for a drink, and then had supper with the rest of the crew. Afterwards, they walked again on the deck, enjoying the starry night and the warm breeze.

'It was a drag about the airport strike,' said Basil, 'but at least we've had the chance to get to know each other, haven't we?'

'Do you really think so?' Misha smiled. 'It seems to me that you know a great deal about me, but I know nothing at all about you.'

'What do you want to know?'

'Well, for instance, how did you get to be a TV correspondent?'

'By a sort of fluke, really. I was at school and university in England, and then I had a very boring job in the British Museum, but I was desperate to get back to France.'

'Why France?'

'My mum lives in Paris, on the Ile St-Louis. I was born there.'

'Really? So, how did you manage to repatriate yourself?'

'I fell in love, with a girl whose father was a big deal in French telly, and he got me a job.'

'Nepotism, Baz?'

'Absolutely!' Basil laughed.

'And did you marry the daughter?'

'Yes, I did. We've been married for eleven years.'

'Have you got a family?'

'No, we haven't.'

Something in this quiet statement made Misha look speculatively at Basil and told her not to pursue the subject of children. 'Tell me about your wife, Baz,' she said lightly. 'Is she beautiful?'

'Ravishing,' said Basil. 'She is also a highly successful artist, and travels all over the world for her exhibitions. We practically have to make an appointment to see each other, nowadays.'

Misha laughed. 'The price of success for you both?'

'Yes, I suppose you could say that.'

For a few moments, they stood together at the rail, watching the lights of a distant ship, going in the opposite direction. 'Ships that pass in the night, Baz. Just like us, isn't it?'

'No, it isn't,' said Basil, turning towards her. 'Or rather, I don't want it to be, Misha. Now that I've found you, I don't want to lose you. At the very least, I'd like us to be friends. Is there anything wrong with that?'

'Baz, you're married,' said Misha quietly, staring out to sea, refusing to look at him. 'The next thing, you'll be telling me that your wife doesn't understand you.'

'You've got it. She doesn't. Or if she does, she doesn't want to know.'

'Come on! Now you're talking in riddles. What the hell do you mean?'

'You'll probably be angry if I tell you, or despise me. As a successful woman with an important job yourself, it's quite on the cards that you'll agree with Olivia, in any case.'

He sounded so morose that Misha almost laughed. Instead, she said: 'Don't jump to conclusions, Baz. Try me.'

He sighed, and looked down over the rail at the fast-moving foam-flecked water below. 'It's silly, really, and pathetically banal. I badly want a family, Misha, especially now I'm forty-four, but Olivia doesn't. She's too committed, too busy, even to consider it.'

Misha looked at him then, seriously. 'And how old is Olivia?'

'Thirty.'

'She's got loads of time, then?'

'But from where I am, Misha, the clock seems to be ticking away pretty fast.'

'Yes, I see that.' She smiled at him, gently. 'I can just see you as a father, Baz. You'd be very good at it, I'm sure.'

'It's what I long for, more than anything in the world. Trouble is, it's not a thing one can do on one's own, is it? At least, not if you're a man.'

Misha covered his hand with hers, as it lay on the rail. 'It sounds to me as if we're both victims of the same situation, Baz. It's very damaging to the human spirit to love someone more than they love you, I'm afraid.'

Basil looked down at Misha's sunburned hand, then at her starlit face as she looked up at him, her eyes full of kindness and comprehension. He found it impossible to believe that a woman of such physical frailty could have found the courage and endurance to carry out her impossible mission in the roasting heat of the desert. A lump rose in his throat. 'If I had been in Paul's shoes, Misha,' he said hoarsely, 'I would have come after you, to the rain forests of the Amazon, or the North Pole.'

'Even if Olivia had cancer, Baz?'

'Yes, even then.'

She withdrew her hand at once. 'This is nonsense, Baz. You don't mean it, and if we're going to be friends, it has to be just that, and nothing else, OK?'

'You're right. I'm sorry,' he replied, abjectly. 'I don't love you really, Misha. It's just my gonads talking; they keep telling me that I do!'

She laughed and gave him an affectionate punch on the arm. 'Ridiculous man! Let's go down and have a nightcap; it's nearly time we were all asleep.'

Chapter Eleven

As September drew to its close, the golden weather turned to cold, sleety rain and wind, and darkness began to fall earlier each day. As he usually did, Paul drove to passage des Ebénistes after work, always hoping to find that Murray-Williams had finally left, but expecting to be disappointed.

On a chill Monday evening, after a long afternoon in the theatre, he parked the car at a little distance from Misha's door, and, looking up, saw at once that the place was in darkness. He sat in the car for an hour, in case Giles should merely be late leaving his office, then got out, let himself into the building, and took the lift to the top floor. Outside Misha's door, he paused for a moment, listening for any sounds of occupation, then put his key into the lock and entered the apartment.

Immediately, he noticed a faint and familiar smell. It was Misha's scent. If she's been here, he thought, why hasn't she been in touch? Is it really possible that she's gone back to that appalling man, after everything he's done to her? He noticed the squashed cushions on the leather sofa, precisely as Giles had intended that he should, and his heart bled.

Reluctant to see any more evidence of this disturbing nature, but driven on by a self-destructive need to know the truth, Paul passed through the kitchen to the bedroom, where his worst fears were horribly confirmed. He stood beside the bed, appalled by what he saw. He went to the bathroom, knowing that it was a foolish thing to do, but incapable of stopping himself. He saw the laundry basket, the lipstick on the collar, and the rest of the evidence of Giles's presence. Paul turned away, entirely convinced that Misha had ended her relationship with him, and was now reconciled to the man she had loved for so long.

Full of despair, he returned to the salon. He saw the note that Giles had left on the glass table, and for a moment he was severely tempted to open it. Instead, he placed the spare set of keys Misha had given him beside the note, and left the apartment. He had fallen absolutely into the trap, exactly as Giles had intended.

The ferry docked in good time for Basil, his crew and Misha to get a cab to the airport and catch the flight to Paris, where they landed in the late afternoon. They were met by the newsdesk's transport and driven into Paris, dropping Misha off at passage des Ebénistes. Basil got out to help her with her luggage.

'Don't worry, Baz,' she said, unlocking the street door, 'I can manage, really.'

'I have to go and debrief now,' he said. 'Is it OK if I come round this evening, when I've finished?'

'Yes, of course. Come when you're ready.'

Blanche de Vilmorin, having confronted Paul with Giles Murray-Williams's letter, and thereby blown apart the pretence that she knew nothing of his affair with Misha ben Bella, was beginning to be seriously concerned about her husband's health. Far from looking better with the healing passage of time, Paul seemed to her to be deteriorating physically and she thought he looked thinner every time she saw him. Curiously, in the last couple of weeks, he had started coming home comparatively early in the evening, though he still refused to share a meal with her, saying vaguely that he had already eaten, and going almost immediately to his own room.

Sometimes, during the day, when Paul was safely out of the house and at the hospital, Blanche could not resist the temptation to poke around in his room, in search of further evidence of his infidelity, in the shape of letters from his lover, or whatever. Long and diligently she searched for the photographs she had thrown at him so dramatically, but could not find them. The drawers of his desk were locked, the keys nowhere to be seen. Short of taking a chisel to the lock, there was no way she could discover what, if anything, he had concealed in there. She searched the pockets of his clothes, as they hung in the wardrobe, and found nothing, not even the poems of Ronsard.

Olivier, the faithful little soul, came to see her on Thursday afternoons, as before, but Blanche felt curiously disinclined for sexual games, and their time together was spent drinking lemon tea, and talking about Paul. Occasionally, she went with Olivier and Catherine to the cinema, or to an exhibition, but she no longer attended the glittering society bashes she had once so much enjoyed. She was not entirely sure of the reason for her reluctance to play her part in these occasions, but Olivier suspected that Blanche was quite frightened of drawing attention to herself, for fear some unscrupulous hack should have uncovered the scandal attached to Paul, and should try to embarrass her in public, by questioning her on the subject.

'Why can't you persuade him to come out with us, sometimes, Blanche?' said Olivier. 'It would be by far the best thing, darling, for all concerned.' He did not choose to add that he was beginning to be bored by the threadbare nature of his social life, now that Blanche so often refused to go out. Tiresomely, it did not seem to occur to her to pass the unwanted invitations on to himself and Catherine, who would have been perfectly happy to go to the functions without her.

Blanche sighed. 'I'll try, but he won't agree, I know.' She gazed at Olivier, her blue eyes bleak. 'Apart from the fact that he hates me, Olivier, anything that isn't connected with medicine bores him rigid. It always has done, you know that.'

Olivier began to make sympathetic noises, then changed his mind. 'He's not bored rigid by goat's cheese, Blanche, is he? Anything to do with Pascal and Emma is of intense interest to him, as I've observed many times, when we've been at Ménerbes with you. He's crazy about Emma, too, you must have noticed that, darling? He worships her, one can tell.'

'It's true,' said Blanche, slowly. She nearly added, 'Though I can't think why, I find her quite boring, personally,' and then stopped herself. 'Maybe I should speak to Pascal, tell him what's happened, see if he could make Paul see sense. If anyone could, I suppose it would be Pascal. The sun shines out of his backside, as far as Paul's concerned.'

'Blanche,' said Olivier, 'that's a very promising idea. You should think about it very carefully, and then write to Pascal. If I were you, dear, I wouldn't abuse Paul in any way. I should take the more in sorrow than in anger line, and say how much you long for the ending of this unhappy interlude, or words to that effect, and ask for their help.'

Blanche looked at Olivier, her blue eyes bright with scorn. 'So you really think I should grovel and whine to my son, do you, Olivier?'

'If it does the business, Blanche, why the hell not?'

So the next morning Blanche sat down at her desk, and wrote a long and rather pathetic letter to Pascal and Emma. When she had finished, she hid it in her blotter, and waited for twenty-four hours, before reading it again, and making a few alterations. Then she made a careful copy of the letter, and went out and mailed it herself, before she could change her mind.

In Mas les Arnauds, the days were getting shorter, but the weather, though colder at night, was crisp and bright, with long hours of warm sunshine. The sky, swept clean by a persistent mistral, was a heart-stopping blue, and the first snow could be seen on the distant alpine peaks.

Emma, almost into the seventh month of her pregnancy, no longer went with Pascal to the market in Apt, to help with the selling of their cheese, but remained at home, preparing for the advent of their twin boys. Slowly, the pattern of their life was changing, in order to adjust to the needs of a growing family. Pascal, not wishing to leave Emma on her own for very long, had not gone up to Col d'Allos to take part in the *transhumance*, the shepherds' traditional long walk, driving the sheep down from the high alpine summer pastures to their winter grazing in the foothills, paddocks, and orchards of their district. Instead, he had used the time to complete the decorating of the room they had chosen for their boys, and to finish the identical cradles he had made for them.

During the summer, he had mended all the holes in the upstairs ceilings, and had replaced the missing and broken tiles of the roof, so that the house was now dry, if not particularly warm. They had replaced their ancient stove with a bigger and much more efficient model, equipped with a back burner. This splendid piece of ironmongery not only heated the kitchen, but had an oven for roasting and plenty of space for cooking on its broad surface. Best of all, it provided plenty of hot water, both in the kitchen and the new bathroom, but they had agreed that central heating would have to wait for the time being. 'After all,' Emma had said comfortably, 'if it gets too cold to sleep upstairs, we can all sleep down here in the warm, can't we?'

Secretly, it was her wish that they should continue to live in the traditional way for as long as possible, and although she had reluctantly agreed with Pascal that with the advent of the children, connection to the mains electricity supply had become essential, she was still resisting the purchase of a refrigerator or even a washing machine.

Walking to the village shops, to pick up her bread, and buy some peppers to stuff with fillets of rabbit, herbs and rice for the evening meal, Emma passed the yellow Post Office van going towards her house, and on the way back she looked in the mail-box screwed to the outside of their gate. Inside, she found the telephone bill, and a letter. Recognizing the distinctive, old-fashioned and spidery hand of her mother-in-law on the envelope, Emma frowned uneasily. Since Pascal had never been on particularly good terms with his mother, their contact with her had always been somewhat tenuous, even reluctant on her son's part, so Emma found it odd that she should write to them now. Presumably, the letter would contain unwanted advice, or some kind of complaint. She put the mail in her coat pocket, opened the gate, and made her way across the leaf-strewn courtyard to the door of the house. I really must find time to sweep up the leaves, she said to herself.

In the kitchen, she put away the shopping and put the kettle on to boil, before sitting down at the table and opening the letter from Blanche.

Dearest Pascal and Emma,

I would not worry you at a time like this, when you are getting quite far on in pregnancy, but I feel it my duty to tell you that your father is very unwell, and causing me much anxiety, even some alarm, as I think it quite possible that he may be contemplating suicide.

Reading these words, Emma's blood froze in her veins, and her eyes widened with terror. My God, she thought, what's happened?

This will no doubt come as a great shock to you, but after more than thirty years of marriage, your father has been going through a mid-life crisis, and has for a few months been involved with a young doctor from the hospital. The woman has evidently decided that their affair must end, and has gone to work abroad, with SMO, I understand. When I heard this, I had hoped that life would return to normal, that Paul would gradually forget about her, and that we could continue to live together in our former harmony.

What former harmony, Blanche? said Emma to herself, recognizing at once that Blanche's disquiet was more for herself than for her husband.

Unfortunately, my hopes for Paul's swift recovery have not been realized, and he seems to me to be in a very unbalanced and fragile state of mind. He does not eat, and I hear him walking about in his room most of the night. Clearly, he is heading for a major breakdown, which is why I am taking the unusual step of asking you both for help, as I am now at my wits' end to know how to cope with the situation, and find a way of helping Paul regain some form of stasis, and self-respect. I know how much your father admires and loves you both, and feel sure that you could help him, if you could find it in your hearts to try.

With my love,
Blanche.

The kettle boiled, and Emma got up from her chair, and made some tea. She stood beside the stove, warming her hands on the mug, and drank thoughtfully. She tried to remember exactly what Paul had said to her, when he had visited them last August. He had told her that he was unhappy, but only because he was temporarily separated from Misha; that he was in love for the first time in his life, and that Misha loved him. What had happened to make the separation permanent? What had happened to drive Misha away? Had it been the work of a busybody at the hospital, or had the mischief-maker been closer to home, perhaps?

At a quarter past six, Pascal came home, and Emma showed him the letter. After he had read it, she repeated to him what Paul had told her in the summer, and they agreed that Blanche was probably responsible, at least partially, for the present state of affairs.

'I'd like to go and see him,' said Pascal, 'and judge for myself how bad things really are, but I'm not leaving you here, darling, all on your own.'

'You won't have to,' said Emma. 'I'll come with you, of course.'

Without telling Blanche of their plans, they caught a fast train from Avignon the next day, and arrived in Paris in the late afternoon. They took a cab to rue de Thorigny, and when Marie-Claire ushered them into the salon, Blanche was taken completely by surprise. Transfixed on the sofa, she stared at her tall, dark-haired son, and his beautiful, grey-eyed and very pregnant wife, and her mouth hung open in astonishment. 'Pascal! Emma! What a surprise!' she exclaimed, and getting to her feet made a pretence of embracing them both. 'I'm so glad you've come! What a relief!'

Marie-Claire brought fresh tea, and Blanche, with a convincing display of touching loyalty to her husband, told Pascal and Emma how worried she was about Paul, emphasizing her ardent wish to see his health and peace of mind restored. 'I am so terrified that he might do something stupid,' she said. 'Sometimes he looks so strange, and his eyes are so wild, it quite frightens me. And yet I dare not consult anyone at the hospital, for fear of them making him take early retirement. It would break his heart, I know.'

Blanche looked at Emma, as she sat on the sofa, so young and so beautiful, still wrapped in her long black cloak, her dark hair glossy with health, and her enormous grey eyes serious and concerned. 'I had so hoped we would have a happy old age together,' she said, with a tremor in her voice, and Emma almost believed her.

It was Friday evening, and Paul, for once, got home before eight o'clock. His astonishment and pleasure at seeing Pascal and Emma was intense, turning almost immediately to alarm. 'What are you doing here? There's nothing wrong with the babies, is there?'

'No, we're all fine, *Père*. We just thought we'd have a last little jaunt before our movements become more restricted.' Pascal hugged his father. 'Actually, we were hoping you'd take us somewhere posh for dinner.'

'Of course I will; terrific idea. If you're sure that's all right for Emma?'

Emma laughed. 'Of course it is, why ever shouldn't it be? That is, if you really think I'm fit to be seen in the sort of grand places you go to?'

'My dearest girl,' said Paul, kissing her, 'there are few sights more attractive than a pregnant young woman. If she is also beautiful, as you are, Emma, it's a bonus. Pascal is a lucky man.'

Pascal smiled, but said nothing.

'Where would you like to eat?' asked Paul. 'I'd better book a table straight away.'

'Somewhere close enough to walk, please,' said Emma. 'After sitting still in the train for quite a few hours, the little guys are a bit squashed, I think.'

'What about Ma Bourgogne?' suggested Pascal. 'I used to like it, there.'

'Good idea,' said Paul, although his heart contracted in his breast at the mention of the restaurant to which he had first taken Misha. He took his phone from his pocket, and looked up the number in his organizer. 'What about you, my dear?' He glanced at Blanche. 'Will you be coming with us?'

'No, no.' Blanche, although mortified by this public display of indifference, had no wish to make it difficult for Paul to speak confidentially to his son and daughter-in-law. 'Marie-Claire is already preparing dinner, and I have to see to the children's room, too, of course. No, I'll be fine here; you three go by yourselves.'

In the end, they drove to Ma Bourgogne, as Paul insisted that it would be too far for Emma to walk there and back. 'You can walk around place des Vosges,' he said. 'Much less difficult and crowded than the busy roads.'

Although, inside himself, Paul's pain was still as intense as ever, his spirits were tremendously boosted by the unlooked-for visit of his son and daughter-in-law, and they spent a happy evening together, in the crowded dining-room of the restaurant that held such poignant memories for him. It was obvious to Pascal and Emma that this was not the place to try to have a potentially emotional discussion, so the conversation remained light-hearted, and mostly centred upon the coming additions to the family.

'Talking of family, *Père*,' said Pascal suddenly. 'Would it be nice to go to Froissy, visit Granny and *Grandpère*, tidy up the graves a bit and take some flowers for them? Emma's never been there, and I think it's time she went, especially with all these new de Vilmorins on board.'

'Pascal,' said Paul, profoundly touched by his son's words, and fairly close to tears, 'you put me to shame. I haven't been near the graves in years. Of course we'll go. Thank you for suggesting it.'

So on Sunday they went to Froissy, just the three of them, and tidied the graves, and put flowers on them. Pascal insisted on getting a scythe from the shed in the courtyard, and mowing the long grass in the little burial ground attached to the de Vilmorin chapel. Emma, taking her cue from Pascal, suggested to Paul that they return to the house and make some tea, since a slight misty rain had begun to fall. 'Would that be possible?' she asked. 'Or maybe there's nothing in the kitchen nowadays?'

'Yes, there is.' Paul, in no way deceived by this little plot to get him alone with Emma, smiled at her gently. 'We could even cook a meal, probably, if you'd really like that?'

'As a matter of fact,' said Emma, 'I'd love it.'

They returned to the house, Emma's long cloak trailing in the damp grass. In the kitchen, Paul lit the fire with the firelighters, kindling and coal already waiting by the side of the stove, and in five minutes it was roaring up the chimney. Then he turned to Emma, as she sat at the table, turning a blue jug in her hands. 'OK,' he said. 'Fire away.'

'No, darling,' she replied evenly. 'You fire away; it's your life we're worried about, isn't it?'

'Yes,' he said. 'I suppose it is.' He pulled out a chair and sat beside her, and slowly and painfully he told her everything that had happened, and how frantic he was feeling about Misha now. He was tormented by the possibility that she had overreacted to the destructive tactics of Blanche and Nina, not only in going to Sudan, but worse, in allowing her ex-lover to re-enter her life.

'But why should you think that?' asked Emma. 'Surely she finished with him completely, didn't she?'

Hopelessly, Paul described his last visit to passage des Ebénistes, and the painful evidence that had seemed to confirm his worst fears.

At last he was silent, and Emma took his hand gently in hers. 'I hope we haven't made things worse for you by coming here, Paul. It's no-one's business but your own, I know, but you're so dear to both of us that we couldn't not come, when I got the letter from Blanche.'

'What letter?'

'She wrote to us, to tell us how worried she was about you.'

'Really?'

'Yes, really. She is fond of you, Paul, in her way. And worried, too.'

They could hear Pascal in the yard, banging the shed door, and Paul got up and put the kettle on the stove. He went to the larder, and brought mugs and a teapot. 'No milk I'm afraid, but at least the tea should be worth drinking.' Then he sat down again, took Emma's face in his hands and kissed her gently on the forehead. 'Darling Emma, if anyone can help me recover from this, it will be you, and those two little guys inside you.'

The kettle boiled, and he got up and made the tea, just as Pascal came clumping into the kitchen. 'Well, that's all done,' he said cheerfully. 'Where's this tea, then?'

'Right here, you cheeky sod,' said Paul, and laughed.

Chapter Twelve

Misha unlocked her apartment, and went in, dumping her backpack just inside the door. She looked around the salon, uneasily, for the place felt cold, and seemed curiously bleak. Well, she thought, it's hardly surprising, after all this time with the heating turned off, and no flowers. She picked up her pack, and went straight through to the kitchen to switch on the heating, failing to notice either the letter waiting on the glass table, or the bunch of keys beside it.

In the kitchen, from force of habit, she looked in the fridge, and was surprised to see quite a lot of food in it; eggs, cheese, butter and some fairly fresh packs of salad. Someone has been here, she said to herself, and her heart lifted at the thought that it was probably Paul. She filled the kettle, and switched it on, then went into the bedroom. What she saw there filled her with revulsion and anger, for she guessed immediately that the blatant exhibition of night-attire was the deliberate mischief-making of Giles, for some bizarre reason of his own. If he thinks this is funny or clever, she said to herself furiously, he has much less intelligence than I gave him credit for. She went to the bathroom and saw the lipstick-stained shirt in the laundry basket. Bloody horrible man, she thought, what the hell is he playing at? Is this some sort of nightmare, designed to frighten me, or what? I can't believe this is happening, I really can't. Why the hell didn't I make sure that he'd taken his stuff away and given me back his keys, before I went to Sudan?

After a moment, Misha remembered that she had put on the kettle, and went back to the kitchen. There, she made a pot of strong coffee, and took her cup into the salon to drink it. Approaching the sofa, she saw both the letter and the bunch of keys. Those are the keys I gave to Paul, she said to herself, and frowned. Why has he left them there? Oh, God, I don't believe this! He must have come round here, gone into the bedroom, and drawn entirely the wrong conclusion, poor man.

Misha drank her coffee, her hand shaking, and knew that she had never felt so alone, so miserable or so bewildered at any time in her life, even when her mother had died. Slowly, and reluctantly, she turned her attention to the letter on the table. She picked it up, and opened it.

My darling Misha,

I hope that by the time you read this, you will have come home, both to Paris and to me. I know that after my accident, that derailed me as much mentally as physically, or so it would seem, you must have thought that my behaviour towards you was less than kind, and for this I am truly sorry. Juliet and Alice have gone to Hollywood, and although, naturally, my responsibility towards Alice remains, I think it unlikely that we shall all live together as a family again. I do so hope, my darling, that we can now resume our former happy partnership, without feelings of guilt, or obligation to others.

Sorry about my little charade, darling, but it seemed like a good way of discouraging that persistent old idiot, de Vilmorin, from breaking into our apartment.

With all my love, and hope for our future happiness together,

Giles

Misha read this letter, twice, with disbelief and a cold anger. Then she tore it into shreds and went to the kitchen, where she dropped the bits into the garbage disposal, washing them down with a long draught of cold water, and a squirt of disinfectant. The savage noise of the metal grinders induced in her a certain grim satisfaction, and made her feel slightly less soiled by Giles's manipulative attempts at reconciliation. Squaring her shoulders, she went to the bedroom, collected every single item of his clothing that she could lay her hands on, together with all his bathroom paraphernalia, and stuffed them into garbage-bags, ready to take down to the rubbish-collection skip in the street.

When she had satisfied herself that every last trace of Giles's presence had been obliterated, always excepting his possessions in the salon, Misha stripped the bed, and remade it with clean sheets and pillow-cases, and renewed all the towels in the bathroom. She made a parcel of the dirty linen, ready to take to the *blanchisserie* in rue de la Roquette, then, rather exhausted, she looked around the apartment to see whether she had forgotten anything, but could see nothing.

Misha looked at her watch: five forty-seven. She had still not unpacked her backpack. It'll have to wait, she thought; I must go out and do some shopping. I need bread, at the very least, and some milk. She put on her jacket, and, picking up her bag and the laundry parcel, let herself out of the apartment, and went down to the street.

She off-loaded the laundry, and did her shopping, buying steak, potatoes and fresh salad, as well as bread and milk. On her way back to passage des Ebénistes, she remembered that Basil was expecting to find her at home, and broke into a run. Sure enough, she found him, propped against the main entrance of number sixteen, waiting for her, having failed to get a response from the entryphone. His heavy luggage was stacked on the pavement beside him, and he had a large bunch of yellow freesias in his hand.

'Oh, dear, I'm so sorry, Baz,' she gasped. 'I've had such an awful time, I completely forgot you were coming.'

'Calm down,' said Basil, gently. 'It really doesn't matter; you're here now, aren't you?' He gave her the flowers, picked up his baggage, and together they went up to the apartment. Once inside, Misha led the way to the kitchen, put away the shopping and began to describe to Basil what she had found in the bedroom earlier. She pointed to the bags of rubbish she had dumped in the roof garden, waiting to be taken down to the public *poubelle*. 'I've put all his clothes and stuff in those bags,' she said, her face red with embarrassment and agitation. 'I can't wait to get it all out of the place. Bloody man, I wish to God I didn't have to see him, or speak to him, ever again.'

'Why should you have to, if you don't want to?'

'He's got a key. He can get in any time he likes.'

'Is that all? No problem; change the locks.'

'It's not quite as simple as that, Baz. He owns a good deal of the stuff in the apartment. Everything in the salon, as it happens.'

'I see,' said Basil, in spite of the fact that he was completely mystified, and furthermore, not at all sure that he wanted to hear the full story. He looked through the windows at the bags of rubbish. 'Would you like me to get rid of these for you, right away?'

'Would you really? You're an angel, Baz. The big *poubelle* is just at the end of the street.'

'Right, I'll go now.'

Basil collected the bags, and Misha went with him to the lift, opening the gates for him. 'Can you manage the front door?' she asked.

'Don't worry; I'll be fine. See you in a minute.'

'Buzz the entryphone, Baz, and I'll let you in.'

'OK, fine.'

More than twenty minutes passed before Basil

returned from his mission, and Misha, arranging the scented freesias in glass jars, began to wonder whether he had put two and two together, come to the conclusion that he was possibly becoming involved in a situation fraught with traumas he could do without, and had therefore decided to back off. Oh dear, she thought, I quite hope he has. I have so much to think about now. I must decide about my job, and I have to get rid of Giles, once and for all.

The entryphone buzzer sounded, and Misha wiped her wet hands on a teatowel, and picked up the receiver. 'Hello?'

'It's me, Baz.'

'OK, come up.'

In a few minutes, she heard his tap on the door, and let him in. 'I forgot to thank you for the flowers, Baz,' she said quietly. 'They're lovely.'

'Not at all,' he said politely. 'I'm glad you like them.'

He followed her to the kitchen, and she got ice and mineral water from the fridge. 'Would you like a drink?' she asked. 'I'm going to have whisky.'

'That'll be fine, thanks.'

She poured the drinks, and they went into the salon, and sat down on the sofa. After a short silence, Basil glanced briefly at Misha, then looked away again. 'I'm afraid I've lost the plot, Misha,' he said. 'You didn't tell me that you were still involved with this man.'

'I'm not,' said Misha defensively. 'At least, not with Giles.'

'I see.'

'No, you don't see, at all. And in any case, what's the big deal with you, Baz? You're married yourself, aren't you?'

'That's true,' said Basil.

Misha did not reply. They sat in silence, slowly drinking their whisky, until she got up, fetched the bottle from the kitchen, and poured herself another drink. 'What about you, Baz? Do you want another?'

'Thanks.' Feeling increasingly unsure of himself,

Basil gazed around the room, recognizing the work of the artists whose paintings and sculptures filled the room, and wondering uneasily whether Misha had got herself involved with some rich old fart that she couldn't afford to dump, for some reason. 'I'm sorry to ask, Misha, but is it possible you really intend to be reconciled with this man, after all? He seems to have played a crucial part in the decorating of this place; presumably your relationship with him must have been a very committed one?'

'Baz, I've told you several times already, I hate the bloody sight of Giles, and I never want to see him again.' She looked at Basil severely, and spoke quite aggressively, her temper fuelled by the whisky she had consumed. 'I feel angry, revolted and humiliated by his assumption that he, or any bloody man come to that, can walk straight back into my life, and repossess me, as if I were that sodding Braque on the wall.'

'Well, he's gone now,' said Basil appeasingly, greatly relieved to hear this robust denial that Misha might still have any residual feeling for her former lover. 'He's gone, and he doesn't have to come back, ever. For a start, we'll change the locks tomorrow.'

'What do you mean, "we"?'

'I thought we were friends, Misha. I want to be near you; to help you. Is changing locks such a big deal?'

'No, of course not. Sorry.'

'Like I said, Misha. I think I love you.'

'Oh, God! Don't start that again, please!' She got up from the sofa and put her glass on the table. 'Would you mind, Baz? I need to be alone, to think things out.'

'Are you asking me to leave?'

'Yes, I am.'

In rue de la Roquette, Basil picked up a cab and was driven to the station, where he bought a ticket to Orléans, then waited on the windswept platform until the train came in. He had not eaten since the inadequate lunch on the plane from Naples, and the two whiskies he had drunk sloshed around inside him uncomfortably. He would have liked to have gone to the buffet to buy a hot snack of some kind, but was extremely reluctant to leave his baggage unattended, containing as it did so much valuable recording equipment, as well as his official documents.

Curiously, Basil did not feel particularly angry or astonished at Misha's behaviour towards him. What he did feel was a dull aching misery, a real physical pain at being so brusquely rejected, and so unbelievably soon, by the woman for whom he felt quite prepared to sacrifice his home, his marriage, and probably the good opinion of his friends and family. As he paced up and down the platform, he told himself that his motives were highly suspect, that Olivia had never done anything to warrant such a betrayal on his part, and that at his age he should stop crying for the moon. He knew perfectly well that an intelligent man of mature years should settle for what he had, and forget whatever it was he secretly longed for.

The train approached with a deep, throbbing roar, doors flew open and passengers descended, hauling out their luggage before hurrying away to the exits. Basil heaved his bags into the carriage, stacked them in the overhead rack, and settled himself in his seat, one of a group of four with a table, which he prayed he would have all to himself. He sat there, huddled in his big black parka, willing the hordes of tired-looking travellers not to sit with him, and to his great relief, no-one did.

All the way to Orléans, he thought about Misha, reliving the time they had spent together on the ferry to Italy. I really do love her, he told himself, but the knowledge did not comfort him in any way. I'm probably on a hiding to nothing, he thought, remembering Misha's anger and bitterness at the behaviour of her ex-lover, and the male sex in general. What the hell am I doing, chasing after a woman who probably has no use for me at all, and intending to destroy Olly in the process? Deep in his heart, he already knew that it was exactly what he was determined to do, and that nothing would stop him.

At Orléans, he took a cab to the barn. The lights were still on, so he guessed Olivia would still be working, or still be up, anyway. He tried the door, but it was locked. He could hear the sound of voices inside: the television must be on, he concluded, and he knocked quite hard, to draw attention to his arrival. In a moment, he saw the heavy curtain to the big window drawn aside slightly, and the questioning face of his young wife peering through the glass. 'Hi! It's me!' he shouted.

'Baz! Why didn't you call me?' She replaced the curtain, and came to the door, pulling back the bolts, and turning the key in the lock.

'Since when did you feel the need to turn the place into Fort Knox, Olly?' Basil dragged his heavy aluminium case inside, and dropped his backpack on the floor beside it.

'Since I realized that I'm nearly always alone, Baz. I need to feel secure, all by myself. Is that unreasonable?'

'No, of course not. Sorry.'

Olivia put her arms round his neck, and raised her face to his. He kissed her gently. 'Hello, again,' he said quietly.

'Hello.' If she was surprised by the lack of warmth in Basil's kiss, Olivia did not remark on it, but put it down to exhaustion. 'Are you hungry, darling?' she asked. 'Have you eaten?'

'Yes, I'm very hungry. And no, I haven't eaten.'

They went to the kitchen, and Olivia melted butter in a pan, and fried some bacon, then broke some very fresh eggs into a bowl, and made him an enormous omelette. 'Bring the bread, Baz,' she said, putting the plate on a tray, with butter, and salt and pepper. 'You can eat by the fire, it's warmer there.'

The flames roared up the chimney, and Basil sat beside it, consuming his delicious omelette, and half a loaf of country bread. Olivia returned to the kitchen, and came back with cheese, a bottle of claret, and glasses. 'Is this the one you like, Baz?' she asked, showing him the wine. 'I got it specially, so I hope it's OK?'

Basil looked at the label: Chateau Segonzac. 'Very nice,' he said, 'but I've already drunk quite a bit of whisky this evening, so maybe I'd better stick to that, if we've got any?'

'Yes, of course.' She fetched the whisky, and some ice, and poured it for him, then sat down beside him on the sofa. 'Are you tired, darling?'

'Yes, I am. I'm knackered as a matter of fact. It's been an exhausting trip, Olly.'

Before coming to unlock the door for Basil, Olivia had turned down the volume of the TV, but had left the vision on, and when she noticed that the news was about to start, she aimed the remote control to increase the sound. 'It's the news, Baz. Do you want to watch it?'

'I suppose so; why not?'

They watched the events of the day; the arrival of a foreign leader in Paris; a demonstration by the unemployed in Marseille, and an interview with a wine producer on the subject of the quality of this year's vintage.

'Not much news, really,' said Olivia, and picked up the remote control, intending to turn off the set.

'Wait a second,' said Basil, suddenly alert. 'Look, it's us.' Olivia looked, and saw a crowd of obviously starving black women and children, shuffling along in an untidy queue, while a fair-haired woman doled out some kind of grain from a sack, into their tin mugs. 'That's bloody Charlotte,' said Basil. 'That's where I've been, Olly. It's our film.'

Onto the screen came Basil, talking to camera, explaining the plight of the refugee Sudanese, and the efforts of SMO to bring food and medical assistance to them. Then came a close-up, of a sunburned, dark-haired woman, trying to insert a needle into the tiny hand of a gasping, horribly bloated baby, whose frantic mother wrung her hands and wailed in despair while this was going on. Then the poor little thing gave a sort of lurching shudder, and collapsed. The mother snatched the child from the doctor's table, and shook it pathetically, evidently trying to restore it to life, but without success.

'Jesus,' said Basil, wincing. 'I thought they might lose that bit.'

The camera then rested on the dark-haired doctor, who was weeping, her hands covering her face. 'Oh, shit,' said Basil. 'Poor Misha, how awful for her. I hope she hasn't been watching this. Turn it off, Olly, I don't need to see any more.'

Olivia aimed the remote control at the TV. She looked at Basil, and was surprised to see how extremely upset he looked. 'I thought you never let these things get to you, Baz,' she said quietly.

'Well, this time it bloody has, I'm afraid.' He turned to Olivia, his eyes blazing. 'Have you got the slightest bloody idea what these people go through, down there, Olly? You sit here, beavering away on another planet, making pretty pictures for rich overfed people to buy, while half the world is starving, or butchered, and some people, like Misha, do their best to bring an inadequate kind of help to them, half-killing themselves in the process.'

'Misha?'

'Yes, Misha. She's the doctor, who was trying to put a line into the baby's hand.'

'She didn't seem to be making a very efficient job of it, as far as I could make out, or perhaps I'm being unfair?'

'Yes, you are, bloody unfair, Olly. And fucking ignorant, too. I'm going to bed. Goodnight.'

* * *

Olivia took the dirty dishes to the kitchen, and washed them up. Then she made herself a tisane, and returned to the fireside. The logs had collapsed into a mass of glowing embers, and she watched their pale blue flames sending occasional sparks up the chimney, promising frost. Staring at the fire, she felt keenly aware that Basil's homecoming had not brought with it the usual excitement and happiness. What's the matter? she asked herself. Is he still cross with me for going to New York? Surely not, he couldn't be as childish as that, could he? In any case, he was shitty to me, not saying where he was, or telling me when he was coming back. Even shittier, saying all that about me being on another planet, pretentious idiot. He's jealous, that's all. Soon, he'll be going on about having loads of kids again, and turning me into his ideal woman.

Suddenly, she recalled that in her recent loneliness and distress at his absence, she had come to the conclusion that perhaps some children would actually enrich their lives, and make their relationship less vulnerable. With this in mind, she had stopped taking the pill. After all, as a means to an end, a couple of kids might be a very good idea. They would certainly bring Basil home more often, even permanently, and would not necessarily mean the demise of her own career.

Thoughtfully, Olivia put the guard in front of the fire, turned off the lights, and went upstairs to bed. She found Basil lying on his back, wide awake, staring at the beams overhead. She went to the bathroom, undressed, washed and cleaned her teeth. Then, naked, she got into bed beside her husband. He said nothing, but turned his head away.

'Baz,' said Olivia, putting a gentle hand on his chest. 'I've been thinking, while you've been away. I agree with you, it would be nice to have some children, so I've stopped taking the pill.'

'Really? What about your work, isn't that the most important thing in your life?'

'Yes, it is, but I've thought it all out. We can have nannies, live-in help, that kind of thing. It doesn't have to be a hassle, does it?'

Slowly, Basil turned his head and looked at her, and his grey eyes were full of misery, and guilt. 'It's no use, Olly. You'll have to know sooner or later. I'm in love with someone else.'

'Who? And since when?'

'You don't know her; she's a doctor.'

Olivia stared at him. 'It's that woman on the telly, isn't it? The one who made the balls of the baby?'

'Please don't talk like that, Olly. Misha is one of the bravest woman I've ever met. She'd been out there in that frightful hell-hole for two months, working all day under a blistering sun, with precious little food or water, and never enough drugs or equipment to make a real difference to the suffering of those poor creatures. It was an absolute nightmare.'

'So you rescued her from this nightmare, did you, Baz?'

'Since you ask, Olly, yes, I did.'

'How romantic! And now, you think you love her?'

'I don't *think* I love her, Olly. I know I do.'

'Have you slept with her, Baz?'

'For Christ's sake!' exclaimed Basil angrily, and turned his back on her.

Olivia stared at the beautiful bare back of the man she loved, and could not believe that he had actually rejected her offer to make him a father, and fulfil his long-cherished hopes of a family. She compared her own still-youthful beauty with that of the scruffy-looking woman she had seen on the telly, sunburned and skinny, with a peeling nose and dull, matted dark hair. I don't believe he has slept with her at all, she reassured herself. It's a gross idea, utterly ridiculous. She's got a face like a dog, and I don't believe it's at all serious. In the morning, he'll feel quite differently, and we can patch things up and start again, I'm sure. Confidently, she closed her eyes and slept.

* * *

In the morning, at first light, she woke. Basil was lying on his back, still asleep, and she told herself what a star he was, and how much she loved him, in spite of his occasional temperamental behaviour. Darling Baz, she thought, I do love you. She covered his body with her own, and kissed him.

Still half asleep, his arms closed around her, and his response to her embrace was swift and passionate. Though his dream-haunted brain was filled with the image of Misha, Basil nevertheless found himself not only willing, but desperately eager to make love to his wife again. For Olivia, the experience was a revelation, and a timely reminder of what she had come very close to losing. When it was over, they lay in each other's arms, sweating and exhausted, and slept again.

When she woke, Olivia found herself alone in the bed. 'Baz?' she called, sitting up.

He came into the bedroom from the bathroom, buttoning his shirt. He had already showered, and washed his hair. 'Sorry, darling,' he said quietly. 'I shouldn't have done that.'

Olivia frowned, drawing her knees up to her chin. 'Why ever not? You're my husband, remember?'

'I told you last night, Olly. I love someone else, and I intend to share my life with her. Now, I feel as if I'd betrayed her.'

Olivia stared at him with disbelief. 'Are you telling me that you've stopped loving me, Baz? Is that it?'

'No, that's not it. Of course I love you, I always will. You know that.'

'I don't understand you, Baz. Why are you doing this to me?'

'Because you don't really need me, Olly, and Misha does. It's as simple as that.'

Swiftly, he pulled on his sweater, and went downstairs.

No amount of pleading or tears could induce Basil to change his mind. Finally she watched in appalled silence as Basil repacked his backpack and metal suitcase with his winter gear, then humped his baggage out to the waiting taxi.

'Goodbye,' he called from the yard. 'I'll be in touch.'

She did not reply, but ran to the window and watched the car go through the gate, and drive slowly away along the bumpy lane.

Chapter Thirteen

For twenty-four hours Olivia lay in bed, alternately weeping with anguish at her husband's abrupt departure, and angrily asking herself what it could be about Misha ben Bella that had persuaded him to behave so outrageously. It sure as hell can't be her looks, Olivia told herself, recalling with contempt the skinny, sunburned legs and arms, the worried face and unkempt dark hair of the woman she had seen on the telly.

Not once in the eleven years of their marriage had Basil looked at another woman, to the best of her knowledge, and never for a single moment had she considered the possibility that he might do such a thing. Equally, Olivia herself, though quite aware of her own considerable powers of attraction, had never felt the need to betray Basil in any way, and to her mind this made it all the more humiliating, as well as surprising, that he should have been the first to break the long-standing trust between them.

From the beginning, Olivia had understood that in marriage, one of the partners invests a lot more emotional mileage in the relationship than the other, and consequently suffers a greater loss of independence. She had never doubted that Basil loved her more than she loved him, or that he had wanted the marriage much more than she. He had good-naturedly deferred to her in all their important decisions, and certainly had never demanded any kind of sacrifice from her. That is, not until his recent obsession about starting a family. In any case, she thought, I even decided to go along with that in the end, so what's the big deal with him? What more could I offer, for Christ's sake, than feeling lousy and messing up my schedules for nine bloody months, and probably doing it more than once, so that he could have a bunch of kids to come home to? Selfish pig, she thought, it would be me, here all the time, having to put up with them in spite of any number of nannies, while he still went on bombing round the world, coming home every now and then, and being the star of the outfit. Sod that, she thought, and, with a sudden burst of energy, got out of bed.

All day long, Olivia wandered around the barn, trying to make some sort of sense of things, missing Basil badly, dissolving into tears of self-pity from time to time, though doing her best to work herself into a state of righteous anger against him.

It was not at all a usual thing for Olivia to agonize too much about her husband when he was away. Once he had departed, it was her habit to get on with her work straight away, and dismiss him from her consciousness. Today, however, she found herself unable to do this, although she unfolded her etching press, and prepared a stack of paper for printing. To her dismay, she could neither concentrate, nor see properly, for tears kept welling up and blurring her vision. In the end, she put everything away, and went out into the garden.

The geese were nowhere to be seen, and she frowned, wondering where they had got to. Shit, she thought, I didn't lock their door last night; I completely forgot about them, bloody things. With apprehension in her heart, she walked through the long dry grass to the shed where they normally spent the night. The door was open, and white feathers were scattered about the entrance, some of them bloodstained. Oh, God, she said to herself, that vile fox must have been here. One quick look through the shed door confirmed her worst fears, for the dead bodies of her little flock were huddled into a corner, their throats ripped out, only one or two of them partially eaten. 'Cruel bloody bastard,' she said coldly, 'you weren't even hungry, were you?' Oh, Baz, she thought, why aren't you here when I need you so badly? How the hell can I bury eight dead geese all on my own?

She went back to the barn, poured herself a whisky, and drank it slowly, standing beside the stove and feeling extremely sorry for herself, and furious with Baz. Then she got a pickaxe and a shovel from the toolshed, and went back to the scene of the massacre.

When she returned to the house, her mission accomplished, she looked again at her press, and knew that for the first time in her life the will to work had completely deserted her. She also knew that she had a compelling need to talk to somebody, to get a second opinion about the disaster that appeared to have overtaken her. I'd really like to talk to Hester, she thought; she'd know exactly how I feel, but it's not on, is it? I can't very well go and tell Baz's mum that he's dumped me, and expect to get any sympathy from her, can I?

Briefly, she considered driving to the farm in Normandy, to see her own mother and stepfather, knowing that they would be delighted to see her, and that their counsel, if sought, would be wise as well as sympathetic. But somehow she felt an extreme reluctance to admit to her parents, so long and so happily married themselves, and rarely, if ever, separated from each other, that her own marriage had failed.

Waking in the middle of the night, she came to a decision, and the next morning, she packed a bag, locked up the barn, got into her estate car, and drove rather fast along minor roads to the A6. There, she joined the southbound carriageway that would take her to Rémoulins, Uzès and Souliac.

* * *

It was just after half past seven in the evening, and already dark, when she drove into place de l'Eglise, and parked her car outside the presbytery. Dead tired after the long drive, tense and near to tears, she took her grip from the back seat, and locked the car. The iron gate gave its customary protesting squawk as she pushed it open, then let it swing shut behind her. She crossed the small courtyard to the big wooden double doors, and entered the house. The familiar old kitchen, with its vaulted ceiling, crumbling limestone walls and long farmhouse table, was empty and dim, though the light over the table was switched on, casting a muted glow on its mellow fruitwood surface.

From upstairs came the faint sound of a piano. Olivia put down her grip, took off her bomber jacket, and hung it on the back of the door. She went into the hall, and stood for a moment at the foot of the stone staircase, waiting until the last notes of a Schubert sonata had faded away. Slowly, she climbed the stairs, and went quietly into the beautiful salon, with its stone Renaissance chimney-piece, and its long windows overlooking the back courtyard garden. The room was furnished with admirable restraint, mostly with the exquisite eighteenth-century pieces collected by her grandparents and her uncle Giò, over the years. A few oak logs were burning in the fireplace, giving off a delicate scent of wood-smoke. One of the table-lamps was lit, and its soft light fell on a pair of feet, encased in coarse grey woollen socks, which protruded from the dropped end of a high-backed sofa standing in front of the fire.

'Hi, Giò,' said Olivia quietly, coming silently round the sofa, and standing beside the fire, offering her cold hands to the blaze.

'Bloody hell, woman! You scared the shit out of me!' Startled, Giò sat up, then immediately lay down again, and Olivia turned from the fire and looked down at him, admiring his wild greying curly hair, spread against the burnt-orange velvet cushions, his dark eyes, and long, thin limbs. Only the hair gave a clue to Giò's advancing years; to Olivia, he seemed to have the secret of eternal youth, and was still the same bachelor uncle Giò of her childhood. He gazed up at her, smiling, curious. 'So, what brings you here, my darling, now that the swallows have gone?'

'I need a shoulder to cry on, Giò.'

'Oh, God! You, too?'

'What do you mean?'

Giò sat up again, and looked at his watch. 'What about a drink, Olly?' Without waiting for a reply, he got up and went to the library table that stood in the centre of the salon. It was crowded with books and papers, a handsome ormolu lamp with a glossy black shade, a very large white azalea in a galvanized iron bucket, and a heavy silver salver on which stood bottles and glasses. 'Armagnac OK for you, darling?'

'Lovely, thanks.'

Giò poured the drinks and came back to the fireplace. He handed her glass to Olivia, and threw another log on the fire. They sat down together, and after a moment's silence, Giò looked seriously at his niece. 'It's Baz, isn't it?'

'Yes, it is.'

'What's happened?'

'He's buggered off, Giò. He came home, told me he was in love with some boring doctor he met at an SMO feeding-station in Sudan, then almost immediately left again. I don't even know where he's gone.'

'A woman doctor, I take it?'

'Yes, of course. What else?'

'Well,' said Giò, 'he certainly does get around, doesn't he?' He took a sip of his drink, observing Olivia's stricken expression as he did so. 'Sorry, Olly, that was a daft thing to say.'

'Doesn't matter. It's only too bloody true.' She looked at Giò, her eyes sad and sorrowful. 'Did he say anything to you, about him and me, Giò, when he was staying with you?'

Giò sighed, rather unwilling to discuss Basil in his absence. 'Well, yes, he did, as a matter of fact.'

'What did he say? Please tell me.'

'Not a lot, really, darling; just that he knows that your work is by far the most important thing in your life, and means much more to you than he does, or ever will.' He lifted his dark eyes to hers, a little shyly. 'He told me you didn't want to have his children, Olly. That's what hurts him the most, I think.'

Olivia passed a hand across her eyes. 'It's quite true, I did say that. I've been resisting the idea for years, until quite recently, that is.'

'Oh?'

'Yes. I stopped taking the pill a while ago, and on the night Baz came home I told him that I thought that perhaps it might be a good idea, having a couple of kids, after all.'

'So what's the problem, for Christ's sake?'

Olivia shrugged her shoulders, hopelessly. 'He didn't want to know, Giò. My decision to start a family came too late, it seems, on account of this Misha woman. He says he loves her, and she really needs him, whereas apparently I don't. So, eleven years of a good marriage is on the back burner as far as he's concerned, and he wants out.' Olivia glanced at Giò, and her blue eyes flashed maliciously. 'And she's not even pretty, that's the really galling thing.'

Giò laughed. 'You're incorrigible, Olly. Why don't you admit that you've brought it all on yourself, darling? Just accept the fact that you're a workaholic; that nothing's more important to you, not even Baz, and certainly not children.'

'Is it such a crime to take one's work seriously; to put it first, Giò?'

'No, certainly not. *Chacun à son truc*, my love. But that's not what Baz wants, and you're not going to change, Olly, however much you try to kid yourself. It's how you are, isn't it?'

Olivia shook her head, and tears filled her eyes,

spilling down her face. 'The trouble is, I really *do* love Baz, whatever he says, and it's terribly painful to me, that he thinks he's in love with another woman, Giò. You must see that?'

'That's just hurt pride, my dear old thing,' said Giò, brutally. 'You'll get over it, and sooner than you think.'

Alone at passage des Ebénistes, Misha's mood swung between relief at being safely back in her own territory, and a terrible exhausted depression that she seemed unable to shake off. After the intense heat of Sudan, the bright, windy October weather felt distinctly cold to her, and did nothing to alleviate her feelings of loneliness and isolation. She longed to pick up the telephone and get in touch with Paul, but recalling the reason for her abrupt departure from his life, Blanche's illness, knew that to try to rekindle their relationship would be a cruel and insensitive thing to do. Poor woman, she said to herself, she needs all the help and support she can get just now, obviously. In the end, she could not bring herself to be the cause of even more unhappiness. I'll just have to tough it out, she thought miserably.

The days crawled by with leaden slowness, and Misha carried out the tasks that seemed to her essential. She had the locks changed on her door, and left the telephone switched to the *répondeur* on a regular basis, so that Giles could not speak to her without her consent. She wrote to him, repeating her request that he should make arrangements to remove his belongings from her apartment. She got in touch with SMO, and, having thanked her for her efforts in Sudan, they regretfully agreed that there was little point in her continuing to work for them, if her health was not sufficiently robust to withstand the conditions in the field.

Choosing her time carefully, in order to minimize the risk of accidentally running into Paul, Misha went to the hospital to see Nicole Christophe, in order to discuss the question of her return to work.

'Misha! You look terrible, my dear! What have they done to you, for heaven's sake? Your poor face, so badly burnt! Didn't you take any sun-block with you?'

Misha looked embarrassed. 'It's better than it was, though it still looks pretty grim, I know. I did try to use sun-block and stuff, but somehow, out there, it seemed a bit irrelevant. I'm quite all right, really. I just need to gain a bit of weight.'

'Well, you don't look all right to me. I think you should go to Tropical Diseases and let them do a few tests, just to be on the safe side.'

'OK, I will, if you really think I should.' Misha smiled shyly, touched by the older woman's concern for her. 'In the meantime, I want to get back to work as soon as possible, and I was wondering if you could find me a place in another *équipe*? I thought, perhaps, general surgery?'

'Of course, I'll look into it, Misha, if you're absolutely sure that's what you want to do?'

'I'm sure.'

'OK. But first, I shall insist that you take some sick leave. Take care of yourself, go to the gym, try to build yourself up, and wait to hear from me.'

'Right, I will. Thank you; you're very kind.' Misha got to her feet, shook hands across the desk, and turned to go.

'Misha?'

'Yes?'

'Are you absolutely convinced that you really wish to make such a radical change? Your reports from Neurosurgery were remarkably promising, my dear.'

'Oh? Whose reports were they?'

'Professor de Vilmorin's, of course.'

Misha swallowed nervously, the blood draining from her face. 'But that was before I left the team, Mme Christophe.'

'No, it wasn't. It was since you took your sabbatical,

Misha. Quite recently, in fact. He told me that, in his opinion, you have a genuine future in neurosurgery.'

'But surely . . . ' Misha stammered, trying to understand what it was that the other woman was telling her.

'His professional regard for you remains the same, Misha. I think you have a right to know that, in the interests of your career. Think about it carefully before you decide on a fundamental change.'

'Thank you,' said Misha quietly. 'I will.'

'Come back and see me, after your leave, and we'll discuss it.'

'Yes, OK.'

The door closed on Misha, and Nicole Christophe sat for a long moment, examining her immaculate fingernails, then she smiled and shook her head. If I've done the wrong thing, she thought, I don't care; not at all. They are two really excellent people, and if they need an ally, they've certainly got one in me.

A week after she had asked Basil to leave, Misha received a call from him. He was still in Paris, he said, waiting for a new assignment. He would like to take Misha out for a meal, if she was free.

Lonely, and bored with her own company, Misha's spirits rose at the prospect of an evening out and she accepted the invitation at once. 'Come and have a drink here, first,' she offered.

'Thanks, I'd like that. I'll come round about eight, OK?'

'Fine, see you then.'

At five past eight, Paul de Vilmorin, as he continued to do from time to time, drove slowly down passage des Ebénistes to see whether by any chance a light was on in Misha's apartment. Since his last visit, when, in his distress at finding the evidence of her apparent reconciliation with Giles, he had put his keys on the table and left, he had told himself a thousand times that he must try to forget Misha, to let her go, if that was what she wanted. In the event, he had found such a thing quite impossible to do, and she remained constantly in his thoughts. The memory of her drew him relentlessly to the place where he still desperately hoped to find her again.

As he approached number sixteen, Paul saw a tall, bearded man speaking into the entryphone. He stopped the car, and watched as the door opened and the man disappeared through it. Paul looked up to the top floor, and at once saw the light shining on Misha's roof terrace. His heart leapt within him. Oh, God, he thought, she's there. In his excitement he very nearly took his phone from his pocket, and dialled Misha's number, then, prudently, thought it better to wait until he was quite sure that the bearded stranger was nothing to do with her, but was visiting someone else. Frowning, he tried to remember where he had seen the man before, for he had seemed vaguely familiar, but could not. He decided to wait, and see what, if anything, transpired. Very slowly, he reversed his car to the other end of the narrow little street, parked close to the high brick wall, and switched off his lights.

After twenty interminable minutes Paul's patience was rewarded, and his fears confirmed. Misha and the bearded man emerged from the building and walked away together towards rue de la Roquette. Despising himself for his actions, but unable to stop himself, Paul got out of his car and followed them. In rue de la Roquette, he found that they had disappeared into the evening crowds. One by one, he checked all the likely places, and finally located his quarry in a bistro he had never been to with Misha. Feeling exactly like a spy, he looked through the small curtained window. They were already eating, and had a bottle of wine on the table between them. The man said something to Misha, and she laughed. They looked happy to be together. Paul turned away, ashamed of his behaviour, in despair at what he had seen. He returned to his car and drove to rue de Thorigny.

* * *

For ten days, Basil came almost every evening to see Misha. Nearly always, they went out to eat, though once or twice Misha cooked supper at home. Aware that she was at a low ebb physically, as well as emotionally, Basil took great care not to pressurize her in any way at all, allowing their friendship to blossom quite naturally. He did not talk about Olivia, or about Misha's previous involvements, knowing that he would get a roasting from her if he did so. Instead, he wove a small spell of jokes and laughter around the woman he loved. He gave her small gifts of flowers; a bay tree for her garden; and because she admired it, a bracelet that he always wore, made of black elephant hair, bound with gold wire.

'No, Baz, I couldn't possibly take it.'

'Of course you can. I want you to have it.' He struck a ridiculous pose. 'As a symbol of my undying love for you, darling Misha.'

She laughed, but took it all the same, and slid it onto her arm.

'Actually,' said Baz, 'I mean it.'

'Of course you don't. This is all just a silly game, Baz. You know that.'

'If you say so.'

'I do.'

On the eleventh day, Basil called and said that he was off to Kabul; he would write whenever he got the chance.

'Don't write, Baz, please. Just give me a call when you get back, if you like.'

'That's probably best, OK. I love you, Misha.'

'Goodbye, Baz. Have a good trip.'

After Basil had gone, Misha was surprised at how much she missed his cheerful company, so that she was extremely glad to get a call from Nicole Christophe, offering her a three-month stint in ENT.

'One of their team is taking maternity leave. It occurred to me that it might suit you to fill in for her, while you make up your mind whether or not you wish to continue in neurosurgery.'

'Thank you very much,' said Misha. 'That would be great.'

'Good, that's excellent. Could you start at the beginning of the week? That would allow plenty of time to go through the procedures with Dr Aumont before she takes her leave.'

'Yes, of course. I'll be there, first thing on Monday.'

Misha slid back into hospital life with very little trouble. At first quite nervous that she might bump into Paul, she quickly realized that such an eventuality was virtually impossible; their departments were so far apart that they might have been working in different hospitals. She quite enjoyed the ENT work, but missed the heightened atmosphere of the neurosurgery unit, and the occasional drama of the more complex procedures. She knew that, ideally, if it were possible to work out an honourable method of co-existence with Paul, her burning desire was to continue in his discipline, and preferably as a member of his team.

Her evenings at passage des Ebénistes were long and lonely. On most days there was a message from Giles on the answering machine, which she erased after listening to the first few words. Once, she received a card from Basil, from Kabul. *Miss you. Hope to be in Paris for Christmas. Love B.* Smiling, Misha propped the card against the glass window in the kitchen.

She usually went early to bed, and it was before she slept that she allowed herself to think about Paul; wondering how he was, and how his wife was, too. Sometimes her need and hunger for him seemed to overwhelm her, particularly when she remembered the last time they had slept together, in that bed.

Sometimes she dreamed that they were together again. When she woke, full of joy, and then found herself alone in her bed, her disappointment and grief were profound. I'll have to get over it, she told herself, over and over again. I must; there's no other way.

Chapter Fourteen

One cold evening, at the beginning of December, Misha walked home from the Métro through lightly falling snow, the delicate white flakes melting as they hit the dark pavement, wet and gleaming under the street-lamps. As she hurried along, the snow settling on her eyelashes, powdering the backs of her grey woollen gloves and the front of her coat, Misha felt a sense of relief, almost excitement at the arrival of this harbinger of winter, the turn of the year and maybe the promise of a less unhappy future. A tentative cheerfulness bubbled up inside her at the possibility of Baz's company during his Christmas leave. Life's not all bad, she told herself, and almost believed it. She put the key into her lock and let herself into the building.

As Misha stepped out of the lift, she saw at once the brooding figure of Giles, wrapped in a long, expensive-looking black greatcoat, waiting at her door. Her heart sank like a stone, for she could tell from the grim expression on his face that he was angry, and that the visit was not intended to be in any way a friendly one. Slowly, she approached her door, without meeting his accusing eyes. Silently, she took her key from her bag, and as she did so, she smelt alcohol on his breath, and a thread of apprehension fluttered in her stomach. I must try not to antagonize him, she said to herself. Doing her best to stop her hand from shaking, she unlocked her door. 'Come in, Giles,' she said, very quietly, and he pushed roughly past her into the salon, without a word.

Still enveloped in his coat, Giles made a silent and comprehensive tour of the room, inspecting each of his valuable possessions in turn, running his fingers over the Japanese carvings, removing imaginary dust from the picture-frames. Leaving him to it, Misha went to the kitchen, unpacked her shopping, and, taking off her damp coat, hung it in the bathroom to dry. She looked at herself in the mirror, observing her unnatural pallor, her green eyes large with disquiet, and her dark hair, wet with melted snow, plastered against her skull. I must stay cool, she thought, and not let him get to me. She took several deep breaths, pinched her cheeks to induce a little colour and went back to the salon. There, she saw that Giles had already poured himself a large whisky, and had taken off his coat. He was sitting on the sofa, staring into his glass.

At Misha's approach, he lifted his yellow eyes, gleaming with malice, and stared at her. 'Sit down,' he ordered.

'I prefer to stand, Giles, if you don't mind.'

'I do mind. Sit down.'

She perched on the edge of the seat, at the other end of the sofa, her arms crossed.

'Have the goodness to explain why you haven't replied to my letters, Misha.'

'I didn't read them, Giles.'

'Why not?'

'Because.'

'What the hell do you mean, "because"? Don't be absurd!'

'I didn't read your letters, or listen to your messages, Giles, because I saw no point in doing so.' Misha turned her head and looked at him, coldly. 'And while we're on the subject of letters, I've written to *you* several times, asking you to remove your possessions from my apartment.'

'I got your letters, of course. That's how I knew you'd got back from your jaunt to Africa.'

'Who told you I was in Africa?'

'The old fart who claims to be your lover, Misha. I caught him here, alone, lying on my sofa as if he owned the place.'

'If you mean Paul, Giles, he had a perfect right to be here. I gave him a key.'

'Did you really? How touching!'

Misha sighed. 'Please answer my question, Giles. Why have you chosen to ignore my repeated requests to come and collect your things, and get out of my life, once and for all?'

'Because it's not necessary. You know perfectly well that we love each other, that there's no reason why we should not patch things up between us and go on as before. I love you, Misha, and I need you in my life. I know you love me, too, when all's said and done. I'm quite aware that I behaved badly towards you, but since that was largely as a result of my accident, I would've assumed that as a neurologist you'd understand that, darling.'

Hopelessly, Misha gazed at him. 'Really, Giles, is it possible that you really believe that I could easily forget about Juliet, and your little girl? That you and I could just paper over the cracks, and go on as before?'

'I can't think of a good reason why not.'

'You can't be serious.'

'I'm *bloody* serious, Misha! What are you playing at, for Christ's sake? I've got rid of Juliet and the kid – what's to stop us taking advantage of that colossal stroke of luck? Nothing at all, *nothing*! You're by far the best shag I've ever had, and I don't intend to let you go, either, even if you are a tad miffed with me at the moment.'

'Miffed is not the word I would use to describe the negative feelings I have for you, Giles.' Misha's voice was subdued, very quiet, but perfectly clear.

'Particularly after the squalid trick you pulled the last time you were here.'

Giles laughed, and took a long swallow of his whisky. 'You surprise me, darling. You used to enjoy jokes like that, I seem to recall, and not so long ago, either.'

'Well, things have changed, haven't they, Giles? My life is no longer any concern of yours, and I'd be glad if you'd leave at once, please.'

Without replying, Giles got up, went to the kitchen rather unsteadily and fixed himself another drink. Still perched tensely on the edge of the sofa, Misha glanced furtively at her watch: ten past seven. Why doesn't he *leave*, horrible man? she said to herself.

'Let me get this straight, Misha.' Giles came back into the salon, speaking in a loud, hectoring tone. 'I take it you're still shagging your elderly boyfriend, is that it?'

Misha stared at him, her stomach churning, her mind a blank.

'Well?'

'Well, what?'

'Well, what have you got to say for yourself, you two-timing slag?'

Giles grabbed Misha's arm, and dragged her to her feet, spilling his drink as he did so. The heavy tumbler slipped from his wet fingers and fell with a crash onto the low table, splitting the glass top from end to end. 'Now look what you've made me do, you stupid bitch!' he yelled, and, drawing back his free arm, punched Misha in the mouth with all his strength. With a sickening awareness, she felt a front tooth crack in her jaw, tasted warm blood, and knew that her upper lip was split. She struggled to free herself from Giles's grasp, but her knees sagged beneath her, until she was kneeling at his feet.

Excited by the idea of punishing the woman who seemed utterly determined to reject his love, goaded by the sight of her bloody and badly damaged face, Giles drew back his right foot and kicked Misha in the side of her stomach, twice, with all the violence of which he was capable, at the same time twisting her arm before thrusting her away from him. With a shriek of agony, Misha fell heavily onto the table, which disintegrated into shards of glass under the weight of her body.

For a few moments, quite surprised by the extent of the damage he had inflicted on her, Giles stood rooted to the spot, staring down at the limp, unconscious form of the woman whose love he had taken for granted. Though he could see only half of her face, he saw that her eyes were closed, and that her skin was deathly pale. Blood poured from her nose and mutilated mouth, as well as from her hands and arms, badly cut in her despairing attempt to break her fall. Stupid woman, he thought, why couldn't she have fallen on the sofa? The bloody table's ruined. He hesitated, trying to decide whether to get Misha some water, or maybe a brandy, to bring her round. Then, suddenly, he noticed that blood was pouring from one of her cut wrists, forming a dark and glistening pool on the glass-littered floor. Jesus! he thought, she's probably dead! Or dying, at any rate.

Terrified, he thought rapidly, then, looking wildly round, saw Misha's bag lying on the floor, and took her organizer from it. With shaking hands, he looked up de Vilmorin's mobile phone number, and dialled it. Paul, about to drive out of the hospital car park, took the call at once.

'*Monsieur de Vilmorin?*' Giles put his hand over his mouth to disguise his voice, and spoke French.

'*Oui.*'

'*Il y a eu un accident, monsieur. Misha a besoin de votre assistance. Toute de suite.*'

'Where is she, Murray-Williams?' asked Paul quietly, not at all deceived by Giles's attempt at anonymity.

'She's at home.'

'I'll come at once.'

Giles Murray-Williams, white-faced and thoroughly alarmed, rang off. He pulled on his overcoat, picked up his bag, and let himself out of the apartment, leaving the door open, since he had no way of knowing whether or not de Vilmorin had a key. Shaking with terror, he went down in the lift, and before leaving the building, jammed the front door open with a telephone directory he found in the entrance hall.

Once in the street, he ran to rue de la Roquette, hailed a passing cab and drove straight to Gare du Nord. There, he bought a ticket to London, checked the time of departure, and, seeing that he would have some time to wait, went in search of a café. Realizing that if he consumed any more alcohol he might be refused access to the train, he drank several cups of black coffee, and ate a *croque-monsieur*.

For the first time in his life, Giles was really frightened by what he had just done. He was in no way ashamed of his behaviour; he felt quite convinced that Misha had brought it on herself, and deserved to suffer. He was, however, terrified that she might die. If she dies, he told himself bleakly, that bastard de Vilmorin has all the evidence he needs to stitch me up, doesn't he?

After the third coffee, he felt less panicky, and somewhat clearer in his mind. Actually, I don't think that's necessarily the case, he thought. They would be a bit pushed to find many clues to my being there, really. Fingerprints on the glass of whisky, I suppose, but that's all smashed and mixed with blood and stuff. Disgusting, he thought, and suddenly, tears filled his eyes. He blew his nose, and picked up the evening paper left behind by a previous occupant of the table. On the front page was an account of a brawl outside a wine-bar, during which a drunken young man had been punched on the chin by another youth. He had fallen, knocking his head against the stone kerb of the pavement, and had, unfortunately, died of his injuries. There you are, said Giles to himself, it was an accident, of course: nothing more or less. Such things happen all the time; it's no-one's fault, is it?

Fifteen minutes after receiving the call from Giles Murray-Williams, Paul arrived at passage des Ebénistes, took his emergency bag from the boot of his car and went up to Misha's apartment as quickly as he could. He passed through the open door, closed it carefully behind him, and looked swiftly round the room. All was silent, and apparently in its usual state of tidiness. 'Misha?' he called softly, but there was no reply. Frowning, thinking that she was perhaps in the bedroom, he began to move towards the kitchen. He drew level with the sofa, and immediately stopped dead in his tracks, frozen with horror. He had been expecting to find Misha injured in some way; he had not expected to find her lying in a chaos of blood and broken glass, presenting every appearance of being dead. He put his bag down, then, pushing aside some of the vicious shards of glass, knelt beside Misha's motionless and blood-stained body, and gently turned her into the recovery position. He placed two fingers on her carotid artery, and to his indescribable relief, felt a faint pulse. Immediately, he took his phone from his pocket and called the ambulance unit from his own hospital. 'Be as quick as you can, please,' he said. 'It's urgent.'

He opened his bag, and took from it several sterile packs, put a temporary suture across the great gash in Misha's lip, then covered it with a dressing. He was, at the back of his mind, surprised at the volume of blood produced by the damage to her face, and it was not until he turned his attention to her hands that he realized that both her wrists were deeply lacerated and bleeding copiously. His hands shaking, he removed the splinters of glass, and sutured the wounds, packing them where he thought it necessary. Then, in order to check for further damage, he carefully cut away Misha's shirt and her track-suit bottoms. At once he saw the extensive bruising to her abdomen, with the imprint of the woven fabric of her clothing clearly marked on the skin. Oh God, he thought, that bastard must have kicked her as she lay on the ground. This almost certainly implies a visceral injury; probably a ruptured spleen.

Meticulously, he examined Misha's limp body for further damage to her back, neck or limbs. Thankfully, all seemed well. He knelt beside her, talking to her softly as he removed the fragments of glass that still clung to her. Once, her eyelids fluttered for a second, and she tried to lift her head. 'Keep still, my darling,' he said. 'You're all right now; don't worry.'

Paul heard the urgent wail of the ambulance siren, in the street below. In a moment, the entryphone buzzed, and he went to the door and pressed the answering button. 'Come up to the top floor,' he said. 'You'll need a stretcher.'

Once in the ambulance and on the way to the hospital, the paramedic inserted a line into the back of Misha's injured hand as best he could in the circumstances, and hung a drip above the cot to which she was strapped. Anxiously, Paul sat beside her head, praying that she had not lost too much blood, willing her to regain consciousness. As the ambulance drew up at the entrance to A and E, and the doors were opened, Misha opened her eyes briefly, and, seeing Paul beside her, tried to say something but slid back into unconsciousness.

'Take her straight to theatre,' said Paul. 'She needs urgent attention, and probably surgery.'

If the paramedic was surprised to find himself in an emergency situation involving the Professor of Neurology and one of the younger women doctors, he did not permit himself to show it, but gave orders to his crew to take Dr ben Bella up to theatre at once, while Paul called the registrar on his mobile to warn him of her imminent arrival and need for blood and immediate attention. 'She has other superficial injuries, François, but this is a question of blunt abdominal trauma, probably splenic rupture, I'm afraid. You are far better qualified than I to treat her. She is not fully conscious, but as she has no relatives in this country, I will sign the consent form on her behalf, if it's a question of surgery.'

'Point taken,' said François. 'I'll go straight to her.'

'Good,' said Paul. 'And thanks.'

Apart from the births of his two children, Paul had never before had to suffer an agonizing wait for news as the responsibility for the life of someone so close to his heart was, of necessity, taken out of his hands, leaving him nothing to do. Rather than hang about until Misha came out of surgery, making a public display of his anxiety, Paul left a message asking François to call him as soon as she was in recovery, and took a cab back to passage des Ebénistes. With a heavy heart, he entered the apartment, and telephoned the police. They arrived with commendable speed, and Paul made a statement, giving them all the information that he had, including the name of the assailant and the address of his place of work.

The officer in charge of the case thanked him. 'In matters of domestic violence, we do not usually proceed unless the victim wishes to press charges. We will interview Dr ben Bella when she has recovered a little, and then a decision can be reached.'

'And if she dies?'

'That would be quite another matter, monsieur. It goes without saying, we would advise London to arrest the man immediately.'

'Good.'

The police took some fingerprints from the whisky bottle in the kitchen, then saluted politely and left.

Paul went out onto the roof garden. A full moon rose over the rooftops, and he stood in the cold air, looking at it with something like horror. It reminded him of the night that he had come to the apartment and listened to Misha's tape, over and over again. He remembered how he had come out here on the roof, and had sat for hours, looking at the moon, and feeling his heart breaking within him. What am I doing here? he asked himself. I should be at the hospital.

He went back to the kitchen and poured himself a small whisky, then put on his coat and prepared to leave. As he came out onto the street his phone buzzed, and swiftly, he took it from his pocket. 'Yes?'

'Paul, it's me, François. Misha's OK. She's quite poorly, but stable. We did a CT scan, followed by a laparotomy and a small splenic repair. She's in recovery now. Her vital signs are OK and her colour's pretty good. I'll transfer her to a private room in a few minutes. We'll keep a careful eye on her, but she'll be fine, I'm sure.'

'Right, I understand. Thank God you were on duty, François.'

'Thank God you got to her in time, Paul, is more to the point. She's a lucky woman.'

Paul laughed, ironically. 'Do you really think so?'

'Yes, Paul, I do, as a matter of fact.'

'Well, thank you very much. It's kind of you to say so, François.'

'My pleasure. Will you be coming in to see her?'

'Yes, of course. I'm on my way.'

Paul got into his car. He sat still for a few minutes, breathing slowly, trying to calm his racing pulse, telling himself that Misha was OK, that the horror was over, that now it would be a simple matter of rebuilding her health and her confidence. The important thing will be to look after her, protect her from Murray-Williams, and make sure that he never sets foot in her life again, though after what he's done, the bloody lunatic, I don't really think he'd have the audacity to try. Paul looked at the car clock: nine forty-two. Incredible, he thought; it seems an absolute eternity since he phoned me.

He drove slowly back to the hospital. He checked with the night sister at the nurses' station, was told that Misha was awake and comfortable, and given the number of her room. He tapped at her door and went in. A dimmed light burned on the wall at the head of her bed, and he found her sleeping peacefully, hooked up to a drip and a blood pack, her battered mouth now neatly stitched, her hands and arms in heavy dressings. Her face was swollen and badly bruised and she had a dark gash across her cheekbone, under her left eye. Her hair lay in damp flakes against her forehead, and from this Paul deduced that she was probably running a temperature.

He sat down on the chair beside the bed, and very gently slid his hand under the fingers that protruded from the dressings of her left hand. Almost imperceptibly, he felt her fingers curl round his hand, and she opened her beautiful green eyes, mercifully undamaged, and looked straight at him. 'Darling Paul,' she mumbled indistinctly. 'I knew you'd come.'

'I'll always be there for you, Misha. You know that, don't you?'

She tried to smile, but could not. Instead tears filled her eyes, and rolled down the sides of her face into her hair.

'Don't cry, darling, please. You're safe now; everything will be fine, you'll see.'

Chapter Fifteen

Olivia unhooked the calendar from her kitchen wall, and turned it to the last page, December. She sat down at the long table, and began to copy all the important engagements from her diary, writing them in red ink on the empty dates of the calendar, to be sure she would not forget them. As it happened, there were not many planned events for the new month: just two exhibition openings, fairly close together, an appointment with the dentist in Orléans, lunch with her agent in Paris, and then it would be Christmas. Whether she would spend the holiday at Souliac, with Giò, or maybe go to Normandy, she had not yet decided. It was quite possible that she would remain here, presumably alone.

It was now two months since Baz had departed so abruptly from her life, and she had not heard from him in all that time. Three weeks ago, she had seen him, briefly, on the telly, so she knew that he was probably still in Afghanistan. Pride, and a residual anger, had prevented her from contacting his colleagues at work to check on his movements, and safety. I guess they'd be in touch if anything happened to him, she had reassured herself rather grimly, and turned her attention, as usual, to her work. October and November had been productive months, and she had completed a new set of twenty-four etchings, in three colours, inspired by the organic shapes she saw in the rocks, woods and marshy ponds around her home. A little stung by Baz's unkind remarks to her on the subject of her supposed occupation of a personal ivory tower, Olivia had deliberately broadened her perceptions, and the themes of her most recent work were corruption and death in the natural world. Even slaughtered geese had found their way into many of her new, tougher images. Already, she was halfway through the lengthy print-run, and felt entirely confident that she had everything well in hand for her spring exhibition.

She turned back to October in her diary, and noted that Baz had left on the second. She also observed with some surprise that she had not made her usual red dot, signifying the arrival of her period, in the middle of the month. Frowning, she turned the page and saw that there was no red dot for November, either. She turned to September. Yes, the dot was there, on the sixteenth, and clearly marked in August, July and June, as well. I don't believe this, Olivia said to herself, feeling the rush of blood to her cheeks; it can't be true, surely? There's no way I could be pregnant, after only one stab at the cherry, is there? She put a hand to her hot face, and shook her head. I can't be, she thought. I don't feel ill, or sick, or anything at all out of the ordinary. In fact, taking everything into consideration, like Baz's rotten behaviour, I feel perfectly well. I'm a bit lonely, of course, bloody man, but OK in every other respect. Really, Baz, she thought, you are the pits: you get me in the club, and then bugger off. She did a quick calculation, and came to the conclusion that she might have been pregnant for a couple of months without realizing it, and suddenly she laughed aloud, imagining Baz's pride and happiness when she told him the news. Actually, she said to herself, I feel pretty good about it myself, in a way. If it's happened, then I'm glad. I can't wait to tell him. I'd better send him a fax.

After lunch, realizing that perhaps a fax was rather a public way of informing Baz that he was an expectant father, Olivia sat down and wrote a long and loving letter to her husband, in the certain knowledge that when he heard about the baby his feelings for Misha would fade pretty swiftly. She sealed and stamped the letter, but decided not to go to the village to post it, for it was raining. She would give it to the postman in the morning. After all, it was not really so very urgent; the baby would not cease to exist, would it?

Olivia spent a strange afternoon, mostly feeling cheerful and triumphant, and as if she and Baz had done something extremely clever. At other times she felt herself to be slightly apprehensive, and still not at all sure that she really wanted a child at all. By six o'clock she had convinced herself that it might be better to delay telling Baz the good news. She would wait until the middle of the month, and then, if her period failed to materialize yet again, she would go to Paris, see her gynaecologist, and have a proper examination to confirm her suspicions. That way, there could be no question of a mistake or a miscalculation. After all, she thought, I don't actually have any of the usual symptoms, do I? Perhaps it's just my hormones up the creek?

Misha lay in her hospital bed, staring at the ceiling, and trying not to move. Though the injuries to her face and hands were healing well, and she could now move her fingers without feeling much pain, her abdomen was still badly bruised and tender, so that she was unable to sit up without assistance. She was still heavily reliant on painkillers, and a sedative at night.

Each evening, after work, Paul visited her briefly, but avoided the subject of Giles and his atrocious behaviour towards her. After a somewhat harrowing visit from the police, and her subsequent decision not to press charges against Giles, Paul saw little point in endless discussion of the brutal and sordid details of the attack, and for this Misha was thankful. Equally, it seemed to him an entirely inappropriate moment to discuss her unlooked-for disappearance from his life, and in any case, now that they had re-established contact, the question had become relatively unimportant to him.

Alone for most of the day, Misha had plenty of time to dwell on the details of Giles's visit, and the horrific beating she had suffered at his hands. Looking back over the seven years of what she had assumed was a civilized and romantic relationship with an exceptionally cultivated man, she found it difficult to believe that her perceptions of Giles could have been so wide of the mark, or that he could have been capable of an assault that might easily have killed her.

Physically weakened, and emotionally shattered, she blamed herself for what had happened. I should have seen him for what he was, years ago, she said to herself miserably; before he became a habit for me, almost a drug, in a way. Silent tears of self-pity, and of shame in respect of some of her less than edifying memories of Giles's sexual proclivities, filled her eyes and soaked her pillow several times a day, eliciting sympathetic noises from the nursing staff, and a fresh pillowcase.

By the third day, Misha's physical injuries were a lot better, and she found that the nightmare of Giles's violence was beginning to occupy her thoughts rather less. Instead, she found herself in a confused state of mind, trying to piece together the implications of the events of the last few days. How was it that Paul had known about Giles's attack? she asked herself. How did he get into the apartment without a key? I must ask him what happened. In any case, we need to talk, to get things straight between us, don't we? She stared at her bandaged hands, as they lay on the thin sheet that covered her painful stomach, and was filled with hopelessness and despair. There isn't anything to get straight, is there? she asked herself. It's over between Paul and me, except as colleagues perhaps. It has to be; Nina was quite justified in what she did for the sake of her mother. I'd have done the same thing myself, in similar circumstances, I'm sure I would.

Late that evening, having worked through a long and difficult list, Paul came to see Misha. She had finished her supper, and was drinking a glass of water through a straw. Desperate for something to eat, for he had had nothing since his early lunch, Paul had bought a packet of crisps from a vending machine, and, tearing the packet open, began to consume them hungrily.

Misha, watching him, smiled. 'You look as if you could do with a drink, too,' she said.

'I could,' said Paul. He took a half-bottle of claret from his pocket, and unscrewed the cap. 'I can't tempt you?'

Misha laughed. 'I wish,' she said. 'But I'd better not, I suppose.'

Paul took a tooth-glass from the basin, and poured himself some wine. He sat down beside the bed. 'When did you get back from Africa, Misha?' he asked quietly.

Misha looked startled at the question, and shot an anxious glance in his direction. She frowned. 'It must be nearly two months now, I suppose. Why?'

'You didn't call me?'

'No.'

'Why not?'

Misha's eyes filled with tears. 'How can you ask me that, Paul? Because of your wife, of course. You must know that already.'

'Why because of Blanche, Misha?'

'Her illness, of course.'

'What illness?'

Misha stared at him. 'Nina came to see me after you'd gone to Ménerbes. She told me that Blanche has non-Hodgkin lymphoma, and hasn't long to live.'

'Did she really? And that was why you left, I suppose?'

'It was a good enough reason, wasn't it? How is she, anyway, poor woman?'

'As far as I'm aware, Misha, she's in excellent health.'

'Paul! Is this true?'

'Absolutely.' He took her hand, very gently. 'So you see, we have both endured months of misery, all for nothing.'

'Is that how you see it, Paul?'

'Yes, I do. Don't you?'

Misha was silent. She felt numb, shaky and confused. At last, hesitantly, she spoke. 'I don't know how I really feel, after all this time.' She looked at him and her eyes were filled with anguish. 'It was hell on earth out there, Paul. Why didn't you try to contact me? Did you know where I was?'

'Yes, I did.' He looked away, not meeting her eyes. 'I thought that you would prefer that I didn't try to reach you, Misha.' Sadly, he looked at her. 'It's too late, isn't it? Obviously, you've moved on; things aren't the same between us, are they?'

'Aren't they?'

'I'm ashamed to tell you, but I have a confession to make, my darling. I've been spying on you, watching your movements. I saw you with your good-looking bearded friend.'

'Oh, Paul, that's only Baz!'

'He seemed to be extremely fond of you, Misha. Is he?'

'He thinks he is. It's just a game. He'll get over it, I'm sure.'

'Tell me about him. He looks a decent sort of chap, anyway.'

'He is. He was very kind to me in Sudan, and got me home sooner than I intended, because I was sick. He's a correspondent on the telly; he came out to do a piece about SMO, that's how we met. He's gone to Kabul, now.'

'I see.'

On his way back to rue de Thorigny, Paul told himself that if Misha had found a new and sympathetic friend, then this was probably the moment for him to try to reconstruct himself into more of a father-figure, mentor and professional colleague; a close friend to her, but not her lover. If, as looked quite likely, Misha was in the process of forming a new liaison, such a change in their relationship would be inevitable. Though his heart might break, at least he would still be able to see her on an almost daily basis. Surely, he could find some happiness in that?

It did not take Blanche very long to notice how much less ill Paul was looking, and to draw the inference that Misha ben Bella must have returned to Paris, and was once more the centre of her husband's life. She realized that her previous efforts at bringing to an end Paul's adulterous liaison, although brilliantly successful in removing Misha from the picture, had proved counter-productive in every other respect, and had in no way improved her own matrimonial relations.

Her first thought was to speak to Nina, before deciding what to do. She picked up the telephone, and then, on second thoughts, returned it to its cradle. She sat at her desk, staring out of the window at the frost-bitten little garden. It's only a week or two before Emma's twins are due, she reminded herself; I'm certain Paul will be really keen to see them. Perhaps we could drive down to Ménerbes together for Christmas, and go over to Mas les Arnauds to pay them a visit. So many new de Vilmorins will make him realize how important his family is to him, and he'll see the ben Bella woman for what she is, merely a bit on the side. Clearly, my best option is to pretend I don't know what's happening, stay cool and earn myself brownie points by being the perfect, super-indulgent grandmother.

With this image of herself at the forefront of her mind, Blanche took a cab to the gardens of the Palais Royal, where she spent a happy couple of hours in a specialist shop in one of the arcades, spending a very great deal of money on exquisite baby clothes for her imminently expected grandsons.

A couple of evenings later, she waylaid Paul as he

entered the house and took him to see the beautiful handmade garments she had bought, and had arranged on a bed in a spare room. 'Mm,' he said. 'Very nice, my dear.' Privately, he thought it more than likely that Emma would have her own ideas about suitable clothing for her little boys, and that these would probably not include things made from silk and lace.

'We could take them over, together, as a surprise for Emma, couldn't we, when we go down for Christmas?' Blanche smiled, pleased to have found a way of introducing the subject without seeming to pressurize her husband. 'Have you thought about which day you'd like to travel, darling?'

'No, I haven't, Blanche. I'm not really sure if I'll be able to get away for Christmas.'

Blanche's face fell. 'Don't you want to see the babies?'

'Yes, yes, of course I do. I might have to make a flying visit, though. You go down with Olivier and Catherine, as usual. Don't you think that would be best?'

'If you say so, Paul, of course.'

Lying awake in the small hours of the morning, Blanche stared at the grey silk of her bed-hangings and rather wished herself dead. He really hates me, she thought, I can tell. He looks through me as though I were part of the furniture, or a slightly irritating dog, fawning all over him, trying to get his attention, and failing, utterly.

It was becoming increasingly clear to her that Paul's feelings for Misha were still deeply serious, and that nothing she could do, short of murdering the intruder, would make any difference. I suppose the next thing will be his asking me for a divorce, she told herself bitterly, and there's not a lot I can do to stop that, either, except delay things for as long as possible. She could visualize only too clearly the spiteful glee of her friends when the news became public knowledge, the sniggering behind hands, the cruel references to her age, compared to that of Paul's mistress. It's disgusting, repulsive, she thought; how can she bear to have sex with a man more than twenty years older than herself? Then, with unusual honesty, she remembered watching Paul last summer, as she sat under the olives pretending to read, though in fact she had been having a good look at her husband's near-naked body as he swam endlessly in the pool at Ménerbes. He had not grown fat in middle age, as Olivier had; his muscles had not yet sagged, as her own had, after the birth of her children. He had not even developed a double chin. Apart from his silver hair, and some quite deep lines around his eyes, he was still the good-looking man she had married. It's not fair, said Blanche to herself, angrily. It's always the bloody same; everything's stacked against us women, even our hormones. Men have it all their own way, the sods. They even have the luck to die first, usually. I hate them all, I really do.

Nevertheless, she recovered her spirits sufficiently to go out to lunch with Olivier the following day, alone, for Catherine was suffering from a migraine. After the second glass of champagne, she told her deeply sympathetic friend and occasional lover that the ben Bella woman had returned to Paris and that she, Blanche, was of the opinion that Paul was on the point of seeking a divorce. 'If that's the way the cat jumps,' she said acidly, 'I'll screw him for everything he's got, the philandering shit.'

'Quite right,' said Olivier and refilled her glass, in anticipation of an afternoon trip to Blanche's bedroom. 'Though, of course, you'll never get that house in Burgundy, darling. It doesn't belong only to Paul, does it?'

'He's welcome to the bloody place,' said Blanche. 'It's falling apart, anyway.'

Giles Murray-Williams, safe and alone in his little house in Chelsea, decided that a bout of flu would be an excellent way of giving himself time to formulate a plan for the reorganization of his life. He therefore telephoned Cunningham's, in order to inform his secretary that he was indisposed, and would be away from the office for a few days.

'It's lucky you called, Mr Murray-Williams. A gentleman from Paris phoned yesterday afternoon, wanting to speak to you, but you'd gone.'

Giles swallowed, nervously. 'Did he give his name?' he asked.

'Yes, he did. And his number. Hang on, I'll get it for you.' After a short pause, she added: 'Right, here we are. It's a Professor de Vilmorin. You can reach him at his weekday clinic, he says, before nine a.m., European time.' She read out the telephone number, then repeated it. 'His extension number is thirty-eight, he says.'

'Right, thanks very much. I'll call him from here.'

'Look after yourself, Mr Murray-Williams. Feel better soon, won't you?'

'Thank you,' said Giles, forlornly, 'I will.'

He replaced the telephone, and looked at his watch: nine forty-six. It's too late to call him today, he thought. I wonder what he wants? The alarming thought crossed his mind that Misha might have died, and a shiver of apprehension caused goose-bumps to erupt on his back, and his throat to contract, making it difficult to swallow. Don't be ridiculous, he said to himself, gazing at his own blurred image in the Venetian mirror that hung on the wall above the telephone table. It's been five days now, and if anything like that had happened, they'd have been on to me by now, that's for sure.

The five days in question had been a difficult and uneasy time for Giles, causing him to jump violently every time the telephone rang, even in the office. He had gone through the motions of his work, even assisting at an auction, but had found it almost impossible not to listen to the sub-text that ran perpetually through his head. After a couple of totally sleepless nights, he had at last decided that there was little point in contemplating any kind of reconciliation with Misha.

Giles found himself thrown into a state of acute disquiet by the message from Paul de Vilmorin, and since he could not endure the thought of having to wait to speak to him until the following morning, he decided to ring the hospital straight away, and leave his ex-directory number with de Vilmorin's secretary, so that Paul could call him back as soon as he was free. Having got through to Paris and left his message without any difficulty, Giles replaced his phone. As he did so he realized that he would now be stuck in the house all day, not daring to go out, or even into the garden, in case the phone rang. He went down to his sitting-room, where there was an extension telephone, and lay down on his chesterfield, to wait.

The phone rang at twelve forty-five. Giles let it ring four times, then picked it up. 'Yes?'

'Murray-Williams?'

'Speaking.'

'Good. I should be obliged if you would make arrangements to remove your possessions from Misha's apartment, before the end of the week.'

'Before the end of the *week*?' Giles's voice rose to a squeak. 'What the hell do you mean, before the end of the week? It's Tuesday now.'

'So?'

'I need more time. Such things take a good deal of organizing.'

'Rubbish. Unless you've been dismissed from your job, Murray-Williams, it's obvious to me that you must have at your disposal any number of removal vans, as well as the necessary workmen. Please arrange to be there to carry out the work on Saturday morning. I will be there myself, at eight-thirty, local time, to let you in, and to look after Misha's interests, since she is still in hospital.'

After a short pause, Giles spoke in a subdued voice. 'How is she, anyway?'

'She is recovering, no thanks to you, you murderous thug.'

'I see.'

'I hope you *do* see, Murray-Williams. You should count yourself lucky that Misha decided not to press charges against you, but if you ever try to pull such a stunt again, I won't answer for the consequences.'

'Are you by any chance threatening me, de Vilmorin?'

'Yes, I bloody am. Just be at passage des Ebénistes with your van, at eight-thirty on Saturday, or you'll find your stuff outside, stacked on the pavement. Understood?'

'Understood,' said Giles faintly. 'I'll be there.'

So terrified was he that de Vilmorin would carry out his threat to dump his belongings in the street, that Giles turned up with his hired van shortly after half past seven, when it was still dark and the streets were comparatively uncrowded. He had brought with him a driver and two removal men from his London office, and they sat huddled together in the cab, trying to keep warm, until Paul de Vilmorin, driving his Mercedes, arrived at twenty minutes past eight.

Stiffly, Giles got out of the van, followed by his team, each of them carrying a tea-chest. Silently, Paul let them into the building, and equally silently, they all crowded into the lift and went up to the top floor. Once inside the apartment, Paul pointed to the broken glass that still lay on the floor beside the sofa. 'I suggest that you remove the glass first, Murray-Williams, and then clean the blood-stains off the floor, before moving your possessions.' Silently, Paul watched as a flustered, red-faced Giles supervised this operation, doing his best to ignore the raised eyebrows and interested glances of his three assistants.

The foreman, Bert, picked up the pieces of chrome

that had once formed the frame of the table. 'Are these to go, then?' he asked.

'Save them, please,' said Giles. 'I may need them, to claim on the insurance. It was a very valuable table; unique, actually.' Shiftily, Giles glanced towards Paul, then immediately averted his eyes, his soul shrivelled by the unmistakable hatred in the dark eyes of the older man.

'You'd better get a move on,' said Paul coldly. 'I haven't got all day.'

By nine-thirty all the major furniture had been man-handled down to the van, and strapped into position, protected by copious layers of bubble-plastic. Then, fussily supervised by Giles, all the loose stuff, the CDs, books, videos, art magazines, small sculptures, the nautilus shells and silver candlesticks, were carefully wrapped and packed into the tea-chests.

Paul looked at the candlesticks. 'You're quite sure those are yours, Murray-Williams?' he asked stonily.

'Are you calling me a thief?'

'Nothing about you would surprise me, after your recent behaviour.'

The workmen looked at each other, eyebrows raised, ears pricked. Giles, turning a ripe shade of beetroot, said nothing, but placed his candlesticks in the chest, taking care not to damage the nautilus shells in the process. In another half-hour the chests were full, and their lids nailed down.

'Good,' said Paul quietly. 'Now, all that remains are the Braques, I take it?' He looked at the collection of drawings and paintings, still hanging on the wall.

'Well, yes,' said Giles, looking slightly embarrassed. 'Though there's still quite a bit of my stuff in the bed-room and bathroom, I believe.'

'No, there isn't.'

'What do you mean, there isn't?'

'Exactly that, Murray-Williams. Misha had the good sense to chuck all your clothes and the rest of your stuff into the public bin when she came home.' Paul stared at Giles with open contempt, choosing not to lower his voice in the presence of the workmen. 'In my view, it was an entirely appropriate action, in the face of your invasion of her privacy. You're lucky that she didn't throw the Braques into the *poubelle*, along with the rest of the rubbish.'

At such an idea, the colour drained from Giles's face, and his forehead shone with beads of sweat. 'Misha would never do such a thing,' he said, with as much dignity as he could muster. 'She is not a philistine.'

'No,' said Paul, and smiled ironically. 'Indeed, she is not.'

When the Braques, with the corners of their ornate frames protected by polystyrene padding, had been wrapped in thick layers of corrugated cardboard and a waterproof outer layer, Paul accompanied Giles and the removal men on their last trip down to the waiting van. There, standing on the pavement and pointedly ignoring Giles, he gave Bert a five-hundred franc note. 'Thank you,' he said. 'You and your men have done an excellent job. I suggest you buy yourselves a good breakfast, before your long drive back to England.'

Bert took the money, with a pleased smile. 'Thank you, sir. It was a pleasure to be of assistance, I'm sure.'

'The pleasure was all mine,' said Paul. 'Turn left out of here, and you'll find a first-class café, in the second street on the right. You can even get real bacon and eggs there. It's called *Le Canard*, you can't miss it.'

Giles frowned, uneasily. 'I don't think that's a particularly clever idea, de Vilmorin. It would mean leaving the van unattended.'

'Of course it wouldn't, Murray-Williams,' said Paul smoothly, permitting himself a small vindictive smile. 'Naturally, you would wish to remain in the van and guard your own property, wouldn't you?'

The van drove off, and Paul returned to the apartment. He opened all the doors and windows, and let the cold air blow through the rooms. He got a broom from the kitchen cupboard, and swept the floor of the salon, so that not a speck of alien material was visible to the naked eye. He stood for a few moments, looking at the slight stain that remained on the floorboards, where Misha had almost bled to death, and an entire flock of geese walked over his grave. He put away the broom, then walked through all the rooms, and the garden, checking that not a single thing remained to remind Misha of her ordeal, when she came home.

When he had satisfied himself that nothing of Giles Murray-Williams was still in the apartment, he closed the windows, turned the heating to low, and drove to the hospital. There, he found Misha not only out of bed, but dressed in the warm trousers, sweater and winter boots he had brought from the apartment a couple of days ago. She was standing by the window, watching some birds in the bare branches of a chestnut tree. When Paul entered the room, she turned. 'They're throwing me out,' she said. 'I can go home.'

'I know. I've come to take you home. Where would you rather go? Your place, or Froissy?'

'Could we really? Go to Froissy, I mean? Wouldn't it be awfully cold just now?'

'I hope not. I got Marcel to order some oil, and turn on the heating. It should be nice and warm by now. Bearable, anyway.'

Misha laughed, and shook her head. 'You're incredible, Paul. You think of everything, don't you?'

'So, shall we go?'

'Yes, please, I'd love it.'

On his way across the Channel, on the Shuttle, Giles had a brilliant idea. Rather than take the van to London and unload the contents into a warehouse, for which he would have to pay rent, he would instruct Bert to make a detour and go to his mother's place, a small seventeenth-century manor house near Tunbridge Wells. There, he would be able to store his furniture and artefacts for nothing, as well as spending a comfortable weekend with his mother.

They stopped at a motorway service station, and while the men ate meat pies and drank tea, Giles telephoned his mother, a thing he had not done for some months. She answered the phone herself: 'Hello?'

'Mama, it's me, Giles.'

'How lovely! How are you, my darling?'

'Oh, not bad, I suppose. Bit tired, you know?'

'Poor you. You work too hard, darling.'

'Mama, I was wondering. I've just given up my flat in Paris, and I thought perhaps you wouldn't mind looking after my stuff for a bit, till I get sorted?'

'Delighted, of course. When would you want to come, darling?'

'Well, now, actually. I'm on my way, if that's OK?'

It was after ten o'clock when Bert and his mates finally left St Ursula's Manor and began the long drive back to London with the empty van. The night was dark, and heavy rain lashed the windscreen, making their progress slow. 'Bloody bloke's a nutcase.' Bert shook his head. 'I've never known anyone fart about like what 'e did, changing 'is mind, you'd think he'd nicked the crown jools or somethink. Didn't even give us a tip, either, did 'e, tight little sod?'

'His old mum was OK, though, wasn't she? Look what she gave me, when we was packing up to go.' Charlie put his hand in his pocket, and took out a flat half-bottle of whisky. He unscrewed the cap, and passed the bottle round. 'She's one of the old brigade, she is; like that nice bloke in Paris. Spoke good English for a froggie, didn't he? The French nosh wasn't too bad, either, was it?'

Chapter Sixteen

Basil Rodzianko sat in the freezing shed that passed for a departure lounge, on the edge of a rather primitive airstrip, waiting for the helicopter that would take him to Kabul, and thence, via a series of fairly unreliable connections, to Paris. Physically exhausted by his tour of duty, he felt completely indifferent to the approaching festive season.

In view of his unforgivable behaviour towards his wife, he thought it unlikely that he would be welcome at Souliac, with or without Olivia, and in any case was quite aware that, at the back of his mind, a plan had been slowly evolving that might give him an excuse to see Misha again. The months in Afghanistan, far from enabling him to put her out of his mind, had been torture for him, and filled with an obsessive longing to be with her. Each night his dreams were a torment of frustrated desire.

Now, as a means of having a base close enough to Bastille to visit Misha on a daily basis, and try to reignite their developing relationship, he thought that he would spend the holiday with his mother, on Ile St-Louis. He had, of course, no way of knowing whether Olivia had spoken to Hester about the break-up of their marriage, but, on balance, he thought that it was likely that she had not. Olivia, like his mother, was not one to broadcast her problems to all and sundry. It would be down to him to offer his mother any explanation he thought appropriate. I'll think of something when the time comes, he said to himself.

He stared through the filthy window at the pale sky, above the encircling snow-covered mountain ranges, his ears straining to catch the first distant sound of the approaching helicopter. Another twenty minutes passed before his vigilance was rewarded, and the brave little machine came clattering out of the sky, landing with the minimum of fuss on the airstrip. Having left his heavy aluminium baggage to follow with the camera crew and the recording equipment, Basil had only his backpack to carry. He ran from the shed, ducking down beneath the still whirling rotors, and climbed thankfully aboard.

It was nearly four o'clock when the car emerged from the woodland track at Froissy, the headlights piercing the already darkening gloom of the December afternoon. The ghostly shapes of white cattle loomed in the frosty fields on either side of the road, turning their heads with unruffled curiosity towards the sound of the engine, their dark eyes gentle. The fencing posts, caught in the twin beams of the headlights, threw their moving shadows over the frozen ground, like long grey searching fingers, exploring the petrified landscape. Beyond the pasture loomed the sombre mass of the old house, its turrets sharply etched against a leaden sky.

Paul drove into the courtyard, and stopped the car. He turned towards Misha. 'Tired?'

'A bit. Not very, though.'

He reached over, undid her safety belt, and placed his hand gently on her stomach. 'How does it feel, now? Still painful?'

'Not exactly painful, just rather tender.'

'It will be, for a while. We must take special care of you. No lifting heavy things; no strenuous exercise. Don't forget, you're here for a rest, so no breaking the rules, OK?'

'You sound just like a doctor, Paul.' She smiled, but her eyes looked exhausted, above her bruised cheeks.

'Anyway, what rules could I possibly break, here?'
'Knowing you, darling, it's quite on the cards you'll think of something.'

Inside the house, the heating had been on for three days and the place felt surprisingly warm and welcoming. While Misha unpacked some of their shopping, and put ham and crusty bread on the table, Paul lit the stove, then carried the rest of the boxes of provisions from the car, and dumped them in the larder. After they had eaten, Misha washed the dishes while Paul, carrying logs and dry kindling, went to light the fire in the sitting-room. He returned to the kitchen, took the drying-up cloth away from Misha and led her by the hand to his favourite room, now basking in the rosy glow of firelight. Tongues of flame leapt up the chimney, and were reflected in the glass of the many pictures and the cases containing stuffed wildlife that hung on the walls. The place seemed enclosed within a circle of fire, and generated a kind of magic.

Paul led her to the wide, chintz-covered sofa, with its heaps of soft cushions. 'Why don't you lie down?' he suggested. 'It's time you had a rest.'

'I'm not tired, Paul, and I don't need a rest.'

'Yes, you do.'

'No, I don't!'

'Doctor's orders.'

'I'm a doctor, too, don't forget.'

'Misha, please do as I say, and lie down.'

'OK.' Meekly, she lay down on the sofa.

Carefully, he pulled off her boots. 'Your feet are terribly cold.' Frowning, he rubbed them between his hands, then took a shabby cashmere shawl from the back of an armchair, and spread it over her legs. 'I really want you to try to sleep, if you can. You won't sleep if you're cold.'

'Paul, you're fussing. I'm really not cold, I promise.'

'Good.' He picked up the long brass tongs, slightly

rearranged the burning logs in the fireplace, then he went to the door.

'Where are you going?'

'Nowhere. Just putting away the shopping, things like that.'

'I wish you'd let me help, Paul. I feel really stupid, lying here.'

'You don't look stupid. You look beautiful.'

Misha laughed, wincing a little as she inadvertently dragged the stitches in her lip. 'If that's a joke, Paul, it's not in very good taste.'

'It's not a joke. Go to sleep; I'll be back in half an hour.'

Misha lay on her soft pile of cushions, and let her eyes wander slowly round the walls of the room, resting on the animals and birds that seemed poised for flight, frozen in their own particular time warp. The flames from the fire drew red sparks from their glass eyes, and the furred or feathered specimens cast shadows of themselves against the back walls of their cases, so that they seemed to move in the shifting light, like living, breathing creatures. In the flickering glow of the wood-smoke scented room, it was not difficult for Misha to imagine herself lying beside a campfire, in some enchanted woodland glade. Any minute now, she thought drowsily, the garden door will open and the seven dwarfs will come in on a blast of cold air, and cover me with leaves.

She smiled, and, turning carefully onto her good side, looked through the glass door to the walled garden in which she and Paul had worked so hard, so long ago, it now seemed. There were no dwarfs to be seen, just the gnarled arching branches of the ancient rose trees, their few remaining leaves dark green and leathery, the serrated edges rimmed with white hoar frost. The heavy wooden barrow lay on its side on the central path, a rake leaning against it. I wonder where the robin has got to, she thought. Tomorrow I'll go out and dig up a patch of earth, and uncover some worms for him, poor thing. Slowly, irresistibly, her eyes closed, and she slept.

Later in the afternoon Paul came quietly into the room, carrying a tray of tea things. He saw at once that Misha was fast asleep, and silently put the tray down on the floor, close to the fire. Taking great care not to make a sound, he added more logs to the blaze, then sat down in the comfortable chair once occupied, more or less always, by his father. He poured himself a cup of tea, then sank back into the depths of the chair, enjoying the warmth of the fire on his outstretched legs.

Slowly, he drank the scented English tea, and as he did so, his dark eyes rested on the sleeping form of Misha, lying absolutely still on the sofa, her eyes closed, her right arm thrust awkwardly away from her body, the upturned hand resting on the floor. Her face was turned towards him, and the long, half-healed scar that disfigured her upper lip, exaggerated by the dried, blackened blood that had oozed between the stitches that held the torn flesh together, filled his heart with terror, for he knew how close she could have been to death; not from the injury to her face, but from the brutal kick in the stomach, the slashed wrists and the subsequent haemorrhage. He also knew that his cold, implacable hatred for the man who had inflicted so much damage on Misha would remain with him for the rest of his life. Will she ever be able to recover from this? he asked himself. Or will the fear always be there, at the back of her mind? Will she ever walk by herself, on the street at night, or feel comfortable, sleeping alone? Will she really be able to go on living in that apartment, with such horrific memories? Perhaps the best thing would be to get rid of it, and find a new place, in another district?

As Paul watched, he noticed that the fingers of Misha's hand were opening and closing, and that, almost imperceptibly, her eyelids were fluttering.

Guessing that she was dreaming, he got up from his chair, and as he did so Misha gave a strangled cry and half sat up, pushing her hair out of her eyes, breathing heavily, blinking. At once, he knelt beside her, and put a supporting arm around her. 'It's OK, darling. You've been dreaming.'

'Oh, God!' she exclaimed, clinging to him. 'It's you, thank heaven.' She drew a deep shuddering breath. 'Why do I keep having this really horrible dream?'

'Tell me about it.'

'It's stupid, really. It's not always the same dream, exactly, but Giles is always in it, and usually he's trying to break down a door and do something frightful to me.'

'What happened this time, can you remember?'

'Yes, I can. He was over there, on the other side of the garden door. I knew it was him. It was awful, he had his nose and his mouth flattened against the glass, and the whites of his eyes were all red, like blood.'

Though disturbed by this turn of events, Paul spoke lightly, doing his best to diminish the distress still manifest in her shaking voice. 'Not a pretty sight, I imagine?'

She half laughed, in spite of herself, and shook her head. 'No, it wasn't at all a pretty sight. Horrible, actually; it scared me half to death, Paul. Bloody man, will I ever manage to shake him off?'

'Yes, you will, I promise. It's probable that the nightmares are triggered by your medication. Once you've finished the course, they will cease to worry you, I'm sure. In the meantime, what about some tea?'

Later in the evening, Misha seemed much more cheerful, and sat at the kitchen table, a glass of wine in front of her, and chatted to Paul, while he roasted a chicken, and made a *gratin* of parsnips and potatoes. 'In January,' she said, 'when the Seville oranges arrive, I'll make you a pilau of rice, with the zest of bitter oranges, cardamom, saffron and toasted almonds. That's lovely with chicken, too.'

'Sounds wonderful,' said Paul. Sounds better than wonderful, he said to himself. She's beginning to look ahead, to plan things, and that can't be bad, can it?

After supper, they sat in front of the fire in the sitting-room for a while, planning the day to come, comfortable, warm and happy, then went early to bed.

'Would you sleep more comfortably on your own, Misha? I can easily go to my old room; it needn't be a problem.'

'It would be a *huge* problem for me, Paul. I hate the idea of sleeping alone; please don't make me.' She looked at him, her bruised eyes desolate. 'What's the matter?' she asked in a small voice. 'Don't you want to sleep with me any more?'

'Of course I want to sleep with you, Misha, more than anything in the world.' Wearily, he sat down on the side of the bed, searching for an explanation for his motives, but anxious not to hurt her feelings.

'So why did you suggest sleeping in your old room?'

Paul looked at her, meeting her eyes, and spoke as honestly as he could. 'As a matter of fact, Misha, it's pretty hard for me to share your bed, and keep my hands off you, so to speak.'

Misha sat down beside him. 'Why do you have to keep your hands off me, Paul? I'm not made of eggshells, you know.'

'No, but you've just been through a pretty traumatizing episode. It seemed to me that you needed space to recover, in your own time. You certainly shouldn't have to put up with sexual advances from anyone, specially me.'

'Why should you think that, Paul?'

'Because it's true.'

'No, it isn't.'

'Misha, you're teasing me.'

'I don't mean to.' She turned his face towards her own, and kissed him very gently on the mouth. He closed his eyes, returning the kiss, and feeling the sharp prickle of her stitches against his skin.

'Dearest, darling Paul,' she whispered. 'Please, let's go to bed. It might interest you to know as far as such a thing is possible at this stage, I would welcome a sexual advance, as you put it, and especially from you.'

'Oh, darling. Would you really?'

'Yes, I would.'

The weekend at Froissy was for them both a time of enchantment, and when they returned to Paris on Sunday night, Misha seemed to have entirely regained her confidence, if not her health. They went out to dinner at their old bistro, and as they ate Paul tentatively brought up the subject of a possible change of apartment. With all her old robustness, she dismissed the idea out of hand. 'Certainly not,' she said. 'If you think I'm going to allow that creep to chase me out of my home, you're wrong. I bought it long before I met him, and I'm not going to allow his gross behaviour to spoil it for me.' Carefully spooning couscous into her mouth, she grinned at Paul. 'In any case, we've had some pretty good times there, ourselves, haven't we?'

Paul laughed. 'Very true, and I hope we'll have a lot more.'

'What do *you* think?'

On Monday, Paul left early for the hospital, happy in the knowledge that Misha felt perfectly safe and secure in her own apartment. She had already expressed herself overjoyed at the sight of the empty salon, and intended to spend the day getting quotes from builders, both to remove the white tiled fittings and to repaint the walls. 'In a day or two,' she said, 'I'll go out and look at furniture and things. What would you prefer, Paul? Modern stuff, or antiques?'

'What I'd really like would be old, squashy, comfortable, relaxed, and not a particularly big deal. But, of course, it's your place, darling. Whatever you choose, I'm sure I'll like.'

'Old and squashy is a good idea,' said Misha seriously. 'Perhaps next weekend, instead of going to Froissy, we could have a trawl through the flea-markets?'

'The best flea-markets I know are in the attics at Froissy. The prices are rock bottom, too, as far as I remember.' He looked at his watch: 'God, I must run. See you this evening.' He kissed her, and touched her face gently. 'I'd better put in an appearance at rue de Thorigny, on my way home. We don't want Blanche sending out a search party.'

'Yes, of course. What will you tell her, Paul?'

'The truth, of course. What else?'

'See you, darling. Have a good day.'

Paul left the hospital soon after seven o'clock, after a normal day by his standards. After his morning clinic, he had lunched early, in order to make his appearance in the theatre before his pupils, to answer their questions and brief them on the afternoon's procedures. While he ate his salad and drank a glass of mineral water, Nicole Christophe joined him at his table, greeting him in a friendly manner. 'I was very sorry to hear of the accident to Misha ben Bella,' she had said. 'How is she, do you know?'

'She's a lot better, thank you.'

'I heard that her face was badly scarred?'

'Yes, I'm afraid so.'

'I'm so sorry. Please give her my best wishes when you see her.'

'I will. Thank you.'

Paul arrived at rue de Thorigny, parked his car and walked to the house. It was a cold night, the wind whipped along the narrow streets of the Marais, and he turned up the collar of his coat, bending his head against the wintry blast. The lights of the house were lit, and he let himself in, slamming the heavy door behind him. He took off his greatcoat, and folded it over the beautiful cedarwood coffer, in the absence of a suitable chair or other convenient piece of furniture. He went swiftly up the stone staircase and opened the door of the salon. There, he found Blanche, seated on one of the grey-silk sofas, reading a glossy magazine. On a small galleried table by her side was a drink; probably a dry martini, to judge by the glass. She was looking extremely elegant in heavy black silk, the cuffs of her jacket edged in red fox, and was clearly ready to go out for the evening.

She looked up as Paul entered. 'Hello, Paul. What brings you here? I hope you're not expecting dinner? I'm on my way out, as you can see.'

'No, it's OK, I don't need feeding.'

'You make yourself sound like a dog, my dear.'

He chose not to respond to this, and, going to the drinks table, poured himself a whisky. 'How are you, Blanche?' he asked politely, very nearly adding: 'I'm very sorry to hear that you've been diagnosed with non-Hodgkin lymphoma,' then thought better of it, knowing that to bring up the subject of Nina's deceit would be counter-productive.

'More to the point, Paul, how are *you*?' She looked at him keenly. 'Actually, you're looking quite a lot better. I take it this means that Misha ben Bella is back in Paris?'

He crossed the room and sat down on the opposite sofa. 'You're quite right, Blanche, she is.' He took a sip from his glass. 'As a matter of fact, Misha's had a rather serious accident. Perhaps you heard about it, through the bush telegraph?'

'No,' said Blanche, quite truthfully, 'I hadn't heard.'

'Well, thank heaven, she's a lot better. She's out of hospital, and making good progress.'

Blanche looked at Paul, trying to figure out the purpose of his visit, and his motive in giving her the details of his mistress's misfortune. It felt to her almost as if they were already divorced, and enquiring kindly after each other's new partner. 'Was she badly hurt?' she asked.

'Yes, she was. She was kicked in the stomach, and had her face smashed.'

'How horrible! Is her face scarred, Paul?'

'Yes, it is.'

Blanche sat very still, gazing at the black silk that covered her knees, expecting to feel a justifiable thrill of triumphant revenge, but, to her surprise, this sensation failed to materialize. Slowly, she raised her china-blue eyes to Paul's. 'I'm very sorry,' she said.

'Thank you.'

'I imagine all this means that we now have serious problems, Paul? Are you thinking of divorce?'

'No, Blanche, I'm not. One marriage is more than enough in a lifetime, in my view, and it clearly doesn't bring a guarantee of happiness with it, does it?'

'I suppose not. So, what are your plans?'

'I don't make plans any more.'

Blanche took a sip of her drink, then looked steadily at her husband. 'Is it your intention to move out of our house, Paul?'

'Not unless you want me to, Blanche. I would prefer to come and go, exactly as I do now, if you have no objection to the arrangement.'

Blanche smiled, a little bitterly. 'Isn't that expecting to have your cake and eat it? What if I found such an idea inconvenient, and decided to seek a divorce myself? God knows, you have provided me with plenty of incriminating evidence.'

'You must do whatever you think best, Blanche. I'm sure Olivier would be very happy to take my place. You've had him on a string for years, haven't you?'

Blanche's cheeks grew pink, and her voice rose slightly. 'How can you even *suggest* such a thing? Olivier would never divorce Catherine, never.'

'Because she controls the purse-strings, perhaps?'

'Really, Paul, what a sordid thing to suggest!'

At that moment, the door opened, and Marie-Claire announced Olivier and Catherine. Paul and Blanche stood up to greet them.

'Are you ready, darling?' asked Catherine, addressing herself to Blanche, and shooting an uncertain glance towards Paul. 'We don't want to be late, do we?'

Paul laughed. 'Go on,' he said cheerfully, 'there's no need to hang about on my account. I'm just collecting a few things from my room, and dumping some laundry. Then I'll be off myself.' He turned to his wife, and kissed her on the cheek. 'Don't worry, Blanche,' he said. 'I won't let you down.'

At the opera, while Catherine was queuing up for the loo, Olivier, full of solicitousness, brought Blanche a glass of well-chilled champagne. He was bursting to know what had been the purpose of Paul's visit. 'What was all that about not letting you down?'

To his huge astonishment, Blanche, after sinking half her champagne, looked at him with cold blue eyes. 'Why don't you mind your own fucking business, Olivier?' she said frostily. 'Perhaps you yourself would do well to think a bit more about not letting Catherine down, don't you agree?'

Misha had spent a satisfactory first day back at work, but had, at the insistence of the head of the ENT unit, left the hospital at four o'clock. 'Take it steadily,' he had said. 'We don't want you back as a patient, do we?'

At passage des Ebénistes, she was delighted to find that her workmen had removed all the white glazed tiles from the salon, and had left the place clean and tidy, and ready for the painters. Cans of saffron-coloured paint stood against the wall, ready for the redecoration of the room. Since the removal of Giles's furniture had left them nowhere to sit, except at the table in the kitchen, Misha had bought a big, comfortable sofa, complete with loose covers of narrow black-and-white striped ticking, with a set of matching cushions. This important piece of furniture was already installed in the salon, covered in a protective sheet of plastic, and marooned in a sea of polished oak floorboards. Old rugs would be nice, thought Misha; shabby ones, with frayed edges. Persian or Indian ones would be lovely.

She put away her shopping, and made herself some tea. It was a Tuesday, and usually on that day Paul's list was a long one, which meant that it was quite likely that he would be very late for supper. Knowing this, and also, from her own experience, understanding that he would be dead tired and not particularly hungry, Misha was planning to make a light dish of grilled coquilles St-Jacques. This, together with some braised endive, could be thrown together in a matter of minutes, while Paul relaxed on the new sofa, a well-earned drink in his hand, trying to stay awake.

At the Italian delicatessen, she had bought a *pane sciocco*, the flat oblong Tuscan bread, and a bottle of Pomino di Frescobaldi. Looking at the bottle as she drank her tea, Misha thought longingly of the summertime, and the hot sunshine of the south.

The entryphone buzzed. Misha, surprised, looked at her watch: ten to six. Surely Paul hasn't finished already? she asked herself. Anyway, he wouldn't buzz; he's got his key. Frowning, wary, she went to the door and lifted the phone: 'Who is it?'

'Misha? It's Basil Rodzianko.'

'Oh. Hello, Baz.'

'Is this an inconvenient time? Or could I come up for a moment?'

'Um, yes, I suppose so.'

'You don't sound very sure?'

'Yes, it's OK. Come up.' She pressed the button to release the street door, then waited until she heard the knock on her own. Before opening it, she looked through the spyglass that Paul had insisted on having fitted, saw that it was indeed Baz, and opened the door. Tall, untidy, massive in his black parka, he stood there, staring at her battered face with horror, seeming bereft of speech.

Misha smiled. 'Come in,' she said quietly. He came into the salon, and she closed the door. 'Would you like a drink?' she asked, for something to say.

He turned towards her, his eyes bright with distress. 'Misha, what the hell have you done to yourself? What happened, for God's sake?'

'It's not as bad as it looks, Baz, and maybe a bit later on I can have plastic surgery.' She gave a strained, ironic little laugh. 'You should have seen me a couple of weeks ago. I *was* a bit of a mess, then.'

'If it was worse then, I'm glad I didn't see it.'

'Yes, well,' said Misha, not wishing to dwell on the subject of her appearance. 'Come through to the kitchen, and I'll give you a drink. It's not very comfortable in here yet.'

Basil did not comment on the dismantling of the salon, but followed her to the kitchen. Misha poured two glasses of wine, and they sat down, facing each other across the table. 'Tell me about your trip, Baz. Was it interesting?'

'No, it wasn't, and I don't particularly want to talk about it,' he replied. 'I want to hear about you, Misha. What happened? Please tell me. And don't say you walked into a door, because I'll know that's balls. I've seen too many faces that've been smashed either by fists or rifle butts not to realize that you've been beaten up. Am I right?'

Misha sighed, and looked down at her hands, the fingers folded tensely round the stem of her glass. 'It's true,' she said. 'I was beaten up. Are you really sure you want to hear about it, Baz?'

'Of course I do. Tell me, please. First of all, who did it?'

'Giles, of course. Who else?'

'The guy whose junk you threw out?'

'That's him. He came to the apartment when I was out, and he couldn't get in, because I had changed the lock. I found him, waiting outside my door, in a foul mood. Like a fool, I let him in. He was drunk, there was a row, and he punched me in the face, as you can see. He knocked me out, and I fell on the glass table. It shattered underneath me, and I was pretty badly cut.' She pushed up her sleeves, and showed Basil her scarred arms. 'He kicked me in the side too, and gave me a ruptured spleen, the brute.'

'Jesus! The bloody man's insane! I hope you told the police, and got him dealt with?'

'Yes, Paul told them at once, of course, in case I died. But as I didn't, we decided not to press charges.'

'We?'

'Paul and me, Baz.'

There was a long silence, during which Basil stared hopelessly into his glass, and wished himself back in Kabul; in Rwanda; in Moscow, doing his job. Anywhere but here, he told himself, face to face with the woman for whom he would gladly give his life, when it was horribly clear to him that she no longer had any need of him, and probably didn't even want him as a friend. After all, he had not even been here when she had been so savagely attacked. Instead, the man who had been the cause of her struggles in Sudan now seemed to have regained his former place in Misha's life. 'I suppose it was Paul who rushed in and saved your life, Misha?'

'Something like that, yes.'

'And I suppose you're together again?'

'Yes, we are.'

'What about the sick wife, Misha?'

Misha sighed. 'Apparently, that wasn't strictly true, Baz. The daughter brewed it up, to get rid of me.'

'A bit shitty?'

'You could say that.'

Basil drained his glass, and stood up. He went to the window, and stared out at the little garden. 'I suppose this has to be the moment when I gracefully bow out, and wish you well, Misha.' He turned towards her, his grey eyes blazing with love and anger. 'But first I must tell you something. I know you always laugh at me, and refuse to believe me, but when I told you that I loved you, it was the truth, Misha. I do love you; I wish we could be together always, have children together. I want to look after you, protect you, and be utterly faithful to you, until death us do part. But it's not on, is it? It's not part of your agenda, or the gospel according to the sainted Paul, is it? But he's not prepared to leave his wife for you, is he? He uses you, Misha, just as bloody Giles did, if you're honest with yourself. But you put up with that, don't you? You'd rather have half a life with him, than a full one with me, wouldn't you?'

'Really, Baz, aren't you being a bit illogical? It's true that Paul is married and has responsibilities, but you're in the same category yourself, aren't you? What about Olivia?'

'Misha, we're not talking the Fifties here, for Christ's sake. If a marriage fails, the parties divorce in a civilized manner and no harm done, especially if they don't have children. No one *chooses* who they fall in love with, Misha. It *happens*, doesn't it?'

'And if you happen to be married, you fall *out* of love with equal facility and lack of conscience, is that it?'

'No,' said Baz, miserably. 'That's not it, you must believe me.'

Misha looked at her watch. 'Baz, it's getting a bit late.'

'Come out to dinner with me?'

'Oh, Baz, what's the point?'

Basil took her hand gently in his and kissed it. 'Just one more time, please, darling Misha.' He gazed at her scarred face, and his heart froze with pity, and fear. 'I have a lot to tell you, if only you'll listen to me. Out there, in places like Afghanistan, one does a great deal of sitting around in cold dark caves, in between bursts of action. I've had a lot of time to dream about you, Misha, and to convince myself that it was fate that brought us together at Talakal.' He released her hand, placing it carefully on the table, and stood up. 'Don't just show me the door, Misha. At least come and have supper with me, even if it's only as friends, OK?'

Misha, touched by his sincerity, relented. 'OK, Baz,' she said. 'I'll come, but strictly as a friend, you understand?'

Basil smiled, and said nothing. He watched as Misha scribbled a note to Paul and left it on the table.

Two hours later, Paul arrived at passage des Ebénistes, and wearily let himself into the apartment. He went into the kitchen, saw the wine and the glasses on the table, as well as the note. *Basil Rodzianko is on leave, and came round. We have gone out to supper. Shan't be late. Love, M.*

Exhausted as he was, and therefore incapable of reacting sensibly to this news, Paul jumped immediately to the conclusion that he had been right in his earlier belief that Misha's relationship with a man of her own age would mean the inevitable decline of his own role as her lover. He looked round the place where he had spent so many happy hours, and his heart bled. I suppose this is what always happens, he said to himself sadly. A younger man comes along, and one gets dumped. Poor Misha, he thought, I don't blame her, really. In ten or fifteen years, I'll probably be dead, and where would that leave her? Alone, with thirty or so empty years stretching ahead of her, with nothing to fill her life but her work. It was selfish of me to want so desperately to believe that we were together again, wasn't it? I have to let her go without a fight, obviously, so the sooner I do it, the better.

Before he could change his mind, he wrote a note to Misha, and left it on the table, beside hers. *See you at work. Be happy. Love, P.*

He left the apartment, and drove slowly back to rue de Thorigny.

* * *

Misha got home just before midnight. She read the note, and burst into tears. They were not tears of sorrow, but of mortification and rage. She dried her eyes, and thought of ringing Paul on his mobile. Then, still angry, she decided against it and went to bed.

Chapter Seventeen

For three days, Misha made no attempt to speak to Paul at the hospital, still hurt and angry at his abrupt departure from the apartment. Each evening when she got home, she found Basil waiting on her doorstep, and felt reluctant to deny herself the pleasure of his company. Scrutinizing her disfigured face in the bathroom mirror each morning, she found it comforting that anyone, but especially a man as handsome as Basil, should not find her physically repulsive, or shrink from being seen in public with her. The livid purple scars had not yet begun to fade, and she was becoming inured to the glances of pity and horror she frequently intercepted in her daily life. The fact that she remained attractive to Basil was an enormous boost to her confidence.

On the fourth day Paul paged her at work, and they lunched together. Misha was the first to bring up the subject of Basil's visit. 'Why did you leave, Paul? It wasn't at all necessary; you should have known that.'

'Should I, Misha?'

'Yes, you should.'

'Is he still here?'

'Yes, he is. He'll be in Paris over Christmas. He's staying with his *mother*, Paul.'

Paul looked sheepish. 'I shouldn't have asked; I'm sorry. Your life is your own, Misha. I have no right to interfere in any way.'

'Why the hell not, Paul?' Misha sounded irritated. She put down her fork. 'Of course, you should express your feelings in any way you think fit, but to tell you the truth, I'm getting really pissed off with you both. I feel as if I'm being driven into making a choice between you, and frankly, I don't see why I should. I like Baz a lot; he's been a very good friend to me, and I don't want to be unkind to him.' She looked crossly at Paul, and frowned. 'Well, I *don't*! I don't belong to either of you, so I don't see why it's not possible to be friends with you both. Is there a law against that?'

'No,' said Paul, after a moment's thought. 'I don't believe there is.'

The next day was cold and foggy. During the afternoon, there was a serious pile-up on the Paris *périphérique*. Many of the casualties were brought to the hospital's A and E unit, most of them with fractured limbs and facial lacerations. Misha volunteered to help out, glad to have an excuse not to spend the evening with Basil. Paul came down to A and E at the end of his day, to check that there were no neurological traumas to be dealt with, and was told there were not. He saw Misha at the other end of the unit, delicately repairing the badly cut arm of a young boy, and went at once to her side. 'Is this wise, Misha? Are you really up to this sort of thing?' he asked quietly.

She raised her eyes to his, and smiled. 'I'm fine, thank you, Professor de Vilmorin. I'm doing exactly what I need to do, and want to do, OK?'

'Yes, of course.' He smiled at the patient, raised an apologetic hand to Misha, and departed.

In the car park, he sat for a few minutes, thinking about Misha's cool reprimand in the face of his intervention, and smiled ruefully. She's absolutely right, he told himself. I'm becoming a fussing old bore, and that's the last thing she needs; from me, or from anyone else.

Without consciously making the decision to do so,

he drove out of the car park and turned the car in the direction of Bastille. When he arrived at passage des Ebénistes, he found Rodzianko on the doorstep. 'Good evening,' he said, and introduced himself. 'Misha's going to be late. She's on duty in A and E. There's been a series of car accidents, so there's a rush on.'

'I see.'

'I was thinking of going round the corner for some supper, Rodzianko. If you've nothing better to do, perhaps you'd care to join me?'

'Um, well. OK, thanks.'

In the bistro, the little waiter greeted Paul with obvious pleasure, and took their coats. 'How is madame? She is not dining tonight?' he asked. 'She is quite well, one hopes?'

'She's very well, thank you,' said Paul. 'Just working late at the hospital.'

'Madame is very conscientious lady.'

'Yes,' agreed Paul. 'She is, indeed.'

'What will it be tonight, sir? The seventy-five franc menu, *comme d'habitude*?'

Paul laughed. 'Why not? Is that OK for you, Rodzianko?'

'Yes, of course. Fine.'

Paul studied the wine list, chose a Burgundy to go with the daube of beef proposed by the menu, and asked for a carafe of water.

Basil sat in silence, while the waiter brought bread, the wine and water, as well as the first course, a terrine of garlicky wild mushrooms. He opened the wine, half filled their glasses, and put the bottle on the table. '*Bon appétit, messieurs*,' he said politely, and left them to their meal. Surprised that the waiter had not offered the wine for Paul to taste, Basil said, rather shyly, 'Doesn't he let you try the wine, before he serves it?'

'No, he doesn't. He is an entirely confident man, the wine comes from his home village, and he knows that it will be excellent. He doesn't need me to tell him his business.'

'I see.'

They ate in silence for a few minutes, then Basil picked up his glass. The wine, as promised, was delicious, and he took a bigger swallow. Suddenly, his feelings of constraint and anxiety left him. 'Poor Misha,' he said, 'what an absolutely ghastly thing to happen. It was lucky you were there to take care of her.'

Paul smiled at Basil over the rim of his glass, but his eyes were cool. 'Taking care of Misha is what I intend to continue to do, for as long as she needs me, Rodzianko. Is that a problem for you?'

'Er, no, of course not.' The realization that Paul de Vilmorin appeared to be fully aware of his feelings for Misha made Basil suddenly wary and defensive, and nervously, he took another deep swig of his wine.

The waiter arrived, took away their empty plates, and brought the daube. For a few minutes, they ate in silence. Then Paul put down his knife and fork, and rested his elbows on the table, with his fingers locked together. 'It seems to me obvious, Rodzianko, that it's crucial for us both to remember that Misha is not a chattel, something to be owned, or bought and sold. We all three have demanding careers, and that's clearly a primary element in each of our lives, you surely must appreciate that? The important thing for Misha is that she should feel herself to be entirely free, to be what she wants to be, to love whomsoever she chooses to love, don't you agree?'

'Yes, yes, I know all that!' exclaimed Basil, impatiently sweeping aside what he privately considered to be Paul's extremely pompous opinions concerning Misha's needs. Then, following his host's example, he, too, put down his knife and fork, and looked Paul straight in the eye. 'The fact is, de Vilmorin, I think you should know that I'm deeply in love with Misha and I've asked her to marry me. Several times, in fact.' Basil hesitated for a second, then went on, candidly: 'The trouble is, she doesn't seem to want that.'

Paul did not at once reply, but picked up his knife and fork, and began to eat. After a while he said gently: 'Misha will be a surgeon before very long, Rodzianko, and in my view, she'll be a very good one. You're not seriously hoping that she'll marry you, and stay at home, housekeeping, are you?'

'Yes,' said Basil, 'that's exactly what I'm hoping.' Deliberately, he stared at Paul, the challenge in his eyes palpable. 'I've even made up my mind to get a desk-job, so that I could come home every night.'

'And did you regard that as a tremendous sacrifice on your part?' Paul's voice was very quiet, his slight smile ironic.

'Yes, I expect I did,' said Basil sulkily.

Observing Basil's sullen face with some irritation, Paul's laid-back manner suddenly vanished. He became deadly serious, his dark eyes brilliant with passion, his voice low and intense. 'I don't think you even begin to understand how much I love Misha, do you, Rodzianko?' he said. 'Or how important her happiness is to me?'

'I don't suppose you love her more than I do,' Basil replied, quite aggressively, feeling himself to be on safer territory. 'Don't forget, I left my wife for her.'

'And you really think that should make a difference to what Misha decides to do?'

'Yes, I do, since you ask.'

They finished the meal in silence, and afterwards Basil, thoroughly upset, took the Métro to St-Michel and walked to Ile St-Louis. Paul drove thoughtfully back to rue de Thorigny, where he spent a miserable night. Misha, arriving home in a cab after midnight, expecting Paul would be waiting for her, was disappointed to find her apartment empty. Feeling tired, lonely and abandoned, she, too, went to bed.

* * *

Olivia came out of the consulting rooms of her gynaecologist, and took a cab to her mother-in-law's apartment. It was nearly five o'clock, and the December afternoon was cold and dark, in spite of the brilliance of the street lamps that illuminated the *quais* as the taxi threaded its way through the riverside traffic towards Ile St-Louis. Olivia had not seen her mother-in-law since the abrupt departure of Basil at the beginning of October, and neither had she been to Paris to attend the various functions to which she had received invitations.

Instead, she had remained at the barn, alone as usual, cocooned in a curious feeling of self-sufficiency, and disinclined to venture far from the house. This desire to wrap her home around her, like a protective shell, had not prevented Olivia from working the long hours that were the norm for her, and the realization that pregnancy need not necessarily diminish her creativity had come as a great relief to her.

She felt fit and strong, and was not adversely affected by the changes taking place in her body. The only thing that seemed at all unusual for her was that she became pretty sleepy soon after supper, and took herself to bed quite early by her standards, usually before ten o'clock.

As she had promised herself, Olivia waited until mid-December before making an appointment to see her gynaecologist and have her pregnancy confirmed. The consultation took place on the twenty-second of December and lasted less than half an hour. 'Your baby will be born in early July,' the gynaecologist told her. 'We'll do regular scans a bit later on, of course, to check on your progress, but at present you are both in excellent shape. What a lovely Christmas present for you and your husband; congratulations.'

In the taxi, Olivia placed a hand on her already slightly rounded stomach, and smiled to herself, rather wishing that she had reached the stage when the child would announce her presence with a kick. She never doubted for a second that the baby was a girl.

The cab drew up at the entrance to Hester's apartment. Olivia paid the fare, then went under the *porte cochère* to her mother-in-law's door and rang the bell. As she waited, she looked into the courtyard around which the seventeenth-century mansion was built, admiring the flawless Renaissance architecture, and the well-maintained lime trees, at present graceful in their bare winter mode. It was not difficult to imagine such a house during its original occupation by one extended family, with their many children and servants, their carriages, horses and dogs filling the place with life. Even now, divided into apartments, the mansion was beautiful and loved, its elegant tall windows rosy with light as the working day drew to a close and families came home.

The grey-painted door in the *porte cochère* opened, and Olivia turned towards it. 'Hello, Hester,' she said. 'How are you, darling?'

'Olly! Where have you been? I haven't seen you for months! Come in out of the cold, child, at once.'

Olivia followed her mother-in-law up the narrow stone staircase to the apartment in the *entresol*, with its very low ceilings and flaking, limewashed stone internal walls, smelling of damp. Hester opened the door to the sitting-room, and they went in. The lamps were already lit, and shone on the many paintings and gilded icons that hung on the walls, evidence of a lifetime's work by Hester herself, and that of her dead husband, George. The room's original windows, uncurtained, overlooked the courtyard. In less severe weather, they frequently stood open, filling the low-ceilinged room with fresh air, sweet with the green scent of summer, the haunting aroma of burning leaves in autumn. Sometimes, when it snowed, Hester opened the casements and leaned on the sill, her eyes closed, inhaling the smell of snow, and mentally transporting herself to the silent winter countryside of Russia.

'Hester,' said Olivia, without preamble, 'where is Baz? Do you know?'

'He's been sleeping here, darling, though I haven't seen much of him. He goes out early and comes back very late. I believe he's been in Afghanistan for some weeks, though he never says much about it, does he?'

'No, he doesn't, Hester, and I haven't heard from him, since he left, nearly three months ago.'

'I'm sorry to hear it, Olly.'

'Hester, if you know where he spends his days, please tell me.'

'I don't really know, dear, and I wouldn't dream of asking him, you must know that? Do you need to see him urgently?'

'Yes, I bloody do,' said Olivia, brusquely. She looked severely at Hester, her beautiful blue eyes stern. 'I need to talk to him, and at once. It's time he got his act together, and stopped fooling around.'

Hester wavered uncertainly for a moment, then came down on Olivia's side. 'Yes, well, I can quite understand your point of view, Olly. As it happens, I do have a contact number for him, somewhere in Bastille, I believe. I'll have a look.' She got up from the sofa, went to her worktable near the window, and unearthed her address book from the jumble of other books and papers. 'Yes, here it is, Dr ben Bella. Do you want to make a note of the number?'

'Thanks.' Olivia joined Hester at the table. 'Would you mind if I tried to get him now, from here?'

'Not at all. Go ahead, darling. I'll go and make some coffee, and leave you in peace.' Moving a good deal more swiftly than was usual for her, Hester scuttled out of the room.

Slightly nervously, Olivia lifted the phone and dialled the number. After three rings it was answered, by a woman. 'Hello?'

'Good evening. I wonder if I could speak to Basil Rodzianko, please?'

'May I know who's calling?'

'Olivia Rodzianko.'

'I see. I'm sorry, but Basil's not here just now. Should I ask him to call you, if I see him?'

Olivia hesitated, then said, 'Would I be wrong in assuming that I'm speaking to Dr ben Bella?'

'No, you would be right.'

'Would you mind very much if I came round to see you? Or, if you would find that intrusive, we could perhaps meet in a café.'

After a slight pause, Misha said, 'I would be very happy to meet you, and of course, you are welcome here.'

'Thank you,' said Olivia. 'I'll come now, if that's OK?'

'Fine. Do you have the address?'

'No, I don't.'

Misha gave her the address. 'How will you come?' she asked.

'I'll take a cab from Ile St-Louis.'

'See you in about half an hour, then?'

'OK.'

Waiting for Olivia to arrive, Misha arranged cups and saucers on a tray, and put the kettle on for tea. She felt more curiosity than nervousness at the prospect of a confrontation with Basil's wife. Possibly, the fact that she was quite a lot older than Olivia may have had something to do with her unruffled attitude, but she did not really think so. Olivia was, after all, a woman of some achievement, and evidently a person to be reckoned with. She thought that it was more a question of first impressions. On the phone, Olivia had sounded very together, cool and unhysterical, the very antithesis of an abandoned wife. Quite right, said Misha to herself, and much more impressive than I was, when Giles dumped me.

The entryphone buzzed. She answered it, then went to the lift and waited for Olivia to appear. The gates of the lift slid open, and out of it stepped one of the loveliest creatures Misha had ever seen. Tall, blonde, stunningly beautiful, her kingfisher-blue eyes brilliant in her pale and perfect face, Olivia was wearing a Mongolian lamb hat, a long russet-coloured coat edged in the same curly brown wool, and soft green-leather boots. 'Dr ben Bella?' she asked politely.

Misha took Olivia's proffered hand. 'My name's Misha. May I call you Olivia?'

'Please do.' Olivia's voice tailed off, and she frowned, staring with horror at Misha's battered face, at the livid scar across her lip, and the yellowing bruises beneath her eyes. 'What on *earth* happened to your poor face, Misha?'

'I got beaten up.'

'*What?* You're not *serious*?'

'I'm afraid I am. Come in, Olivia. I've made some tea.'

They went into the salon, and Misha closed the door. 'It's a bit of a mess here, as you can see,' she said. 'I'm in the throes of redecorating, but do take your coat off, and make yourself comfortable on the sofa. I'll just get the tea.'

Thoughtfully, Olivia took off her hat, folded her coat across the back of the sofa, and sat down on the soft yielding cushions, resisting the temptation to pull off her boots and draw her knees up to her chin, as she would have done at home. Confusingly, she felt herself extremely attracted to the slight, dark-haired, frail-looking woman with the shattered face, and found herself responding to the air of vulnerability that Baz himself had found so appealing about Misha, in the first place. Olivia had, of course, come to passage des Ebénistes expressly to challenge her presumed rival, but now felt unexpectedly loath to raise the subject.

Misha brought in the tray of tea things, and put it on the floor in front of the sofa. She poured for them both, offering milk and lemon, then sat down herself. For a few moments they both drank their tea, silently, then Misha turned to Olivia. 'You want to know what my relationship is with Baz, don't you?'

Since she had supposed that it would be she, if either of them, who first mentioned Basil in such a context, Olivia was slightly taken aback by this unambiguous approach. 'Yes, I do,' she stammered. 'But only if you feel like telling me, Misha. Please believe me, I haven't come here to pick a fight.'

'I didn't really think you had.' Misha sat curled up at her end of the sofa, and looked very steadily at Olivia. 'I think it would be best if I told you the whole story from the beginning, otherwise you won't understand how we became close friends.'

'Are you really sure you don't mind?'

'I'm sure.'

So, beginning with the accident to Giles, and ending with the flight home from Naples, Misha told Olivia exactly what had taken place between herself and Basil.

'You must have had a ghastly time,' said Olivia quietly. 'No wonder Baz fell in love with you, Misha. You're just the kind of victim that he can't resist making himself responsible for; it's his thing.'

Stung, Misha asked, 'Are you mocking me, Olivia?'

'No, of course I'm not, I'm telling the truth as I see it. Basil loves all frail defenceless creatures: birds with broken wings; refugee children.' She turned her brilliant blue eyes on Misha. 'Children, especially,' she added.

'But I'm not a child.'

'No, but you *are* a bit of a victim, aren't you?'

Misha stared at Olivia, wondering how Basil's wife knew so much of his involvement with her. 'Did Baz tell you about me?' she asked.

'Yes, he did. We saw that piece about your work in Africa, on the telly. He told me then how wonderful you were, and that he loved you, but I didn't really believe him. I certainly didn't see you as a threat, then.'

'And now?'

'Now, I suppose I do.'

Misha smiled, and shook her head. 'You shouldn't, Olivia. Basil's not in love with me, he only thinks he is, poor guy. To tell you the truth, he's been giving me quite a hard time, especially since the man I really love is Paul. The trouble is, Baz refuses to take that on board. Paul isn't much help, either. When things start getting complicated, he simply removes himself from the frame, silly man. It's a mess.'

'And all the more of a mess because I am nearly three months' pregnant. Sod's law, isn't it?'

Misha stared at Olivia, so beautiful and radiant in pregnancy. 'Are you really?' she said, sounding awed by the news. 'How wonderful for you, and for Baz, too. It is Baz's child, of course?'

Olivia laughed, not at all offended by the question. 'Of course it is, what else?'

'Sorry.' Misha shook her head, acutely aware that Olivia's announcement made her own failure to take a firmer line with Basil now seem incredibly feeble. 'What a strange man Baz is,' she said quietly. 'He's very keen to be in control, to organize the lives of the people he thinks need him, and take care of them. But underneath all that, there's still an insecure little boy, demanding attention and love, as his right, isn't there?'

'You've got it, Misha, and that's probably the fundamental reason for his need for children of his own. When you have kids to provide for, and love, you don't have any more excuses not to grow up yourself, do you?'

'You're right.' Misha smiled. 'And looking after people does seem to be an obsession with him, doesn't it?'

'You've noticed?' Olivia laughed. 'As a matter of fact, I used to despise that, on principle, but it's actually one of the most endearing things about Baz. That is, it is if you love him, and I do.' She looked at her watch: nearly five forty-five. 'I must go,' she said, 'or I'll miss my train.' She stood up, and slipped on her coat.

'There's just one thing, Misha. Please don't tell Baz that I've been to see you. If he does decide to come home, I don't want it to be because he knows I'm carrying his baby. I'd much rather not use the pregnancy as a kind of bargaining chip. I'm sure you understand?'

'Yes, absolutely. Of course I won't tell him, don't worry.'

They went together to the lift, and Olivia said, 'Goodbye, Misha. I'm glad we met.'

'Goodbye, and take care of the baby, won't you?'

'I will.'

Misha went back into the apartment, and closed the door. Thoughtfully, she took the tea things into the kitchen, and put them in the dishwasher. She switched on the outside light, and gazed unseeingly through the glass walls of her kitchen at the row of empty terracotta pots, evidence of her long neglect of her little garden. She did not know whether to be glad or sorry that Olivia had been to see her. She was, however, quite aware that her friendship with Baz must, of necessity, come to an end, and at once. The question was, how to bring this about, without being too brutal, and without betraying Olivia's confidence in the process? It's all very well for her, Misha said to herself, frowning. She goes prancing off to wherever it is, leaving me to find a way of dealing with the whole thing without involving her. It's not only ridiculous, it's impossible.

Chapter Eighteen

On the twenty-third of December, Blanche de Vilmorin travelled to Ménerbes for the Christmas and New Year break, driven by Olivier, and accompanied by Catherine, as usual. She took with her the many expensive gifts she had bought for Pascal and Emma, and their twin boys, now expected any day. They arrived at the house a little before eight in the evening, and had scarcely got through the door before the telephone began to ring. Blanche answered it. '*Oui?*'

'Mother? Hello, it's me, Pascal. I tried to get you at rue de Thorigny this morning, but there was no reply. Just to let you know that the babies arrived last night, and everyone's in good shape. We can probably go home tomorrow.'

'Oh, darling! How lovely! I'm so pleased for you.'

'Is *Père* with you?'

Blanche hesitated. 'No, not yet, darling, but I'm expecting him, maybe tomorrow. He had an urgent case to deal with. He'll be coming, I'm sure. I'll call him tonight, to let him know about the babies, of course. I'm sure he'll be thrilled by the news.'

'Thanks, that would be kind of you, because I'm using the hospital payphone, and I've run out of change. When you speak to *Père*, tell him Emma sends her love.'

'Yes, of course, I'll do that, darling.'

'Thanks very much. Talk to you soon.'

Blanche cleared the line, then dialled the number of Paul's hospital, and asked to speak to him. 'It's Mme de Vilmorin,' she said.

'I'm afraid he's still in theatre, Mme de Vilmorin. Can I get him to call you when he's free, or perhaps you'd prefer to leave a message?'

'Ask him to call me, will you? Tell him I'm at Ménerbes.'

It was after eleven o'clock when Paul left the theatre. He was hungry and very tired, and felt extremely disinclined to spend another night sleeping alone at rue de Thorigny. He longed for the soothing touch of Misha's arms around him, and the smell of her hair, and the warmth of her body close to his. He stripped off his scrubs, took a shower, then prepared to leave. On his way out, he was stopped by the girl on the theatre switchboard. 'I have a message for you, Professor de Vilmorin. Will you call your wife, please? She's at Ménerbes, she says.'

'Thank you. Goodnight.'

In the car park, he called Blanche on the mobile. She answered at once. 'Hello, Blanche. You called me at the hospital. Is everything all right?'

'Yes, darling, everything's fine. Pascal rang from Aix. Their twins were born last night, isn't that marvellous news?'

'Yes, Blanche, it is. Thank you for telling me.'

'Will you be coming down to see them?' A wistful note crept into Blanche's voice. 'It would be lovely if you could find the time, darling.'

Paul hesitated for a second, then he said, reassuringly, 'Yes, of course I'll find the time; don't worry about it.'

Blanche did not press him, or try to pin him down in any way. 'Pascal said that they might be allowed to go home tomorrow, Paul,' she said. 'They'll be so happy to see you, I know. They sent their love.'

'Good night, my dear. Thank you for letting me know.'

'Well, it's not every day that your son has twins, is it?'

'Indeed not,' said Paul. 'Good night.'

'Good night,' said Blanche softly. 'Sleep well, Paul. It's so late, you must be exhausted.'

Paul switched off his phone, and drove to rue de Thorigny.

He ate an extremely boring supper, a dish of frozen monkfish which he cooked rather doubtfully in the microwave oven, having read the instructions on the packet. While he waited for the statutory number of minutes to elapse, which seemed an eternity, he drank some whisky and ate a piece of cold pie from the fridge. The bell of the microwave rang, and he took the dish from the oven. He ate it standing at the counter, and burning his mouth in the process.

He left the dirty dishes in the sink, and went to the salon, which was gloomy and cold, for the central heating had turned itself off. He thought about calling Misha, then, looking at his watch, decided that it was too late, she was probably asleep. He poured himself another whisky, and went to bed.

He turned on the television at the foot of his bed, doubled up a pillow beneath his head, and watched a very old black-and-white movie. He gazed at the flickering images but after a while ceased to connect, for his mind and his heart had regressed more than thirty years, to the time of the birth of his own son, Pascal. What a magical moment that was in my life, he said to himself, smiling at the recollection of the red-faced, angry little baby whose screams had disrupted their lives for months, and driven Blanche to distraction. Poor old Blanche, he thought, she wasn't cut out for maternity, was she? In his mind's eye, he saw his beautiful daughter-in-law, Emma, so calm and relaxed, and knew that for her the challenges of motherhood would seem perfectly natural, and easily overcome with patience and love. But then, he said to himself, she does have Pascal by her side, all the time, supporting her in every way, doesn't she? I was hardly ever at home, and never more than a part-time husband to Blanche, was I? No wonder she's become so brittle and bitter. Her marriage to me must have seemed like two per cent of bugger all, poor woman.

Early the next morning, he called Misha at passage des Ebénistes. 'Sorry I didn't call you last night,' he said. 'I was terribly late, leaving the hospital.'

'You poor thing,' said Misha. 'I hope you're not having to work today?'

'No, thank God, I'm not. Misha, something has come up. Pascal and Emma's babies have been born, and I feel I should go down and see them.'

'How lovely! Are they OK, Paul? No problems?'

'No, they're fine. They're coming home today, I think.'

'Great, you must be thrilled. Of course, you must go and see them. Will you drive down?'

'Yes, I thought so.'

'Today?' she asked.

'Yes.'

'That's good; you'll be with them for Christmas, won't you?'

'That's one of the things I want to talk to you about, Misha. Are you working, over the holiday?'

'No, I've got a week off.'

'Good. I imagine Rodzianko will be around to keep you company?'

'I don't know, Paul. I haven't discussed it with him.'

'Well, anyway, have a happy Christmas.'

'You too, Paul.'

Paul packed an overnight bag, informed the hospital that in the event of an emergency he could be reached either at Ménerbes or Froissy, then got into his car and drove to Froissy, with the intention of cutting a fir tree for the house. Quite why this small winter ritual seemed to him important he did not attempt to explain to himself. Perhaps it was a gesture of welcome to his new grandsons; perhaps, and more likely, a salute to his own distant boyhood.

It was ten days since he and Misha had stayed together at the house, and it felt a little cold. Paul went into the boiler-house, checked the level of the oil, and turned up the thermostat. Then he got an axe from the woodstore, put on his gumboots and walked across the frosty fields to the wooded slopes beyond. The frozen grass crunched beneath his feet as he climbed through the trees to the small planting of firs, halfway up the hill. When he reached his goal, he sat down, resting his back against a tree for a few minutes, to regain his breath and to look down over the land and the house that he loved.

Christmas is a rotten time, he said to himself sadly. It's bloody depressing, filled with reminders of long-ago happiness, and a vanished innocence. You look back to your own childhood Christmases, the magical times your parents gave you, and later, you remember seeing the reflection of that special joy in the faces of your own children. Then they grow up, and it's down-hill all the bloody way, just a time of over-eating and hangovers. It's strange, he thought, but Nina never once suggested bringing her children here for Christmas, did she? I suppose Gérard's family is much more important to her. Blanche always hated coming here, of course, and doubtless Nina agreed with her mother.

He looked at his watch: nearly midday. I must get a move on, he thought, and got to his feet. He chose a nicely shaped, not very big fir tree, and with four strokes of the axe, cut it down. He carried it down the hill, and back to the house. There, he took the tree to the hall, and rammed it firmly into a fire bucket, already filled with damp sand. He stood beside it for a moment, his head bent, inhaling its therapeutic smell, and seeing in his mind's eye his mother hanging the decorations on a rather taller tree, in exactly that place. He remembered the excitement of Christmas Eve, and returning to the house after midnight mass, when the real candles that adorned its branches were lit for the first time. I suppose it's unrealistic to expect happiness like that to be permanent, he said to himself. I found it again with Misha, but the way things are, it seems quite improbable that we can really find a way of sharing our lives. I keep forgetting how young she is, and how bloody old I am. If I'm losing her, I must try to be happy with what I've had, which is a lot, when all's said and done. Nothing's ever perfect, or lasts for ever, how the hell could it?

He locked up the house, got back into his car and drove south to Avignon and Mas les Arnauds, to see his grandsons.

Misha replaced the telephone, frowning, and bewildered. What is Paul trying to do to me? she asked herself. He seems hell-bent on steering me into a relationship with Baz that I neither need nor want. It's high time I sent Baz about his business, particularly now, after Olivia's visit. On the two previous evenings, she had made several vigorous attempts at convincing Basil that it was time for him to go home to his wife, but this he had flatly refused to do.

It was now blindingly obvious to Misha that the only way of getting rid of Basil would be to renege on her promise to Olivia, and spill the beans about the expected child. I'll just have to tell him the truth, she said to herself, and if he's going to get home by Christmas, there's no time to lose.

The first thing she did was to telephone a car-rental firm and hire a car for ten days, arranging that they would deliver the car to her at passage des Ebénistes, at noon. She put a couple of books of Basil's, his camera and some rolls of film into a plastic bag, then packed a suitcase for herself. She telephoned the TV centre and left a message for Baz, inviting him to lunch with her at *Le Petit Zinc*.

The man arrived with her car, and he came up to the apartment to do the necessary paperwork, then helped her carry the luggage down to the street, stowing it in the boot. She drove him back to his office, then made her way to rue de Buci. She parked in a side-street, and walked to the restaurant. The place was packed, since it was Christmas Eve, and people were there in force, enjoying the seasonal fresh seafood that was the restaurant's speciality. She waited in a short queue, looking around for Basil, and then was given a table in a corner, near the door. As she sat down, Baz came through the door. She called his name, and he installed himself opposite her, hanging his parka over the back of his chair. 'I got your message, Misha,' he said. 'What a lovely idea. I took the afternoon off, so we don't have to hurry over lunch.'

Misha said quietly, 'My pleasure,' and picked up the menu. 'Everyone seems to be having oysters, Baz, or maybe you'd rather have something else?'

'No, oysters would be terrific. What a treat.'

Misha ordered the oysters, and a half-bottle of Chablis. 'Or would you prefer champagne, Baz?'

'No, Chablis would be perfect, thanks.' Basil looked guardedly at Misha, as she sat opposite him, for she seemed to him to be somewhat on her dignity, and behaving in a curiously formal manner towards him, almost as if he were a stranger. She appeared confident and very sure of herself, as she discussed the wine with the waiter. It was clear to Basil that she was far from being in a celebratory mood, and for the first time he was obliged to recognize aspects of Misha of which he had little or no experience. What he saw was not the frail, vulnerable child-woman of his fantasies, but someone quite different, cool, well dressed, self-possessed and rather formidable. Into his head came Paul's words: Misha will be a surgeon before very long, Rodzianko, and in my view, she'll be a very good one.

When the waiter had departed, Misha sat back in her chair, and folded her arms. She looked directly at Basil, her green eyes serious, and now that the bruises were fading, beautiful. 'I had a visit from your wife, Baz,' she said.

'You *what*?'

'I had a visit from Olivia. As I'm getting very tired of telling you, Baz, it's time you went home. She thinks so, and I agree with her.'

'I can't think of a single good reason why I should, Misha. Didn't you tell me that Paul would probably be going to Provence, to see his family? I've no intention of leaving you alone in Paris. You need me, here.'

'No, I don't need you, Baz, not at all. I'm really not the pathetic and feeble creature you seem to think I am. But quite apart from that, there's a much more compelling reason for you to go home, and at once.'

'Oh? And what might that be?'

'Your wife is pregnant.'

'What did you say?'

'I said, Olivia is pregnant; very nearly three months pregnant, in fact. She must have conceived at around the time we came back from Sudan.' Misha laughed, and her manner became less severe. 'Really, Baz, you do put yourself about, don't you? You offer me marriage in the afternoon, then go to bed with your wife that same night!'

Red-faced and guilty, Basil dropped his eyes, as the memory of his moment of weakness with Olivia came flooding back. 'It wasn't meant to happen,' he mumbled.

'But it did, Baz, and the upshot is that you're going to be a father after all, you silly man. Aren't you at all pleased about that?'

The colour drained slowly from Basil's face, and he stared at Misha, shattered, and quite unable to think of anything to say. A welcome distraction arrived, in the shape of the waiter with their lunch, and this flurry of activity gave him a little time to recover his wits, and rearrange his thoughts. In silence, they ate the delicious oysters, and drank the wine. Slowly, Basil began to feel slightly less like a halfwit, and more like a human being. Conflicting emotions filled his easily moved heart, of sadness and regret, but equally a swiftly growing elation and joy. He felt like shouting and bursting into tears simultaneously. Instead, he put down his glass, and looked at Misha, his glance at the same time tender and unhappy. 'It's over, isn't it, darling?'

Misha smiled softly, and touched his hand. 'Yes, it's over, Baz. Though it never really happened, did it?' She raised her glass. 'I hope you both have lots of children, and a happy life together.'

'I suppose I'd better come back with you to pick up my bits and pieces, if I'm going to get home in time for Christmas.'

'It's already done. I hired a car for the holiday, and your stuff is in the boot. I'll drive you to the station, if you like.'

He smiled, a little bitterly. 'You must have been pretty sure you'd get rid of me without a fight, Misha?'

'I didn't think you'd want to hang about, once you knew about Olivia's baby.'

'It didn't take you terribly long to persuade me, did it? You must think me a bit of an emotional grasshopper.'

Misha laughed. 'You're OK, Baz. You'll make a good father, too.' She looked at him seriously. 'Olivia loves you. You're very lucky to have her. I hope you realize that.'

'Yes, I do. I've been a fool, I know that.' He took her hand. 'I only hope I didn't make a fool out of you, Misha?'

'No, you didn't, not at all.'

'Sure?'

'Quite sure.'

They finished their lunch, and Misha took Basil to the station. They got out of the car.

'Sorry about the sordid plastic bag,' said Misha, taking it from the boot and handing it to him.

'It's OK.' He took her hand. 'Tell me something, truthfully, Misha.'

'What?'

'It was Paul all the time, wasn't it? And always will be for you, right?'

'Right.'

'Never me, at all?'

'No.'

'Good.'

He raised her hand to his lips. 'Goodbye, darling Misha. Take care of yourself.'

'Goodbye, Baz. Take care of Olivia, won't you?'

'I will.'

'There's just one thing, Baz. I nearly forgot. You'll have to pretend that you don't know about the baby, or Olivia coming to see me. I promised her I wouldn't tell you. I hope you can handle that?'

He stood for a long moment, looking down at her, but his expression told Misha nothing. Then, without speaking, he turned, and walked away without looking back.

Paul arrived at Mas les Arnauds just before ten o'clock. He drove slowly through the silent village, the stone houses shuttered against the wind and cold, their courtyards hidden behind high stone walls and massive iron gates. At the end of the main street he entered the narrow winding lane where Pascal and Emma lived, and presently saw his son's battered old van parked outside the entrance to the house. Good, he said to himself, they're home. He stopped the car, switched off the lights, and got out. He looked up, over the top of the high wall, and saw that there was a light burning in an upstairs room. Perhaps they've gone to bed, he thought. If they have, I mustn't disturb them.

He turned the handle of the gate, half expecting it to be locked, but it swung gently open on its well-oiled hinges and he went into the courtyard. A cold, brilliant moon shone on the walls of the house and garden, bathing them in incandescent white light, so that their stones were drained of colour, and seemed transparent and ghostly in the still, anaesthetized air. Paul closed the gate quietly, and, looking towards the house, saw that the kitchen windows showed bright strips of light around the shutters. Without hurrying, he walked through the courtyard, and as he passed the mulberry tree he noticed that hundreds of surprisingly long and slender icicles hung from its leafless branches. He stood for a moment to examine the petrified tree, amazed at the power and intensity of the frost that gripped it. As he gazed, transfixed, marvelling at the crystalline beauty of the gnarled old tree decked in its wintry splendour, Paul could hear all around him tiny shatterings of sound, the faint tinklings of exploding ice. It seemed to him that the frozen world slept, spell-bound.

He tapped on the kitchen door, and Pascal, carrying a small black-haired baby in his arms, let him in. 'How lovely to see you, *Père*,' he said. 'Have you come straight from Paris?'

'Yes, more or less.'

Pascal closed the door, then kissed his father. 'Take off your coat, and come by the stove,' he said. 'This must easily be the coldest night this year, so far. Aren't you frozen?'

The doors of the big stove stood open and the logs inside burned brightly, their flames giving off a comforting heat. Emma sat close to the fire, bathed in its rosy glow, nursing the second baby at her breast. She raised her grey eyes to Paul's as he drew close, and gave him a slow, delighted smile. He bent over, and kissed her cheek. 'Well done, my darling,' he said.

Gently, Emma detached the baby from her breast, and winded him. He rewarded her with a milky burp. 'Good boy,' she said, then handed the small bundle to

Paul. 'There you are, Paul. You hold him, will you, while I give his brother a go?'

Paul took the baby from her, sat down in a chair and cradled the child in his arms. He watched, mesmerized and deeply touched, as Emma fed the other baby, and an intense happiness filled his soul, for the two little boys were not only identical twins, but images of Pascal, and of himself.

When the feeding was finished, Emma put the babies into their cribs, one by one, talking to them reassuringly in her soft, gentle voice.

'A glass of wine, *Père*?'

'Thanks, I'd love one.' Father and son smiled at each other. They had no need of elaborate congratulations, or a blow by blow account of the birth of the miraculously perfect children. Each of them knew exactly how the other felt, and the extent of their love for and pride in each other. They sat together in front of the fire, drinking their wine, until Emma had settled the babies, and came to join them.

'I'm so glad you came, Paul,' she said, sitting down. She looked at him, critically. 'Actually, you're looking a great deal better, thank God. Not so thin.'

'I'm OK, darling. Fine, in fact.'

'And less unhappy?'

He smiled. 'Happiness is relative to a multitude of things, Emma, isn't it? I have much to be glad about, and thankful for. If that's a kind of happiness, then, yes, I am happy.'

Pascal said, 'Have you eaten, *Père*? There's some bread, and sausage, if you're hungry.'

'Thanks. Bread and a bit of sausage would be great.'

Emma touched his hand. 'I hope you'll stay with us, tonight? We can easily make up a bed for you.'

'I'd love to, Emma, but I won't. I must go to Ménerbes in a minute. Blanche will be expecting me.'

Misha arrived at Froissy at six-thirty, having shopped in Vézelay. It was dark and cold, but she found the key without difficulty and let herself into the empty, silent house. The basket of kindling and logs was full, and she lit the stove, as much for the sake of cheerfulness as anything, since the place felt quite warm. She went back to her little car to fetch the shopping, and humped the two bulging bags into the kitchen, disregarding Paul's orders concerning the carrying of heavy loads. She kicked open the larder door, unpacked the bags of provisions, then returned to the car, and retrieved her grip from the boot.

After the emotional switchback of the morning, followed by the long drive to Froissy, she was beginning to feel extremely tired. I'll go upstairs now, she thought, and put the immersion heater on. Maybe a bath would be a good idea, before I make myself some supper.

Carrying her bag, she went along the corridor to the hall, switching on the lights as she went. She turned towards the staircase, and immediately the little green fir tree caught her eye. It looked small and lonely, stuck in its bucket, the only living thing in that vast, chilly stone chamber. It stood in front of the tall glazed French windows that screened the great double-leaved doors that opened onto the ruined vineyard, the meadows, and the woodlands beyond. Misha's thoughts flew back to the day she had first come to Froissy, and Paul had pushed open those enormous wooden doors, letting in the sunlight, a warm gust of summer air and the sweet smell of trampled grass, bringing the neglected old house to renewed life. He must have been here, she thought, on his way to Ménerbes. It must have been quite a detour. I wonder if he's got there yet? Perhaps he's still on the road?

Suddenly, the image of Paul driving fast, alone on the dark *autoroute*, or on icy country roads, sent a cold chill of apprehension down her spine, and she found herself looking into a future without him, a long and lonely life after his death. It was like staring into an abyss. If the future holds that sort of horrible emptiness for me, as the penalty for loving him, she thought, then that's the price I'll have to pay. I love him, now and for ever, until the day he dies, and after his death, too.

Upstairs, in the bedroom that held such vivid memories for her, Misha turned on the lamps on either side of the bed, and the water heater in the bathroom, to boost the heat supplied by the kitchen stove. She pulled back the counterpane, kicked off her boots, then lay down on the bed to rest for a few minutes. The farewell lunch with Baz, and the amount of nervous energy she had invested in expelling him from her life, had taken more out of her than she would have believed possible. Added to that, the long drive to Froissy, alone, in heavy traffic and on frequently icy roads, had proved to be quite a challenge in itself. She closed her eyes, letting her limbs grow limp, and trying to relax into the warm curves of the bed.

Slowly, in spite of her exhaustion, Misha began to feel curiously liberated in her spirit, and had the feeling that she was floating a little way above the bed; it was as if a door had opened in her head, releasing her from the trap she had probably set for herself. What a fool I was, she thought drowsily; I need never have allowed Baz to monopolize me the way he did, it was stupid of me. Thank God Olivia had the sense to come and see me. She's a very remarkable young woman. I hope Baz never forgets that, for both their sakes.

She turned her head, and smelled the faint scent of Paul's hair on the pillow, and her heart dissolved with longing for him. I'll never love anyone as I love him, she thought. I must get up, and make some supper, or I'll fall asleep with my clothes on. I'm too knackered to have a bath now – I'll have it in the morning. She turned slowly onto her side, opening her eyes, and without any reaction of shock or surprise, saw a tall, silver-haired woman in a blue dress, hanging a delicate wreath of green leaves in the window. The woman turned towards her, and Misha saw that she had large brown eyes and delicately arched dark eyebrows.

'Hello, Jane,' she whispered softly, not daring to move.

'Hello, Misha,' the woman replied.

Slowly, Misha sat up, and put her feet on the ground, but when she raised her eyes, the vision vanished. She looked more closely, and saw that the circle of green leaves was still hanging in the window. Perhaps it was there all the time, she said to herself. Maybe Paul put it there?

Full of happiness, she went down to the kitchen, stoked up the fire, made herself an omelette, and poured herself a glass of wine.

Misha woke at sunrise, after a long and dreamless sleep. She had not drawn the heavy *toile de Jouy* curtains when she went to bed, unwilling to obscure the beautiful little circle of leaves, which, on closer examination, had revealed themselves to be mistletoe, bound to a circle of wire. It was a quarter to nine when she opened her eyes, disturbed by the low sunlight that streamed through the window. It was a perfect midwinter morning, the sky a deep azure, the countryside frozen, crisp with frost, each twig coated with ice, each leaf edged with white.

As a city-dweller, Misha had never had any particular occasion to study the urban weather patterns, and thought of spring, summer, autumn and winter strictly in terms of heat or cold, the length of the hours of daylight. She had never been especially conscious of the subtle changes that took place within the rhythmic turning of the year. If anyone had said to her 'a beautiful day', she would immediately have called to mind a fine day in summer. Now, she got out of bed, wrapped herself in Paul's dressing-gown, pulled on a pair of his thick winter socks, and went to the window, delighted and astonished at the shimmer and sparkle of the sunlit, frost-bound land spread out before her. Below her, on the wire of the fence that bordered the old vineyard, a mistle thrush perched, his feathers puffed out to insulate him from the cold, and from his open throat poured his aggressive, challenging song, each note a separate diamond in the unpolluted air.

Dragging herself away from the window, Misha took her bath, and got dressed in the warmest things she could find, some of them belonging to Paul. In the kitchen, she stoked up the still-burning stove, made herself some coffee and boiled an egg.

After breakfast, she went into the larder, and looked at the fat duck she had chosen. I really can't eat this silly bird all on my own, she told herself. It would be mad, wouldn't it? I think I'll eat the steak I bought, for my supper tonight, and keep the duck till later. Maybe I could cook it with wine, in a casserole, or something, so that it will make several meals. It's so cold in here, I'm sure it can't possibly go off, or anything. In any case, I've got better things to do here than waste time preparing anything elaborate. Like what, Misha? she asked herself. The answer came at once: like decorating the tree, for a start.

It took a very long time to find the decorations, but at last she discovered them, hidden in the drawers of a small pine chest, in the cobweb-festooned attics at the very top of the house. Dusty and dishevelled, but triumphant, she carried the boxes downstairs to the hall and opened them, carefully. The glass balls, birds, angels and stars were the prettiest and most delicately made Christmas baubles that she had ever seen. One by one, she took them from their nests of tissue-paper and hung them on the branches of the fir tree, until she had used every single one and the tree had been transformed into a shimmering mass of silver and gold. Reaching up, Misha fixed the last star to the topmost branch, then stood back to admire her handiwork. It was after three o'clock, and the sun had left the sky, but the tree seemed to glow with a magical light. 'It's absolutely *beautiful*,' said Misha, softly. 'Darling Paul, I do wish you were here to see it.'

When it grew dark, the magic faded from the tree, because there were no fairy lights to bring it to life again, much less the old-fashioned real candles that would have been clipped to the branches in Jane de Vilmorin's time. Undeterred by this misfortune, Misha went to the kitchen and diligently searched for, and found, several boxes of household candles, kept in case of a power failure. In the larder, on a high shelf, she found a dozen empty jam jars, and pressed them into service as makeshift candlesticks. She put everything onto a tray, then carried it to the hall. She stuck the candles in the jars, then lit them, and placed them in a circle round the tree. At once, the tree reappeared, a glowing beacon in the sombre gloom of the hall. Misha stood back and gazed at it, entranced by the flash and gleam of the gilded treasures that seemed to turn her tree into a spellbinding, insubstantial illusion, shining in the light of the flickering candles.

By the time she had finished, it was too dark to go outside, or to attempt any more decorating. Instead, Misha went into the sitting-room and lit the fire, having found that it was already laid. Tomorrow, she thought, I'll go out and cut some holly and stuff, and make it a bit festive in here, too. She decided to have her supper there, sitting on the floor in front of the fire. She drank some claret with her steak, offering a silent toast to her father and her dead mother, and to Paul and his little grandsons. She did not feel unhappy, or alone, for the strong presence of Jane de Vilmorin seemed all around her, in the firelight, in her pictures on the walls, and in the watchful eyes of all the woodland creatures. I don't think she minds me being here, Misha said to herself. I hope she lets me see her again, sometime.

Basil did not catch the next train to Orléans. Instead, he went down into the Métro, took a train to Courcelles, and walked along rue Daru to the Russian Orthodox Cathedral. Dusk was already beginning to fall as he reached the black iron railings guarding the tall white building with its gilded onion domes, and went into the church, following a trio of old ladies with shawls over their heads.

Inside, the darkness was partially relieved by hundreds of flickering orange-coloured tapers, tall and smelling of beeswax, their smoking flames carrying the prayers of the faithful high up into the dome, to add yet another layer of soot to the smoke-blackened, scarcely visible icon of the Creator, painted on the ceiling high above their heads. The old ladies lit their own candles, then moved away into the open central space of the church, each of them standing alone, silently whispering her prayers, crossing herself and bending down from time to time to touch the floor.

Basil did not light a candle, but leaned against a thick stone column, making himself as inconspicuous as possible. Since leaving Misha at the station, he had felt himself to be falling inexorably into a state of spiritual limbo, a kind of numbness; a profound desolation of his soul. It was true that in the restaurant he had felt a rush of excitement, even a fragile joy, at the news of Olly's baby, but his mood had reverted swiftly to his desperate need to cling to his love for Misha, and he found himself unwilling as well as unable to exorcize from his mind the small ghosts of the imaginary children they would have conceived together, had his heartfelt longings been fulfilled.

Basil leaned against his pillar for a very long time. His old ladies departed, to be replaced by others, and later, from behind the carved screen that hid the priests from the congregation, came the baritone rumblings that told him that a mass had begun.

Eventually, he roused himself, put francs into a box, and added a new taper to the dozens of others, burning in a round brass candleholder. He crossed himself, then folded his arms and stared at the floor beneath his feet. If you're really there, God, please give me a sign; tell me what to do, he prayed silently. But in his head Basil was miserably aware that there wasn't a glib and easy answer to the grief in his heart, or to his sense of shame towards his wife. He knew that for himself it would necessarily be a question of a long and private forgetting, and for Olivia, a lifetime of forgiveness, if that was how she chose to deal with the situation. In his innermost heart, Basil knew that Misha would always remain the love of his life, that he would never cease to mourn her loss. Equally, and bitterly, he reminded himself that, for the sake of Olivia and their future children, it would have to remain a secret and solitary tragedy, endured alone, and shared with no-one.

It was after midnight when Basil got home, and found the barn in darkness. He got out of the cab, carrying the flowers he had bought at the station, and paid the fare.

'*Merci, monsieur,*' said the driver. '*Joyeux Noël, monsieur,*' he added, not sounding as though he really meant it.

'*Vous-même,*' Basil responded half-heartedly, and they exchanged a bleak smile. The driver raised a hand, did a swift U-turn, and drove away.

Basil turned towards the barn, carefully checking all the windows for any sign of a light, but could see none. Maybe she's gone away, he said to himself. Perhaps she's gone to her mother's, or to Souliac. Straining his eyes, he peered across the yard towards the open byre, and saw that Olivia's car was parked there, as usual. He stood for a moment by the door, hesitating, unable to decide whether or not he really wished to be reunited with his wife, or would be quite relieved to discover that she had gone away.

He put his key in the lock, let himself into the house, and turned on the light. She didn't bolt the door, he thought; she must be expecting me. He looked around at the familiar room. All was quiet, and extremely orderly. The big press had disappeared, together with the plan-chests and the bench for the acid baths. Why? Basil frowned uneasily, and for a second felt as if he had come to the wrong house, so uncharacteristically neat and tidy did the place seem to him. Olivia had not decorated the room for Christmas, and had not even bought a tree. The logs in the fireplace were still glowing, though burned quite low, and he crossed the room and put another log carefully on the embers. He was still holding the bunch of lilies in his hand, and he tried to remember where Olly kept the glass jars and vases she filled with wild flowers in the summertime. As he passed the table on his way to the kitchen in search of them, Basil saw the note Olivia had left for him. *I left some supper for you, in the low oven, in case you haven't eaten. I expect you will be tired, but I won't mind if you wake me up.*

Exhausted as he was, and emotionally wiped out, Basil felt the prick of tears behind his eyes as he read these words, and blinked rapidly. He looked towards the top of the staircase, and saw Olivia standing there in her nightdress, wrapped in a large red Spanish shawl. Her feet were bare. 'What lovely lilies, Baz,' she said, and smiled timidly.

'They're for you, darling; that is, if you'll have them.'

Olivia came slowly down the stairs, took the flowers from Basil and put them on the table. She turned towards him, and slid her arms round him, underneath his parka. 'I have something to tell you, Baz,' she said, gently.

'If you mean the baby, darling, I already know about it.' Basil looked tenderly down at his wife's fair head, and put a protective arm around her shoulders, holding her against his chest.

Swiftly, angrily, Olivia pulled away from his caress. 'Misha must have told you!'

'Yes, she did.'

'How utterly *shitty* of her! She absolutely *promised* that she wouldn't!'

Basil smiled. 'Does it matter, if it means I'm here, with you, Olly?'

'Well, I suppose not, really.' She looked at him

severely. 'I imagine it was the only way she could get rid of you, you philandering bastard!'

Basil did not deny this. He looked at Olivia, and his eyes were full of shame and sorrow. 'Misha took me out to lunch, and then told me to piss off,' he said. 'Afterwards, I went to the Russian Cathedral, Olly, on a sort of pilgrimage. It's eleven years, almost to the day, that we exchanged rings there, do you remember? I told you then that I'd never betray you, but I did, in my head, anyway. Can you ever forgive me, darling?'

Olivia had rehearsed this scene of reconciliation many times in her mind, and had intended to concede that the sins of marital omission had been as much hers as Basil's. Now that the critical moment had arrived, however, she decided that such apportioning of blame was pretty pointless, and said nothing. She led the way to the kitchen, put the lilies in water, and took the casserole containing Basil's supper from the oven.

Much later, lying in bed, warm in her husband's arms, Olivia counted her blessings, and put a cool hand against his face. 'Baz?' she murmured softly.

'Mm?'

'Would you have come back to me, darling, if Misha hadn't kicked you out?'

'Yes, of course I would,' he lied, and kissed her gently. 'You're my wife, remember?'

At Ménerbes, Blanche was in her element, happily engaged in hosting her annual post-Christmas drinks party. The large, sunlit salon vibrated with the roar of the raised voices of her many friends, most of whom, like herself, had migrated south to their holiday houses for the end-of-year festivities. Olivier and Catherine, too, were in good form, renewing their summer acquaintance and enthusiastically discussing the events of the Paris season.

Paul, endeavouring to maintain some kind of

benevolence towards his wife, had behaved impeccably throughout Christmas Day, and was even now circulating in the conventional manner, exchanging polite seasonal greetings with Blanche's guests, and replenishing their drinks.

At ten to one, his head bursting, he slipped out of the noisy room, and went to his car. There, he took his new, and much more powerful mobile phone from his pocket, and called Misha, unable to endure another day without speaking to her. There was no reply. Frowning, he dialled her mobile number, and she answered at once.

'Hello, darling,' he said quietly. 'Where are you?'

'I'm at Froissy. It's pretty lonely here, all by myself.'

'What do you mean, "by yourself"? Where's Basil?'

'He's gone home to his wife, Paul. I sent him away.'

'You're not serious, Misha?'

'Never more so.'

'I don't believe it!'

'You'd better believe it, because I'm fed up with sleeping in our bed on my own, Paul. I miss you.'

'It'll take me about seven hours to get to you, my darling; depending on the weather, of course.'

'Are you sure that's all right? Won't you be expected to stay a bit longer?'

'I don't give a stuff whether I am or not. I've done my duty, so now I'll tell Blanche I've been called away on an urgent case.'

Misha laughed. 'Well, you have, haven't you? The urgent case is me, Paul.'

'Is it true, darling? Do you really need me, as much as I long to be with you?'

'I love you, Paul. I need you with me.'

'I love you too, Misha. I'm on my way.'

Misha spent the afternoon, as she had promised herself, out in the cold sunshine, cutting holly from the hedgerows. She arranged the prickly green branches over the chimney-piece in the sitting-room, and on top of the pictures and glass cases on the walls. She lit the fire, choosing thick long logs, and plumped up the cushions on the sofa. When it grew dark, she switched on the lamps and drew the curtains.

At half past six, she stuffed the duck with herbs, lemon and garlic, ready for roasting later, and peeled potatoes and baby turnips. She set the kitchen table with the heavy silverware and candlesticks, and some beautiful old wine glasses, then put her small jar of *foie gras* on a silver dish, ready for the first course. She took the kitchen torch, and went down to the cellar. There, after a little searching, she found a half-bottle of Muscat de Beaumes de Venise to go with the *foie gras*, and chose a bottle of red Rully to drink with the duck. Back in the kitchen, she uncorked the Rully, and put the Muscat in the fridge, to keep cold.

At seven o'clock, she put the bird into the oven, then stuck fresh candles in the jam jars around the Christmas tree, and lit them. She pulled on her boots, put on a thick tweed coat she found in the cloakroom, and turned off the electric light in the hall. Taking care not to create a draught, she opened the French windows, and then, one by one, slowly pushed back the heavy outside doors. She turned, and looked back. Inside their makeshift storm-lanterns, the flames of the candles trembled very slightly as they bloomed in the darkness, casting their golden light on the fragile decorations, and bringing her tree to magical, shimmering life.

The moon was high, and Misha had no need of a torch as she made her way along the driveway between the pastures, then walked along the frozen rutted lane until she reached the entrance to the woodland road. It was a lot darker under the trees, the moonlight casting a slightly sinister shifting pattern of branches onto the ground below, and she regretted not bringing a lamp.

Cold, her hands thrust deep into the pockets of her coat, stamping her feet to keep warm, Misha waited. At last, far away, half hidden in the trees, she saw the twin points of probing light advancing towards her. She stepped out into the middle of the road, waving her arms up and down, smiling.

The car stopped, the driver's door opened, and Paul got out. They stood together in the beam of the headlights, clinging to each other, too happy to say anything sensible. At last Misha lifted her face, to receive his kiss. 'We'd better get home quickly,' she said. 'Or our goose will be cooked, literally. Well, actually, it's a duck.'

They got into the car and drove on. As they came out of the woods and turned into the lane, Misha said, 'I've got a surprise for you, darling. I just hope it hasn't set the place on fire!'

'Misha! What the hell do you mean?'

'Look! There it is!'

Paul stopped the car, and looked across the pasture, and what he saw made his heart overflow with the happiness he had believed had gone for ever. He undid his belt, turned towards Misha, took her face in his hands and kissed her, very tenderly. Then he said, 'Let's leave the car here, and walk, shall we?'

They got out of the car, and, hand in hand, made their way across the frozen meadow towards the house they both loved, their quiet voices insubstantial, vanishing like the whispers of ghosts into the thin echoing air.

THE END

THE COUNTER-TENOR'S DAUGHTER

Elizabeth Falconer

Dido Partridge's life as the daughter of an exotic operatic soprano and her counter-tenor lover, Signor Pernice, has been a strange one. A childhood spent mainly in the dressing rooms of the great European opera houses had led naturally to her present bohemian existence in a grand old houseboat, once her mother's, moored on the Thames. This unusual home she shares with Jacob, a film director and her erratic but long-term partner, until her friends' hints of Jacob's frequent infidelities are proved true by her discovery that he had been entertaining another woman on the houseboat. Disposing of his belongings overboard and booking the first flight out of Heathrow that she could find, she ends up in Corfu, in a beautiful, unspoilt bay where she reads, swims and eats the lovely but simple food prepared for her by the local taverna keeper.

Gradually, as the peace and tranquillity of Corfu begin to work their magic on her, Dido becomes aware of Guy, an attractive lawyer who left London for the solitude of the island when his disability – the result of a childhood accident – became too much for him to bear. Guy's resentful sister Lavinia, who may know more about Guy's accident than either of them is prepared to admit, can never forgive Guy for inheriting the great family mansion in Ireland where, by coincidence, Jacob is now directing a film. As Dido and Guy start to heal the wounds which each of them has acquired through the years, they both begin to see how their lives can change.

0 552 99624 6

BLACK SWAN

WINGS OF THE MORNING

Elizabeth Falconer

Christian and his younger sister Emma, children of a wealthy but spectacularly ill-matched couple, had been brought up by their mother Flavia in the hope that one of them, at least, would find a vocation to the religious life. Their father Ludovic, meanwhile, was absent from their lives for a great deal of the time – an absence which, as they grew up, became all too readily understandable. But while Christian lived in London and Gloucestershire with his wife Phoebe and their two small children – a shamefully irreligious life, according to Flavia – Emma followed her heart's desire by training to be a fresco painter in Italy and then, bowing to the incessant pressure from her mother, became a nun in an enclosed order.

A tragedy in the family brought them all to crisis point. Flavia fell apart, becoming increasingly and fanatically religious. Phoebe and Christian had to rebuild their family life, while Emma became gloriously, unexpectedly free – finding love of a more earthly kind in the glorious countryside of Provence.

'A GORGEOUS, INSPIRING NOVEL . . . ELIZABETH FALCONER TREATS OF LOVE, PASSION, DREAMS AND DUTY WITH THE ABSOLUTE ASSURANCE OF A CONSUMMATE STORYTELLER'
Sarah Harrison

0 552 99755 2

BLACK SWAN

A BAREFOOT WEDDING

Elizabeth Falconer

Two families, both with secrets in their pasts . . .

Phyllida loved the magical Channel Isle of Florizel, where she had been spending summers since she was a small child. But this year she was in disgrace – expelled from school in the middle of her A Levels – and not looking forward to the family holiday at all. But then she met Andras, a handsome young fisherman whose family was hiding a secret from the wartime occupation of the islands, memories of which still divided the tiny community.

Meanwhile Rachel, trapped in a loveless marriage with a tyrannical Oxford academic, decided to make a sudden bid for freedom. She travelled to Italy and discovered passion for the first time; she also, inadvertently, stumbled on the clue to an old wartime tragedy. A clue which led Andras and Phyllida to Tuscany – and to the discovery which would change their lives.

'FALCONER'S BOOK IS OPTIMISTIC ABOUT THE HUMAN SPIRIT'
Women and Home

0 552 99756 0

BLACK SWAN